THE REBELS: SONS OF TEXAS

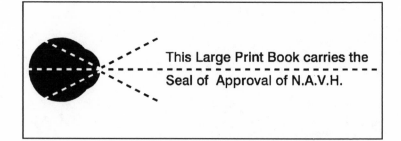

This Large Print Book carries the
Seal of Approval of N.A.V.H.

EK.

THE REBELS:
SONS OF TEXAS

ELMER KELTON

THORNDIKE PRESS

An imprint of Thomson Gale, a part of The Thomson Corporation

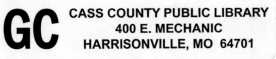

THOMSON
—————✦————— ™
GALE

Detroit • New York • San Francisco • New Haven, Conn. • Waterville, Maine • London

LIBRARY OF CONGRESS CATALOGING-IN-PUBLICATION DATA

Kelton, Elmer.
    The rebels : sons of Texas / by Elmer Kelton.
        p. cm. — (Thorndike Press large print western)
    ISBN-13: 978-1-4104-0316-2 (lg. print : alk. paper)
    ISBN-10: 1-4104-0316-5 (lg. print : alk. paper)
    1. Pioneers — Fiction. 2. Texas — Fiction. 3. Large type books. I. Title.
PS3561.E3975R43 2007b
813'.54—dc22
                                      2007038641

Published in 2007 by arrangement with Tom Doherty Associates, LLC.

Printed in the United States of America on permanent paper
10 9 8 7 6 5 4 3 2 1

THE REBELS: SONS OF TEXAS

■ ■ ■ ■

PART I:
THE NEWCOMERS
TEXAS, 1830

■ ■ ■ ■

CHAPTER 1

His boots sinking deeply into the freshly turned earth, Andrew Lewis reached the end of the row and hollered, "Whoa," at the big blue ox. The muscular old work animal sometimes required a fair amount of coaxing to start pulling the wooden plow, but the slightest hint would bring him to a stop. Balancing the plow handle against his leg, Andrew took off his floppy, sweat-stained hat and rubbed the sleeve of a homespun cotton shirt across his forehead. Spring had brought the heat early, he thought. He had never completely become used to the fact that spring came earlier here in Texas than it did back in Tennessee.

He looked around for the black dog that had spent much of the morning trotting alongside the plow, watching for mice or rabbits that occasionally popped up, startled. He thought the dog might be off seeking mischief, a trait at which it was discouragingly talented, but he saw it dozing in the shade of a rail fence that kept cattle out of the field. Were the dog not an eager protector of the children, Andrew would long since have tried to give it to some passing stranger.

As he had done regularly for most of a month, he let his gaze run expectantly over the trail that came westward from the town of San Felipe de Austin. *Damn it,* he chided himself, *it's still a way too early to be looking for them. They're probably not halfway here yet from the old state.*

His back ached from the hard labor of planting. He stretched, placing both hands above his waist and pushing, trying to straighten out the kink that seemed to have found itself a permanent home. Late rains had delayed his starting, and it was high time the corn seed was in the ground. Plant it too early and it was likely to freeze. Plant it too late and it might be caught by a long summer dry spell. Farming had never been an easy life anywhere, but it seemed sometimes that Texas weather had a special grudge against the plowman.

He turned slowly, looking across the expanse of land he claimed for his own. At twenty-eight, he already owned more hectares here in Mexican Texas than the acres he might reasonably have expected to put together in a long lifetime back in Tennessee. The government in Mexico had been generous to its American settlers and he felt grateful. He had done well, especially in the four years since he had married Petra Moreno. She had given him a reason to work, to build, to grow.

He looked across the field toward his log cabin, where smoke curled from the tall stone chimney. It promised him a good dinner later, when the sun rose to midday and his shadow lay close to his feet. He had lived in that cabin alone his first several years here. He had added a second section after his marriage to Petra. He saw her now, a distant, slender silhouette, standing in the open dog-run that divided the two sections of the cabin. She probably wondered if something was wrong that he had stopped the ox and the plow.

He had better start moving soon or she would come striding down to the field to be sure he was not sick or hurt. He waved to let her know he was all right. He did not like the idea of her leaving the two young ones at the cabin alone for even that long. Texas was benevolent in many ways, but it harbored special hazards for children: rattlesnakes, coral snakes, scorpions, and

11

centipedes. There were bears and mountain lions as well, but they seldom ventured too close anymore. The ever-growing numbers of new immigrants into Stephen F. Austin's American colony had pushed those sorts of predators back farther and farther to the west. The ax and the plow were doing to them what the rifle alone probably never could.

"Come on, Blue," he said. "We've lazed long enough."

He had no more than raised up the heavy-handled plow than the dog barked, and he eased it down again. Two riders approached from the direction of his older brother Michael's farm. Andrew smiled at the sight of eight-year-old Mordecai Lewis, carrying a rifle across his saddle longer than the boy was tall. Little Mordecai was making a start toward becoming the spitting image of his lanky father, who sat on the other horse.

Andrew called, "Where you-all goin' with all that artillery? You already got your corn plantin' done?"

He knew they could not have, for it had rained on Michael's place as much as on Andrew's.

The gaunt Michael pointed his chin westward, toward the heavy forests that lay along the river and beyond, where no one had yet settled. That land was being saved for other Lewis kin. "We're gettin' almighty tired of eatin' hog. We're fixin' to see if we can scare up some venison."

Mordecai put in eagerly, "Or maybe even bear."

It was like Michael to leave the planting unfinished and go traipsing off into the woods, forgetting everything but the hunt. Andrew was glad Michael was taking little Mordecai, for the boy would give him reason to come home in a timely manner. Alone, Michael sometimes would stay out for days, even weeks, roaming, searching for God knew what, listening to calling voices that Andrew had never heard. Chances were that little Mordecai would turn out just like him. He ought to be in school, but no schooling was to be had out here so far from San Felipe except that which his mother gave him from her small collection of books and his father gave him in the field and the woods.

Somehow the work seemed to get done in spite of Michael's restlessness. Nobody had ever gone hungry in Michael Lewis's cabin. But Michael would never be as much a farmer as Andrew, and Andrew would never be the natural woodsman that Michael was.

The black dog sniffed around the horses'

heels until Michael's horse lifted a foot to kick at it. The dog retreated hastily to the rail fence and barked from a safe distance.

Andrew asked, "How's Marie and the young'uns?"

"They're fine. Marie said she might come over this evenin' and set a spell with Petra. Ain't likely that me and Mordecai will be back before dark."

"Petra'll be tickled to have her," Andrew said. Marie was French and Spanish, out of the old Louisiana town of Natchitoches. She usually fetched along samples of her cooking when she came visiting. It differed in some ways from Petra's East Texas Mexican. And both women had learned a lot of American dishes. Between the two of them there was always something good to eat.

He said, "If you can take the time, I'll walk up to the cabin with you and drink a little of Petra's coffee."

Michael shook his head, as Andrew had expected he would. When he was headed for the woods, Michael had little interest in anything else. "I expect we'll be gettin' on. Mornin's half spent already." He looked eastward. "You ain't seen any sign of them, have you?"

Though he had done the same thing just a few minutes ago, Andrew said, "No use wastin' your time lookin'. We can't even know for sure that they've left Tennessee yet."

"They've left," Michael said confidently. "They're kin of ours, so they'd've been itchin' to leave as soon as the snow melted. They're apt to come rollin' in just about any day now."

"Maybe. But they might run into trouble along the way."

"Ain't no trouble ever stopped a Lewis when his mind was set. And mine's set on a little huntin'." He turned to his son. "You ready, Mordecai?"

The boy nodded enthusiastically. He carried his late grandfather's given name and already had much of his grandfather's look. There was an old family story that when the first Mordecai Lewis had been six months old he had crawled out of his crib and taken hold of a rifle. It was certain that from the time he became big enough to carry one, a rifle was never far from his reach. Mordecai, the father of Andrew and Michael, had been the first Lewis to come west into Texas, back before 1816. It had been Spanish then, and Americans were unwelcome. Fatally unwelcome. Mordecai died in Texas, a Spanish officer's bullet in his brain.

Much had happened in Texas in the fourteen years since; it was a different country now. Mexico had shaken off the Spanish imperial yoke, winning its independence on the battlefield, much as the United States had won its freedom from England. In an effort to settle Texas and put a buffer between itself and hostile Indian tribes, Mexico had welcomed Stephen F. Austin and other impresarios who brought American colonists into the thinly-populated land. She had granted them freedoms she did not allow even her own people down in the interior of Mexico. She had been generous with her lands to those who would live on them and make them fruitful.

It had been a mercurial, often-changing government, however. From the beginning, there had been those in the Mexican hierarchy who counseled for caution. There had been those who declared Americans to be an acquisitive and grasping people, unworthy of trust. They said that when Americans became too numerous, they were likely to want more and more land, until at last they took it all. Stephen Austin had often felt compelled to travel the long, hard road to Mexico City to plead the colonists' case, to pledge their loyalty, and to vouch for their gratitude.

There had been worrisome stirrings. Back in 1825, Andrew and Michael had helped Austin and Mexican troops put down a short-lived, overblown rebellion by certain land seekers at Nacogdoches, who had declared themselves the independent republic of Fredonia. Many would have considered it laughable in its pretensions and its futility, but lawmakers in Mexico City had not laughed. Those who distrusted Americans had pointed to it as an ominous forerunner of things to come.

Life had remained peaceful here on the Colorado River west of San Felipe, headquarters of Austin's colony. Seldom did Andrew think about the Fredonian rebellion anymore. His mind and his efforts were directed toward developing his farm, enlarging his fields, increasing his little bunch of meat hogs running free in the woods, and expanding his modest herd of cattle. Lately he had been thinking about other Lewises, his kin, on their way here from Tennessee. They would find Texas different from the settled land of their birth. It was big and mostly undeveloped, a wilderness except for scattered clusters of settlements. They would probably think his Mexican wife Petra talked funny, as did Michael's wife Marie. But they would come to love both

17

women when they got to know them. They would come to love this land as Andrew and Michael had learned to love it. Once they knew Texas, they would never want to leave.

After a time he heard Petra clanging a piece of iron against a broken section of wagon tire hanging in the dog-run. It was her signal for him to come to the cabin for dinner. The black dog jumped to its feet and made a start toward the house, then stopped and looked back expectantly. Andrew glanced up at the noon sun for confirmation, then unhooked the plow and left it standing in the row while he walked the blue ox down to the river for a good watering. When the animal drank its fill, Andrew took him to a pen to feed upon last summer's grass hay until it was time to go back to the field. The dog paced impatiently back and forth until Andrew said, "Go on." The dog left him and trotted toward the cabin, willfully scattering the multicolored chickens that Petra treasured above all except family and cabin.

Petra waited in the dog-run and uptilted her chin for Andrew to kiss her. More than four years of marriage had not diminished that welcome ritual. She looked at him with eyes big and black and happy. "You are hungry?"

"I could eat the south end of a mule."

She laughed. "Today we eat pork instead." She had learned a fair amount of English, though she sometimes used the wrong word, put it in the wrong place, or mispronounced it. His Spanish fell short of perfect, so he could not fault her English. What mattered was that they understood each other in either language. Everybody else would just have to make the best of it.

He kissed her again, because he felt like it, and gave her a fierce squeeze. She laughed and said in Spanish, which came easier, "This is not the time. This is the middle of day."

"I'll feel the same way come night."

"Then wait for the night. The children are hungry."

Their oldest, three-going-on-four, played in the dog-run with a pup Michael had brought him. The boy was named Ben, after Andrew and Michael's Uncle Benjamin back in Tennessee. In the kitchen was the youngest, a girl, Rose to Andrew, Rosa to Petra. She sat in the high chair Andrew had first built for Ben and munched on a piece of flat bread, freshly baked on the hearth. Her eyes lighted at sight of her father, and she gave him a wet kiss, well flavored with the bread. Andrew felt fortunate that both children were healthy; that this isolated life could be hard on the little ones was painfully evidenced by a small grave above Michael and Marie's cabin.

Petra said, "I saw Michael and Mordecai. Why did they not come to the house?"

Andrew explained their mission. Petra smiled at the news that Marie would be coming over in the evening. Though the two women lived hardly two miles apart, they had not seen one another in a week or more. Each had her own work to do, work enough to last from daylight until well after dark. Life in frontier Texas granted women even less leisure than the men.

The field labor had made Andrew hungrier than he realized. He ate a considerable helping of pork and finished the meal by using some of the flat bread to swab up cane molasses he had traded from a farmer down near San Felipe.

The black dog sat in the doorway, forbidden to enter the cabin, though the pup was allowed. The dog had perfected a silent but plaintive form of begging. It usually worked better with Petra than with Andrew, who knew the dog had already made a good meal from a cottontail rabbit it had caught in the field.

The dog started barking and left its post

at the door. Andrew glanced questioningly at Petra. It was too early for Michael to have returned, but travelers on the dim road between San Felipe and San Antonio de Bexar often stopped at Andrew and Petra's cabin. Andrew pushed back from the table and walked out on the dog-run, ready to invite a visitor to come in to the table.

He stopped short, the invitation stuck in his throat. An old animosity flared. He tried to suppress it and be civil to the two black-bearded men who sat on horseback in front of the cabin. He forced a semblance of a greeting. "Howdy, Finis. Howdy, Luke."

One-armed Finis Blackwood seemed fatter every time Andrew saw him. It was no surprise, because his greatest exertion was in rushing to the dinner table. He said, "Good day to you, Andrew. See you been busy plowin'."

Luke echoed, "Been plowin'." Luke, broad and muscular, had always been a little slow in his thinking. Mostly he did whatever his older brother told him to, and took as gospel anything Finis said. For whatever he had been shorted in brains, Luke made up in meanness. Finis sicced him onto his enemies the way he would sic a dog. There had been a time Andrew would have met them with a rifle, but that was futile. When

21

the Blackwoods looked for trouble, they never came in the open, as now. They sneaked in from behind when nobody was looking. That had been their style when they and the Lewises had grown up as reluctant neighbors back in Tennessee. It was still their way.

Finis said, "Me and Luke, we been huntin' for a milk cow that strayed off. She was a-springin' heavy with calf. We figure she's had it somewheres by now and is a-hidin' it out. Big brindle cow, she is. We was wonderin' if by chance you've seen her?"

It was Andrew's opinion, which he kept to himself, that the cow's rightful owner had come along and found her and had taken her home. That is, if there had been a cow in the first place. It was strongly probable that the Blackwoods had been hog hunting in the woods and had decided to come over for a free meal. That was ironic because it was probably Andrew's hogs they were hunting. His pig crop always weaned smaller than it should. He had long suspected that a percentage of his hogs ended up in the Blackwoods' smokehouse.

He said, "I haven't seen any such cow. We was just finishin' up our dinner. Long's you're here, you'd just as well come on in and have what's left." It was hardly a gracious invitation, but it was the best he felt like giving them.

Even as Finis was saying, "We ain't come to impose," he was dismounting. Luke followed his lead. They tied their horses to a post in the sun. Andrew would have tied them in the shade of a tree just a few steps farther away, but the Blackwoods had their own ways, and he felt no compulsion to try to educate them to higher standards.

Petra was painfully civil to the two brothers while they finished everything she had cooked and looked around for more. She asked, "How is Nelly?"

"Fatter'n a hog," Finis said, wiping the last piece of bread through a plateful of molasses. "I declare, I never did see anybody who loved to eat like she does." He gave Petra a condescending look that said he had as soon not talk with her at all. She was Mexican.

Petra seemed to understand the look, and Andrew suspected she continued the conversation just to aggravate Finis. That was not difficult to do. She asked, "And the three children, how do they do?"

"Noisy, hungry all the time." Nelly had been shelling out children at the rate of one a year, a trait admirable in cows but not always so desirable in women. Fathering babies was the only kind of planting in which Finis found any pleasure. Hard work around the Blackwood farm was left mostly to younger brother Isaac, the only one of the three Andrew considered worth the powder it would take to dispatch them to a better world. Even Isaac would bear watching, for he was a Blackwood.

Finis and Luke finished, not so much that they had eaten all they wanted but that they had eaten all there was. The two children held their distance. The little girl was always timid around strangers. The boy Ben was more sociable, but he distrusted these dirty-bearded, unkempt neighbors from across the river. Andrew took that as a sign of his son's good judgment.

He followed Finis and Luke outside, not so much to bid them good-bye as to be sure they did not pick up something and carry it away. The necessities were hard to come by in the isolation of colonial Texas; he didn't want any of them stolen. Finis said, "That wife of yours is a fair to middlin' cook, Andrew, even if she is a Mexican. I wisht Nelly could take some lessons from her."

From the looks of Finis's soft belly, Nelly fed well enough.

Finis said, "But there's one thing bothers me about you bein' married to a Mexican.

The day's comin' when us Americans is fixin' to have to fight them. When that day comes, Andrew, I'm wonderin' which side you'll be on — ours or theirs."

Firmly, Andrew said, "I don't see it comin' to that. But if it ever does, I'll be on *mine.*"

He watched the Blackwoods ride west, skirting along the river. Their farm was on the other side and some miles to the east. Not until the two brothers were out of sight did he return to his field. They remained on his mind after he set the blue ox back to pulling the plow. He had long wished for the Blackwoods to fail on their farm and move somewhere else, to be someone else's worry. Were it not for Isaac Blackwood's stubborn diligence, it would have happened long ago. Without Isaac to carry the load, Finis and Luke would not remain long.

He became so absorbed in his work and his thoughts about the Blackwoods that he did not see the other two horsemen who arrived on the faint trail which led from San Antonio de Bexar, capital of the Mexican state of Texas. He heard Petra clanging the piece of wagon tire hanging in the dog-run. She did not often use it except to call him to a meal, and this was midafternoon. He left the ox standing in the field, picked up his rifle that leaned against the pole fence, and trotted anxiously toward the cabin.

He saw two strange horses in the corral, three counting a sleek brown colt. The saddles on the fence were of a Mexican style rather than American.

As he walked up to the dog-run, he saw a thin dark-skinned man of forty or so years standing there, white teeth shining, his smile broad and friendly. *"Qué pasó?"* the man greeted him.

"Elizandro," Andrew exclaimed, his voice glad. Relief swept over him. "You are a long ways from home."

They gripped each other's arms in the *abrazo,* the Mexican manner of greeting between two old friends. "It has been a long winter since I have seen you," Andrew said in Spanish. Elizandro Zaragosa had learned considerable English, but he was more comfortable using his own language. Andrew had learned to be at ease with Spanish; Petra had been a good teacher. When he found himself at a loss for a word, he would throw in English and hope it was understood. "I saw two horses in the corral."

"My son Manuel came with me. You saw the colt?"

"I did."

"We have brought it for Michael's oldest."

"Mordecai will be pleased."

"The colt is not much in return for the many favors you Lewises have done for me and mine. When your boy is a bit older, I shall bring him a colt also, for the good American milk cow you brought me last fall."

"The cow was a gift."

"So is this colt, and the next one."

Petra came to the door. Her large eyes, almost black, took pleasure in the friendship between her husband and this former soldier, retired now to a quiet life as a farmer and livestock raiser at Bexar.

Manuel, eleven, seemed to have grown half a foot taller since Andrew had seen him in Bexar the previous fall. He was a handsome youth, thin, dark-skinned like his father, his eyes large and brown and full of life. He had the look of the outdoorsman about him, though Andrew knew his mother made him attend the church school and brooked no excuses that might let him stay out where he would rather be, with the cattle and horses. Manuel stood up quickly as his father and Andrew entered the room. He bowed slightly, with the good manners of his people, then shook Andrew's hand with a vigor he had learned from his association with *americano* frontiersmen like the Lewises.

This Manuel Zaragosa was going to grow up into a considerable man, Andrew thought. He shared the pride of his friend Elizandro.

Little Ben had already made friends with Manuel. Rose, barely two and shy around strangers, remained in a corner. She watched Manuel with misgivings.

Zaragosa said, "A wonderful family you have, Andrew."

Andrew hugged Petra and smiled. "We may not be through yet."

She blushed, which made him wonder. She was not pregnant so far as he knew, though no one could accuse him of not try-ing. She said, "You have worked enough for the day, Andrew. Take time now for a visit with our friend."

Andrew nodded. The same thought had come to him. When all the questions had been asked about Zaragosa's family in Bexar, his wife Elvira, and the children younger than Manuel, he said, "I left the ox in the field. Would you like to come with me, Elizandro, while I bring him up and turn him loose?"

Elizandro nodded and glanced toward his son. Manuel said, "Papa, I will stay and play with Benjamin."

Walking away, Andrew looked back to see the two boys on the dog-run, where Ben was petting his pup. Manuel was making a show of admiring the awkward little animal that had a hard time moving around without falling over its own feet.

Andrew said, "That's a fine boy you have, Elizandro. Is he going to be a soldier like you were?"

Zaragosa vigorously shook his head. "No, I came to hate the life of a soldier. I have no wish to see Manuel be a soldier, ever. Better that he become a good farmer and feed people instead of killing them."

They brought the blue ox to the shed, where Andrew put out a little hay and opened the gate so the animal would be free to go to the river for water and then drift away to graze. The ox never strayed far. He knew where the feed was.

Back in the cabin, sitting at the table and drinking coffee they saved for company and special occasions, Andrew asked, "What is the news in Bexar?"

Zaragosa frowned, pondering a while before he answered. His voice carried a tone of regret. "There is troublesome news from Mexico City, my friend. You know there have always been those there who have distrusted you Americans. Do you remember the General Mier y Terán, who was in Texas last year?"

"I heard of him."

"He did not like what he saw. He said visiting the American colonies was like visiting the United States. He found nothing of Mexico in them. He said the Americans are winning Texas without a battle and the central government should take steps. Now it has. Drastic steps."

Andrew felt a foreboding and set his coffee cup down. *Those damned Fredonians. What they did'll keep coming back to haunt us.* "What kind of steps?"

"It has ordered a stop to all further immigration by Americans. Only those who have their proper land papers or a proper passport can enter Texas."

Andrew's stomach began to burn with the rising of anger. "What about the ones already on their way?"

"They will be stopped unless they bring the papers."

Andrew saw the quick misgivings in Petra's eyes. He said, "We have relatives coming from Tennessee. Austin promised they could have land next to ours."

"Did he send them the papers?"

"No. They were to get those when they arrive."

Zaragosa shook his head regretfully. "Then it is too late. Unless they somehow miss the soldiers, they will be turned back. They will never reach here."

Andrew forgot he had been speaking in Spanish. "This is a hell of a damned thing," he declared angrily. "We were promised —"

"Promised by Austin, not by Mexico City. I wish there were something I could do. If I were still in the army — in the army I could do things, or I could overlook things."

Andrew walked to the door, worriedly staring out past the dog-run toward the trail to San Felipe. "I dread seeing Michael when he hears this. He will bust a gut."

Petra came up behind him and placed her hands gently on Andrew's shoulder. "Perhaps they will miss the soldiers."

Andrew shook his head. "They can't. We wrote them to travel the main trail to Nacogdoches."

She leaned her head against his shoulder. "I am sorry, Andrew. I know how much you and Michael wanted them here."

He turned, his troubled eyes on Zaragosa. "Maybe there is something I can do. I will ride to San Felipe tonight and get Austin to make out the papers in the morning. I will go then to Nacogdoches and take the trail east toward Louisiana. With luck, maybe I

31

can find them before the soldiers do."

Zaragosa arose. "It will be a long and hard trip. And it may be for nothing."

"It is the only answer I can see." Andrew touched a hand to Petra's cheek. He saw sadness in her eyes at the thought of his going. He went to English. "The plantin' has to wait, *querida*. I've got to go see if I can help my kin."

"Michael will be here tonight. Wait and talk with him."

He shook his head. "You know Michael and his restless ways. If I wait, he'll go instead of me. And once he's gone, Lord knows how far he'll ride or when he'll find his way back home. But if *I'm* gone, he'll have to stay here and look after things."

Zaragosa said, "I wish I could go with you. I still know many of the military in Nacogdoches. If one speaks to the right officers, anything is possible." He looked regretfully toward his son. "But I have Manuel with me."

Petra offered, "Manuel could stay here with us."

The boy said hopefully, "Or I could go with you, Papa."

Zaragosa said to Petra, "If he would be no imposition —"

"He would have a good time with Ben and

Mordecai. And they could learn much from him."

Zaragosa was not long in making up his mind. "While I am gone, son, you will remember that you are a gentleman."

Covering his disappointment, Manuel replied, "Yes, Papa."

Andrew smiled, grateful for having Zaragosa's company on the long journey ahead. "Fix us somethin' to take along, Petra. I'll go fetch up my horse."

CHAPTER 2

The United States lay most of a day behind them. They had crossed the two canvas-covered wagons over the Sabine River shortly after dawn, the rising sun at their backs. They were many miles into Texas now, and James Lewis was not sure he could see a big difference from the Louisiana side. Texas did not appear to have many people in it, at least not this part along the trail that meandered through the dense shade of tall pine trees and the formidable canebrakes that at times seemed to extend for miles. The wagon ruts had been cut deeply through years of passage by heavy, iron-rimmed wheels, moving westward toward Nacogdoches in Texas or eastward toward sister town Natchitoches in Louisiana. More headed westward than eastward, James would judge by the stories he had heard. People who went into Texas usually stayed. Certainly his two older brothers had. Now

34

James was going to join them and the excitement tingled within him again the way it had the day he and the others had set out from their old home in Tennessee.

Texas! The word had a ring to it, a sparkle, a magic that conjured up all manner of exotic images, even if so far the country looked the same as much of the land they had already passed through. It was the name that made the difference.

Riding a long-legged bay horse named Walker, James Lewis was a tall, thin, wiry man crowding twenty-one. He eagerly studied this new Texas with the restless, searching blue eyes that had run in the Lewis strain from as far back as the oldest could remember. Though James recalled little of his father, his mother had told him he had the same strong jaw, the same lean and sturdy frame. James supposed it must be true, for he remembered that look in his older brothers. He remembered it especially in Michael, who in a sense had taken his father's place. Woodsman Mordecai Lewis had put a strong stamp upon his sons.

That stamp went beyond the look. After a youth spent meeting the challenge of the fields and forests in Tennessee, James felt he was unlikely to encounter anything in Texas that he could not handle, given a little helpful counsel by Michael and Andrew to set his feet firmly upon the ground. His older brothers had one advantage: nearly a decade of experience in Texas. But James thought his youth should make up the difference. By his reckoning, Michael must be thirty now and Andrew about twenty-eight. In Tennessee that was regarded as almost middle aged. He supposed people must wear out at about the same rate in Texas.

He rode fifty yards in front of the lead wagon, watching for anything that might cause difficulty, such as a tree fallen across the trail or a washout that might break a wheel. Indians were in the back of his mind, but he had been told in Natchitoches that they were not likely to create trouble on this leg of the journey. The ones in eastern Texas were generally friendly. Folks had said it was renegade white men he should watch out for. Some, whose presence was greatly desired by the authorities in Louisiana and farther east, had found refuge in the redlands of eastern Texas, where the Mexican army force was small and mostly ineffective. Well, sir, they would be sorry if they came looking to prey upon these wagons. James held his long rifle across his saddle, ready for whatever might come. Folks back home claimed he was as good a shot as his brother Michael had been. He had kept the family table well supplied with meat after Michael left to go west. Though James had never been called upon to squeeze the trigger against a man, he did not doubt that he could do it. He wouldn't need the Mexican army to defend him and his.

The Mexican army. That was the only thing which gave him pause about coming to Texas: It belonged to Mexico. That made it a foreign land, with laws different in some ways from those he had known. He had often wondered how Michael and Andrew had made the adjustment. In Michael's letters, which James suspected had been written for him by his Louisiana French and Spanish wife, Michael had assured him that this was no particular obstacle. American settlers far outnumbered those from the Mexican interior, and most local laws in the American colonies were patterned after ones familiar in the old states. In many ways it would be as if James had never left home except that most of his family had remained far behind him.

But not all. He looked back at the lead wagon where his sister Annie drove the team of four big, strong mules that their Uncle Benjamin had selected from the best he owned. James never had understood why

Annie wanted to come along except perhaps that she thought she might find a better husband in Texas than the many prospects she had passed over in Tennessee. She was twenty-two, well on the way to becoming an old maid by Tennessee standards. Most men considered her uncommonly handsome, and many a likely lad had come calling. The best James could figure, she had measured them all by the memory of her brother Michael. As a girl she had idolized Michael, just as James had done. None of the young suitors cast a shadow as long as Michael's.

Older sister Heather had married at seventeen, as a young lady properly should, and she had four children now, as a young married woman properly should. Naturally she had not entertained any of this foolishness about going to Texas. But Annie had always been of an independent mind; you never could tell her anything she did not want to hear.

Following in the second wagon were cousin Frank and his family, moving lock, stock, and barrel to Texas. Frank Lewis was the same age as Michael, thirty or thereabouts. To James that seemed a little old to be setting out upon a new life. He was unsure of Frank's reason for leaving Tennessee, for Frank had just about everything there that a man could reasonably want, and he was by all odds the happiest-natured of the Lewis clan. It was said of Frank Lewis that you could set him down in Hell and he would find something to enjoy about the warm climate. James supposed Frank's restless, questing spirit had brought him here. Frank had been talking Texas for years, ever since Michael and Andrew had gone there. He talked Texas during his waking hours, and James suspected he dreamed about Texas when he slept. As Uncle Benjamin's oldest son, Frank stood to inherit a considerable amount of land back home someday. Nonetheless, Frank had said a man could amass far more land in Texas than he ever could in Tennessee. Ambition, he called it. But James suspected it was an adventuresome spirit, like brother Michael's. As a young man, Michael had never been able to stay in one place long. James wondered sometimes how his brother had remained in Texas for most of ten years. It would have been like him to have kept moving west until he came to mountains he could not climb or an ocean he could not swim.

James's heartbeat quickened with excitement when he thought about finally seeing Michael again after all these years. Never had anybody had an older brother quite the cut of Michael.

He heard a whistle from the wagons. Annie hailed him, waving her arm. She could stick two fingers in her mouth and whistle like a man. Heather never would have done that; she had too much feminine dignity. But anything Annie saw a man do, she took as a challenge to go him one better. She was even wearing a man's hat now instead of a conventional woman's bonnet. To James, that one fact was a pretty good indicator of her nature. He rode back to the front wagon and turned the bay horse around, keeping the steady pace of Annie's mule team. Annie stared expectantly at him with big blue Lewis eyes as if he should already know what she wanted. "What you need, sis?"

"I was thinkin' you ought to be ridin' ahead and findin' us a likely place to camp the night. We don't want to still be travelin' when dark catches up with us."

It was *his* place to decide when to start hunting a campsite, he thought, a little shy on patience. He had done a pretty good job as outrider all the way from Tennessee. Their coming into Texas was no excuse for Annie to start thinking she had to take charge just because she was a year or so

40

older. "There's a-plenty of daylight left," he said.

"Just don't you be crowdin' our luck."

James turned back and pulled up beside Frank Lewis's wagon. Frank was tall and rangy like all the Lewis men, like James himself. Being some ten years older, he was starting to show the lines and furrows that came from mature responsibilities, work, and worry. Not that Frank ever acted like he worried much. As far back as James could remember, Frank had always liked to tell stories and laugh and slap his knee. He, almost alone among the Lewis men, seemed always to have a book somewhere within reach. He had a boxful of them in the wagon. Just about anything in the world interested him. He could tell you the histories of foreign kings and queens. He could tell you what made the lightning flash and the thunder roll. At least, he claimed to know from the books he had read. That didn't keep him from being a good farmer and a middling hand with a hunting rifle, though not as good as Michael had been.

Michael! Like Annie, James always seemed to be holding men up to compare them with Michael, and they never measured quite so tall. Not even close kin.

One thing about Michael, though, he had

never smiled much, not like the next oldest brother, Andrew. Cousin Frank, now, he could be provoked to a smile over the least little thing, a toadfrog hopping across the road, or the way a mule cocked its ear over crooked. Some people back home had mistakenly thought he never took anything seriously. But Frank was serious about his family, his wife Hope, his two small boys who rode horseback behind the wagons, pushing along three extra horses and a pair of milk cows. Hope would be needing those milk cows, because anybody with half an eye could see that she was showing. In three months, maybe four, there would be another little Lewis. Frank had been anxious about their getting to the Austin colony in Texas and putting their cabin up before that event took place. A wagon was no place to birth a baby.

Hope Lewis sat beside her husband on the wagon seat. She wore a respectable cloth bonnet and a plain gray homespun cotton dress, practical for traveling like this because it did not show the dirt too much, and there was no way to keep clean on a long trail. James asked her, "You gettin' tired, Hope?"

"I'm doin' fine," she said. She had never been one to indulge in complaint or to tell her husband or James what they ought to

42

do next. She accepted what life sent her and acted as if it was exactly what she had ordered. But James saw fatigue in her eyes. He knew Annie was right, though he would not admit that to her until some snowy day in July. He had better be finding them a stopping place pretty soon.

"How about you, Frank?" James asked.

Frank's blue eyes sparkled. "If I grinned any bigger my face would bust and fall off. You ever see a prettier country?"

"Looks about the same so far as Louisiana."

"You're just goin' by what you see. I go by what I can feel. And I feel like this is a day we'll remember the rest of our lives. I just wisht them people that dropped out behind us had stayed all the way to see it."

The Lewises had thrown in their lot with a considerable string of wagons when they left Tennessee, but one by one the other travelers had reached their destinations or turned away onto other trails. Since Natchitoches there had been just these two wagons, just these Lewises, bound for a new life in a new land. James knew Hope missed all that company, for she had made a lot of new friends among the other wagon people. So had Annie, for that matter. But in truth James felt almost relieved that they were all to themselves now. It heightened his sense of responsibility, his sense of a challenge met and mastered. He had been but a ten-year-old boy when Michael and Andrew had left. He had to shoulder a lot of the responsibilities that had been theirs. He was a man now, and this trip gave him a chance to demonstrate it. He felt that Michael would approve. Michael's approval was important to him.

He dropped back a minute to check on Frank's two boys driving the loose stock, and to marvel at the pair of rough wooden cages that held Hope's precious laying hens at the rear of the wagon. He had thought for sure that those hens would get out somewhere along the way and make a meal for the wolves. Frank's books and Hope's chickens — quite a combination.

As he rode by Annie's wagon again, she asked anxiously, "How's Hope lookin'?"

"She looks fine to me," he said, knowing Annie was telling him in her own way that they ought to stop soon for Hope's sake. "She could probably travel half a day yet."

He heeled the bay horse into an easy lope, putting the wagon behind him before Annie could offer any more advice. He slowed the animal as soon as he was safely out of earshot, for he had inherited a love of horses from his father. He would not push one to the point of exhaustion without a strong reason. Horses were valuable property here in Texas, people said. A man would be a fool to abuse one, especially one as willing and able as Walker. James had raised Walker from a colt out of Uncle Benjamin's stock, had broken and trained him under his uncle's wise teaching. There hadn't been a better horse within twenty miles, maybe thirty. James had matched him in races several times against various horses brought up — stolen, probably — by the young Blackwood boys. They had never finished within a length and a half of Walker. The bay would have folks in Texas blinking their eyes, too.

Texas! James could remember when the word had brought dread to the Lewis family, for his father Mordecai had been killed in Texas almost fifteen years ago by Spanish soldiers who regarded him as an armed intruder. But conditions had changed by the time Michael and Andrew had moved to Texas nearly ten years ago. Mexico had won independence from Spain and had opened the gates for immigration. Texas offered a start for the young, like himself, and a renewal for the older ones like cousin Frank.

He was not sure what it offered Annie; probably not as much as she expected.

He came, after a mile or so, to a clear-running creek. The gray ashes and cold, blackened remains of old campfires told him that many travelers had made camp here in the past. A good day's wagon journey from the Sabine, it seemed a likely place to pause for the night. Deadfall timber nearby offered plentiful firewood. He dismounted, tasted the water, and found it good. After letting the horse drink, he tied it and began dragging up dry branches, breaking them over his knee. He wadded several handfuls of moribund grass left from last year's growth and struck fire into them with flint and steel, blowing the faint spark gently into a blaze and adding small chips of wood. By the time Annie and Frank pulled in with their wagons, he had a good fire going. An hour or more of sunlight was left, but an hour did not mean much on a journey of this length. He watched Frank gently help Hope down from their wagon. "Easy, little mama," Frank cautioned her, smiling. "The two of you have traveled far enough for one day."

Annie surveyed the campsite, and James waited to hear her make some complaint about it. She disappointed him, for she said,

"Nice place you found, James. I'm proud of you."

"I always find us a good place," he said defensively.

He unloaded the cooking vessels they would need to make supper. He had shot a young buck in the cool of dawn, so they had fresh meat. They had bought flour in Natchitoches, and corn they could grind for bread to save on the flour. They even had coffee, though they were careful to stretch it. There was just enough money for the real necessities. James was sure their journey to Texas had been much easier than the one Michael and Andrew made together a long time ago.

He and Frank's boys watered the horses and mules, then staked them where they could graze on new spring grass. The older and most dominant of the two milk cows had a calf, so all they had to do was tie the calf to a tree; the cow would not wander far. The younger cow would stay close to the older one. Her udder was dry, but she was starting to show some, like Hope. James left the milking chore to Frank's oldest boy. Milking cows was one job James had never relished, though he had done it often enough. Hunting was more to his liking. A cow's teats fit his hands about as poorly as a plow handle.

"Better hurry up, Edward," James told his nephew. "Smells like they've near got our supper ready."

Edward, hands already strong at eight, finished his milking and turned the calf loose to finish whatever was left. The red cow never let down all of her milk until the calf was punching at her udder; it was her instinct to save some for her offspring. When she held back too much, Frank would turn the calf with her for just a minute, then remove it to let Edward finish the milking. "It doesn't take much to fool a cow," Frank said, "so long as you're just a little smarter than she is."

The smell of frying venison drew James to the campfire. He realized how hungry he was. When the venison was cooked, Annie poured off most of the grease and dropped corn dodgers into the skillet. Bubbling on a bed of red-hot coals was a pot of beans that had already served them for two days. A man could get almighty tired of beans, but they came in handy on the trail. A big fresh pot, cooked overnight, could last for several days. All it needed was a little heating each time they made camp.

They all bowed their heads while Hope gave thanks to the Lord for delivering them safely into Texas after such a long journey. She beseeched His continuing guidance while they found their way down into the American colonies to settle beside those Lewises already there. "We hope you'll keep a-lookin' out for us, Lord, for we are Thy loyal servants, a-travelin' through a savage wilderness. Look with favor upon these young'uns here and the young'un soon to come. Protect us if Thou will from any who would come a-wantin' to do us harm. Amen."

James said, "Amen," and raised his head. He noted that his bay horse and a couple of the mules were staring fixedly toward the west, their ears pointed. He turned, searching. He saw a dozen or so horsemen moving in their direction on the trail.

"Hope," he said quietly, "maybe you'd better say the last part of that prayer over again." He went to the wagon wheel where he had leaned his rifle. He raised it up and cradled it across his left arm.

CHAPTER 3

As the riders neared, he saw that they were soldiers. Their uniforms were the worse for wear and dusty from traveling, but the man in the lead bore himself with the dignity James had always associated with lieutenants and captains and such. He did not remember that he had ever seen anyone higher in rank than that. His father had served with Andrew Jackson once, long before James's time, but all James knew about that was the stories he had heard in the family. He could not picture Mordecai Lewis in a uniform. He had most often worn buckskins.

The men were brown-faced, like some he had seen in Natchitoches. This was part of Mexico, so these must be Mexican soldiers, he reasoned. At least they were not the white renegades he had been warned about. But Spanish soldiers had shot his father a long time ago, probably not far from here.

He did not know how much difference there might be between Spanish and Mexican, so he kept the grip on his rifle. He was re-assured when cousin Frank stepped up beside him. Frank had a rifle too, but he carried it at arm's length, presenting no overt threat to the riders. Frank's genial countenance had fooled some people back home into believing they could crowd him as much as they wanted and never have to pay the fiddler. Frank's fighting streak was well hidden behind his smile, but that smile could turn cold just before lightning struck.

James asked, "What do you reckon they want with us?"

Frank shook his head. "Nothin' I can think of. They couldn't've known we were here till they seen us. Was I you, I'd lower that rifle and let them know we're friendly."

"I *ain't* friendly till I know what their intentions are."

Frank's smile froze, and his voice took on a tone of command. "Lower it."

James had always been taught to defer to age. He eased the rifle down. "I'd like to know first that *they're* friendly."

"It's their country."

"Ours too, now."

The riders crossed the creek, splashing water liberally. The man in command said something sharp in a language James could not understand. The soldiers spread out, reining up in a half-moon configuration around the little camp. The leader looked first at James, then at Frank. His black eyes revealed no friendliness. His accent was thick, but his words were clear. "Who is in command here?"

James considered telling him that Annie thought she was, but levity seemed inappropriate. Frank said, "Nobody is, exactly. We all just do our part."

"You are the only men here?"

Frank replied, "We're all there is. Two men, two women, two boys. Welcome to our camp."

"And where do you think you are going?" The question was voiced like a challenge.

James took it as one and was about to reply in kind, but Frank cut him off with a voice still calm and easy. "We're goin' to Nacogdoches, then on down to a place called San Felipe, in Stephen Austin's colony."

The soldier gave them a long study. If anything, his eyes seemed increasingly hostile. "You have the papers, then? Papers from the Esteban Austin?"

James gave Frank a questioning glance. Frank shrugged. James said, "We got a letter from my brother, sayin' Austin is holdin' us some land."

"But nothing from the Austin himself?"

"Just that letter, is all."

"Then by the new federal law which has come to us from Mexico City, you have no right to be here. No more Americans are allowed into Texas if they do not have already the papers from the Austin himself." He spoke quickly in that other language, and soldiers on either side of him drew their sabers. He said in English, "You are under arrest!"

James's face warmed in a flash of anger. "I've never been under arrest in my life! I ain't fixin' to start now." He tightened his grip on the rifle, though he still held it at arm's length. He shivered as he thought how one of those sabers would feel, run through his stomach.

A voice spoke from behind the soldiers. "You'll get used to it, friend. Happens a lot in this country."

A youngish American-looking man in buckskins sat slouched on a dun horse behind the soldiers. James had not noticed him before. The man's face had not felt a razor in many days. It was brown, but the color came from sun, not from Mexican blood. He wore a crooked grin that indicated he was taking a certain perverse pleasure from all this.

James declared, "You don't look like one of these soldiers."

The young man pushed his horse forward, stopping abreast of the soldier in charge. "You could say that Sergeant Díaz has made me his guest, if you wanted to put the best face on it."

The sergeant said firmly, "He is under arrest. You are all of you under arrest." At a command, one of the soldiers swung down from his horse and reached out for Frank's rifle. Frank reluctantly gave it up. As the soldier reached for James's rifle, James stepped back, bringing the weapon up into both hands. Several more soldiers swiftly drew swords. James saw the threat in their eyes and felt his heartbeat quicken, but he did not give up the rifle.

The American stepped down lazily from his dun horse. He still had that crooked smile, but the humor had faded from it. "I never was swift with figures, but I could always count up to twelve, and that's how many soldiers there is, friend. If I was you, I'd give up before they hurt you."

"We come a long ways to get here. My brother's letter said he had everything fixed up for us. We got a right."

"You're in Mexico, friend, and in Mexico it's the man with the rifles who tells you what rights you've got. If you won't give that gun to one of them, then give it to me, but be quick. Sergeant Díaz there, he's got no patience with Americans."

James backed up another step. "Nobody's takin' my —"

He saw the fist coming, but he was too late to dodge it. It struck him squarely on the chin, snapping his head back. He felt the rifle jerked from him as he staggered, then went down on his hands and knees. Streaks of lightning flashed in his eyes. Pain lanced from his chin up through his head and back down his neck. He would have sunk flat onto his stomach had cousin Frank's strong hands not grabbed and held him.

He heard the American say, "Here's the rifle, sergeant. The boy's just headstrong and don't understand the situation."

"He is arrogant, like all you *americanos*. But he is not in your country now. He is in mine."

James could hear Frank's voice. "What do you figure on doin' with us, sergeant? My wife here, she's in a delicate condition, as you can see."

"I will escort you back to the Sabine River

and see that you cross it."

"That's a whole day's trip. My wife is awful tired."

The sergeant gave Hope a moment's sympathetic study. "We will camp here tonight. We will take you tomorrow." He said something in Spanish, and his men dismounted. He asked Frank, "There are other guns?"

Frank was not smiling. "One more in each wagon."

James protested, but he could not tell that anyone heard him; at least no one paid attention to him. He saw Annie hand over the rifle she carried beneath her wagon seat. Frank fetched his second one, holding it with his hand away from the trigger guard to demonstrate that he had no intention of using it. It was probably not loaded, anyway.

The sergeant said, "No one will leave this camp tonight."

To James, that seemed a needless statement. With a dozen soldiers camped beside them, they weren't going to sneak two wagons, eight mules, the extra horses and two milk cows out of here.

The American knelt and gingerly touched James's chin. "I didn't go to hurt you, friend."

James angrily pushed the man's hand

away. "Sure didn't feel like you meant to do me any good. And don't call me *friend*."

"I meant you nothin' *but* good. Another minute and they'd've gutted you like a cat-fish."

"But we've got a right —"

"East of the Sabine you've got rights. Over here, Díaz holds all the cards, and he's got a hard feelin' towards Americans. If you don't want to lose your health awful sudden, you'd better be playin' the game by his rules. Come on now, let me help you up off of the ground."

James curtly shrugged him away. "I can get up by myself." He did, but he swayed a little. His jaw ached.

The man said defensively, "All right, so you've got a sore chin. But you're still breathin'. Ain't my fault you got caught."

"Seems to me like if they wasn't escortin' you back to Louisiana they wouldn't've come across us."

"You was goin' to Nacogdoches, wasn't you?"

"To register like my brother said, before we set off down to Austin's colony."

"Then it wouldn't've made any difference. They'd've turned you back when you got to Nacogdoches."

"Nobody in Louisiana told us there was a

new law."

"They probably ain't heard yet. Seems like the government in Mexico City taken a bad case of the itch about so many Americans settlin' in Texas. After all, it ain't been long since the Mexicans took their country away from Spain. Now they're afraid the Americans might take Texas away from Mexico the same way. So they've passed a law to stop any more from comin' in. A letter from your brother don't mean a damned thing to Díaz."

James's voice was bitter. "It meant several hundred miles in a wagon to us."

"There's good land to be had in Louisiana."

"We didn't come for Louisiana, we come for Texas. And one way or another, we'll get to where we was headed."

"I wouldn't let Díaz hear you say so."

James's stomach roiled in anger and frustration, and he still felt unsteady on his feet. He seated himself on a wagon tongue and watched resentfully as the Mexican soldiers unsaddled their horses. Hell of a thing this was, to travel so far and then be escorted back to Louisiana like criminals.

Annie had been studying the American with more curiosity than James thought was proper. She said, "I don't believe we heard your name."

"Díaz has got a name for me, but it's in Spanish, and you don't want to hear it. My mother named me Daniel — Daniel Shipman. Over home they just call me Sly."

"Sly?" Annie seemed intrigued. "How'd you come by a name like that?"

Shipman grinned. "Because folks say I'm pretty good at what I do."

"And what do you do?"

"I'm a merchant, you might say. I take American goods over into Texas and I trade for Texas goods to take back and sell in Louisiana."

James said grittily, "What you're sayin' is that you're a smuggler."

"I never did like that word myself. Truth is, I do the folks a service. There's people on one side of the river got goods that people on the other side would like to buy or swap for. But there's overfed lawyers a thousand miles away sayin' they mustn't do it. Now, show me in the Bible where it says I can't go around a mudhole when I find one in the road. I simplify people's lives, is all."

James saw irony in the man's nickname. "Folks call you Sly, but you wasn't sly enough not to get caught."

"This time. But it's been close to two

years since the last time they caught me. I been over here twenty, thirty times since and never let them even see my tracks. I wouldn't've got caught this time if a jealous competitor hadn't turned me in."

Annie pressed, "How did it happen?"

"I taken several mule loads of goods to some of my Cherokee Indian friends up above Nacogdoches. There's a trader over yonder who'd rob the Indians if it wasn't for me. He fetched Díaz and the soldiers. They confiscated my mules and throwed me in the Nacogdoches jailhouse."

James thought Annie seemed unnecessarily sympathetic. She said, "Mighty expensive for you, wasn't it?"

Shipman shrugged. "Not bad. The Cherokees stole the mules back from the soldiers. They'll keep them for me. I've always tried to make friends wherever I go. It's the Christian thing to do. And anyhow, it's good for business."

James grunted. "You ain't made a friend of Sergeant Díaz."

"Díaz is a good man, after his own lights. You can bribe most of these soldiers and they'll let you go. But Díaz is an honest man. Got a ramrod for a spine so that there ain't no bendin' him. And he ain't got much use for Americans."

60

Frank asked, "If he hates us so much, how come he talks pretty good American?"

"He lived in Louisiana a while. Way I heard it, his family had to run from the Spaniards because of their politics, and American renegades made life mighty hard for them on the other side of the river. Soured him against us all."

James frowned. "It ain't fair to judge everybody by a few."

Shipman smiled. "We all do it, don't we? I'll bet you've already laid a mark against all Mexicans because of Díaz."

James started to say this was different, but he reconsidered. He had always been made uncomfortable by people who forced him to back off and take a look at himself. They made him see things he would as soon have overlooked.

Annie said, "We were fixin' to have our supper, Mr. Shipman. We'd be tickled to share with you. Invite Sergeant Díaz, too. Maybe he'd feel a little better towards us."

"He mightn't take it kindly, ma'am. He'd figure you was tryin' to bribe him. He'd still put you across the Sabine tomorrow. Was I you, I'd save my venison. But me, I'd be much obliged to join you and your husband."

James was about to tell him Annie was his

61

sister, but Annie hastily beat him to it. "I have no husband. This hotheaded young man is just my brother."

Just her brother, like that didn't mean much. James grimaced. He would like to have seen Annie get this far without him along. If it had been up to him, she would still be at home in Tennessee.

Shipman removed his hat and bowed slightly from the waist. "Well now, ma'am, I must say that comes as a surprise to me. I'd've figured a handsome young woman like you to already have herself a husband. Must be a lot of blind men back where you-all come from."

Annie smiled like the sun had just come up.

Shipman said, "I believe you have the advantage of me, ma'am. You know my name, and I don't know yours."

"I am Annie Lewis. This is my brother James and my cousin Frank and his wife Hope. And those are their boys, Edward and David. We were on our way to join our brothers Michael and Andrew, down in Austin's colony."

Shipman frowned. "Michael Lewis. That name's got somethin' familiar about it." He pondered a moment. "Would he be the Michael Lewis that married Old Man Villaret's daughter, from over in Natchitoches?"

Annie said eagerly, "The same. We stopped for a day and got acquainted with the Villarets. Do you know Michael?"

"No, but Old Man Villaret taught me most of what I know about my business. He was in it hisself for a long time. And what he didn't teach me, Old Eli Pleasant did. I've heard Eli speak of Michael Lewis. They was good friends."

Frank smiled, remembering. "Eli visited us in Tennessee."

"I still miss that old reprobate. He was killed by some renegade, you know, down in Austin's colony. Him and me, we used to make trips together, tradin' goods. Wasn't nobody slicker when it come to goin' around the authorities. Made no difference to Eli if they was on the Mexico side or the other one. He forgot more than most of us'll ever know."

Annie said, "If he was here, maybe he could figure some way to help us get out of this mess. We didn't come this far to just turn around and go back to Tennessee."

James said with irony, "While he was teachin' you so much about smugglin', I don't suppose he taught you a way to go around *our* problem."

Shipman made that crooked little grin.

63

"Maybe he did. But things are a little close in this camp, and you don't know how many ears are listenin'. We'll talk about it on the other side of the river."

Frank showed quick misgivings. "I've got my family here. I wouldn't want to do anything that'd put them in danger."

"Friend, you taken them into danger as soon as you left home." He turned to Annie. "Ma'am, reckon it would strain hospitality too much if I was to ask for another little piece of that venison?"

Supper finished, they sat around the campfire. Frank asked Shipman a lot of questions about Texas. James listened closely. They were questions he would have wanted to ask if he felt more kindly toward the young smuggler.

Annie climbed down from the wagon with a pencil and some papers in her hands. She sat a little way back from the fire and started sketching. James wondered what she found here that was worth drawing pictures of. Annie had always been something of an artist. Before she left home she had sketched a couple of pictures of their mother to give to Michael and Andrew. She had sketched others of the family, and the old family cabin. Along the trail from Tennessee she had sketched scenes they encountered and wrote notes about the things they saw. At least, when she was sketching she wasn't giving him the jaw about something or other.

Shipman was eventually nagged by curiosity enough that he pushed to his feet and went over to see what Annie was drawing. He declared in surprise, "Why, that's me."

She nodded. "As near as I can draw you."

"I didn't think I was all that handsome."

Annie seemed to blush. "I draw things the way I see them."

James said, "It's gettin' dark. You probably can't see very good."

James slept little that night. He was always conscious of the Mexican soldiers camped beside them. He did not know what manner of men they might be, how far they could be trusted. He insisted that Annie sleep in the wagon, though it was cramped and uncomfortable because of the farming equipment and few pieces of cookware and furniture they had hauled all the way from Tennessee. He rolled his blankets on the ground close beside the wagon, where he could hear if anyone tried to sneak into it. Nothing happened. He heard the Mexican soldiers talking quietly at each change of the guard. He noticed that the guards faced into the camp rather than outward from it.

They were more concerned about keeping their prisoners than about any threat that might come upon them from outside. They need not have worried, James thought. He saw no way to escape.

If he had been by himself, it might be different. He almost wished he had come alone like Michael and Andrew, carrying nothing that he could not pack on a horse. These soldiers would have played hell catching him, or holding him if they *had* caught him. Unencumbered, he could have given them a run for their money. Once into the woods he would have been gone like a red fox.

They were up at daylight and fixed a hasty breakfast. Sergeant Díaz impatiently prodded them to be done with it so they could set out upon the trail. He spoke harshly to James and to Sly Shipman, but he was civil to Frank and chivalrous to the two women. He seemed particularly solicitous about Hope's welfare.

Shipman said to James, "See what I told you? He ain't a bad man, that Díaz. He's just got his own notions about things, is all."

"I wish he didn't have such a strong notion about sendin' us back into Louisiana. If we could just get to San Felipe, my brothers would see to it that we had all the papers we need."

"This is a long ways from San Felipe."

"We'll get there. I swear we'll get there!"

The afternoon sun was low at their backs when they returned to the banks of the Sabine. The teams were tired, and Hope looked exhausted, but Díaz would not permit them to camp another night in Texas. He pointed to the shallowest ford and declared, "We will camp here. You will be closely watched, so do not think you can wait until we are gone and then cross again."

James thought, *Watch till your eyes fall out, damn you, but we'll be coming back.*

Díaz seemed to read his mind. Frowning darkly, he said, "I would not advise it."

James felt more angry than frightened. "What about our guns? We'll need them to find meat on our way back to Tennessee."

The soldiers had tied the confiscated rifles to a pack mule. Díaz ordered them untied. He made sure they were unloaded, then gave them to Frank rather than to James. He told Frank, "You should counsel this young one. I have no wish to see him buried in Texas."

Frank said, "Stubborn runs in the family. We outgrow it, most of us."

Díaz turned to Shipman. "I do not waste my time with advice to you. I know you will be back."

Shipman simply smiled.

Díaz said, "I will be watchful, and I will have a cell waiting for you. It will be deep and dark."

The Lewises put the teams into the river, and in a few minutes the mules and the wagons were dripping water on the Louisiana shore. James looked back. True to his word, Díaz and his men were making camp on the Texas bank.

To travel so far and be turned back — He smacked a fist into the palm of his left hand.

Shipman said, "Don't bust your fingers for nothin', friend. Like I told you, there's ways."

CHAPTER 4

James looked west, across the river. He could see Sergeant Díaz's campfire on the Sabine's far bank. His resentment still simmered. He turned back to his own fire, where Annie had made coffee. They did not drink it every day, for it was scarce and expensive, but she had decided tonight it might help take the edge off their disappointment. Or maybe she was trying to impress Sly Shipman.

Two nights ago they had camped on this same Louisiana riverbank. The smell of spring's rebirth was in the air, and the birds had sung prettily up in the trees. James thought it must be a different set of birds tonight, for they were making noise, not music.

Annie was acting very pleased because Shipman had agreed to camp with them the night instead of riding on, as if he were doing them a big favor. James had a feeling that they could not have chased him away with a club, not when he had a chance to enjoy another woman-cooked meal or two. And he seemed taken with Annie's company. Quite a few of the young men back home had shown a similar departure from good judgment. Had they been watching Annie for twenty years from a brother's close perspective, seeing her critical moods without being swayed by her handsome looks, they might not have tarried.

James said grittily, "Look at him over yonder, that Díaz. I expect he'll stay there as long as we stay here."

Shipman glanced up from his coffee. "Longer. He'll want to be sure you don't turn around and go right back across."

"That's pretty much what I had in mind."

Shipman had taken time to shave off his several days' growth of whiskers. It probably made him look better to the women, but James did not see it as much of an improvement. James's jaw was still sore.

Shipman said, "Try to look at it the way he does. He figures that you'll figure that very thing. So if you move your wagons east tomorrow, out of his sight, he'll figure you're figurin' that he'll turn back to Nacogdoches. He'll figure you're figurin' to go back across as soon as you figure he's left.

So he'll pull off a ways into the woods and wait out of sight, figurin' to catch you. Like as not, he'll stay close to the river for two or three days, tryin' to outsmart you."

"So how long do you think we'll have to wait?"

"Was I you, I wouldn't wait at all. I'd just pull back where they couldn't see me from across the river, then head south on this side. There's other good crossin's down yonder a ways. Then, while he's still wastin' his time up here, you head southeast and light a shuck straight for San Felipe. There's been people crossin' this river for a long time — folks that didn't want the authorities lookin' over their shoulders."

James looked at his cousin Frank, asking with his eyes.

Frank said dubiously, "Sounds too easy. Things that're too easy never work like they're supposed to."

Shipman shook his head. "Ain't but a handful of soldiers in all of northern Texas. Them tryin' to shut off the whole border is like tryin' to wipe out an ant-bed with a sharp stick."

Annie and Hope were washing the supper tinware in a pan. Annie said, "I don't suppose there'd be a regular trail?"

Shipman sipped his coffee, then shook his

71

head. "If there was a trail the soldiers'd know about it. No, you'll have to make your own way. All you need is a good sense of direction."

James straightened his back to show his confidence. "You don't need to worry, sis. I've led you this far."

"You had a marked trail to follow. I just wish Michael or Andrew could've come and met us. Things'd've been a lot easier."

"If you'd wanted it easy, you ought to've stayed home like I told you."

Annie turned to Shipman. "Reckon we could persuade you to go with us and show us the way?"

James was about to protest that they could make it on their own, but Shipman did not give him the chance. "I wish I could, ma'am, but I got business responsibilities. I'll go with you a ways in the mornin', as far as my cabin, to point you right. Then I'll have to bid you *adieu,* as they say in Natchitoches. I must say, I'll miss you ladies' good cookin'. A man gets kind of lank bein' on the trail most of the time, doin' for hisself."

James was mortified to hear Annie say, "You should get yourself a good wife, Mr. Shipman." It was almost as if she were hinting for the job.

"Yes, ma'am, many's the time I've thought

72

about that. But bein' married to me would be like bein' hitched to a boat captain who's always at sea. I wouldn't wish that off onto any woman I thought a lot of. And if I didn't think a lot of her, there wouldn't be no point in me marryin' her, would there?"

Annie smiled. "You'll run into somebody someday who'll make you want to keep your business close to home."

Shipman nodded, staring at her in a way that James thought bordered on being indecent. "That could sure be, ma'am."

They were on the trail as soon as breakfast was finished. The wagons backtracked eastward a couple of miles, the way they had originally come from Natchitoches, until they reached a dim trace that turned off to the south. Shipman, on his dun horse, tipped his hat to Annie on the lead wagon and told her — not James — that they should follow him. James looked back. The river had long since fallen out of sight.

James said suspiciously, "What if Díaz sent a scout over here to keep an eye on us?"

"Mexican soldiers can't cross into Louisiana, and American soldiers can't cross over into Texas. There's a treaty."

"Did Díaz sign it?"

"Sergeants don't get to sign treaties or

73

make laws. They just get sent out to do the dirty work. No, Díaz'll be waitin' in the timber, watchin' for you to try and sneak back across the river. But you-all're fixin' to fool him."

Toward noon the wagons reached a log cabin that stood high above the river. James was a little nervous about being back within sight of the Sabine again. What if Díaz had sent a scout downriver to watch the crossings? He sat on his bay horse and studied the opposite bank and its timber for some minutes. He saw no sign of life.

Shipman seemed to know what James was thinking. "Was I you I wouldn't be in a cold sweat. Everything'll be all right."

James was not convinced. "You seem to know a lot about how Mexican soldiers think."

"Ever since I was fourteen years old I been makin' my livin' outguessin' them."

The cabin was old and not nearly so well built as one the Mordecai Lewis family once had back in Tennessee. It was a single small cabin without a dog-run to divide it into two sections. The place sure needed some patching up, James thought. "You build this yourself?" he asked Shipman.

"No, I fell into it by inheritance, you might say. It belonged to Old Eli Pleasant.

Him and me, we worked out of here a lot of times. When nobody showed up to claim his property after he died, I reckoned Old Eli wouldn't mind me goin' on and usin' it."

Frank noticed a white locust tree in front of the cabin, flanked on either side by a cactus-like plant known as the Spanish dagger. He remarked that it was an odd match, somehow.

Shipman grinned crookedly. "You'll find a good many places in this part of the country have got the same arrangement. Sort of a custom here, you might say."

James suspected from his manner that there was more to it than that, but Shipman volunteered no additional information. He turned to Annie. "This is my place," he said. "You-all'll want to stop here for dinner and rest your stock a while." He pointed toward a small barn and lean-to shed and a set of horse pens. "There's corn out there for the mules. I'll unhitch them for you."

Annie smiled warmly. "Much obliged." She waited for Shipman to help her down from the wagon seat. James had seen her get down from it by herself several times a day all the way out from Tennessee. He had never noticed her needing help.

Frank was particularly interested in the place, for he remembered Eli Pleasant much

75

better than James did. While the three of them unhitched the mules and led them to the pen, Shipman and Frank took turns recounting stories about Eli's exploits. Frank's two boys walked along and listened, their mouths wide open. The stories made Eli sound nine feet tall. James thought it a wonder that the old man had managed to live as long as he had, because skirting the laws of two countries had been a way of life for him. James deduced that smuggling on this frontier was a crime only in the eyes of the authorities; it was regarded as a welcome service by the common people who lived on both sides of the Sabine.

Frank said, "I've heard stories about the outlaws who stay close to the river so they can swim quick if they have to. How could Eli have operated here so long without some of them robbin', maybe even killin' him?"

Shipman said, "There's a kind of unwritten treaty amongst us who live here. We don't bother one another. We don't see nothin' or hear nothin', and we sure as hell don't tell nothin' if the authorities from either side come pokin' around. Eli lived up to that code and so do I. Anybody breaks it is apt to have trouble catchin' his breath."

James frowned. "Is it thataway down in Austin's colony?"

"No, it's so law-abidin' that they ain't even built them a decent jailhouse. Anybody tries to start a ruckus, Austin and his people run him out so quick his shadow is a day late catchin' up with him."

By the time they got the mules unhitched and watered and fed a little corn, they found Annie and Hope sweeping out the cabin. Shipman admonished them, "You ladies don't need to be doin' that. It'll just get all dirty again."

Annie said accusingly, "I never have understood how a man can live in a place like this and never straighten it up."

James smiled inwardly. Now she was showing Shipman a little of her true self. They would be seeing the last of him pretty soon now, for a little of Annie's lecturing went a long way. The man would be glad to wave them good-bye.

Shipman said, "I don't exactly live here. I just use this for a startin' and stoppin' place. Out on the trail is where I *live*."

Annie gave him a look of pity. "Just the same," she said, "it won't hurt this cabin to feel the broom now and again."

Shipman nodded amiably. "I'm mighty glad to've run into you ladies. Makes me realize there's a whole other world back yonder, and I been missin' out on some of

77

its finer blessin's."

Before long the women had smoke coming out of the chimney and venison frying in the fireplace. At the rate Annie was cooking up the meat, James thought he was going to have to leave the wagons and go hunting again. But Shipman went into a lean-to and brought out a couple of cured hams. "I'm puttin' these into your wagon, Miss Lewis."

She protested that his generosity was unnecessary. Shipman said, "It's mighty little for the good meals I've eaten with you-all and for the kindness you ladies done me in fixin' up this cabin. Why, it almost looks human again."

"It needs a woman in it," Annie said.

"Eli used to have one once in a while. He'd fetch them out of Natchitoches and one place and another. Widder women, mostly, lookin' for a new husband. They would pretty soon decide Eli wasn't the one they was lookin' for."

Hope was a little shocked. "You mean they came here without even the benefit of clergy?"

"You have to understand, ma'am, that the clergy ties a hard bind. Eli was always partial to a slipknot. That way, there wasn't no harm done if the match didn't fit. And it

78

never did."

Annie's eyebrows arched. "Do you feel that way too, Mr. Shipman?"

"It worked mighty fine for Eli."

James noticed that Annie didn't talk much after that. She looked as if she were on the verge of giving somebody a stern lecture, but she kept it to herself.

Shipman helped James and Frank reharness the mules after dinner. The boys poked around all the way down to the river, exploring. Frank hated to leave, for Hope had been able to stretch out and rest a while on a real bed; in her condition, Lord knew she needed it. But James itched to get started. He was not nearly so confident as Shipman that Díaz would remain at the other crossing. Up here on this high bank, the wagons would be visible from across in Texas.

Hitching Annie's team, Shipman said, "You'll camp tonight on this side. Sometime tomorrow afternoon you'll come to a place where the river shallows out, and you can cross over without much trouble."

James asked, "How'll we know the place? Is it marked?"

"Not exactly. Nobody wants to let the authorities know about it, because there's been folks crossin' it both ways. But there's the leavin's of an old cabin that some fool let catch afire, and a burned-up tree that stood beside the cabin. The ford is about two hundred yards farther on. You'll know when you come to it."

Annie did not say anything, so Hope said it for her. "You would not reconsider and go along with us, Mr. Shipman?"

"Ma'am, I got to go to Natchitoches and see about a new stock of tradin' goods and some pack mules. Apt to be a while before I can get my others back from my Cherokee friends."

"A pity," James said, not meaning it. "We was just beginnin' to know one another."

Shipman said, "When you get across the river, it'd be a kindness, if you'd take pains to smooth over your tracks the first little ways. That'd help others who might cross later. What the authorities don't know ain't apt to get anybody hurt. Besides, it might keep them from trailin' after you."

James would not want to admit he had not thought of that. He supposed he lacked the devious mind of a man like Shipman who made his living dodging detection.

Shipman waved to the boys, shook hands with the men — Frank first — and tipped his hat to the two women. Hope smiled and thanked him. Annie just nodded, a little cold. She had little to say as they moved south on a dim trail that paralleled the river but was never quite in sight of it. James suspected the trail had been used mostly by people like Eli Pleasant and Sly Shipman, who had no wish to be seen from the other side.

And people like us, he thought.

That idea gave him pause, for it put him in the company of smugglers. But of course the Lewises were not smugglers; they were just illegal immigrants. He gathered from what Shipman said that Texas had a lot of those.

The trail had not been used heavily. At times it was so dim that it was not actually a trail at all. Often he had to pick a slow and cautious way through rough, washed-out terrain and deadfall timber that threatened to stop the wagons. Annie curtly asked him if perhaps he had lost the trail entirely.

"You can't lose somethin' that nobody ever found in the first place," he retorted.

He became half convinced that Shipman had sent them on a fool's errand, but every so often he would find enough of a trace to indicate that others had negotiated this same route. If they had, he could.

He noticed the bay horse's ears turn suddenly forward. The animal had a knack for seeing everything that moved. James

81

blinked, sweat burning into his eyes from the effort of picking a path. He saw half a dozen horsemen moving toward them from downriver. He wondered for a moment if Díaz might have brought soldiers across in defiance of treaty prohibitions. Well, if he had, there was little they could do on this side except threaten. Here, east of the Sabine, the Lewises were on their own country's ground.

He saw in a minute that the men wore no uniforms. Uneasily, he turned back toward the wagons. He found an open spot and motioned for Annie to halt there and for Frank to bring his wagon up close to Annie's.

"We got company comin'," he said, "and there ain't no tellin' if they're friendly. Annie, you and Hope better get down and stay behind the wagons — you boys, too." He gave cousin Frank a questioning glance. "Got your rifle loaded?"

"It's always loaded," Frank replied. There was no hint of a smile in his eyes. He fetched Hope's from beneath the wagon seat and loaded it as well. Annie did not have to be told. She poured fresh powder into her rifle's pan. She asked, "What could anybody want with us?"

James replied grimly, "They might want

what we've got with us — the wagons and what-all's in them."

It was in the back of his mind that they might even want the two women. He had heard of such things. Out of earshot of Annie and Hope, Shipman had told James and Frank that just such an atrocity had befallen Sergeant Díaz's sister, one reason the soldier resented Americans so bitterly.

Frank said, "I count six — no, seven. If they really want these wagons, won't be much me and you can do except try to keep the women and young'uns from gettin' hurt."

Defiantly, James replied, "We can fight them."

Frank shook his head, his normal good humor replaced by a grimness that made him look a little like James's memory of his older brother Michael. Frank said, "We got one shot apiece. Two, if you figure the women's rifles. If me and you get ourselves killed, what happens to Hope and Annie and the boys?"

"We can't just let them people take us over."

"We can let them have the wagons, if it comes to that."

"We brought these wagons all the way from Tennessee. I ain't givin' them up without a fight."

"You're just shy of twenty-one, James. You got a long life ahead of you if you don't throw it away. You can earn back everything that's in those wagons. You can't earn your life back."

James did not feel like arguing. But he was convinced that his brother Michael would not back away in a situation like this, and James had no intention of doing so, either.

James put his and Annie's wagon between him and the approaching horsemen, letting the long barrel of his rifle extend up and over the wagon wheel where the riders could see it.

The men reined up. There were seven, just as Frank had counted. They were a rough-looking set, all bearded except for a youngster on one end who had not started to grow whiskers yet. Something about him reminded James of the Blackwood family back home, about as shiftless a lot, all in all, as one was likely to encounter anywhere besides a county jailyard.

James's and Frank's rifles seemed to have gotten the riders' full attention. They held back fifty to seventy-five feet. All of them seemed to look to a tall, gaunt man with a gray-salted black beard that reached a long way down the front of a dirty cotton shirt.

The man raised one hand, then touched his heels gently to the ribs of a black horse and rode forward alone, toward the wagons. "Howdy, folks," he said affably. "Ain't no need you-all bein' so free with them weapons. We're just travelin' people, like you-all. We mean you no violence."

James said, "Fine. Just go on around, then. Way around."

"Well now, we'd do that, but we'd feel ashamed because we had throwed such a scare into a set of pilgrims without cause. We'd feel like you thought we was outlaws of some kind, and maybe give others a bad report about us on down the trail. We couldn't just leave here with such a misunderstandin' hangin' in the air."

Frank muttered, "They're out to rob us, James. You can see it written all over his face. He's playin' with us, tryin' to set us off of our guard. Let's just back off into the timber and let them have what they want, except they can't have *us*."

"I can shoot him right where that beard stops."

"You ever shot a man?"

"No. He'd be my first."

"And your last. Them others'd be on us in a second. Let's just get the women and young'uns back into the timber."

85

"*You* do it. I ain't lettin' them have our wagons."

Frank was angry. James had not often seen him that way. "Damn it, James, listen to somebody, will you?"

James was listening to something else, a horse coming in a run behind them. In dismay he said, "They've sent somebody to go around us." He wanted to kick himself for not being more alert to such a move. Michael would not have made such a mistake.

He glanced back over his shoulder and saw a dun horse. He knew the rider. For a moment he wondered if Sly Shipman might be in league with these renegades, that he might purposely have sent these wagons south into a trap.

Shipman slowed his dun horse to a walk. He carried a long rifle across his saddle. He gave the Lewises a quick glance, then turned his attention to the horsemen, especially the dark-bearded one who had moved forward. "Well now," he said, "good evenin', friends. I hope I have interrupted somethin' here that looks like it could cause considerable grief."

The tall, bearded man said, "If you're part of this bunch, I wisht you'd tell them to put their rifles away. I never was partial to havin'

86

a rifle pointed at my brisket. Makes me all-fired nervous."

Shipman said, "But I believe you can see how a bunch of you bustin' in here like this would make these people nervous, too. Was I you, I'd just ride on around and forget whatever it was you had in mind."

The tall man squinted. Gone was any false friendliness. "And just who might you be, a-givin' out advice so free?"

"I'm Sly Shipman."

The man blinked in surprise at the name, but suspicion quickly crept back into his eyes. "Anybody could say they're Sly Shipman."

"Who else besides the real one would want to claim such a thing?"

"You got a point there," the man conceded.

A young horseman called out, "He's Shipman all right, Clem. I've seen him before."

Clem seemed to wilt a little. He gave the wagons a long, disappointed study. "And I suppose these people are with you?"

"They're friends of mine. I'm askin' safe passage."

Clem glanced regretfully over his shoulder at the men behind him. "Since it's you, Shipman —" He backed his horse a step or two, then turned him. He waved his arm

87

over his head. The riders took a long swing around the wagons and proceeded north-ward.

Frank let out a long-held breath. "I'll declare, Sly, you get better-lookin' every time we see you."

"I got to thinkin' about it," Shipman said. "I was afraid you might happen upon some of these old boys."

James said stubbornly, "We was fixin' to take care of things by ourselves, without help."

"And just what was you fixin' to do?"

"I was fixin' to shoot that tall one and let them know our intentions was to not give an inch."

Shipman frowned. "Have you always been so damned mule-headed, or is this an ail-ment that's just lately come over you?"

CHAPTER 5

James thought Annie might mellow again to Sly Shipman in response to his rescuing them from the Louisiana renegades, but she remained cooly civil. When she took offense, she was not lightly moved to forgiveness. James also remained suspicious. He rode beside Shipman, who knew the trail and picked an easier way for the wagons than James had been able to do. James suspected he had ridden it often, mostly in the dark.

James weighed the proprieties and decided to ignore them. He said, "Those robbers backed off real quick when they heard your name. Who'd you kill to make them so afraid of you?"

Shipman seemed surprised at the question. "Who says I killed anybody?"

"Stands to reason. Otherwise they'd've just gone ahead and tried to take us over, and you with us."

"I told you there's an understandin', kind

of, among all us that lives in the strip between Natchitoches and the river. We leave one another alone. Everybody in the strip knows me by name, even if they don't know my face, same way they always knowed old Eli. Nobody ever messed around with Eli more'n once, and that protection shed off onto me. The locust tree and them Spanish daggers you asked about — Eli put them there. They was always a symbol in the strip. They meant you was to be left the hell alone."

James was almost disappointed. "You never killed anybody?"

Shipman's face seemed to darken. "I never killed anybody the world wasn't better off without."

As he had promised, the wagons reached the burned cabin about the middle of the afternoon. A rock chimney stood like a grave marker amid blackened coals and a remnant of gray ashes not yet washed away by the rains. The charred trunk of a tree stood beside the ruins. Frank said such a scene deserved a good story. "Who done this, robbers? Indians?"

Shipman grunted. "Nothin' so adventure-some as all that. Couple fellers I know got liquored up on Kentucky squeezin's they bought from a wagon peddler in Natchitoches. One of them knocked a candle over and was too drunk to find it. Said he seen two of them, but the one he kept reachin' for wasn't real. Him and his partner got out with nothin' much except their britches, and them scorched pretty bad."

Frank laughed. "A pretty good story, but it'd make a better yarn if it had some wild Indians in it."

Shipman shrugged. "We do the best we can with what the Lord sees fit to give us."

He didn't ask James, but he spoke to Frank, Annie, and Hope. "You can either cross the river now and travel a good ways before night, or you can rest here and get a fresh start in the mornin'. I'll see you safely across before I go home."

Frank was more sparing of James's feelings. "What do you think, James? Reckon we hadn't better be goin' on?"

James was grateful for the recognition from his cousin. "I say we go now. We can make a few miles with the daylight we've got left." The longer they waited, he thought, the greater the chance Díaz would find them.

Frank nodded at Shipman. "That's how it is, then. We're all anxious to get over into Texas."

Shipman looked pleased. "That would've

been my choice, but it's your family." He started down the slope toward the river, letting James and the wagons and the livestock follow after him. Shipman rode back and forth in the edge of the water, seeking the place where the bottom would be firmest. By the time the wagons reached the river, he had found it.

James feared they might have to double the teams and take the wagons across one at a time, but the ford was shallow and made that unnecessary. He rode close to Annie's wagon, ready to help her if an emergency should arise. None did. Annie was as cool as a professional mule skinner. She talked the mules across, her voice steady and reassuring, without the profanity he would have felt obliged to use. Mules were dependable most of the time, if somewhat on the stubborn side. But water could throw them into a quick panic if anything went awry, if their feet suddenly failed to reach bottom, and especially if they began to flounder and get water in their ears. James had seen mules go crazy and drown themselves. Given a little bad luck, they could take somebody with them.

The crossing was uneventful. James rode back to where Frank's two boys waited with the loose stock and helped drive the animals across in the wake of the wagons. As they came up onto the opposite bank, Edward asked, "Is this Texas?"

"It is."

"What if they catch us and throw us out again?"

"We'll keep comin' back in spite of them. But this time we don't aim to let anybody catch us. Get down, Edward, and help me brush out these tracks."

James found a heavy branch that the wind had broken from a tree. He dragged it back and forth across the wet tracks left by wagons and animals. Edward came along behind him with a much smaller branch and finished the work. It would be almost impossible to get the ground completely smooth, but sunshine would soon sap the water from the sand, and wind would shift enough of the dry surface that only the most observant could know someone had passed this way.

James and Edward continued their work until the wagons passed out of their sight. A little way from the river, Shipman had directed Annie and Frank onto grassy ground where the tracks were less conspicuous than in the sand, though the weight of the wheels crushed the grass down. James told the boy, "Not much we can do here except hope that if any soldiers come along they ain't lookin' real close. The grass ought to straighten itself in a day or two. We better lope up."

He thought Shipman was simply going to see them across the river, then turn back. But he found that Frank had talked the man into staying with them to the night camp and sharing a last good supper. Young Edward said, "I'm sure glad. He's a lot of help, Mr. Shipman is."

"He eats a lot," James replied.

He admitted to himself, though he would not to anyone else, that Shipman helped steer them around a dense canebrake that might have cost them a lot of time had they wandered into it. They would have had to hack their way through or turn around and backtrack. They were traveling southwest-ward, the proper direction. But knowing the right direction was not enough. Shipman took them around the southern edge, rea-soning that any soldiers who might come looking this way would probably approach from the north and would not care to invade the heavy growth of cane, even on horse-back.

As they came upon a creek and prepared to make camp, Frank cheerily echoed his son's comment. "Mighty lucky we are to have Sly with us."

James frowned. "I'll bet there's some sheriffs that would like to have him, too."

Frank grinned and led his mules down to the water.

Annie said nothing. James thought she tried hard not to look in Shipman's direction.

James expected to see Shipman turn back as they broke camp the next morning and set the wagons on a southwesterly course. But Shipman beckoned him off to one side and said, "I'm hanged if I can figure out what I done to provoke your sister. I hate to go off and leave her feelin' ill towards me."

James knew Annie had bowed up over Shipman's comment about not needing to get married when the benefits could be had without the tether. But he simply said, "She's always been kind of touchy. Half the time you can't tell what she's thinkin'."

Frank suggested to Shipman that they might need his guidance a little farther, for this one more day, at least. There were bound to be some more canebrakes ahead. Shipman's experience in traversing this part of the country would be a great help and would earn the family's everlasting gratitude.

"I'll do it," Shipman said, giving in much

easier than James thought was necessary, "but I'll want somethin' in return."

Now we're coming to it at last, James thought. He had felt all along that Shipman's help had not been given simply out of the kindness of a big heart.

Frank asked, "And what might that be?"

Shipman looked at Annie. "That picture Miss Annie drawed of me. I'd sure admire to have it. When I'm old and gray and all hunched over, I can show everybody what I looked like when I was in my prime."

James doubted that Shipman would ever get old. Somebody was bound to shoot him long before then.

Annie did not smile. "*I* certainly have no use for it."

Shipman added, "I don't reckon you've drawed a picture of yourself, Miss Lewis? If so, I'd admire to have that, too."

The flushed color of Annie's face told James that Shipman had touched her despite her resistance. She stammered like a girl in school. "N-n-no, I've drawn pictures of everybody else, but I wouldn't know how to draw one of myself."

"It'd be a mighty pretty picture," Shipman said. "You'd ought to try."

Annie blushed and looked away. James saw a flicker of victory in Shipman's eyes.

We may never get rid of him now, he thought.

They traveled past long stretches of forest, skirted numerous canebrakes and sometimes traversed open stretches of prairie land where the spring grass was tall and green and James thought the soil must be deep and black. Much of it would be good farming country, probably fine for cotton like so much of the Louisiana land they had passed through. He wondered at times why Michael and Andrew had gone so much farther to the southwest, passing up all this likely-looking ground where so far as he could tell no one had set a plow in the ground or built a cabin. They traveled all day without seeing a person or any sign that a human had ever passed this way except for occasional traces of old wagon tracks, gullied out by the rains.

He brought himself to ask Shipman why no one had yet settled here. The young smuggler shrugged. "You'll find some squatters hidden back in yonder if you look real good. They had just as soon you wouldn't, though. The Mexican government says where it wants people to live. They ain't opened this up because it's a long ways from where the soldiers are at, and they don't trust people too far out of their sight, not even their own people. They've tried to hold the settlers in colonies like Austin's and De-Witt's and DeLeon's. Easier to keep watch on them that way."

"Looks like they don't want us *anywhere*."

"I been expectin' this to come. It's hard to take people as different as Americans and Mexicans and mix them up together. They don't talk alike, and they don't think alike. Americans are used to goin' where they damn well please and doin' what suits their fancy. The Mexicans have been ruled hard by first one and then another. They're used to havin' to take orders whether they like them or not. My guess is that this is liable to blow up into a fight if the government don't ease off on that new law."

"They can sure have a fight with me if they want it."

Shipman's voice held a tone of reproach. "Fightin's easy to talk about when you're a long ways off, but it can get damned bloody when you're right there in the middle of it." He turned away from James, moving his dun horse back to Annie's wagon. He rode along and tried to talk to her. He did not appear to be getting much response. James would have given a right smart to know what he was telling her, but he would not compromise his dignity by dropping back to listen. He let his mind run free over this big, rich-looking land and his plans for making part of it his own.

Shipman was still with them when they stopped for night camp beside a spring he had said would be there. Smuggler Spring, he called it, voicing his disapproval of the name.

If the shoe fits — James thought.

Shipman ate more supper than anyone else. Afterward, he and Frank enjoyed swapping jokes and tall stories. Frank gloried in having a new audience for some that everyone in the family had already heard many times. James had not seen his cousin glow so much since the last of the other wagon people had pulled away. Shipman told stories James thought must be outrageously exaggerated about life in what he called the neutral strip, about adventures shared with old Eli Pleasant, about narrow escapes from the military authorities on both sides of the border.

Annie said little but listened with rapt attention. James suspected that if Shipman were to ask her when he turned back tomorrow, she would probably swallow her resentment and go with him. But he felt confident that Shipman would not ask her. He did not appear the type to be burdened down by a woman, especially one as full of sass as

Annie could be at times when things did not go her way.

Suspicious of Shipman's intentions, James rolled out his blankets not far from Annie's. He was almost disappointed that nothing untoward happened during the night because the vigil kept him from getting much sleep. Shipman slept at a considerable distance from the wagons and, so far as James could tell, never left his blankets once. At dawn they were all up, the women fixing breakfast while James and Frank and the boys prepared to break camp.

James saw Shipman hurriedly saddling his horse. The smuggler swung up onto the dun's back and rode into camp, his eyes showing strain. "Folks," he said, "I'm afraid I can't stay for breakfast. I'm fixin' to see just how fast this dun of mine can run."

Annie was dismayed. "What's the matter?"

Shipman said, "I've got to apologize, ma'am. I misfigured the way Sergeant Díaz was goin' to figure. He's right yonder with his whole detail, comin' this way in a good smart trot."

James felt his heart leap as he saw the horsemen coming across the prairie, no more than two hundred yards away.

Frank asked, "What can we do?"

Shipman said, "Ain't much you *can* do

except surrender. About the worst he'll do to you is to maybe haul you into Nacogdoches. Might even keep you in jail a few days before he takes you back to Louisiana. But he's got a deep, dark dungeon cell waitin' for me. I'd likely be an old man before I seen sunshine again."

James was suddenly outraged. "You're fixin' to run off? You ain't goin' to stay and help us fight them?"

"Fight them hell! Didn't you ever learn how to count?" Shipman turned to Frank. "You-all better educate this young fightin' rooster before he gets everybody killed. Good luck, folks, and *adiós*."

He spurred the dun horse eastward toward the Sabine. Several soldiers split off to follow him.

Annie cupped her hands in front of her mouth and shouted, "Run, Sly! Run!"

James had a feeling that the soldiers would catch nothing except the smell of Shipman's dust.

A damned pity.

Turning to Frank, he found that his cousin appeared resigned to whatever fate Díaz planned for them. Frank's rifle leaned against a wagon wheel. He looked at James's, his eyes giving advice that he did not have to speak aloud. This time James counted the soldiers and knew resistance was useless. "Double damn the luck!" he swore, and leaned his rifle against the wheel with Frank's. He stood beside his older cousin and waited for Díaz to rein up.

"I'm gettin' almighty tired of this," he said.

Nacogdoches was not a large town, nothing to compare with its French sister Natchitoches to the east. In the last of the two days it took the wagons to reach the old Spanish-Mexican outpost, James began seeing a fair number of small farms, most apparently operated by Mexican people. Disappointment and anger rode with him as steady companions. He silently cursed Díaz a while, then Sly Shipman. For the first time he began to develop a strong feeling of being helpless in a foreign land. The feeling was reinforced by the soldiers who rode on either side, and by Sergeant Díaz, who had lectured the Lewises severely on the penalties for breaking Mexican law. Díaz had also talked about their poor judgment in aiding and abetting a fugitive from justice. James had restrained himself from commenting on the soldiers' use of slow horses.

Díaz said, "A few days in our jail will teach you respect." But whatever the sergeant's resentment about their slipping back into

Texas, James noticed that he remained solicitous about Hope's health, and he camped early the first evening when he saw she was becoming tired. The second afternoon brought them through the tall pines and into the outskirts of town while the sun was still more than an hour high in the west.

Frank said with concern, "Me and James can stand some time in the jailhouse if we have to, but you wouldn't put the women-folk and the boys in there, would you?"

Díaz shook his head. "My family was once badly mistreated in your country. Yours will not be mistreated in mine."

James said defensively, "We was way back in Tennessee when all that happened. We didn't have nothin' to do with it."

"You are of the same blood. It is a blood that has no place in Mexico. I wish none of you had ever been allowed here."

Díaz had sent a messenger to Nacogdoches the day before to let the garrison know his detail would be bringing in prisoners. A couple of dozen soldiers were lined up in front of an old stone building that appeared to be the most substantial in the small town. James assumed it was a jail or a courthouse or something of that type. An officer came out of the building. Díaz saluted him and gave a report. James did not understand the words, but he understood the accusing look Díaz kept flinging in his direction. He glanced at Frank. Though his cousin was not smiling, his face was composed, resigned. Frank Lewis was a hard man to discourage for long. The officer listened impassively to Díaz's report, his dark eyes studying the wagons, the two men, and the boys on horseback. At length the officer turned to look behind him.

James saw another man standing in the doorway. By the darkness of his skin James knew him to be Mexican. Evidently he was not a soldier, for he wore no uniform. Yet he bore himself in what James took to be a military manner, his back and shoulders so straight that they must have hurt. The officer beckoned him. The civilian stepped out into the dirt street, giving James and Frank a thin smile and nodding affirmatively as if he knew them.

James glanced at Frank, silently asking a question. Frank shook his head. "Never saw him before, but he looks friendly. Right now we could sure use a friend."

The man walked up near Frank's horse. He asked, "Your name is Lewis?" His accent was thick, but the words were clear.

"It sure is. Frank Lewis. This here is James. He's a Lewis, too."

The man nodded, his smile broadening. "I can see it. Which is the brother of Michael and Andrew?"

"That's me," James said, puzzled. "You know them?"

"For many, many years. Turn. Look."

A man came striding up the dirt street, a tall man with a smile as broad as an ax handle. James began to tremble. He would know that lanky frame anywhere, for it looked much like his own, like Frank's, like all the Lewis men. James dismounted, ignoring Díaz and the soldiers. He took a couple of steps forward, tears suddenly blurring the man who approached him. He said in an unsteady voice, "Michael?"

"You're close," came a happy reply. "I'm Andrew. And you'd have to be James."

They threw their arms around each other. James heard a squeal of joy from the front wagon and saw through a blur as Annie sprang nimbly down from the seat in a flare of gray skirts. She pushed James aside in her eagerness to hug Andrew.

"Don't you know me?" she cried, kissing him twice.

"It's been almost ten years. You've changed, both of you. You've grown up."

Annie backed off to arm's length to stare at him, tears coursing down her cheeks.

"You've changed, too, but I'd know you from a mile away, Andrew."

James felt disappointment that it was not Michael who had come, and a little shame for not realizing this was Andrew instead of Michael. The Michael he remembered had to be taller than this. Stronger, too, and fiercer of eye.

Frank pumped Andrew's hand and then hugged him. Seeing the two cousins together, James was struck by how much they looked alike. Some Lewis a long way back in their heritage must have planted mighty strong seed.

"Where's Michael?" James asked urgently.

"He's home where he's supposed to be, and where we'll all be goin' soon as we get some paperwork done."

James looked toward Sergeant Díaz, who watched without pleasure. "The sergeant yonder, he's got a different notion. He's wantin' to throw me and Frank in the jailhouse, a while, then send us back to Louisiana."

Andrew shook his head, still smiling. "I know Sergeant Díaz. But what's more important, Elizandro Zaragosa knows the *comandante*. He's got everything fixed for me to take you-all to San Felipe, and then on out to the Colorado River."

Annie said joyfully, "You mean we won't be sent back to Louisiana after all?"

Andrew hugged her again. "No, you're in Texas to stay."

Zaragosa embraced Sergeant Díaz in the traditional *abrazo.*

Díaz said, "It is good to see you again, lieutenant."

"Not lieutenant, not anymore. Just plain Elizandro Zaragosa. I am a farmer now, not a soldier."

"You will always be lieutenant to me, sir." Díaz looked toward the *americano* wagon people with misgivings. "I have gone to much trouble to teach these foreigners a lesson. Have you and the *comandante* come to an agreement to let them go?"

"I am sorry to disappoint you, old friend, but I could do no less. These are family to the Lewises, Andrew and Miguel. You know they once saved my life."

"And you once saved Miguel's. I understand, sir, even if I do not agree with you. But every *americano* we allow into Texas now is one more *americano* we must fight when the war comes."

"You talk as if war is inevitable. So long as men of good will prevail, it is not. There are many good Americans in Texas, loyal to the government of Mexico. They want to preserve the friendship."

"Do they? Already there is much resistance to the new law that says no more *americanos* are allowed into Texas except by special permission."

"The law was poorly conceived. I am sure it will be repealed when cooler heads are given time to reconsider."

"And what do you think your *americano* friends will say when the government sends more soldiers into Texas and sets up more garrisons among them? Especially when they discover that the government is sending convict soldiers taken from the prisons of Mexico, and that when the convicts' service is done they will be expected to settle among the *americanos?*"

Zaragosa's eyes narrowed. "I had not heard of this."

"You will hear much more, I think, when it becomes generally known. I wonder how your friends the Lewises will like having convict soldiers sent to watch over them?"

Zaragosa frowned darkly. "They will not like it. But as I told you, they are loyal to Mexico."

"For how long, my lieutenant? For how long?"

CHAPTER 6

Texas got to looking a lot better to James as he and Andrew and Zaragosa rode south-westward, the wagons and the loose stock trailing behind them through the dark pine woods, through the clearings where small farmers struggled to gain even a meager subsistence. Andrew insisted on their spending the first night out of Nacogdoches at one owned by a Mexican family named Moreno. Remembering Sergeant Díaz, James had reservations about associating with anyone who looked Mexican, including even Zaragosa. He was taken by surprise when a short, heavyset matriarch threw her arms around Andrew. Andrew explained that this dark-faced woman who talked in happy torrents was his mother-in-law. James did not understand a word, for she spoke no English. He stood by uncomfortably, not knowing whether to nod *yes* or shake his head until Andrew translated for him. On this farm, Andrew recounted, he had learned to know Petra and her family at the time of the abortive Fredonian rebellion.

Here, too, some ten years earlier, sixteen-year-old Michael Lewis had fought for life against a wound given him by a Spanish soldier in the slaughter that had felled the first Mordecai Lewis. Only the care and attention of the widow Moreno and old Eli Pleasant had pulled him through. And the vigilance of the two larger Moreno boys, at considerable risk to themselves, had prevented him from being retaken by searching Spanish troops.

"I came here in pretty bad shape myself," Andrew said. "Some of those Fredonians like to've beaten me to death in Nacogdoches. Old Eli came along and taught them the Scriptures. Mother Moreno and Petra took care of me till I got on my feet, the same way they took care of Michael."

James dimly recalled hearing a little something about the Fredonian rebellion. "From what we heard in Tennessee, it didn't seem like much," he remarked. "Just a handful of people who declared an independent republic or some such of a thing."

Andrew's brow furrowed. "They took it serious down in Mexico. You can blame that new immigration law on the Fredonians.

Just goes to show what trouble a few hot-heads can cause."

James suspected that Andrew was trying to make some kind of point. He had probably been talking to Annie.

Andrew introduced the newcomers to brothers-in-law Carlos, Ramón, and Felipe, and to a pretty young sister-in-law named Juanita, who appeared to be within a year or so of James's age. The younger Morenos seemed pleasant, but they spoke little more English than their mother. Annie and Juanita traded a lot of sign language and confusion and laughter. Frank eagerly pressed Andrew to translate for him while he questioned the Moreno men about their farming and stock-raising methods. Frank tried telling them some stories out of Tennessee, too. James suspected a lot was lost in the translation, for they often laughed in the wrong places.

Frank kept telling James, "You'd ought to strike up a friendship with that girl Juanita. She ain't a bit hard on the eyes. If I wasn't a married man —"

James was not ready to start thinking in serious terms about a woman, and when he did she would be American. "She seems friendly enough," he conceded. "But it's probably just because I'm Andrew's brother.

How are a man and a woman supposed to get to know one another if they don't even speak the same language?"

Frank smiled. "Some languages are the same anywhere you go." He was an incurable romantic. From the time he had been twelve years old, Frank had been something of a ladies' man. He still could be, if Hope didn't keep a watchful eye on him.

James could not feel really comfortable among these strangers. Their darker skins and their foreign language reminded him not only of the unpleasantness with Sergeant Díaz but of the fact that James had come into a land alien to him. He would not have expressed it — indeed, he did not quite even understand it — but he felt a little bothered as he observed the warm affection, the earnest caring, the laughter between his brother Andrew and these Morenos. He saw that Andrew had established strong family ties here, ties James could not help feeling properly belonged to blood kin, the Lewises. He even felt a degree of loss because these people had shared in Andrew's life the last five or so years, and probably Michael's as well. All James had had of Andrew or Michael in almost a decade had been boyhood memories and infrequent letters that found their

112

way to Tennessee.

He was confused about his feelings toward Elizandro Zaragosa, too. On the one hand he was grateful that the man had helped smooth the way for their remaining in Texas, and he recognized that a strong bond existed between Andrew and Zaragosa. Even so, Zaragosa still seemed foreign to him, unfamiliar, like this land. Much as James wanted to accept him as a friend, he held something back. It was the darker skin, the strange language, the culture so different from anything he had known. He remembered what Sly Shipman had said about the difficulty of Mexicans and Americans understanding one another, much less living in total harmony, for their heritages were a world apart.

Andrew appeared to have bridged the gap between those heritages and to feel at home among the Mexicans. James wondered if *he* ever could. Right now it seemed unlikely. He would ask Michael, when he reached the Colorado River. In the old days, Michael had always seemed to know whatever James had needed to find out. Michael the quiet one, Michael the solitary man of the woods, Michael the man James wanted desperately to become.

As they moved down the trail toward San

Felipe, Andrew rode much of the time beside Zaragosa. James would pull in beside them, only to find more often than not that they were talking in Spanish. That language seemed to come easier to Andrew than English came to Zaragosa. Though James understood the problem, it left him feeling shut out. He would pull back beside Annie's wagon. She would want to know what Andrew and Zaragosa were talking about. Rather than admit he did not know, James would tell her something innocuous and drift on back to Frank and Hope's wagon. He could always depend on conversation with Frank, even though it was usually one-sided.

He was amazed to see virtually no people, though they traveled several days. They met a few travelers, but they saw no sign of permanent dwellings, of farms, or other settled human activity until they reached the borders of the Austin colony. Then, suddenly, James could almost pretend that he was back in Tennessee. Nothing had the Mexican appearance he had expected. The farms, the houses, the fences, and fields looked pretty much like the ones he had left at home except that most had the look of being new. No legal American settlers had yet been here as long as ten years. Some of the late arrivals were just beginning to break their first ground, plant their first crops. James would ride out to look over the rail fences at the fields, to examine the newly-turned earth. It looked rich, smelled rich. He felt he ought to be out there with a plow, though he had always been more at home with the rifle. That was a Lewis blessing, or perhaps it was a curse, that most of the menfolk were torn between the woods and the field.

They came, in time, to the village of San Felipe de Austin, headquarters for the Austin colony. James had heard much about Austin over the last several years and especially on this trip. He had looked forward to seeing the noted impresario, to determine if he was real or if he was simply a legend. He had heard so many stories back home about Old Hickory Jackson and David Crockett that he sometimes suspected they did not even exist except in the minds of certain shameless old liars. It might have been the same way with Austin.

But Austin was real, for Andrew pointed out his cabin, a double structure with the traditional dog-run in the center and a rocked-up well in front. The place was surrounded by heavy live oak trees, their branches strewn with beards of Spanish moss that waved gently in the breeze.

The town had nothing much Spanish or Mexican about it so far as James could see. It could have been an out-of-the-way Tennessee settlement on the edge of the old frontier from its outward appearance. Most of the buildings were built of logs, for timber was plentiful here along the broad, muddy Brazos River. The style of construction was strictly frontier American.

"I thought this was supposed to be part of Mexico," Frank remarked to Andrew. "It looks to me like we must've gone in a circle and found our way back home."

"Don't be sayin' that too loud," Andrew said. "The Mexican authorities have noticed the same thing. Some of them say we're an American island in a Mexican sea. They say we're fixin' to crowd everybody else out."

James offered, "Maybe that wouldn't be a bad idea. I feel better amongst our own kind."

He was surprised at the reproach in Andrew's voice. "Those people didn't have to let us come in here. They could just as well've kept all this themselves. But they opened it to us, and I feel real bad when I hear anybody talkin' ungrateful."

James retreated quickly. "I didn't mean it that way." He had, but Andrew's adverse reaction made him wonder. Andrew had been here long enough to know the country; James was just going by first impressions. He admitted to himself, but not to anyone else, that he could be wrong.

He was disappointed when Andrew told him Austin had left for Mexico City to see what, if anything, he could do about getting the new immigration law liberalized. Damn it, the man was going to remain a faceless mystery to him after all. Andrew introduced the family to Austin's partner, Sam Williams, who went over the legal documents with them and accepted the money James and Frank had brought to make the required payment on their land. Because both presented themselves to be livestock producers as well as farmers, they received a liberal grant of grazing land. They were stockmen without livestock, except for the milk cows and the few loose horses. Frank, being married, received much more acreage.

Williams told James, "Under the colonization laws as established by Mexico, when and if you find yourself a bride you will qualify for additional land."

James cast a baleful glance at Annie. "I already got a sister who gives me hell enough. I sure ain't lookin' for a wife to make it worse."

Annie said nothing but indicated by her expression that the matter would be explored at more length outside.

Williams said, "Well, it is just a thought to keep in mind should one of our beautiful young Texas ladies catch your fancy. There is a great deal to be said for matrimony, as your brothers Andrew and Michael can tell you."

James had not seen any beautiful young Texas ladies so far, other than Juanita Moreno, and he had not been able to hold any kind of sustained conversation with her. "Don't you be holdin' up supper waitin' for me to come in married, Mr. Williams."

Annie, being a single woman, did not qualify for land. *She'll have to marry hers,* James thought.

Annie protested, "It doesn't seem fair that I'm left out just because I'm a woman. I know how to farm. I know how to make my own way."

James was not surprised that Annie protested; she usually had something to say on just about anything that came along. But Williams was taken aback. "I can understand your feelings, young lady, but that is the way the laws of Mexico are written. They assume you will marry, and at that time your husband will qualify for ad-

118

ditional land."

"Him, not me," Annie said pointedly. "What do *I* get?"

"A home, children, a husband who will no doubt love and cherish you — just what every woman wants."

"Not *every* woman," Annie snapped. "I've gotten along twenty-two years without a husband."

With that kind of attitude, James figured, she would probably have to do without one for another twenty-two. Her only chance would be to grab one quickly, before he had time to discover her snappish nature.

On a large map Williams showed the location of Michael's and Andrew's land. He had penciled in parcels for James and Frank adjoining those and fronting on the Colorado River. "Michael and Andrew hand-picked these parcels," he said, "so you can rest assured that they will be good ones."

James figured if Michael had done the picking, there would be plenty of woods for a man to hunt in.

Frank fretted a little about the lateness of the season, whether there would still be time to break out land, get seed in the ground and make a crop before frost. Andrew assured him there was. "We don't generally have the first freeze here till way down in

November," Andrew said. "The main thing is to get your plantin' done in time to catch the spring rains."

Frank said, "That means the plantin' has to come first, and the buildin' of a cabin'll have to wait. But Hope *can't* wait. She'll be due about June or so."

Andrew grinned. "Me and Michael, Marie and Petra, we took care of that back in the winter when there wasn't any farmin' to do. We put up a cabin for you and Hope and the boys. It's waitin' for you."

Hope gave Andrew a strong hug. Andrew turned. "James, me and Petra figured you could double up with us a while. Annie, we didn't figure on you at all. We had no idea you were comin'."

James said dryly. "Neither did anybody else. She always did have strange notions."

Annie replied defensively, "I figured I had to come along to watch out for James. He'd've probably taken the wrong trail and wound up in Canada or some other foreign country."

James glanced out the door of the cabin, where he could see Zaragosa standing with Frank and Hope's boys beside the wagons. "This one is foreign enough for me."

CHAPTER 7

Annie liked most of what she had seen of Texas so far, aside from the Díaz incidents. The Spanish language was a mystery to her, but she had felt an immediate openness and kinship with the Moreno family because of Andrew. She had been a little frustrated by her inability to talk to them without Andrew or Zaragosa to interpret. She had been given to understand that without the kind and — for the Moreno family — dangerous help by the old Señora Moreno, her brother Michael would probably have died fifteen years ago. She had tried to express her gratitude, but she doubted that the translation had carried the true depth of her feeling. And she had felt that she could have built a solid friendship with the girl Juanita if they had only been able to communicate better. Perhaps it would go easier with Andrew's wife Petra; Andrew said she had acquired a fair command of English.

Annie suspected that James had not been forthright when she asked him what Andrew and Zaragosa were talking about. She had heard things, just enough to intrigue but not enough to know their full import, about difficulties between the American colonists and the Mexican authorities, and speculations about their implications for the future. She made up her mind that as time permitted she was going to learn Spanish from Petra and Marie. Be damned if she was going to remain shut out of things just because she did not understand the language!

The trek westward from San Felipe out to the new land took much longer than was really necessary. Andrew seemed to know every settler for miles on either side of the trail, and a stop at each place was made mandatory by the eager hospitality which isolation had instilled in these Texas pioneers. It was a breach of etiquette, almost a cruelty, to pass by a place without stopping for at least a howdy, a chance for the womenfolk to learn what was new back in the old states, time for the menfolk to spit and whittle and talk some politics. Frank seemed especially to enjoy it, for he had always been one to whom no man remained a stranger long, and no woman if she was comely, though being married to Hope had

122

tamed that aspect of his personality somewhat. Annie found the settlers eager to see
more of their own kind moving in around
them. She mentally calculated that if she
lived up to every return visit she had promised the women along the way, she would
spend much of the summer at it.

Zaragosa left them at the first stop they
made beyond San Felipe. He was eager to
pick up his son and return to his family and
duties at Bexar. He would let Michael, Marie, and Petra know the wagons were coming. Annie could see that Andrew genuinely
regretted seeing him go. Frank was lavish
but sincere in his gratitude for all of Zaragosa's help. James shook Zaragosa's hand
and said, "Thanks," but Annie thought he
had to work at it a little. She wondered
about James sometimes.

Andrew reined in beside her wagon and
pointed toward a long log structure to the
left of the road. "That's the Willet farm," he
said. "I promise you, this is the last place
we stop. But Widow Willet wouldn't forgive
us if we passed her by."

James asked, "Widder? What happened to
her husband?"

Andrew was hesitant in his answer, looking uneasily at Annie. "An Indian raid. But
that was about five years ago. Been mighty

little Indian trouble in this colony for a long time."

Annie read more into his words than he had said. "You're wishin' I hadn't come."

"I never said that. I've got a family, and so has Michael. If we didn't feel like it was safe, they wouldn't be here."

James volunteered, "I never did encourage Annie to come. I was against it from the start."

Andrew gave Annie a thin smile. "I'm glad she did. She'll be good company for Petra and Marie. As for me and Michael, she's our baby sister."

James declared, "Been a long time since she was a baby. Back home, they was already figurin' her for an old maid."

Andrew's smile widened. "I think it's a little early yet to be callin' her such a thing. She's just now come into full bloom."

Mrs. Willet reminded Annie a little of Mother Moreno, though she was several years younger and much lighter of skin. Whatever the nightmare of losing her husband had been, she had long since made peace with the world. She had her children about her, and a couple of small grandchildren from her son Zeb and a willowy young woman called Birdy. Mrs. Willet talked at length about their plans for expanding the farm, their bright hopes for the future.

Annie asked her, "You don't mind livin' here in a different country, under a foreign government and people who talk a language you can't understand?" She had determined that Mrs. Willet did not speak Spanish. She had already learned that most American settlers here did not.

"Law, child, no. *Our* government is in San Felipe, and it's American. Out here we don't often see a Mexican soldier or anybody from the Mexican government. For all you can tell we're the same as back in Kentucky, only we got a lot more land than we'd've ever got back yonder. The livin's been pretty good, all in all."

Annie asked, "You wouldn't want to go back to Kentucky?"

"Law, no, not and leave all this." Mrs. Willet made a broad sweep with her chubby arm and hand. "This is home now. I finished raisin' up my young'uns here and had two grandbabies born on this place. I got a husband buried out yonder. This is our home, bought and paid for with blood, and we wouldn't leave it for nothin' or nobody."

"Not even if Mexico took a notion to turn you out?"

Her brow furrowed. "They wouldn't try.

125

There's enough of us in Texas already to whip them plumb to Mexico City, and they know it." Her smile slowly returned. "Anyway, nothin' like that is fixin' to happen. They've gone to a right smart of trouble settin' up these colonies. There's no reason they'd want to move us now." She gave Annie a long study. "One thing I can't understand is why an unattached young lady would come out here. Women with their husbands, sure, but you?"

Annie had often been asked that question along the trail. "My brothers are out here," she replied, "and I hadn't seen them in most of ten years. I'd begun to feel like I might never see them again if I didn't come. And then there's James —" She looked out the door at her youngest brother, who was studying with much interest a beautiful black horse that Zeb Willet had led up from the barn; the Willets were horse people. "James means well, but in some respects he's not full grown yet. He's got a way of fallin' into trouble that's over his head if somebody's not standin' there to pull him back out of it."

She had long suspected that James was trying to emulate their older brother Michael. Going by a memory that was perhaps more creative than it should be, he would try to decide what Michael would do under similar circumstances, then act accordingly. He had it set in his mind that Michael was never afraid of anything and would never brook insult or injustice. That belief had carried James into many a fight, sometimes at odds that insured his losing in a big way. His wounds would heal, and he was always ready for the next fight. For a smart boy, he seemed almighty slow at learning certain lessons.

Beyond her strong desire to see Michael and Andrew, Annie had made this trip in the hope that she might keep somebody from killing James before he finally matured enough not to attack bears with a willow switch. She could not depend upon cousin Frank to do it; he had a family and problems enough of his own. She suspected her mother had sensed the same thing, for Patience Lewis had put up little opposition when Annie had announced her intention of going to Texas with James and Frank's family. If anything, she had seemed almost grateful.

"The key to handlin' your little brother," Patience Lewis had said, "is to make him think everything is his idea and not yours. Don't try to boss him, or he'll rebel."

That part of her mother's advice Annie

had not been able to take very well. It was not in her nature to be devious. When something came into her head, she spoke it straight out. In short, she herself was a lot like James. She was Mordecai Lewis's daughter.

Mrs. Willet said, "A pretty young woman like you, it's hard for me to imagine that you didn't have a lot of willin' young bucks pressin' for your hand back home. I doubt that you're single for lack of opportunity."

Annie forced a smile. "There was opportunity, all right, but nobody I could see livin' a long life with. Most of them couldn't talk about anything except corn and chickens and cows. They hadn't been anywhere and didn't want to go anywhere. I wanted to see somethin' before I got myself hemmed inside of a field fence."

"I expect you've seen a right smart on this trip."

"I didn't know the country was so big."

"It is, and there's a lot more of it yet to see. Get your brothers to take you to Bexar sometime. It's like another part of the world."

Much as Annie enjoyed the company of Mrs. Willet, her daughter-in-law, and the two babies, she itched to be back on the wagon and making the final few miles to the place that would be her home, where she would finally see Michael again after all these years. She tried to picture how her brother would look, for she had only memory to go by, and imagination. Andrew's appearance had given her some idea. The heritage of Mordecai Lewis had always shown strongly in Michael and Andrew, as it showed now in James. She loved all her brothers, but Michael had always been special, for in a way he had been her father's image. She had always clung tightly to Mordecai, and after his death she had clung to Michael. Texas had taken Michael from her. Now Texas would give him back.

Andrew had told her the trail would lead by Michael's place first, so she knew when the wagons topped a small hill that the double log cabin she saw down toward the river was the place where her brother had made a home. From the distance it looked much like the Tennessee farm where the family had lived during the final years of Mordecai's life. Consciously or unconsciously, Michael had probably copied that pattern when he built the cabin, the barn and sheds, the livestock pens. Even the pole-fenced field lay in much the same relationship to the cabin as the old field had done back home, except that this one had more open country around it. The only deep woods were along the rivers. She saw a man working in the field, following an ox and a plow. A boy walked along behind him, dropping seeds into the freshly-turned rows. The boy stopped suddenly, seeing the wagons. He pointed, and the man halted the ox to look up the slope. Though the distance was considerable, Annie knew instinctively that this was Michael, the lost brother she had come so far to find again. She felt tears well up and spill down her cheeks, wet and warm. Blinking them away, she saw that Michael was taking the ox up to the shed while the boy ran toward the cabin.

By the time the wagons made their way around the field, Michael had turned the ox loose and stood waiting in front of the log house. Beside him were the boy and two women, as well as three smaller children. Andrew set his horse into a lope and hurried ahead of the wagons. He stepped down from the saddle and took one of the women into his arms. That, Annie knew, would be Petra. The other must be Michael's wife, daughter of the Natchitoches Villarets.

James could not wait for the slow-moving wagons. He raced ahead, dismounting to throw his arms around Michael. He received a hug from each of the two women in turn, looking a little awkward about it.

Michael strode out to meet the wagon as Annie drew the team to a stop. She tried to get a good look at him but could hardly see through the second rush of tears. She heard his voice, a voice that had lived in her memory for most of ten years. "Annie. My little Annie. Come, let me help you down."

She trembled so that she almost fell as she started to climb down on the wagon wheel. Michael caught her in strong arms and pulled her against his lean, tall frame, holding her for a minute without a word. Whatever the hardships, whatever the frustrations of the long trip had been, they were as nothing now. She clung to him as she had clung to him on their parting a long time ago, trying not to cry but unable to help herself.

"It's all right," he said in a gentle voice. "You're home now."

She felt it as she had not felt it in a long, long time, not since the family had left Mordecai Lewis's old log cabin home to move in with Uncle Benjamin on his much bigger farm. This was a different land, far distant from any she had ever known, but somehow she felt that Michael was right: She was at home.

He said finally, "There's family here that I want you to meet." He introduced her first to Marie, a slightly-built young woman with the largest, darkest eyes Annie thought she had ever seen, and a smile that left no doubt why Michael had fallen in love with her. Michael said, "This lady gave me life when I thought I'd lost it."

Annie embraced Marie and said, "For that, I've loved you for fifteen years. It is good finally to see and touch you." She pulled back a little. She had met others of the Villaret family in Louisiana, and she thought she could see a little of their look in Marie's face. It was the eyes that struck her most, that she knew must have struck Michael. "All of us Lewises are eternally grateful to you, Marie."

Marie replied quietly, "Whatever I did, I did because I loved Michael. I would do it all again."

"Let's hope you never have to, that none of us ever have to."

She met young Mordecai, who already bore some of the marks of his Lewis name. "You're a fine-looking young man," she told him. "You'd do your granddaddy proud."

Mordecai was shy and ill at ease at the appearance of these relatives who were strangers to him. "Thank you, ma'am." Annie met the small girl named Angeline and started to ask where the baby was, then suddenly remembered a letter telling that Michael and Marie had lost it. It had seemed unreal to Annie at the time she had received word, to have lost a little niece she had never seen. It was real now.

She came then to Andrew's Petra, and their two young ones. Annie said, "I met your mother and your brothers a few days ago. And your sister Juanita."

Petra forced a smile, as ill at ease as Mordecai had been. "It is good. You like them, I hope."

"Very much. And I'll love you too, Petra." She reached down for the baby girl and lifted her up into her arms. "You and your little ones. Everybody! We're all goin' to be family." She watched Frank and Hope and their boys gather around to be introduced one by one, and she felt a warm glow rise from within.

Yes, she was home. Tennessee was in the past. This was Texas, it was now, and it was home. She had a strong feeling that it would be home for as long as she lived.

Marie and Petra had started supper. Annie pitched in to help, despite their protests that she was company and should rest after the long trip. "I'm not company. I'm family."

She listened, she asked questions, she tried to study her two sisters-in-law for some idea of who they were as individuals. She had quickly seen the Villaret features in Marie, and Petra was a slightly older version of the girl Juanita Moreno. Marie was darker in complexion than the women Annie was used to in Tennessee, and Petra was a little darker even than Marie. Marie's English was better, tinged though it was with Louisiana French. Petra struggled to make herself understood, and Annie resolved to try never to smile when Petra's words came out backward. One might laugh *with* family, but never *at* them.

In the course of the talk Petra mentioned that her milk cow had disappeared shortly after Andrew had left to try to find Annie and James and the rest. Michael and Mordecai had hunted for her but had had no luck. For a cow to stray was not strange under ordinary circumstances, but this one had a calf, kept penned up behind the shed. It was unusual for one to go off far and leave a calf behind.

At length Annie heard a dog bark. Curiosity took her to the door, where she stood with a dish-drying cloth folded over her arm. Out beyond the dog-run she saw a

134

man approaching on horseback. She stepped outside, shading her eyes with her hand and looking around to see where the Lewis men had gone. She saw Michael and Andrew walking up from the pens, James and Frank trailing along behind them.

The man reached the cabin before them. He sat on the horse, staring at Annie. Much of his face was covered by a dark beard, but his eyes looked friendly. And they looked familiar, though Annie could think of no reason she should know him. He said, "I don't believe I know you, ma'am, but by the look of you, I'd bet this horse and saddle that you're a Lewis."

"I'm Annie Lewis," she said, wondering. "Michael and Andrew are my brothers."

The man's brown eyes widened. "Come all the way from Tennessee? That explains the wagons, then. They's a bunch of you, I'd surmise, judgin' by the load them wagons is a-carryin'."

"My brother James, my cousin Frank, and his family." She wondered, once she had said it, if she ought to be telling so much, not knowing who he was or on what business he had come. She was troubled by the familiar look about him and her inability to place a name to him. She was troubled, too, by the way he stared at her, as if he were looking through her eyes and into every thought that lay behind them.

He said, "I'm Isaac Blackwood."

Blackwood. She had all but forgotten that three of the Blackwood brothers had moved to Texas and had settled near Michael and Andrew, to her own brothers' great disgust. They had left plenty of troublemaking kin behind in Tennessee, however, and she had known *them* well enough — too well. When a Blackwood came around, you counted your fingers lest you come up short. She wondered now why she had not recognized him as Blackwood; the look was there, plain enough to see now that she knew who he was.

He said, "You're a mighty handsome lady, Miss Annie Lewis."

The Lewis men back home would not long tolerate forward behavior by a Blackwood toward their womenfolk. But this was Texas, and perhaps things were different. Moreover, Annie doubted that Isaac meant to take liberty. He was just speaking what had come into his mind, and she accepted it as a compliment. Andrew and Michael were near enough to have heard, but they did not challenge the man directly. Michael only stared at him, no welcome in his eyes. Andrew nodded civilly and said, "Isaac."

Isaac nodded back. "Andrew." He silently studied the other two Lewis men, James and Frank. He knew both from back in Tennessee, though James had been but a boy when Isaac and his brothers had left there. "Welcome to Texas," he said.

Frank came nearest to smiling, "Howdy, Isaac." James said nothing.

Isaac brought his attention back to Andrew. "You missin' a milk cow?"

Andrew blinked in surprise. "So my wife just told me."

"I brought her back. Left her at your place just a while ago."

Andrew looked suspicious. "Where was she, Isaac?"

"Over on our side of the river."

Michael's suspicion was more palpable even than Andrew's. "Reckon how she come to be on your side of the river?"

"I couldn't tell you about that. I just fetched her home. And now I'll be biddin' you-all a good day. I'll be missin' my supper." His gaze went back to Annie. He touched fingers to the floppy brim of an old hat that once had been white. "Like I said, ma'am, welcome to Texas. Mighty welcome." He turned his horse and started toward the river.

James was the first to speak. "He sure

looks like all them other Blackwoods to me. But if he stole the cow, how come him to bring her back?"

Andrew said, "It wouldn't've been Isaac stole her. It was Finis and Luke, if anybody. Notice his knuckles? They was bruised and beat up some. I'd bet you he had to fight Luke to get the cow and fetch her home."

James demanded, "Why would he do that, one Blackwood fight another to return somethin' to a Lewis? Don't sound like the Blackwoods we know back home."

Andrew said, "Isaac's no saint, but he's better than the others. If he could get away from his brothers he could probably make himself into a middlin' decent man."

Annie remembered the way the man's eyes had softened when he looked at her. Maybe Isaac Blackwood was already a middlin' decent man and nobody had noticed it. She said, "He's missin' his supper for fetchin' the cow home. Couldn't you-all have invited him to stay and eat with us?"

Michael looked at her as if she had lost her mind.

It was full dark by the time Isaac Blackwood reached the homestead he shared with his brothers and Finis's fat wife Nelly. The oldest boy was out in the yard chunking rocks at a stray cat. "I wouldn't be doin' that, young'un," Isaac scolded him gently. "Them cats keep the mice and rats away."

The boy was about four. It always bothered Isaac, trying to figure out who he looked most like. He was accepted as Finis's, because Finis and Nelly had married shortly before the boy's arrival. But Nelly had never been known for being very bright or very selective. The boy could as easily have been Luke's, or even Isaac's own. Times, when Isaac looked into the boy's brown eyes, he thought he saw a reflection of himself, looking back. That thought brought him a mixture of pleasure and sadness. The last thing he would want would be a son of his following after Finis. The young'un wouldn't have a chance for any kind of upbringing. Jerked up, would be all, not *raised* up.

But there was damned little he could do about it, since Finis considered the boy his own and would like as not kill anybody who suggested otherwise — or at least sic Luke on to do the killing for him. Being shy of one arm made Finis depend on Luke for most of the dirty work. Luke had been born some shy on brains. Their mother had always said it was because their father had been dead drunk when Luke was conceived, but Isaac had never thought that explanation held much water. Old Cyrus Blackwood had been dead drunk a lot.

Isaac was the only one of the three brothers who ever stopped to wipe his feet on the rough floor of the dog-run before he walked into the cabin. The dirt he tracked in wouldn't add much to what was already there, for Nelly was not any great shakes as a housekeeper, but the move was instinctive with him. He hated living in a hog wallow. Moreover, the noise would serve to alert his brothers and Nelly that he was coming. It kept Finis or Luke from poking a rifle into his face as he opened the door, their usual greeting to any stranger who happened upon the place.

A candle flickered on the rough table, and a fire burned low on the hearth where Nelly had fixed whatever had passed for supper; he figured he had already missed his and would have to take whatever he could find. In the glow, he could see that Luke's face was swollen a little.

Finis glowered at him from behind his thick black beard. Sarcastically he said, "I'm surprised you seen fit to come home. I thought maybe them Lewises was so grateful for you bringin' their cow home that they might ask you to stay and live with them."

Isaac did not condescend to answer him. He asked Luke, "How's your face?"

"It hurts," Luke complained. "You didn't have no call to hit me so hard."

"The way you come at me, I had to. When you ever goin' to learn not to do everything Finis tells you?"

Finis said, "You know we needed that cow. These young'uns ain't had no milk since our own cow up and left on us."

"You ought to have better sense than to steal from a nigh neighbor. They'd've come over here and found that cow, and like as not there'd've been a fight. And a fight can lead to a killin'."

Finis shrugged indifferently. "That'd be fine with me. I wouldn't mind seein' one or two of them Lewises layin' dead."

"It might not've been them layin' dead. Might've been one of us." He turned to Nelly, who stood over against a wall, washing the supper plates in a pan. She looked bigger than a three-year-old heifer. He wondered how he could ever have brought himself to climb into bed with her. It had been a long time since he had.

"Got anything left that I can eat?" he asked.

Finis put in sharply, "He ain't gettin' nothin', Nelly. He had no business whuppin' up on his brother thataway."

Nelly just stared open-mouthed, confused by the contradictory signals she was receiving. Saying nothing, she kept rubbing an old cloth against the plates.

Isaac took a plate and a spoon and went to the pots that sat on the hearth. He found there a remnant of squirrel stew and helped himself to it.

Finis declared, "I told you there wasn't no supper here for you. If you want to eat, go back to your friends the Lewises."

Isaac looked his brother squarely in the eye. There was nothing Finis needed so badly as a good whipping, but Isaac had never brought himself to do that to a one-armed man. He just said, "You go to hell, Finis," and carried his plate out onto the dog-run so he could eat in peace. He could hear Finis inside, cursing first Nelly and then Luke, and Nelly railing back at him in her whining voice.

If I had a lick of sense I'd just go off and leave them, he thought. But the boy came and stared at Isaac while he ate, and Isaac knew there was at least one good reason he could never leave.

The image of Annie Lewis crossed his

142

mind. He could not help making a contrast between her and Nelly. That led him to an even broader contrast between the Lewis family and the Blackwoods. There had always been a closeness among the Lewises that had never existed among his own battling kin. He wished for just once in his life that he could experience that kind of closeness.

He set down the plate and beckoned to the youngster.

"Come here to me, boy," he said gently.

The boy declared resentfully, "You whupped up on my Uncle Luke." He walked off into the yard, picked up a rock and hurled it at Isaac.

CHAPTER 8

During the summer James Lewis had no roof he could properly call his own. Andrew and Petra had intended to let him sleep with the children in one side of their double cabin, but Annie's unexpected presence had changed that plan. Annie slept in the room with the children. James slept on the ground outdoors most nights. He was accustomed to it because of the many hunting trips that had kept him in the woods for a night or more back home, and because he had rolled his blankets on the ground all the way to Texas from Tennessee. When the weather was benign, that suited him. The air was always better outside than in a cabin, even one where chinks between the logs let the wind find its way through. When it rained, he could either sleep on the dog-run or climb up into the wagon and be protected by the canvas, still drawn down tightly over the wagon hoops. Andrew's black dog was

144

slow at first in accepting James as a member of the family but eventually began lying down beside James's blankets, keeping him company through the night.

The first priority was planting. The families had to finish Michael's and Andrew's fields and break out enough land for cousin Frank to raise a crop and a garden that would feed his family, their animals, and Hope's precious laying hens through the first winter. Because James was a bachelor without a family depending upon him, and Annie had been granted no land of her own, there was less urgency in their case. They could look to their brothers. The men and the three boys large enough to help combined their strengths, moving together from one farm to the other for the work. As Michael, Andrew, and Frank forced the wooden points of their plows into new ground on Frank's place, James and the boys followed behind, dropping seed into the freshly-turned earth. Frank's two sons and Michael's Mordecai had not been long in cementing a solid friendship that went beyond their being blood kin. The two fresh arrivals from Tennessee were the only boys Mordecai had had around him near his own age.

It was imperative that the crops be planted

early enough to mature before frost bit them down. James remembered stories in the family — from before his own time — about his restless father Mordecai, ever itching to find new land, ever moving his wife and children without considering the length of the growing season. Sometimes only Michael's skill with the rifle had kept the family from going hungry through the long winters. With Michael at home there had always been meat, even when there was no bread.

James was curious about their neighbors but saw little of them during those early weeks, for the neighbors had work of their own to do, work of the same urgency as the Lewises'. Visiting could come later, when the crops were planted and the weeds hoed out. There would be a lull of sorts before the harvest. Not until this lull would James have time to do much about putting up a cabin for himself and his sister Annie. James had always heard it said that one kitchen was too small for two women. He wondered how Petra and Annie kept on good terms with one another in such close quarters. He never saw Annie display the snappish side of her nature to Andrew's wife; that seemed to be a sisterly trait reserved for James alone. Petra's English improved considerably through her constant association with Annie, and Annie picked up a smattering of Spanish. James figured it was probably just enough to get her misunderstood and into some kind of trouble if she ever found herself in need of it and nobody like Petra was around to translate.

Hope's baby came along in due time. As if there weren't already women enough — Annie and Marie and Petra — plump Mrs. Willet, the Kentuckian, came over to provide midwife services. For a woman who displayed such a sweet and kindly face, it seemed to James that she could give an unreasonable number of orders and find an ungodly heap of things that the men ought to be doing to help. James decided it was time to see more meat hanging in the dog-run, so he went off hunting for a couple of days. When he came back, he found the Frank Lewis family blessed with another boy.

"Texas just keeps on a-growin'," said Andrew Lewis, smiling. It seemed to James that Andrew smiled a lot. He always had, back in Tennessee. Michael had been the moody one. At times, he still was. The only time James saw him smile was when Marie unexpectedly came into his view, or Annie or the boy Mordecai. James supposed he would be moody, too, if he had lived through what Michael had, seeing his father killed in cold blood and himself being left to die on the prairie.

Times when Michael was around, James ached for conversation with him. But Michael had been taciturn back in Tennessee, in those years after that first disastrous trip to Texas with his father. He was older now, lines starting to show in his face, but that dark, quiet manner still clung as it had in his youth. In the absence of talk, James watched. He tried to do as Michael did, to look as Michael looked.

He found himself liking the Texas country more all the time. Listening to stories back home, he had visualized a golden land teeming with wildlife and a soil so rich that you just scratched a spot in the earth, dropped a seed and jumped back to keep from being struck by the fast-growing plant. The reality fell considerably short of that image, but it was good enough. The soil looked fine and dark, and it gave off a pleasant smell when a plow turned the original sod for the first time. Michael and Andrew agreed that the game was no longer as abundant as they had first found it, but James could only compare it to Tennessee. There the land was increasingly crowded with people, and game was being killed off or driven away at a disturbing rate. Texas — this part of it, anyhow — was still years away from reaching that point. West of the Lewis farms, where nobody yet lived, James could always find something to level his rifle sights on. He never failed to bring home meat. That kept Annie from lecturing him at length about his absence from the field.

He took Michael's eight-year-old son Mordecai with him when Michael could spare the boy. James found the lean young Mordecai keen of eye and short on talk, just the way James liked for boys to be. Mordecai would respond politely if James initiated a conversation, but he seldom spoke first except to draw James's attention to a deer or something else of interest. Annie could well take lessons from him, James thought. He felt the boy's eyes following him often, studying him, perhaps making some kind of appraisal but never betraying the nature of it by word or expression. He had a solemn manner much like the one James remembered in Michael back in the old days before Michael and Andrew had come to Texas. By the time Mordecai was grown, James thought, he would be the spitting image of his father. Anybody with half an eye could already see that he was a Lewis. The family features were stamped strong and clean. The only thing different that James could see was that the boy's complexion was a little darker. Came from the Spanish on his mother's side, James figured.

Mordecai often spotted game before James did. When James let him take the first shot, there was no need to reload for a second; Mordecai hit whatever he aimed at. Michael had trained him well. Or maybe it was in the blood, a legacy from the Tennessee grandfather whose name the boy bore.

Though Mordecai did not say much, James became aware that he could say it in either of three languages. He had French and Spanish from his mother, English from his father. James was in no position to judge how good the boy's French and Spanish were, because he had not learned more than a dozen words of Spanish himself, and no French at all. But he noticed that when an occasional Mexican happened to ride by, Mordecai had no trouble talking with him.

James puzzled, "It's all just noise to me. How do you know what you're sayin'?"

Mordecai shrugged. "Everything's got a name. To me, everything's got three names. I'll bet I could learn you Spanish in just a little while."

James shook his head. "I don't know what

use it'd be. Just about everybody I've seen in Texas talks English like I do."

"But we belong to Mexico."

"No sir, I don't belong to nobody. The Lord put me on this earth a free American."

"You stopped bein' an American when you come into Texas and taken up Mexican land. Least, that's what the law says."

"I'll *always* be an American. They can come and throw me in jail if they can catch me, but it won't change what I am."

Mordecai showed a flicker of concern. "They might decide to come and try if they hear you talkin'. Folks say there's some Mexican soldiers moved in over at San Felipe. Never been any there before except just passin' through."

"I've got no quarrel with them. All they've got to do is let me alone."

"But they get ants in their britches when they hear people talk like you do."

"I come from Tennessee, and in Tennessee a man can say anything he wants to if he's stout enough to back it up."

"You're not in Tennessee anymore."

James frowned. "I'll bet your daddy ain't afeared of no Mexican soldiers."

Mordecai took his time in framing a careful answer. "He ain't afeared of anybody. But soldiers always make him nervous.

151

Mama says it's because they remind him of when the Spanish soldiers went and killed my granddaddy. Says soldiers are trained how to kill people." He added defensively, "That ain't bein' scared, that's just bein' watchful."

James nodded. "A wise man is always watchful. Still, I'll bet your daddy never ran from anybody lookin' for a fight."

"He stays out of their way when he can. But I don't know as he ever turned and run from them."

"Well, I ain't goin' to either. I'll say what I please, wherever I please. Anybody doesn't like me the way I am, he can go around. Us Lewises don't back off for anybody." He thought he saw a positive response in the boy's eyes.

Mordecai asked, "You ever been in jail?"

"Just once, in Nacogdoches. Why?"

"Uncle Andrew says we'll probably have to go and get you out of jail one of these days."

They were in the midst of cutting corn that fall when the soldiers first came by. The Lewis men and the three boys were working in Andrew's field. He had planted earliest, so his corn was the first ready for harvest. They lopped the heads from the stalks and dropped the ears into long cotton bags dragged behind them. It was young Mordecai who first spotted the riders and came running to tell his father. James counted six soldiers, mounted on small, ribby horses that didn't look as if they had ever seen any corn, and not a lot of anything else. The unexpected appearance of the uniformed men caught Michael in midstride and seemed to stagger him a bit. James saw something in his older brother's eyes, a darkness he dimly remembered from a time back in Tennessee when the Blackwood family had put Michael under a threat of death that was a hazard to all the Lewises.

Michael turned to Andrew. "They look like they're wantin' somethin'. You talk the language better than I do. Why don't you go down and see what they're after?"

Andrew seemed to accept without question his brother's reluctance to approach the soldiers. Anyway, it was his farm. "Sure, they're probably just lookin' for directions to someplace."

Michael said firmly, "Give them directions to someplace a long ways from here."

James said, "I'll go with you, Andrew, in case of trouble."

Andrew gave him a surprised glance. "Trouble? There won't be any unless you're lookin' to start some."

"I've never been one to cause trouble."

Andrew smiled. "That's not what Annie says. But just you let me do the talkin'."

James couldn't have done any talking if he had wanted to, for the conversation was all in Spanish. He stood in awkward, confused silence, listening to Andrew and a couple of the soldiers, watching the elaborate movement of their hands as they augmented their words. James thought the visitors were a hard-looking lot, all eyeing Andrew's cabin as if they would like to see what was in it. Their uniforms were dirty and threadbare. One man was knife-scarred, two had misshapen noses which James guessed had been broken fighting, and one was missing part of an ear. He wondered idly if it had been bitten off or sliced away with a knife. Neither way was much of a recommendation. He had seen better-looking men on a chain in a Tennessee prisoner work gang.

Though not a word had been said that James could understand, James had a strong feeling that Andrew was uneasy. A couple of times one of the men pointed toward the cabin, and Andrew shook his head, pointing off in another direction.

At last the men turned their horses and rode away, down toward the river. Andrew leaned on the rail fence, watching them intently. James knew he had not been mistaken; something about the soldiers had struck a raw nerve in his brother. James said, "They had the uniforms, but they didn't look much like real soldiers to me." He had heard tell of outlaws using soldier uniforms to gain an advantage over the unsuspecting. "You think maybe they're somethin' else?"

"They're soldiers, all right, but they're not like the ones we've seen around here before. I'm afraid Zaragosa was right. He told me they were fixin' to send convict soldiers up here to watch over us."

"What did they want?"

"They asked how many people are settled in this part of the country, and if we're the last ones to the west. But all the time they kept lookin' at the cabin. If there hadn't been so many of us here, I expect they had in mind to rob it."

"What're we goin' to do?"

"Nothin' much we *can* do. Maybe they won't be back."

James doubted that. He had seen for himself the way they looked toward the cabin. Andrew and Petra didn't have much, but even that little must look like a lot to someone who had nothing at all. "We can run them the hell off if they do show up here again."

Andrew turned, his eyes grave. "You don't understand this country. Mexico has given us a lot, but it could take it all back. There's people down there more than ready to try. They don't like us and never did. Zaragosa said that's why these convict soldiers were bein' sent, to see if we could be provoked into doin' somethin' that would give them the excuse."

"It'll take more than the likes of what I just saw."

"They've got more; don't let anybody tell you different." Andrew turned his attention back toward the river. The soldiers had watered their horses and were turning east in the direction of San Felipe. Andrew looked relieved. "Do me a favor, James. All Michael needs to know is that they asked for directions. If he thought there was more to it — well, you don't know Michael like I do."

"I know him. He'd fight."

"There are times when the hardest fight a man has to face is with himself. Michael's been down that road too many times. One of these days he's liable to fight that fight and lose. Let's go head some more corn."

■ ■ ■ ■

From the first, James had harbored reservations about his brothers' wives. To his Tennessee ear they both talked a little oddly, especially Petra, and they were darker complexioned than the women he had known back home. Times, he wondered why his brothers couldn't have gone back to Tennessee and found brides a little more like themselves. He guessed that when a man was in a foreign country, he accepted what that country offered.

However, he had no complaint about the women's performance in the kitchen. When all the Lewis men worked together, the Lewis women did likewise. Put Annie, Hope, Marie, and Petra all in the same kitchen and the only thing totally predictable was that something good to eat would come out of it, whether it was Mexican, French, or American.

Both of his brothers' wives were small women, shorter by half a head than Annie, and the constant work of a frontier existence had not let them put on any more weight than their small frames demanded. James thought he could almost reach around Marie's waist with his two hands, though he would not be so bold as to do it. Times he caught a sadness in her eyes, and he wondered if she might be thinking about the baby buried up the hill from her cabin. But other times she laughed, and her laugh was as clean and light as the tinkle of a silver bell.

Petra was a quiet sort, but James seldom saw her looking sad. Whenever Andrew was around, her gaze would follow him, her dark eyes soft and loving. Andrew looked the same whenever he was around Petra. There was a contentment about that pair, one James wondered if he would ever find for himself. He often had a feeling that Michael had never quite found it. Michael could be darkly moody, though he always seemed to brighten when Marie put her hand on his arm or around his shoulder.

James decided his brothers could have done worse, even if they *had* gone a long way from home to find their wives. But despite their example, he wasn't sure he ever wanted to marry. He might get somebody as easily dissatisfied as Annie and spend the rest of his life looking for reasons not to go home.

Though the families worked together in daytime during the harvest, they went to their own homes at night, for they had cows to milk, chickens to tend, and hogs to feed. Andrew and James had caught up several of Andrew's free-running pigs from the woods and penned them to fatten on corn and whatever minor leavings the kitchen table might yield. Come winter's cold, the pigs would be converted into hams, bacon, and sausage. The hens ran free in the daytime, but at night they roosted within a tall picket enclosure as varmint-proof as Andrew had been able to make it. There were plenty of four-legged predators around which had a taste for chickens, or whatever else they could catch.

It was the two-legged variety that started the trouble for James. One starry night he spread his blankets as usual some distance from the house. The black dog preferred the children's company in the daytime, but when they were put to bed in the cabin at night, the animal would join James, lying down beside him. The dog was company of sorts, though given to getting up in the night and running around a while, barking at any varmints he found prowling. When he came back he would often lie there and chew noisily on a bone he had preserved for that purpose until James would curtly tell him to go to sleep.

This night a low growl awakened James.

"Shut up, dog," he said irritably. But the dog kept growling until James decided there was something different in his manner this time. A wolf, maybe, or even a bear. James reached for the long rifle he kept just beneath the edge of the blanket to protect it from morning's dew. He pushed to his bare feet and felt around for his boots. The dog moved out away from him a little, back arched, the growl coming from deep in the throat.

From down at the hog pen, James heard a sudden squealing. Nothing put up a noise like a pig caught and unable to break away. It had to be something bigger than a raccoon or even a coyote to grab hold of a half-grown pig, he thought. In his underwear, he held the rifle against the poor light of a quarter moon and primed it. Then he set off in a trot toward the sound of the squealing.

He saw a dark form coming out over the top rail of the hog pen and knew immediately that this was no wolf or bear. This was a man, holding a squealing, kicking pig in his arms while he broke into a run.

James shouted, "Let go of that pig!" and struck a long trot in an effort to head the man off. He could hear the sound of horses' hoofs. He heard a man's excited voice, though he could not make out the words. He could see that the man had no intention of turning the pig loose. James dropped to one knee, brought the heavy rifle to his shoulder, and tried to aim without being able to see the front sight clearly. The rifle belched fire and kicked back hard against his shoulder. A man shouted in surprise. The pig squealed, kicked free, and went running desperately back toward the pen from which it had come. While James reloaded the rifle, handicapped by the darkness and the momentary blinding of the flash, he heard horses running. He could see the outlines of two horsemen, riding away as hard as they could go. He saw no need to waste powder and ball on a second shot that would almost certainly miss. Besides, the pig had gotten loose.

Andrew shouted from the dog-run. "James! What's the matter? What you shootin' at?"

James turned and started back toward the cabin, though he took time to go by his blankets and put on his trousers. He did not intend for Petra to see him in his underwear; it would be an embarrassment to them both. He heard Annie shouting at him. With Annie it wouldn't make any difference; she was hard to embarrass.

Andrew came out to meet him. "You see some varmint out there?" he asked.

"A pig-stealin' varmint. One that ran on two legs. Him and another one got away a-horseback."

Andrew appeared incredulous. "A man? You sure?"

"Didn't you hear him holler when I fired that shot? You ever see a four-legged varmint jump on a horse and run off?"

Andrew pondered. "By any chance did he just have one arm?"

"No, I'm pretty sure he had two." James realized Andrew's first thought was of Finis Blackwood. Stealing pigs was about the level of accomplishment expected of the Blackwoods back home. From what he had heard around here, the Texas branch wasn't any better. "Could've been one of the other two, though."

"Luke maybe. Not Isaac. He's got his faults, but I doubt he'd stoop to pig-stealin'."

James could see the two women standing on the dog-run. They were too far away to hear the conversation. He said, "It might not've been the Blackwoods at all. Remember, we seen some of them convict soldiers pass by here this mornin'."

Andrew stiffened. "You don't suppose you

162

hit him, do you?"

"I sure as hell tried. I'd've killed him if I could."

Andrew's voice was stern. "For a pig? Damn it, James, we reckon human life a little higher than that. If it *was* soldiers, we could be in for a right smart of trouble."

"A man's got a right to protect himself from thieves."

"Not when they're soldiers. If one of them shows up with a bullet in him, the law is goin' to take his side and believe whatever story he wants to tell."

James felt the sting of Andrew's implied rebuke. With a touch of resentment he said, "I'll bet Michael would've shot to kill."

"For somethin' important, maybe. Not for a pig."

James said, "Maybe we'd better hope it was just the Blackwoods. The world could stand a few less of them, anyway."

CHAPTER 9

Though he and Andrew tried to make light of the matter, James could tell by the women's expressions that they were not fooled, especially Petra. Despite the men's casual recounting of the incident, which betrayed no concern, she shuddered. She could remember back to another time when Spanish soldiers had been the terror of the countryside, taking whatever they wanted, arbitrarily killing those their officers suspected might be sympathetic to the native Mexican movement against Spanish rule. They offered no trial, heard no evidence. They had murdered her father, who was one of their countrymen, just as they had murdered Mordecai Lewis, who was not.

She said, "Better, I think, if we gave them the pig — if we gave them all the pigs."

Andrew agreed with her, but James replied stiffly, "You can't give in to a thief. The more he gets away with, the more he'll come back. That's how it was with the Black-woods back home. We never did let them get away with anything."

Andrew put his arms around Petra and tried to hug the worry out of her. "Even if it *was* soldiers, chances are James didn't hit one of them. It was too dark to see good."

James declared, "I hope I did, so they'll take roundance on this place from here out. They'll know there's light sleepers around here."

But it was not to be that way. Early the next morning, seven soldiers rode up to the farm, the rising sun at their backs. Andrew and James were tending to the livestock before they went into the field to harvest corn. Michael, Frank, and the boys had not arrived to help.

James saw the dark foreboding in An-drew's face and said, "I got my rifle over against the shed. I'd better fetch it."

"No," Andrew said sharply. "Worst thing we could do would be to show them a weapon. Stand quiet and let me handle it."

James knew little about rank in the Mexi-can army, but one of the soldiers wore a bit more tattered finery than the others, so he figured him for an officer or something. To James, he looked no better than the men around him. It was hard to see much of his face because of a huge and menacing black moustache that seemed to cover almost everything except his dark eyes and the point of his chin. As to the hard-eyed men with him, James doubted their own mothers would claim them. Whoever had opened the prison gates and turned them loose upon the public had made a grievous mistake.

Andrew said the man in the lead was a sergeant, the same rank as the one named Díaz who had caused the immigrant Lewises so much trouble west of the Sabine River. James did not take the rank as any recommendation. Unlike Díaz, this one did not speak English, or at least gave no sign that he did. It was left to Andrew to do the talking in Spanish. James listened, trying in vain to catch a word here and there. Whatever Andrew told the sergeant, the men around him answered with loud and angry denials. The sergeant's expression was accusatory, and so was his tone of voice.

James impatiently nudged Andrew's arm. "What's he sayin'?"

Andrew did not take his eyes from the soldiers, for their manner suggested violence was in some danger of breaking loose. "He says they were camped a little ways down the river last night. Says somebody taken a shot at one of his soldiers that was on

166

outside guard and creased him across the shoulder. He doesn't exactly say so, but it's plain he figures one of us done it. He was askin' if we've seen anybody suspicious come by here."

"We have, and they was all soldiers."

"I told him we shot at somethin' last night that tried to steal a pig. I didn't tell him we knew it was a man. I said it was dark, and we thought it was probably a wolf, or maybe a bear."

"Like hell we did. I knew damned well what it was."

"Sometimes, little brother, it pays to tell people what they want to hear. Especially soldiers."

The sergeant evidently understood more than he let on, for he pointed to James and asked a question. James demanded, "What is it now?"

"He's askin' if you're the one that fired the shot."

James braced himself defiantly, his feet a little apart. "Tell him I did, and I'll do it again if I catch another wolf around here."

Andrew tried to soften the sense of it, but James could tell that the sergeant understood what he had said, enough at least to know his meaning. He saw angry challenge in the man's black eyes. He said, "Tell him if he wants to fight about it, to climb on down here."

Andrew gave James an exasperated glance. "I don't know how we're goin' to keep you alive long enough to ever make a crop on that place of yours."

"I just don't like thieves, and this whole bunch looks to me like fugitives from a hangin'."

The sergeant gave James a crackling look that said he would be back. James imagined he could feel heat from the man's eyes, like the heat from coals banked for a long winter night. The sergeant spoke to the men, and they, too, fastened surly attention upon James. James wished again for the rifle, but it was well out of his reach. After what seemed like several minutes the sergeant gave a sharp command. His men pulled their horses around and rode away, some turning in their saddles to look back.

Andrew watched them a few minutes before he faced James with trouble in his eyes. "I'm sorry to say this, but it may've been a mistake for you to come to Texas."

"If you think I'm afraid of a bunch of pig thieves like that, you're mistaken."

"I know you're not. The thing is, you ought to be. If you halfway knew this country, you *would* be."

James stiffened defensively against Andrew's implied criticism. "I'll bet Michael would've done the same thing. You couldn't catch *him* takin' any sass off of them soldiers. Michael would stand up for himself."

Andrew just stared at him a moment, shook his head and turned back to feeding the livestock. James felt his face warm, for he wanted his brother's approval. But devil be damned if he was going to back down from a bunch of convict soldiers to get it.

When they weren't harvesting one of the fields and nobody had a great need for fresh meat, James had begun going into the woods and cutting down trees to provide logs for the cabin he intended to build for himself and his sister Annie. It would be more than a mile upriver from Andrew and Petra, and fully a mile from the new cabin of cousin Frank and his family. James had gathered perhaps half enough for the job, cleaning them of branches with his sharp ax, dragging the logs up and stacking them at the place where he planned to build. He hadn't asked Annie's advice about the site. She would probably want to build somewhere else out of pure sisterly contrariness. He didn't see where it mattered anyway; she would probably snare some poor unsuspecting soul and leave here before long, properly married. Let somebody else try to please Annie!

A time or two, his bay horse Walker looked off toward the timber as if he saw or smelled something. James glanced in that direction. Probably a deer, he thought, foraging at the edge of the heavy cover. When he had finished the day's work here he would take his rifle and see about fetching some fresh venison for the table.

He didn't see the three soldiers until too late; he was busy, using the horse to shag a log out of the woods with a thick rawhide rope he had laboriously made for himself in the evenings after the field work was done. The bay horse jerked its head around, snorting loudly, pricking its ears forward in alarm. Two soldiers were bearing down on James, spurring their horses viciously. A third — he looked like the sergeant — sat back shouting orders. One of the soldiers waved a saber that blinked a split second of reflected sunlight. James felt his pulse quicken, and he looked around desperately for something with which to defend himself. He had left his long rifle leaning against the stack of logs. All he had was the ax, its blade buried into the log he was dragging. He grabbed it, wrenching it free. He gripped the handle in both hands and brought it up to catch the saber's savage downstroke. His wrists quivered at the impact as the sharp blade bit deeply into the hard wood. He thrust the ax upward, shoving the sword back toward the man who held it, then gave a quick twist, trying to wrest the blade from the dark brown hand. It came free from the ax handle, but the soldier retained his grip on it. He gave an angry shout and raised the saber again. The second soldier had no saber, but he held a blunderbuss.

James used the ax to shield himself from the second swing of the saber, this time twisting the handle's end around and driving it with force against the soldier's ribs. Breath gusted from the man. James dropped the ax and grabbed the sword arm, giving the man a hard pull. The soldier was already off balance, so James managed to yank him from the saddle and bring him crashing to the ground. The man landed atop the sword. The point of it drove into his leg. He screamed in surprise and pain.

The other soldier brought up the blunderbuss. James stepped quickly behind the downed soldier's horse, trying to put it between him and the man with the firearm. He heard the blast and felt the horse take the impact. The animal screamed, jumped twice and went down, its thrashing hind legs striking the soldier who was on the ground. The soldier cursed.

James saw that the man still on horseback was trying hard to reload the weapon. James picked up the ax and flung it in that direction, spooking the horse and causing the man to lose the gunpowder he had poured in the palm of his hand for placement down the hot barrel. James made a quick dash across the open ground toward his own rifle. Grabbing it, he dodged behind the pile of logs and dropped down. He brought up the rifle, cocking the hammer back. He took a quick bead on the soldier still on horseback, but judgment stayed him from squeezing the trigger.

If he fired, he would be defenseless during the moments he was reloading. That blunderbuss would almost surely get him. And if it missed, the sergeant had moved up closer with a weapon of his own. But this way, his rifle loaded, James remained a lethal threat to the horsemen. The nearest soldier swung quickly to the ground and put his horse between James and himself.

One horse was dying, though it was not of James's doing. It would be useless for him to kill the second. That would only leave him vulnerable, an empty rifle in his hands.

The matter went to a standstill for a minute or two. James watched the soldier over his sights, the rifle leaned against the top log of the stack. The soldier had his blunderbuss leveled across the seat of his saddle, though his nervous, fidgeting horse made it impossible for him to hold the barrel still.

The other horse still thrashed, fighting death as its blood pumped upon the ground in measured spurts. The soldier whose leg was cut crawled behind the downed horse, trying to use it for a shield from James's rifle but also trying to avoid the hoofs that lashed out in blind agony.

The sergeant held back, still shouting angry orders that went unheeded.

James's bay horse had spooked and dragged the log at the end of the rawhide rope until it caught against the others and wedged, stopping him beside the stack. He pitched, fighting in vain against the rope. James tried to talk to him in a soothing voice but dared not step out to grab the reins.

He could hear the two soldiers shouting back and forth to one another, the sergeant shouting at both of them. The one who had taken the sword's edge in his leg was evidently in pain. His voice had a pleading tone. The other was mostly angry. The sergeant was livid but did not move closer.

Son of a bitch is a coward, James thought. *Sent those other poor bastards to do the job.*

He remembered Andrew's warnings about caution, about watching what he said and to whom he said it. Andrew had been right. But if the situation arose again, James knew he would do nothing differently. All his growing-up years, he had remembered how sternly Michael had faced whatever challenges came along, and he had tried to follow that example. He might sometimes wish things would turn out in another way, but anybody waiting for him to apologize had better bring enough vittles for a long camp.

At last the soldier still on his feet began moving toward the one who was down, leading his horse, keeping the animal between him and James. By this time the wounded horse was dead. The led horse snorted and tried to jerk back, spooked by the scent of blood. It was all the soldier could do to hold him. The wounded man began crawling on hands and knees, which only frightened the animal more. James could hear the man cursing.

James shouted, "Put your gun down and I won't shoot you."

The soldiers did not understand him. He

tried a couple of times making motions as if to lay down his rifle, then pointing toward the blunderbuss. The message got through, finally. The soldier laid the weapon down at his feet, and James rested his across the stack of logs, in plain sight of the soldiers but well within his reach if he needed it. He had no intention of letting sympathy for a wounded man jeopardize his own survival. They raised them smarter than that in Tennessee.

The soldier who had held the rifle used a knife to cut away part of the other's trouser leg and bind it around the wound. Then he helped his wounded companion up into the saddle. The wounded man pointed toward his own saddle, still buckled to the dead horse. The second one struggled with the animal's weight and managed to worry the saddle loose and take the bridle. He handed them to the wounded man to hold while he swung up behind him on the horse, the blunderbuss in his hand.

The sergeant made no move to help them. He held his distance, sulking over their failure.

James wondered how far they had to travel. The wounded one was going to have a mighty sore leg before they went many miles, and they'd have a very tired horse, carrying double. The second soldier would probably have to get down and walk a right smart of the way. The sergeant probably wouldn't help them any more than he already had. The privilege of rank, and the arrogance.

Well, the hell with them! He hadn't invited them here.

As the men rode away, the sergeant turned and shouted at James and shook his fist. James wished he had a little Spanish of the right kind so he could make a proper reply. All he could do in the way of communication was to raise his rifle over his head and shake it.

Three men, and he had run them off. He wondered if Michael had ever done better than that. Trouble was, they might not stay run off. That sergeant looked like the kind of man who would keep bringing more soldiers until he got the job done, no matter how many of them got hurt in the process.

This might be a good time to go hunting for a few days.

They wouldn't be back for a little while, at least. He had two or three more trees felled out in the edge of the wood. Be damned if he would let a few soldiers stop him from getting a day's work done. He dragged those in before he mounted the horse and rode eastward to let Andrew know what had happened.

Andrew already had an inkling, because he rode out to meet James, his thin face dark with worry. He gave James a quick look up and down before demanding, "Are you all right?"

James nodded. "Didn't nothin' happen to me. It all happened to *them.*"

Andrew's voice was strained. "The soldiers rode by the field, two of them on one horse and one of them lookin' like he was bad hurt. I tried to ask them what happened, but all I got was a cussin' out by that sergeant. I was afraid I'd find you layin' up here dead someplace. You oughtn't to've shot a soldier."

"I didn't. That soldier fell on his own damned sword. Bled like a stuck hog. Goin' to be a while before he gives anybody much trouble."

"There's aplenty more where he came from. What happened?"

James told him. "They just come at me out of the woods without so much as a howdy-do. It's their good luck that I didn't kill one of them."

"And yours. But it's bad enough. You'll have to get away from here."

"I figured on that. I'll go huntin' for a few days."

"A few days?" Andrew's eyes narrowed with exasperation. "You'll have to be gone a lot longer than that. They won't be forgettin' about you, and if they find you they'll chop you up into little pieces."

"I didn't do nothin' except defend myself. I didn't go chargin' into *their* camp."

"This isn't Tennessee. You've got to put some country behind you, and the sooner the better."

James thought about the logs piled up for his cabin. He had hoped to move into it before winter's cold and stop depending so much upon Andrew and Petra. "But what about my farm? I don't want to give it up."

"You want to be buried on it?"

"Maybe, in fifty or sixty years."

"It's not even a farm yet anyhow, it's just raw land. If it's not still vacant there'll be another for you someplace when you get back."

"From where?"

"I don't know. Home to Tennessee, maybe, for a year or so till these soldiers have moved on somewhere else."

"A year!" James felt as if Andrew had struck him in the stomach. A year seemed like a life sentence, especially in view of the fact that he had not been here nearly that long. "Maybe if I just go off for a long trip huntin' — maybe go west and see what San Antonio de Bexar looks like —"

"Not Bexar. That's where the soldiers are sent from. No, I think you'd better clear out of Texas for a while. Maybe over around Natchitoches, Louisiana, if you don't want to go all the way home to Tennessee. You can probably find some kind of work to do. Maybe Old Man Villaret, Marie's papa — he might have somethin' for you."

James slumped in the saddle. "You're makin' a lot out of this, Andrew. It was the soldiers started it all."

"And they'll finish it if you give them the chance."

He rode with his brother back to Andrew's place, resisting all the way, thinking up arguments. By the time they reached the cabin he had just about made up his mind not to go at all. They couldn't do anything to a man who had acted only in self defense!

He expected Annie to wade into him with a lot of her sisterly scolding, but she only stared at him with sad blue eyes that appeared about to break into tears at any moment. It was Petra, for once, who did the talking. She took both his hands in hers and told him of the terrible day the soldiers had killed her father while her half-grown brothers stood by and could do nothing. The younger Moreno children, like herself, had huddled in terror with their mother inside their cabin.

Andrew had already talked himself out. He could only stand and nod agreement with what Petra said.

She declared gravely, "If they come for you, James, it will be again as with my father. You will die here. And for what? For a pig?"

"It ain't just the pig," James argued. "It's that a man ought to stand his ground and not run like a rabbit."

"And what then? You stand your ground, and you die on it. The soldiers win. They always win."

He looked at his sister. "Annie, I didn't want to bring you here in the first place. But I did it anyway. Now you want me to run off and leave you?"

Annie said, "I want you alive. The rest doesn't matter."

Andrew said, "Don't you be frettin' yourself over Annie. We'll take care of her — me and Michael, Petra and Marie."

James heard the sound of running horses. *Damn them, have they come already?* he wondered. He stepped out onto the dog-run. He saw his brother Michael, and someone else. A black-bearded man dismounted from a sweat-lathered sorrel. James had not seen much of the Blackwood family in his months here, but he remembered this one as Isaac.

Isaac fixed James with a solemn stare. "You'd be the one they're after, I reckon."

"Who's after me?"

"Them Mexican soldiers. I was over to the Willet place just now. There was a bunch of them soldiers there, takin' their siesta and robbin' the old lady's garden when three more rode in from this direction. One of them had his leg butchered up some. They was mighty mad. Best me and the Willet boy could make out from their talk, they'd had a run-in with some young buck over this way. They was fixin' to come back and get him. I skint out and come by Michael's place; didn't know but what you'd be there."

Michael had said nothing. He just stared at James with a sad look much like Annie's. It struck James as odd that Michael would ride with a Blackwood under any circumstances.

James said, "Michael, everybody's wantin' me to run away. I told them *you* wouldn't. You'd stand your ground and fight."

Andrew looked up at his brother. "Tell him, Michael. Make him see that he's got to go."

Stubbornly James said, "You never did run, Michael."

Michael's eyes were grim. "Run? You're damn right I've run. I've found that there's a time to fight, and there's a time to retreat. This is a time to run, and run like hell."

James was conscious that the women had come out onto the dog-run. They had heard what Isaac and Michael said. "How many soldiers are there?"

Isaac replied, "I'd expect there was a dozen. Maybe one or two more. More'n you'd be wantin' to tangle with, I'm thinkin'."

Andrew pressed, "How far are they behind you, Isaac?"

"Can't rightly say, but not too far. I don't know how fast them soldiers' horses are."

James frowned suspiciously. "You're a Blackwood. How come you'd want to warn me, a Lewis?"

Isaac's gaze went for a moment to Annie, then lifted to the sky. A gray look had built up, clouds moving in from the Gulf way to the east, as if it might shortly rain. Isaac said, "It ain't goin' to be no pretty day to die. If I was you, I'd be ridin' away from here mighty quick."

Petra turned back toward the kitchen. "James, I will put together something for you to eat. Andrew, you put together the things he will need."

James felt a chill, for the cold reality was finally sinking in. He was truly going; there was no choice.

He still half expected Annie to blame him, to send him away with her recriminations ringing in his ears. But she put her arms around him, and he felt her tears wet against his cheek. "Please, James, don't let anything happen to you."

Petra came with a sack of food. Andrew tied James's rolled blankets behind the saddle and led the long-legged bay horse up to the dog-run. "What clothes you've got are inside the blankets," he said. He went into the cabin's kitchen and came out again with a few coins in his hand. "It ain't much because we don't have much," he said. "But maybe it'll see you through if you find yourself in need."

James thought he could see something moving on the eastern horizon, but it might have been the tears he was trying to force back. "I didn't go to bring trouble down on you-all. All I intended to do was to stop a thief."

"Just don't stop any bullets."

He looked at Michael. "I wish I could say good-bye to your family. To Marie and Mordecai."

Michael nodded. "They'll understand."

Isaac Blackwood had been watching the horizon. He turned. "They're comin'. Boy, was I you I'd skin out yonderway, across the river, then stay in the timber at least till night catches you. You know where our place is at?"

James knew only vaguely; he had not been there.

"Well," Isaac said, "was I you I'd go around. It'd be like Finis to try and turn you in to get himself better fixed with the authorities."

The man was a Blackwood, but James felt obliged to say, "I do thank you, Isaac." He hugged Petra and then his brothers. "I don't know when, but I'll be back."

He turned to Annie, who was weeping silently. He touched her wet cheek with the palm of his hand. "It'll be all right, sis. Now, don't you go marryin' the first old boy that comes along."

He swung up onto Walker, having to lift his leg high to clear the roll of blankets. He rode down to the river in a long trot and put the horse into the water. Over the sound of the wind he heard a shout and turned to see the soldiers spurring hard to catch him. He leaned over Walker's neck to make himself less of a target. He heard a couple of musket balls whiz by, missing him by a comfortable margin. He tried to push the horse for more speed, but Walker was swimming, doing the best he could.

The swimming speed was much less than the running speed on the ground, and the soldiers quickly closed the distance. Before James was out of the water on the north bank, some of the soldiers had put their mounts into it from the south. A couple held back to fire at him before he could disappear into the woods. The first shot went wild.

He did not hear the second shot. He felt it like a mule had kicked him in the ribs, knocking most of the breath out of him. He almost fell from the saddle and grabbed and held on, struggling for breath. He brought a hand up to his right side and felt blood there, warm and sticky. The wound burned as if it were being seared by a branding iron. The pain was sharp; the bullet had glanced off, but he suspected its impact had cracked a rib. His head swam; he was not sure he was going to be able to stay on the horse. But he had no choice. He sensed that those men back there had every intention of killing him. Self-defense didn't mean anything if a man never lived to get to the courtroom.

Damn it all, maybe Andrew was right. Maybe he *shouldn't* have come to Texas.

He headed the horse into the heavy woods. "Come on, Walker. If you ever had to win a race in your life, this one is it!"

CHAPTER 10

Pain shot through his body like a lance with each stride the horse made, but James held to the saddle and urged Walker to keep moving, dodging his way through the timber. The soft mat of old leaves left little or no track, though it produced a rustling noise beneath the hoofs. In a while he stopped, partly for momentary relief from the pain, partly to listen. He heard no sound of pursuit. Somehow he had shaken loose from the soldiers. But James knew he had meandered in the woods. He had not spent much time on this side of the river, so he did not know his way.

He let the horse move in a walk. That eased the jolting, afforded the horse a chance to recover its wind, and gave James a better chance to hear if the soldiers approached him again. He did not know which direction was safest for him to travel. If the soldiers had gone around him, he faced the hazard that he might run into them again no matter what direction he followed.

The persistence of the pain and the slow but steady trickle of blood forced him finally to dismount and lie down for a bit after kicking together a bed of old leaves. They felt almost as soft as a cornshuck mattress. When he pressed his hand to his side, the sharp pain almost took his breath away. He remembered that once, when he was twelve or thirteen, he had fallen from a horse and cracked a rib, possibly the same one the musketball had struck. His mother had wrapped his rib cage tightly with cloth. That had given him some ease. But he had no cloth here, unless he were to tear up his homespun shirt or empty the bag of food Petra had given him. He was reluctant to do either.

He thought of the rawhide rope he had used to drag logs to the cabin site. He pushed carefully to his feet and took it from the saddle. He found the process awkward because he had to keep circling the coiled rope around his body, shifting it from one hand to the other. Invariably he lost its tautness, and it slipped down to his waist in a tangle. He gave up and lay down again for a little while, until another idea came. He tied one end of the rope to a tree, backed off to the end of it and began turning slowly in circles, keeping the rope tight, winding it around and around his body like a windlass as he moved closer to the tree. The overlapping coils prevented slippage. He tucked the end of the rope under them, wincing at the pressure on the cracked rib.

It still hurt, but less intensively now. He felt as though his upper body was encased in a tight barrel, or he was stuck in a hollow log. It was a poor solution to the problem but better than no solution at all. He found himself exhausted by the effort and lay flat on his back for a while, looking up at the heavy canopy that blocked out most of the sunlight. He let his mind run back over the events of the afternoon. He gave in to alternate bouts of regret and anger: regret that he had been forced to leave his new home, his brothers and their families, even Annie; anger over a mistaken government policy that sent convict soldiers to police honest people. It was like sending a wolf to guard the lambs.

One frustrating conclusion kept coming to him, that there was not a damned thing he could do about it. He had done too much already. Right and wrong were no longer the immediate concern. Survival was.

He rested as long as he dared, ate cold venison and bread from the sack Petra had given him, then remounted and set Walker in an easterly direction. Each time the trees thinned and he seemed to be coming to the edge of the woods, he drew in again. After dark he would break out into the open and try for speed, to put this place as far behind him as he could before daylight. Right now, concealment was his first concern.

He came unexpectedly upon a clearing and a cabin. Caution told him to pull back into the timber and keep riding, but the wound had produced the beginnings of fever. His mouth was parched. He saw a stone-walled well ten paces from the cabin. Seeing no sign of Mexican soldiers, he pushed Walker toward the well. He dismounted unsteadily, leaning against the circular stone wall for support. He began cranking the creaky windlass, bringing up the bucket from the bottom.

He sensed uneasily that he was being watched. He saw a boy peering with curiosity around the corner of the cabin. As they made eye contact, the boy quickly disappeared. James could hear his voice calling, "Papa! Papa!" and the creaking of a wooden door dragging its way across a threshold.

As the bucket came to the top, James swung it out to rest on the flat top of the wall and eagerly dipped a drinking gourd that hung from one of the posts supporting the windlass. The water was cool and sweet and brought a sense of relief as he gulped down all the gourd could hold.

A rough voice said, "Stranger, that's a private well."

James had trouble bringing his eyes to focus on the face. He rubbed an arm across them and saw two men, both black-bearded. The fatter of the two had but one arm. He carried a rifle in the other, cradling it across the stump. Dismay nearly took James's feet from under him as he realized he had done just what Isaac Blackwood had warned him against: He had blundered onto the Blackwood place.

Finis Blackwood looked at the rope wrapped around James's torso. "Who the hell tied you up, and how'd you get away?" Then his eyes narrowed as recognition slowly came to him. "By God, you look to me like a Lewis. You ain't Michael or Andrew, but you got the look of them about you."

"The look of them, all right," Luke Blackwood chimed in. James remembered that folks said Luke was strong of body but weak

191

in the head. He sensed that the best thing would be for him to get on Walker and ride. "Much obliged for the drink." He edged toward the horse.

Finis stepped closer. "You got blood on you. By God, you been shot, that's what it is." He brought the rifle to bear on James. "Luke, I know now what it was them Mexican soldiers was tryin' to tell us when they came by here a while ago, jabberin' at us in Spanish. They was lookin' for somebody, and this here is him."

James put a foot in the stirrup, though the effort brought fresh pain. Finis moved quickly for a fat man, jabbing the muzzle of the rifle against the rope that bound James's ribs. Finis said, "You ain't a-goin' no place. You step back away from that horse without you want another bullet in you."

The man's muddy eyes told James that he meant it. James weighed his chance of knocking the rifle aside and knew it was poor. He was a Lewis. Finis Blackwood would kill him without hesitation and be grateful for the opportunity. He eased his foot back to the ground. Knowing it would do no good, he said, "I never done you any harm."

"You're one of *them*," Finis answered. He motioned with the rifle. "You come on over here to the house. Luke, you take his horse and turn him into the lot. And saddle mine. I'm goin' to see if I can find them soldiers."

Luke blinked, not quite comprehending. "What you want the soldiers for?"

"They'd think a right smart better of us was we to catch this boy for them, wouldn't they? Might even give us more land, you never can tell."

Luke said, "We ain't used up all we already got."

"Land is money. Ain't never been no rich Blackwoods. We just might git to be the first ones."

Luke stared hopefully at James. "You reckon they'll hang him?"

"I don't know. I ain't rightly sure what they want him for."

"I ain't ever seen a hangin'. I'd *like* to."

"Maybe they'll give us an invite. Go do what I tell you." Finis poked James again, on the side that hurt. "Now, you git along into that cabin."

It was a double cabin, like so many in the Austin colony, modeled after those back where most of the settlers had come from. A heavy woman stood with the boy in the open dog-run. James could not tell whether she was pregnant or just fat. She wore an old homespun dress that fitted her like a sack, reaching down almost to her calloused feet. She stared with the same uncomprehending expression as Luke's. The boy appeared to be five or six years old. He had all the markings of the Blackwood boys James had known back in Tennessee, though his eyes looked brighter than most. There must be some outcross blood in him, James thought.

The woman asked, "What you doin' with that feller, Finis? And what you got him all tied up for?"

"Somebody already tied him up before I got him, but they left his arms out. Ain't no wonder he got away from them. But he ain't gittin' away from us."

She studied James from his head down to his feet as if he were a studhorse or something. "He ain't a bad-lookin' feller. Nice and young. What would anybody want to tie him up for?"

"He's the one them soldiers was a-huntin'. I'm goin' to fetch them here and see what they'll give us for him."

She showed misgivings. "They'll probably shoot him. Ain't good for the young'uns to see such as that."

"This is a Lewis. It'd do the young'uns good, let them see what life is all about."

"He's been a-bleedin'," she observed.

194

"I ain't never seen a Lewis bleed enough to suit me."

Luke brought Finis's horse. He said, "Finis, why don't you let me go after the soldiers?"

"Because you'd get lost in a mile and I'd have to go hunt you." He handed Luke the rifle. "Now, don't you let him get away, or them soldiers'll be mad at *us* instead of the Lewises."

"You want me to shoot him if he tries to leave?"

Finis looked exasperated. "That's what I give you the rifle for, ain't it?"

The woman kept staring at James, studying him boldly. "Seems like a shame, him so young and handsome and all."

Finis warned her sternly, "And don't you go gettin' no ideas about him. You already got man enough to take care of what you need, and that's me." He started to mount the horse but paused to tighten the girth. "Damn you, Luke, can't you ever learn to cinch a horse up tight? It's a wonder the saddle didn't turn under him with me."

Luke mumbled as he watched Finis ride away. "Always cussin' me, he is. I got a mind to just shoot this feller and see what Finis says about *that.*"

The woman quickly shook her head. "You

don't want to go and do nothin' like that, Luke." She moved up close and touched the rawhide rope that bound James's ribs. Dried blood had seeped out through the shirt and the tight coils. "Poor boy, you been hurt."

James tried to watch her but found himself watching Luke's rifle. "Musketball broke a rib, I think. The rope was all I had to bind it with."

She said, "You come on in the house and I'll see what I can do for you. Ain't right, leavin' a man to stand out here and bleed to death."

James didn't think the wound was bleeding anymore, but he did not argue.

Luke demanded, "What you fixin' to do with him, Nelly?"

"See if I can patch him up."

"Finis wouldn't like that."

"Finis ain't here. You comin' to help, or are you goin' to stand out here with your mouth hangin' open?"

"I reckon I'll go in. Finis told me to watch him."

She led James into the bedroom side of the double cabin. It was a Spartan hovel to say the best for it. The fireplace at the east end was about as crudely put together as James had ever seen. He thought it a wonder that the cabin hadn't burned. The furniture was rough and splintery, homemade by careless hands. The floor was of dirt. James could remember living in a dirt-floored cabin when he was small, but at least his mother swept it every day. This one showed no experience with a broom.

The woman motioned him toward a lop-sided bed that was only a rawhide-tied timber frame and a cornshuck mattress. "Have yourself a sit-down. Let's get that rope off of you and see what you look like."

He saw two more children, one a boy of about two or so, the other a baby lying asleep in a crib.

It seemed to him that Nelly rubbed her hands against him a lot in the process of removing the rawhide rope. She leaned so near that he could smell her breath and feel the warmth that emanated from her large body. She said, "Ain't no fat on your ribs at all. You're thinner'n a hard-wintered pony." When the rope all lay on the packed dirt floor she pulled his cotton shirt up to just beneath his armpits. She looked at him a minute, and he was not sure he liked what he saw in her eyes. It was hunger, of a sort.

She said, "You kind of put me in mind of Isaac. He never was one for no extra weight neither. I always kind of liked a man that was all muscle." She rubbed her hand over his chest and his rib cage, ranging far beyond just the spot torn and angry from the bullet. She pushed gently against the hurt rib. He sucked in a lungful of air, letting it hiss between his teeth.

She said, "That hurt, didn't it? Rib ain't busted in two, but I don't doubt that it's cracked." She cleansed the wound with corn whiskey, which made James want to climb the log wall for a minute until the fire burned down.

Luke protested, "That's our drinkin' whiskey."

She tossed him the jug. "Then drink." He did, a long double swallow, and then another, and a third after that.

Nelly took her time washing the area around the wound, her hands moving slowly, caressing. She dried him with a piece of cloth, taking her time about that, too. From a box she took more homespun cotton cloth and bound James's ribs. The cloth was more comfortable than the rawhide rope had been. But her hands worried him. They moved up above the binding, and down to his leg where he had not been hurt. James had not had much experience with women, but it was clear to him that her interest went beyond any nursing instinct.

He was not sure how to respond.

"Luke," she said, "why don't you go outside and keep a watch for Finis?"

"He knows his way home."

"Take the jug with you. And the two boys. You and the young'uns can play games."

"What about this feller? Who's goin' to watch him?"

She smiled. "I'll do that. Now, you-all git. This man needs his rest before the soldiers come."

Luke took another drink from the jug. "You sure this is the way Finis would want it?"

"Finis ain't here to say otherwise."

As Luke and the boys went out the door, she closed it and slid a wooden bar into place. She turned back toward James, and he *knew* he did not like the look in her eyes. She studied him as if she were a bear and he a chunk of red meat.

The bed groaned as she sat down beside him on the edge of it. Her hand went to his leg. "You a married man?"

He shook his head.

She said, "I didn't much think so. You look a little young yet for that, but you never can tell. They get to wantin' what a woman's got for them, they sometimes marry awful young." Her hand began moving suggestively up and down his leg. "It's a pity how many bachelors there is in this country that don't have no idea how good a woman can be. How's that bindin' feel?"

"Hurts some. I think I need some air." He tried to get up from the bed, but she put an arm around his shoulder and held him.

She said, "What you need is to lay down a while. Rest easy."

"What I *really* need is to get away from here before them soldiers come back. They're set to kill me."

She kept her hand moving. "That'd be a waste, sure enough. Ain't near enough good-lookin' men in this country as it is." She leaned, her large breasts pressing against him. "Yes, sir, sure would be a waste. You really one of them Lewises?"

He was sweating. "From across the river."

"I never did rightly know how come Finis hates the Lewises so much. What little I ever seen of Michael and Andrew, they seemed like good men. Handsome, too; the both of them. Always kind of wished I'd seen them before Finis come along."

James tried to imagine Nelly in Michael's or Andrew's cabins instead of Marie or Petra. He would have laughed were he not so ill at ease. "Then how come you to marry Finis?"

"Had to marry *somebody.* The baby was comin' on. Isaac never asked me, and Luke, he ain't bright. Never was sure which one of them was rightfully the baby's papa, but I reckon it don't make no difference. We're all family anyway. It's like they was all my husbands."

James blinked. "*All* of them?"

"Well, Isaac don't do me no more. Mostly it's Finis, and now and again Luke when Finis ain't around. Ain't neither one of them very good-lookin'. Not like you, anyway." She kissed him boldly. "I wouldn't mind a change, if you was willin'."

She had both arms around him. He felt trapped, smothering in her heavy embrace. He knew her aim was seduction, but his reaction was nearer panic than arousal. "Please," he said. "My ribs."

She relaxed her hold. Her voice was sympathetic though disappointed. "I didn't go to hurt you none. Almost forgot for a minute. I reckon you don't feel up to doin' nothin' right now."

He took advantage of the moment to free himself from her and get to his feet. "No ma'am, I'm afraid I hurt too much."

"Well," she said in resignation, "maybe another time. If you get away from the soldiers."

"I don't know how I'm goin' to do that when Luke's waitin' outside with that rifle."

"That won't be no trouble. Luke's half drunk by now, and probably forgot what Finis told him to do. You just stand by the door, and when Luke comes in, you slip out right quiet. I'll keep him busy a while."

"I'm obliged to you, ma'am."

"It ain't no strain. I've got in the mood anyway. Since it can't be you, Luke'll do."

"I don't know how I can ever pay you."

"You can come back around someday when Luke and Finis ain't here, and when there ain't no soldiers after you. Like I said, there just ain't enough good-lookin' men in this country."

She lifted the bar and opened the door while James coiled the rope. "Luke," she said quietly, "you want to come in here?"

"What for?" Luke's slurred words indicated that he had been tilting the jug considerably.

"I just want you to. Finis ain't here. Been a while since it was just me and you, without Finis around."

Luke suddenly showed a lively interest. "That's a fact." His boots clomped across the wooden threshold. He blinked at James, as if he had forgotten about him. "Wasn't we supposed to be guardin' this feller?"

"He's a growed man," Nelly said, taking the rifle from Luke's hand and leaning it against the rough wall. She took Luke's hand and brought it around behind her. "Let him take care of hisself."

James stepped outside. He heard the wooden bar slip back into place. The older of the two boys stared up at him. James tried to decide which Blackwood he resembled most. He guessed it was as Nelly had said: It didn't make much difference.

He tousled the boy's hair. "You take good care of your mama, young'un. Ain't many like her around."

He hurried to the lot, saddled Walker and set him into a slow but steady lope, putting this place behind him. He forgot, until he was a mile or two away, that his rib still hurt.

CHAPTER 11

He rode most of the night, stopping occasionally to rest. The tight binding Nelly had wrapped around his ribs was more effective than the crude one he had formed with the rawhide rope, but it did not block all the pain. He tried not to think about what he was leaving behind, but the image of it kept running through his mind, over and over. Maybe if he had listened to Andrew more — maybe if he hadn't been so quick to antagonize the damned sergeant — maybe if — The *maybes* went on and on. The frustration hurt almost as much as his cracked rib.

Well, he wouldn't stay gone, they could count on that. He'd be back to reclaim what belonged to him. Michael's first experience in Texas had been disastrous, but he had come back. For James to do less would be to fail his older brother.

He avoided well-traveled trails and roads,

crossing the Brazos and skirting north of where he knew San Felipe to be. But as he sensed that he was nearing the edge of the Austin colony, the sharp pangs of regret deepened. He wished to delay that final separation as long as he dared. Because of last spring's trip down from Nacogdoches, he knew that when he left the Austin colony he was likely to travel for days without seeing so much as a farmhouse. The food Petra had hastily sacked for him was gone.

He saw a farmer and several young boys gathering corn in a field neatly fenced with rails. The long, rambling log house, the pens, and the sheds reflected relative prosperity. This was probably one of Stephen F. Austin's original Three Hundred, here long enough now to have set his roots deeply in the rich soil of this new land. James felt reasonably confident that he had temporarily outdistanced pursuit or any word of his fugitive status. He argued with himself only a little before he turned Walker's head away from the woods and over toward the field. The wound had not bled since he had been at the Blackwood place, and he had rinsed all the blood from the shirt. The bullet hole remained. He reasoned that these people probably would not notice it. Clothes worn and torn, even ragged, were common in this fledgling colony. Reality and practicality took precedence over form and fashion.

He raised his hand in greeting as the middle-aged farmer trudged down a row of head-high corn to the rail fence. The boys had stopped working, staring at James in curiosity. "How do?" the farmer said. "Light and rest a spell." He had rusty-colored hair and a round, happy-looking face, red both from his nature and from exposure to the Texas sun.

"I'm obliged," James responded. He motioned toward a cloth-wrapped water jug hanging from the fence. "Mind if I have a swig of that? Been a long ways since the last creek."

"Help yourself and welcome," the farmer said jovially. "You headin' for Nacogdoches?"

"That direction, anyway." James intended to swing south of Nacogdoches and hit the Sabine River in some isolated area where he was unlikely to encounter soldiers. Sergeant Díaz there was almost sure to remember him, as much trouble as they had given one another last spring.

The farmer told his sons to resume work, then turned back critically to James. "You don't look well fixed for a ride that long. I see blankets, but I see nothin' in the way of vittles."

"Got my rifle. Figured I'd find enough game along the way. Had squirrel last evenin'."

The farmer glanced up toward the sun. "Gettin' toward noonday. My wife and the girls'll be a-ringin' the bell for dinner pretty soon. It's plain, but there's always aplenty if you'd care to stop with us a spell."

James looked behind him. He did not expect to see soldiers, but one never could be sure. His stomach reminded him that none of the squirrel had survived last night's supper, and breakfast had consisted of the last piece of dry bread from Petra's sack. "My horse could stand a rest. We been travelin' pretty hard."

The farmer frowned. "I hate to say this, but you've got the look of a man who's watchin' back over his shoulder. That hole in your shirt looks like it could've been made by a rifle ball. You runnin' from somebody?"

James was caught by surprise. He hadn't thought anybody would notice. "To tell you the truth, sir, I run afoul of some Mexican convict soldiers. I had to up and leave what was rightfully mine. You seen any soldiers over this way?"

The farmer nodded darkly. "They've taken what they wanted and then left. I figured it was better to let them. I just look on it as an extry tax."

"I guess that was my brother Andrew's way of lookin' at it, but it wasn't mine."

"Andrew?" The farmer studied James's face. "Would that be Andrew Lewis? Seems like I see a resemblance, now that I look at you a little closer."

"You're right, sir. I'm James Lewis."

"Good man, that Andrew."

"Michael's my brother too."

"I've met Michael, but he's a hard man to get to know. Andrew, now —" The farmer smiled. "If you're a brother of Andrew Lewis, you're more than welcome at this place." He extended his hand. "I'm Marcus Caldwell. Them yonder's my boys."

James shook with him. "I got to tell you, sir, there's a chance the soldiers will come lookin' for me."

"You kill one of them?"

"Creased one a little, is all. Caused another one to fall on his sword and stick it in his leg. They *acted* like it was a killin'."

The farmer nodded gravely. "A mistaken policy, sendin' convict soldiers here. But Austin has gone to Mexico to talk to the officials. He's always been able to get things straightened out."

"I hope he hurries."

James did not intend to eat without contributing something. He took his knife and started heading corn, dropping it into a sack he began dragging for a boy who looked to be eight or nine, about the age of Frank's oldest. The exercise brought an occasional stab of pain from the rib, but it was no longer so bad as the first day and night. He heard a clanging sound from the house after a while. The boys began eagerly dropping their sacks. "Dinner, Papa," shouted the one whose sack James had taken.

"I heard," said Caldwell, "but we'll work to the end of our rows before we stop. You'll be wantin' to eat next winter, too."

That, James surmised, was why the family looked prosperous. They were a working people, like his Uncle Benjamin back in Tennessee, who had married James's mother and had seen to the raising of the family after Mordecai's death in Texas. Uncle Benjamin had never been one to deny pleasure in its own due time, but the work had always come first.

Caldwell grinned as he watched his boys put down their sacks at the turn-row and climb over the fence to start an eager race toward the house. "I could've let them go at the sound of the bell, but it's good trainin' to let them know that they'll not starve for workin' a few minutes longer. They learn patience, and application to duty."

The log house, like many James had seen in the colony, showed the rambling effect of several additions as the family had grown. The whole place had a well-tended look, a look that bespoke comfort, as comfort was measured in the relative isolation of the Austin colony from the old states back home. It reminded him of Widow Willet's place some distance east of Michael's. These people had dug in here to stay.

He found that at least one of the boys had overheard his conversation with Caldwell about his trouble with the soldiers. Caldwell's wife stood on the narrow porch waiting for her husband and the company her sons had told her was coming. Caldwell said, "Martha, this here is another of the Lewis boys, brother to Andrew. You remember Andrew."

"Name is James, ma'am. I'm mighty pleased to meet you."

Her response was to touch his shirt, examining the hole left by the musket ball. "If you'd like to put on one of Marcus's shirts, I'll patch this for you right after dinner. The boys didn't say if you were wounded."

"Nothin' to talk about, ma'am. I reckon the ball was purt nigh spent by the time it struck me."

A girl with red hair stood half a pace behind her mother. James took her to be about fifteen or so, and some plainer than a few girls he had known back in Tennessee. She seemed not impressed by him. "What if the soldiers come lookin' while he's here? They won't take it kindly, us feedin' him."

Mrs. Caldwell, a plump woman with gray in her hair and authority in her voice, said, "He's a brother of Andrew Lewis. If the soldiers are after him, it's the soldiers who are wrong."

"But they're the ones with the guns," the girl said. "Maybe we'd ought to just give him somethin' to take with him and let him be on his way. If they catch him, let it be somewhere else."

Mrs. Caldwell said sternly, "They won't catch him while he's here because some-body's goin' to watch and give warnin' if they come. Since you're the one most wor-ried about it, Libby Caldwell, that's a fit and proper job for you."

James protested, "Ma'am, I don't want to be no trouble. Not to you and not to this little girl here."

He saw a flash of resentment in Libby's blue eyes over the *little girl* reference.

Mrs. Caldwell declared, "There'll be no trouble. Libby can eat when somebody else is done and can take her place." Her manner showed that the subject was closed. James shrugged at the girl and went inside at Mrs. Caldwell's beckoning. The girl's eyes indicated that he had not made a friend.

The house was of logs, but it was well finished inside. He looked at the fine stonework in the fireplace and remembered the haphazard one he had seen in the Blackwood cabin. The homemade furniture was plain, probably done by Caldwell and his sons, but it bespoke care, skill, and time. What this family had, they had built for themselves and built well. The food on the table was plain, as Caldwell had said, but it was plentiful, including fresh corn roasted in the ear, and pork from the family's own free-ranging herd of hogs.

The sons and daughters were seated on benches along the length of the table, girls on one side, boys on the other. The mother and father took chairs at either end. Mrs. Caldwell assigned one of her daughters — evidently Libby was the oldest — to give the blessing. The boys were ravenous from the morning's work in the field, and Mrs. Caldwell called them down, admonishing them that they were displaying poor manners before company. One of the boys asked James about his trouble with the soldiers, purposely looking away from his father's disapproving stare. Leaving out some of the details he thought not appropriate at the table, James told of the two soldiers' attempt to steal a pig, and the incidents that followed.

The oldest of the boys appeared to be around sixteen or seventeen. He declared, "Mr. Davis down at the forks of the creek says we're goin' to have to fight Mexico one of these days and show them they can't boss Americans around."

Caldwell cautioned the boy, "Hush with that kind of talk, Thomas. The Mexicans let us come here and take up land and own it. We can look to Mr. Austin to watch out for our interests. Us talkin' too much will just make that job harder for him."

"But Mr. Lewis here, *he* didn't let them boss *him* around. I'll bet Mr. Davis would sure like to meet him."

In deference to Caldwell, James felt obliged to point out to the youth that because he had resisted, he was on the run. "My brother Andrew agreed with your papa. If I'd listened to him, I wouldn't be in this fix."

"And you'd be short a pig. Maybe a bunch of pigs. I wish *I* could've shot at them."

"Thomas!" Caldwell said sharply. "We'll have no seditious talk in this house. It can only lead to trouble."

James saw in this family a diversity of opinion that he suspected was growing all over the Austin colonies, and probably in the other American settlements. He also saw that his presence here was fueling the disagreement between father and son. He thought he had eaten enough. He pushed away from the table and stepped back from the bench. "I'm mighty obliged for the good dinner, but I'd better be movin' on."

Mrs. Caldwell said, "I was goin' to mend your shirt."

"The shirt'll be all right. I'll do it myself when I get past the Sabine."

Mrs. Caldwell gathered up some of the food left on the table and began putting it into a sack. "It's a long ways to Louisiana. I'll not let you leave here without you take somethin' along to eat."

Caldwell stood up and shook James's hand. "I'll find some way to get word back to your brothers that you passed this way and that you were all right."

"That'd be more than kind of you, sir."
He shook Caldwell's hand. He paused to
look at this family. They reminded him a lot
of the Lewises back in Tennessee, of his
mother, of Uncle Benjamin, and all the rest.
They gave him a feeling, almost, of being
home. He hated to leave.

"I'm glad to've met you folks," he said. "I
hope I'll see you again someday, without
any soldiers behind me."

He had unsaddled Walker in a pen with
plenty of water, and Caldwell had given the
horse some heads of maize in a trough. The
maize had been eaten, and Walker nosed at
the water without drinking. He had had his
fill. James caught him and began to put his
saddle on him.

The red-haired Libby watched him
through the rails of the corral fence. "You
already fixin' to leave? Thought you'd probably spend the rest of the day and
somebody'd have to stand guard to keep
the soldiers from catchin' you."

He saw no lessening of her earlier resentment. "You can go in and eat now."

She pointed her chin at the sack of food
Mrs. Caldwell had gathered up. "I'm surprised you left me anything."

Testily he said, "*I* didn't ask you to stand
guard for me. That was your mama's idea.

Now go on in yonder and eat your dinner like I said."

"I'll go when I'm ready. You don't boss me around."

She reminded him of his sister Annie — not in looks but in manner and sharpness of tongue. He finished the saddling, opened the gate, and swung up onto Walker. He said without meaning it, "I hope we'll meet again someday."

"We won't unless you catch me unawares."

He remembered no particular landmarks from the trip the previous spring. Texas — that part of it, anyway — had no mountains or even any sizeable hills that might set themselves firmly in his mind. It had been a succession of forests, rolling open lands, canebrakes, streams, and rivers without any particularly distinguishing characteristics. It was a feeling rather than any tangible evidence that told him he was nearing the eastern edge of Texas. If he had ever crossed over the track they had followed before, he was not aware of it. But he came at last to a trail that appeared to have carried some horse or mule traffic at times in the past, though it revealed no sign of recent use. It led him almost due eastward.

He was not sure how far the Sabine lay

ahead, probably a few miles. Seeing a squirrel, he thought ahead to his next meal and shot it, and then another. He wondered whether he would eat them on this side of the river or the other.

The question did not linger long, for the appearance of four Mexican soldiers to the northwest postponed the next meal indefinitely. They quartered toward him out of the late-afternoon sun. Evidently they had heard the shots and had come to investigate. They pushed their horses in a stiff trot. A patrol out of Nacogdoches, he figured, watching for smugglers or illegal immigrants. Surely they had not had time to hear about his trouble down in the colony. But chances were they would take him to Nacogdoches for investigation, and that bloodhound Díaz would find out.

"Come on, Walker," he said, touching his heels to the horse's ribs. "Let's see how good their horses are."

As he moved into a lope, the soldiers did likewise. Not knowing how far it was to the river, he pushed Walker no harder than necessary to keep the soldiers beyond rifle range. If it should come to a real horse race, he wanted to reserve Walker's strength. The soldiers' horses were of mediocre quality. They presented no great challenge.

The run was shorter than he had dared hope. The river appeared unexpectedly. Remembering how Walker's slow swimming in the Colorado had given pursuing soldiers a chance to get within firing distance, he pushed for all the speed he could get to widen the distance before they reached the water. The soldiers trailed by at least two or three hundred yards when James paused to look behind him at the Texas he had entered so eagerly last spring, not once but twice. "It's a damned shame to leave it now," he spoke aloud, as if the horse could understand how he felt. "But I'll be comin' back." He put Walker into the water.

Across the river and well up on the Louisiana bank, James could see a small cabin, its old logs almost orange-colored in the last moments of the setting sun. He swam the horse across, holding his rifle high to keep it from getting wet. On the Louisiana side, he dismounted again to let Walker shake off some of the water. The soldiers had reached the river's edge and stopped there, watching him. At the distance he could not see their expressions, but he presumed they were of frustration. For that, he was duly thankful.

He looked up toward the cabin. He could not see if it was occupied. No matter; it was shelter. Thunderheads were building in the east. Likely as not it was going to rain tonight. At least it had not rained on him during the days and nights of his retreat across Texas. Let it rain the bottom out now for all he cared; this was not his country. He might be obliged to remain here a while, but Texas had become his country, and it would remain so no matter where he had to go.

He led the horse up the long, high bank to a shed and a set of log pens that looked familiar. He had been here — by here, anyway — last spring. He saw two Spanish dagger plants flanking a white locust tree and remembered. This had been old Eli Pleasant's place. From here Eli had conducted his smuggling operations into and out of Texas, between Natchitoches, Louisiana, and the Nacogdoches region. James had struck the old smuggler trail and had followed it.

He put Walker in the pen and found some corn for him in a wooden barrel beneath the shed. The trip had drawn the horse down some; he had traveled hard and had not had time to graze enough. Well, James had no plans now. He would stay here a few days to let the horse rest. Eli had been a good friend to the Lewises; he would have approved.

Wearily, James walked to the cabin, looking up at the chimney but seeing no sign of smoke. He had held onto the squirrels whose demise had attracted the soldiers. They would make him a good supper.

Rounding the corner of the cabin, he was startled to see a man standing there, waiting for him. James's hands tightened on his rifle until he recognized the face and the voice.

Sly Shipman said sarcastically, "I thought you was fixin' to bring them soldiers on over here. They ain't quite the kind of company I need."

James recovered quickly from his surprise. After all, this *was* Shipman's cabin, informally inherited from Eli Pleasant. At least his claim on it was probably as good as anybody's. He tried to match Shipman's sarcasm. "I expect they've chased *you* across that river aplenty of times."

Shipman did not try to answer the comment. "I never expected to see you again, James Lewis. I figured somebody'd've shot you before now."

"You're always figurin', and figurin' wrong."

"What did you do to get the soldiers after you? Did you punch Sergeant Díaz in the face or somethin'?"

Shipman listened to the explanation with more sympathy than James had expected. The young smuggler asked, "What you goin' to do now? Fugitive or not, a man has got to eat."

"I brought two squirrels for supper."

"I'm figurin' farther down the road than just supper. I'm figurin' next week and next winter and on past that."

"I ain't had time to sort things out. Gettin' to this side of the river was my main worry. Now that I'm here, I'll have to figure what my next step is goin' to be."

Shipman studied him until James became uneasy under the young man's solemn gaze. He felt that Shipman was looking through him plumb to the gizzard.

Shipman said, "I know me and you didn't get along very good when we met before. We may not get along good now, because it strikes me that you still jump first and think about it later. But I could use some help, if you'd like to join up with me."

"Doin' what?" James asked, though he knew well enough what Shipman's business was.

"Handlin' merchandise. Bein' a merchant to the people. Whatever needs sellin', we sell. Whatever needs buyin', we buy."

"Smugglin', you mean?"

Shipman grimaced. "I was right. You ain't changed a bit. If I had any sense I wouldn't even ask you."

"But you did ask me, and I've got nothin' better to do."

Shipman nodded, the matter settled. "Now, you said somethin' about some squirrels?"

The squirrels were reduced to a stack of bones on the rough table, and James felt fuller than he had been since he had stopped at the Caldwell house. The two men leaned back in a pair of crude chairs. Shipman lighted up a long, black cheroot. James eyed him with curiosity.

"Shipman, you said yourself, you don't especially like me. You could get somebody else to help you. Why'd you ask me?"

Shipman took his time, and when he spoke it was not a direct answer. "How's that good-lookin' sister of yours?"

James decided that was direct enough.

CHAPTER 12

Annie's heart was in her throat as she watched James swim the bay horse slowly across the river while the soldiers fired at him from a rapidly decreasing range. She was encouraged to see him leave the water and set the horse into a hard run toward the timber while the soldiers struggled with the swim. By the time the troops reached the north side, James had put a considerable distance behind him. She turned and grabbed Isaac Blackwood by both arms, thinking he was Andrew.

"I believe he'll make it! I believe he'll make it!"

Isaac smiled thinly through his surprise. "I do hope you're right, ma'am."

Annie's face flushed hot as she realized the mistake she had made in the moment of excitement. "I'm sorry," she said quickly. "I was so relieved I didn't know what I was doin'."

Michael's grim expression dashed her sudden exuberance. She knew he was remembering another time, other soldiers, and a race that had ended in the murder of their father. Michael said, "I don't count him free till I know he's in Louisiana."

Andrew pointed out. "He's got a good lead on them, looks to me like."

Michael grimaced. "It's a long ways to the Sabine." He turned toward his horse, then thought better of it and came back. "If they don't catch him, they're liable to come here huntin' for somebody to take it out on. I reckon I'll stay a while."

Isaac said, "I'm in no hurry to go home, either."

Michael gave him a curious glance. "It ain't none of your fight, Isaac. He's our brother, not yours."

"There's times us Tennessee folks have got to stick together."

Annie felt her face warm again as Isaac's gaze momentarily touched her. She knew Isaac was not staying out of concern for Michael or Andrew. She said, "Your brothers may be wonderin' where you are."

"They'd be just as happy if I never came back."

Annie could not quite understand that, for she had known only the eternal closeness that existed among members of the Lewis family. True, she sometimes spoke sharply to James, but it was out of a wish to point him in better directions. It was out of love. Love must be a stranger in the Blackwood family, she thought, feeling sorry for Isaac. She sought out Petra with her gaze. "We'd best be fixin' some supper, don't you think?

Michael took his plate and stood in the doorway, staring darkly toward the river. He ate but little. Annie had seen the turmoil in his eyes, the haunting by old and terrible memories. He said, "I wisht the world didn't have any soldiers."

Just before dark, Annie saw Michael stiffen, then take a few long strides out past the dog-run. Fear constricted her throat, and she quickly followed after him. She knew Andrew, Petra, and Isaac were behind her, but she did not look back. She stopped beside Michael and watched the soldiers coming across the river. She saw no sign of James.

"Do you think —" She could not finish the question.

Michael made no comment for a minute or more. Finally he said, "By the set of their shoulders, I'd say they was mighty disappointed."

Annie had held her breath. Now she let it go, slowly. "Then he did get away."

She thought the soldiers would probably come up to the cabin, perhaps seeking some sort of retribution. She knew by the worry in Michael's and Andrew's faces that they had the same idea. The soldiers might have lost their quarry, but the family was still here. They made no such move, however. They set about making camp on the river. Annie could see them starting a fire. Dark came, and they made no move toward the cabin.

Michael looked relieved. "They ain't comin'."

Andrew agreed.

Annie asked, "What would you have done if they had come?"

Michael cradled his long rifle in his arms. "Whatever we had to do." He seemed to realize the sense of threat his voice carried, and he softened it. "Marie'll be worried. I'd best get on home before she sends Mordecai over here huntin' me." He gave Isaac Blackwood a questioning glance.

Isaac said, "They might decide to come up durin' the night. I think I'll stay. I can sleep here on the dog-run."

Annie could see that Michael was not keen on that notion, nor was Andrew, but she felt grateful. Had Isaac not brought warning, James would not have escaped. "We can find you a couple of blankets, I'm sure."

She saw pleasure in Isaac's eyes as he replied, "I'd be much obliged to you, ma'am."

Andrew warned her, before she went to bed, "It wouldn't hurt if you was to bar your door tonight."

She said, "Since the soldiers haven't come already, I don't think they'll come at all."

Andrew admitted, "I wasn't thinkin' about the soldiers."

"Isaac came to help us," she argued.

"A dog can help you too, but some of them you don't let in the house."

Morning came, but no soldiers. Annie opened the wooden window and looked toward the river. They were still camped down there. She walked out onto the dog-run. The blankets were neatly folded, but she did not see Isaac Blackwood. Unaccountably, she felt disappointed. He had probably sensed Andrew's disapproval.

Andrew came up from the cow shed, carrying a bucket of milk. Annie asked him, "When did Isaac leave?"

"He was saddlin' his horse when I went out to milk."

She felt a momentary impatience with her brother. "Didn't you at least ask him to stay for breakfast?"

"He seemed bound on goin'. I didn't argue with him."

"I suppose, no matter what he does, you'll never be able to forget that he's a Blackwood."

"It's a hard thing to overlook. I look at him and I see Finis and Luke. I also see Old Man Cyrus, who never was worth the rope it'd take to hang him with. Blood tells, Annie. Isaac shows a few good tendencies now and again, so maybe he's some kind of an outcross. But he's still got enough Blackwood blood to taint him. Was I you, I wouldn't waste any of my time feelin' sorry for Isaac."

"But I do, and I can't help it."

He gave her a worried look but said only, "Let's go have some breakfast. I got lots of work to do today."

They were cleaning up the dishes afterward when Petra went to the doorway and looked outside. "The soldiers go," she said.

Annie hurried to her side. She saw several soldiers riding downriver, toward San Felipe. Her feeling of relief was dashed, however, when she discovered that two remained behind. She could see them and

228

their staked horses, still down there in camp. "They've left a guard," she said, "to watch over us, I reckon, and to see if James comes back."

Petra gave her a concerned glance. "Will he?"

Annie shook her head. "It wouldn't be smart." She would have to admit, if pressed, that not everything James had ever done was smart. But Michael and Andrew had made it clear to him that he had better go to Louisiana, and that he had better remain there. He had seemed to accept their advice.

Andrew came up from the field at noontime, his brow furrowed. "Those soldiers look to me like they're fixin' up to stay. They're buildin' themselves a *jacal* out of some timber and brush." A *jacal* was a rude type of shack, a shelter of sorts from the weather. "They must figure to watch till James comes home."

Annie frowned, for sadness overtook her. "Then I hope he's gone for a long, long time."

The cabin was short of meat, except for salt pork Andrew and Petra had put up themselves. Andrew badly needed to go out into the forest and find some game, but he was concerned about leaving the two women and the children alone while the soldiers were posted down on the river. But days passed, and the soldiers made no untoward move. He decided at last that they probably would not, so he took rifle, powder, and ball and rode off west.

Evidently the soldiers had been watching. Not an hour after Andrew left, Annie saw them walking up toward the cabin. "Petra," she said tightly, "we may be fixin' to have trouble."

Andrew's rifle was gone from above the mantle, but Annie had her own in the room in which she slept. She loaded it quickly, for she had grown up in a family where the girls as well as the boys were taught a familiarity with firearms, along with the hoe, the ax, and the skinning knife.

Petra eyed the rifle nervously. "You will shoot them?"

"Depends on what their intentions are." Annie moved out past the dog-run, where she could see the soldiers clearly. Petra shut the children in the kitchen and moved out to stand beside Annie. She had no rifle, but she provided a moral backing by her presence. It took nerve, Annie thought, for she could see that Petra was genuinely frightened. Like Michael, Petra had a strong personal reason for dreading soldiers; years ago they had butchered her father for no better reason than a suspicion that he was not loyal to Spain.

It quickly became clear to Annie that the soldiers were not coming to the cabin; they stopped at the pen where the pigs were kept. "They're fixin' to try and steal a pig again," she exclaimed.

"Let them," Petra said. "We have more pigs."

"But it's the principle of the thing. James's trouble started when he stopped them from stealin' one of the pigs. Now they're settin' out to do the same thing again, to show us who the boss is."

"A pig is just a pig."

"Not these pigs. It's because of them that James had to run. Damned if I'll stand by and let a bunch of convict soldiers make it be all for nothin'." She strode briskly toward the pen, Petra hurrying after her.

The pigs were squealing and the soldiers laughing as they chased the fattest one around in the pen. Annie yelled, "You, climb out of that pen and let those pigs alone!"

One of the soldiers glanced at her and snickered, then resumed his pursuit of the panicked animal. He managed to grab the curly tail while the pig made a terrible racket and scrambled for footing. The second soldier took hold of the thrashing beast and lifted it from the ground.

Annie said, "I'm not goin' to say it again. Turn that pig a-loose!" They might not understand the words, but they understood the meaning well enough. Petra repeated in Spanish, for emphasis. One of the men replied to her in an insulting tone. Whatever he said, Annie knew it was obscene because of the flush of color in Petra's face. The soldiers held onto the pig.

Annie brought up the rifle and aimed the barrel through the fence. "You put that pig down or I'll shoot you!"

The fun went out of it for the soldiers, and their laughter turned quickly to anger. They did not take her seriously; she was a woman. It was an affront to them that she would so much as threaten them with a rifle.

From the corner of her eye Annie saw a movement. She was almost afraid to take her gaze from the two soldiers, but she risked a quick glance. A horseman had just crossed the river and was coming this way. It was not the right direction for Andrew, nor the right color horse. She wondered if it might be another soldier. She already had more than enough. If she fired she might stop one of these, but she would have no chance against the second.

The soldiers became aware of the rider. By their sudden concern Annie knew he was not one of their own. The soldier who held the squealing pig dropped it. It scurried off into a corner to join its fellows, grunting as it pushed its way deeply into the bunch. The soldiers cursed Annie and Petra but climbed out over the fence and trotted off toward their rough camp. The rider stopped his horse and watched them pass cautiously behind him, perhaps more intimidated by the rifle he carried than the one Annie had pointed at them. He brought the horse around and continued to watch them until they disappeared into their *jacal.* Then he came on toward the two women.

Annie thought she recognized the horse and the way the man sat the saddle, but the face was different.

"Is that Isaac Blackwood?" she asked Petra.

Petra nodded. "It is. He has no more whiskers."

Isaac had shaved away the heavy black beard, leaving his face clean, the lower part pale compared to the upper because the whiskers had so long sheltered it from the sun.

Isaac reined up and touched fingers to the floppy brim of an old hat. "Mornin', ladies.

You-all havin' trouble?"

Annie felt so relieved that she could have kissed him. "I'm afraid we were fixin' to. You came along just in time."

Petra turned, hearing the youngest crying, unaccustomed to being left shut up in the cabin. "I must go. Thank you, Mr. Blackwood." She turned and hurried to see about the children.

Isaac said to Annie, "I don't know as I done anything, except just ride up."

Annie said, "That was enough. You couldn't have timed it any better."

"Ain't Andrew around?"

"We needed meat. We hadn't had any trouble with the soldiers, so he thought it was safe to ride out. And then I guess they decided it was safe to come in here and take a pig."

Isaac made a thin smile, staring at Annie's rifle. "I don't know if it was or not. Would you really have fired that thing?"

"I was about to find out when you showed up."

His smile widened. "You've got a look in your eye. I wouldn't ever want you after *me* with that rifle. I do believe you'd use it."

She glanced toward the little *jacal* on the river. "I hope I never have to find out." She studied his face then. She had never really seen Isaac's features before; they had always been half hidden by a growth of black beard. She would not call him handsome, even now, but she could see strength in the set of his square jaw. "What went with your beard, Mr. Blackwood?"

"I decided to get rid of it. And I wisht you'd get rid of that *Mr. Blackwood.* We're neighbors. Everybody just calls me Isaac."

"Are you hungry, Isaac? It wouldn't take us long to fix up somethin'."

"I'd be much obliged." He dismounted and began walking beside her toward the cabin. "One thing I don't understand. Looks like it would've saved a lot of trouble if you'd just let them carry off a pig. One pig ain't worth much."

"These pigs are. My brother James paid a high price for them."

Isaac nodded thoughtfully. "I never looked at it that way." He held a brooding silence until they reached the dog-run. "I'm afraid it's a lot bigger problem than just pigs. I hear there's been a right smart of trouble with the soldiers, one place and another. If the government don't do somethin' before long there's apt to be a killin' somewhere. One killin' leads to more killin's. Ain't no tellin' where it'll stop."

Annie had heard enough to sense that he

could be right. "You think this could eventually lead us into a war?"

Isaac shrugged his broad shoulders. "I just know that you ain't come to no happy country."

■ ■ ■ ■

PART II:
THE SEEDS OF
REVOLUTION
TEXAS, 1832

■ ■ ■ ■

CHAPTER 13

James Lewis decided at their first meeting that William Barret Travis was a potential troublemaker, a firebrand who spoke his mind regardless of consequences. He liked him on sight.

Travis stood six feet tall, weighed 175 pounds and had a touch of red in his hair as well as in his temperament. About the same age as James, he was a lawyer rather than a farmer. He had left Alabama after a brief and unhappy marriage and sought new surroundings in which to make a fresh life. He came to Texas with a wagon train from New Orleans headed for Nacogdoches. James and Sly Shipman, with a pack train of mules, happened across the westbound wagons east of the Sabine River in Louisiana. A couple of the wagons were bogged to the hubs in mud. James and Shipman unpacked the mules and lent them to the task of dragging the wagons up onto firm ground. Invited to camp the night and share supper, they willingly accepted the offer to eat a meal prepared by someone else. Neither had more than passable skill as a cook.

Sitting at the campfire, watching the reflected red light of the flames play across Travis's animated face, James found himself spellbound. Being a lawyer, the man had a gift with the language. Though he had not yet seen Texas, he had already learned much about it through diligent reading and inquiry. He talked of the land and its promise. He voiced a strong opinion that Texas should break its bonds with feudalistic Mexico and attach itself to the United States.

James declared, "I do believe you're right, sir." Not to many did James say *sir,* but Travis had the look and manner of an educated man, yet one who adapted with ease to the role of frontiersman. "I've thought along the same lines ever since I had a run-in with them convict soldiers. We wouldn't've put up with such as that back in Tennessee. We wouldn't've had to."

But Sly Shipman took a different view. To Travis he said, "I don't reckon there's any law can stop a man from thinkin' what he wants to, so long as he keeps his thoughts

240

in his head and don't let them all spill care-less out of his mouth. But you go talkin' that way down in Texas and you're liable to find yourself settin' in a dungeon cell where you can talk all you want to and there won't nobody hear you."

Travis was taken aback. "You believe in Mexican rule over Americans, do you, sir?"

"I don't believe in anybody rulin' over anybody. But that's the way the world is set up, at least in Texas and the rest of Mexico. Back where you come from, you could say what you wanted to so long as you could whip anybody who took offense and wanted to test your mettle. The law didn't mix in it. But once you cross that river you're in another country. They got a whole different way of lookin' at things. Say the wrong word and they'll figure you're tryin' to poke up another revolution. They're sensitive about revolutions; they've had so many. Some army officer is liable to hang your ears up over his mantle."

Travis gave Shipman's advice a courteous hearing but did not take it to heart. "I have crossed many rivers, sir, and I have found that however I felt on one side, I still felt on the other. I do not believe the Sabine River will effect any change in my principles."

"Maybe it won't, but I hope it'll make you

careful who you're with when you speak your mind."

The next morning James and Shipman watched the wagon train move on westward. Their own destination was Natchitoches, to the east, where they were to pick up goods from merchant Baptiste Villaret for another trading trip over into Texas. The trade was still clandestine, but many of the Mexican soldiers seemed to have wearied of trying to stop it, for it was like trying to halt the flow of the river with their hands. The two tradesmen could take their pack trains within shouting distance of Nacogdoches and run little risk of challenge. They had a little more difficulty down on the Gulf coast because a stricter officer controlled that part of Texas. The way James heard it, Mexico was beset by rebellions, one following another, to a point that the soldiers were never sure who their president was. Communications were slow and uncertain. To a degree, therefore, each commandant at an army garrison was a law unto himself. Some exerted this power like lions. Others turned their backs to trouble and pretended it did not exist.

Watching the departing wagon train, Shipman grumbled, "One thing Texas don't need any more of is lawyers. It needs farmers and carpenters. It needs more teachers and merchants, but it's already got a plentiful sufficiency of lawyers to muddy up the waters for honest workin' folks like us."

He and James were regarded by some as smugglers, but they looked upon themselves simply as merchants, ministering needs that would not be met were they not there to meet them. James had never known much about lawyers. He had been brought up too far out in the country to see them at work. He said, "I guess they're not a bad thing to have sometimes. They're good at settlin' disagreements."

"Who do you think stirs up most of the disagreements in the first place?" Shipman demanded. "Come on, we got work to do."

James looked back once before the wagons passed out of sight. "You don't reckon he'll have any trouble gettin' into Texas?"

"I doubt it. But I won't be surprised if he causes a lot of trouble after he gets there."

The Mexican government's prohibition against further immigration into Texas from the United States of the North remained officially on the books, but after a few months it had begun to be honored mainly in the breach. Newcomers filtered across the border in ever-growing numbers, or arrived by ship at the mouth of the Brazos and other ports. They were hampered but little by a small military force that at first could not begin to catch them all and after a time did not seriously try. Officials in Mexico's interior wrung their hands over the Americanization of Texas, but they could do little. Internal power struggles and recurring revolutions kept the central government hamstrung. It could not control the upheavals close at hand, much less do anything of consequence in distant Texas, a northern adjunct to the border state of Coahuila. One after another, presidents and statesmen deplored the fact that Texas had become more American than Mexican, but concern over their own individual survival took precedence over this affront to national honor.

James paid little mind to the turmoil that kept festering to the surface deep in Mexico except as it might affect the trading business he conducted in a loose partnership with Sly Shipman. He found many settlers in agreement with him that this instability was a potential hindrance to the peaceful settlement of Texas, and he wondered aloud sometimes if Travis might be correct in saying that Texas should attach itself to the United States and cut its ties to Mexico. He found many of the newcomers to be of that mind. The older settlers, in the main, were more inclined to bide their time and hope that conditions in Mexico would finally settle down. Mexico, they said, had been good to them in terms of generous grants of land. They had much to lose by angering Mexico into punitive action.

That, he remembered, had been the sentiments of his brother Andrew. He had never heard Michael express much of an opinion on politics. Michael was a doer, not a talker. On matters of this kind, James pondered what Michael would do, and did likewise.

James had traveled over much of settled Texas in his trading enterprise, though he avoided San Felipe and the upper Colorado where his brothers and sister lived. Messages relayed to him by Michael and Annie through old Villaret warned him that the army officer who had sought his blood was still around, still appearing periodically at the Lewis cabins without warning in hopes of catching James there on a visit.

"We would love to see you," Annie had written, "but we fear the time is not yet. Wait and have patience. Officers change stations. The land does not move away, nor do we. Someday, dear brother. Someday."

The months had passed and stretched into a year and more. His mind went back often to the Colorado River, though he could not, to the land into which he had been given no time to sink his roots.

Someday.

They were uneasy partners, James Lewis and Sly Shipman, quarrelsome with one another over small things but usually together on matters of major import. Shipman, because of his much longer experience, expected to lay the plans and give the orders. James, a quick learner, soon decided he knew enough about the business to be a full partner in every respect. It became his habit to greet most of Shipman's suggestions with vocal skepticism, though usually when he thought them through he found them to be of merit. It was not that he distrusted Shipman's judgment; he simply did not want to be subordinate. He had not taken well to orders in Tennessee. As Travis had put it, James usually felt the same after crossing a river as he had felt on the other side, so he did not take well to orders in Louisiana or Texas either.

Though he and Shipman quarreled and sometimes seemed in danger of dividing the mules, they managed always to find a point of compromise and remain together. Shipman would say, "The way I figure, if I was to go off and leave you to your own devices, you'd probably get yourself killed. That good-lookin' sister of yours would never speak to me again."

"She wouldn't speak to you now," James would retort.

They found themselves in the spring of 1832 carrying goods down the coast near Galveston Bay, into a seething cauldron of trouble. James had heard rumblings about it but had taken only a passing interest in the reports except as they concerned a stringent effort by the authorities to extract tariffs on all goods brought into the region. Working there, he and Shipman took special precautions to be seen only when they wanted to be. The situation confirmed James's feeling that Mexico had no business bossing Americans around.

It was ironic that the first big confrontation came not from a Mexican but from an arrogant and dictatorial transplanted American named John Bradburn, Kentucky-born and a veteran of many years in service of the Mexican government as a soldier of fortune. He had begun going by the name Juan Bradburn rather than John. For whatever reason, he was hostile to the American settlers moving into Mexican Texas and he harassed them whenever his office gave him the opportunity. He was assigned to command the garrison at Anahuac, near Galveston Bay. That afforded him ample occasion to vent his contempt for his former countrymen.

It happened that William Barret Travis had set up a law practice not far from Anahuac in a new town called Liberty, made up largely of newcomers like himself. Even the name of the town hinted at resistance to the government. Many of its residents, including Travis, were illegal in the eyes of Mexico. Like the other latecomers who had no legal status because of the immigration proclamation, Travis was not entitled to acquire land or other property under Mexican law. He had to live in a rented room and subsist on what small bits of legal practice he was able to stir up. He was not hesitant in expressing his opinion about that law, about the convict soldiers who served under Bradburn, and about Bradburn himself, considered a turncoat by most of the American Texans for having committed himself wholeheartedly to the cause of Mexico.

James and Shipman had no inkling that rebellion was bubbling toward a boil when they led their mule train down the coast, though they knew about Bradburn and were taking particular care to avoid his soldiers.

They had been traveling mostly by night, laying up in the daylight, until they neared their destination at Liberty. There they expected a lucrative trade. Sunrise had caught them still on the trail, looking for a suitable hiding place to spend the daylight hours. Suddenly they saw a considerable body of horsemen coming toward them. It was too late to hide.

"Whip them up!" Shipman commanded, pointing toward a heavy forest a mile or so to the east. Once in the forest, they should have some chance to elude the horsemen, who looked at the distance like cavalrymen. James shouted and set the mules into a hard run. But he saw the riders pull out of the trail and quarter across to intercept them. He popped the trailing mules with a whip and shouted encouragement, but he felt dismay as he realized the horsemen were going to overtake them before they could reach the wood. Shipman, riding in the lead, could see it, too. He gave James a sign to slow down.

"We can fight them," James shouted, but he realized Shipman could not hear him. It would have made no difference if he had. Shipman was too cautious a man to fight odds that appeared to be seven or eight to one. Reluctantly James slowed, and so did the mules, once he stopped pressing them. He remembered the smell of that cell in Nacogdoches and wondered what kind of jail they had in Anahuac.

His despair and anger gave way to relief as he realized the approaching riders were not soldiers. They were civilians, settlers by the look of them. They were all armed. For a fleeting moment he considered the possibility that they might be robbers, but that was unlikely. There had been little of that kind of deviltry down in the interior of Texas, though it still went on in the no-man's-land strip between Natchitoches and the Sabine River and occasionally spilled over onto a little of Texas along that border.

Shipman raised one hand as the first of the riders reached him, showing that he intended no fight. James circled the mules to be certain they would not keep running and perhaps be lost. That done, he reined Walker to Shipman's side. Shipman had quickly established that the riders meant no harm.

The leader was a broad-shouldered man, fierce of eye and straight in the saddle. He had all the bearing of a man in charge. "We did not mean to give fright," he said, not so much in the manner of apology as simply in explanation. "We thought you might be a couple of Bradburn's soldiers bringing supplies."

Shipman had regained whatever composure he might have lost. "No sir, we are but honest tradesmen, goin' about our business."

"Honest?" one of the other riders asked. "Smugglers, you mean."

James had long since decided that Shipman could sell overcoats in Hell. Shipman put on his best salesman's manner in the same way he might put on his gloves. "Only because of unjust officials who would rob the poor to enrich themselves. Our only interest is to give the honest settler an honest deal. We ask no profit for ourselves except what little we need to feed our animals and keep hunger from our camp."

The leader turned to the rider who had spoken. "We have no quarrel with these men. They serve a useful purpose and earn whatever reward may fall into their hands." He studied Shipman and James for a moment. "You have come from the north?"

James did not intend to let Shipman do all the talking. He said, "We come from Natchitoches, then along the Sabine as far as it carried."

"Have you seen any Mexican soldiers the last day or so?"

Shipman was about to reply; he considered himself the leader in their enterprise. But James answered first. "No sir, but then we wasn't lookin' for any. We try not to get in their way and hope they stay out of ours."

The leader seemed relieved. "We were afraid they might be sending reinforcements from the north, Nacogdoches perhaps. Is it possible you gentlemen have not heard about the trouble?"

Shipman answered ahead of James. "No sir, in our line of business we make it a point not to see more people than we have to, so we don't hear a lot. What's happened?"

"You've heard of Juan Bradburn?"

"Yes sir, he's another we try not to see, or be seen by."

"He has presumed himself to be all-powerful. He declared the land grants around Liberty to be void, and he ordered the town itself abolished. When the citizens protested, he arrested Patrick Jack and a lawyer named Travis."

"Travis?" James demanded, remembering well the man he had met on the trail. "The one from Alabama?"

"The same."

Shipman gave James a glance. "I told you. I knew he'd open his mouth too wide and fall into it himself."

The leader of the horsemen declared, "No man should be arrested for saying what he believes. Free speech has always been an inalienable right for all Americans."

"Not when they're in Mexico," Shipman said. "And this is part of Mexico."

"Bradburn declared martial law over ten leagues of land. He intends to send Jack and Travis down into Mexico for trial. They'll never come back. The Mexicans will shoot them."

"That's too bad," Shipman said, meaning it. "Except for talkin' too free, he seemed like a decent feller. Especially for a lawyer."

"We do not intend to let it happen. Men are gathering from all over this part of Texas, even from as far as San Felipe. They have commandeered a schooner and loaded cannon upon it to attack Anahuac from Galveston Bay."

James began to feel excitement. "So you're goin' to Anahuac?"

"Yes, to attack from the land side as the schooner attacks from the water. But first we ride to Velasco to attack the garrison there. Its guns are trained on the Gulf. The schooner cannot pass to Anahuac until the Velasco garrison is taken."

Shipman's face had frozen into a hard frown. "You folks really thought through what you're doin'? If you fire on Velasco and Anahuac, you've declared war on Mexico."

"Freedom-loving men have never shrunk from war if that is what is demanded to preserve their freedom. The soldiers are mostly convicts with no great stake in whether Texas rebels against Mexico or not. We believe they will lay down their arms when they see the seriousness of our intentions."

Shipman's frown was undiminished. "And if they don't?"

"We will do what we must. The Lord loves freedom, and He will be at our side."

Shipman demanded dryly, "You've asked Him about that?"

"Prayer has its place in all our counsels."

"I hope so, because you're goin' to need a lot of it if you get Mexico mad enough to send some *real* soldiers up here."

The horseman clearly had already passed judgment on Shipman, and it was not favorable. "We would invite you two to join us in this mission, but I can see that you have no such inclination."

Shipman shook his head. "We're merchants, not lawyers and not soldiers. I don't see where we've got any reason to bog ourselves down in somethin' that don't concern us."

James's blood had been aroused by what the leader said. He exclaimed, "It concerns *me*. I say we go give those soldiers a whippin'. They've got it comin'."

"These won't be the same ones who ran you off of your land."

"They belong to the same outfit. Fight one, you fight them all."

Shipman's face showed a growing impatience. "Damn it, we've got a business to take care of. We've got goods here that we're responsible for. We can't be ridin' off and leavin' them to take up somebody else's fight. We'd be lettin' down Baptiste. Travis talked his way into jail. He's a lawyer; let him talk his way out of it."

The leader of the riders said, "We are wasting time. Whoever would go with us should come along. Whoever chooses not to do so may remain behind. We are better off without him." He turned and rode away at a stiff trot. James counted fourteen men following him.

He went to one of the pack mules and loosened the pack, opening a sack that contained their traveling rations of coffee, flour, and bacon. He transferred a little of it to a leather pouch on his own saddle.

Shipman glowered. "It's a fool's errand."

"I like Travis. It ain't right, them puttin'

him in jail for sayin' what he thinks."

"That's a real battle they're fixin' to have. You ever been in a battle before? An honest-to-God fight with gunpowder goin' off around you and bullets whistlin' around your head like hornets?"

"My brothers have been. My ol' daddy was. I figure if my brother Michael was here, he'd go."

"I wish he *was* here, so you could ask him. He might tell you to stay behind and mind your own business."

"Not Michael. He's a fighter."

For a moment James wondered if he was going to have to fist-fight Shipman. They had come close to it more than once but had always managed to back away from the edge just in time. One of these days he was going to have to find a more congenial working partner or maybe just do for himself. He didn't really need a partner, anyway.

Shipman got down from his horse, looking as if he contemplated trying to stop James. "I hate to see you get killed before you even have a chance to grow up."

"I'm twenty-one. That's grown."

"Your body may be, but your head is still about sixteen. I owe it to your family to knock some sense into it."

"I'm ready any time you figure you're big

enough." James knotted his fists in preparation.

Shipman took a couple of steps toward him, then stopped, shrugging. "Go ahead, if you're bound and determined. I done right well for myself before you ever come along to aggravate my life. I'd probably be better off if they was to blow a hole through you and get you out of my misery."

James remembered the way Shipman had run off the time Sergeant Díaz's troops were closing in. In effect, he was running now, James thought. "You never did have stomach for a fight."

"I've had my share. Maybe it's just as well you go ahead and get this out of your system. If you live through it, you might even come out a little smarter — which I doubt."

James mounted his horse. "Wish me luck?"

"I wish you some *sense*. I hope you come back with more than you're showin' now — if you come back."

"I'll be back. Don't you be runnin' away with our mules." James spurred off into the dust left by the riders on their way to confront the garrison at Velasco.

CHAPTER 14

In later times it would be said that the first shots fired at Velasco the night of June 25, 1832, were the opening salvo of the Texas revolution against Mexico, though the full-blown revolution was yet more than three years away. There had been individual confrontations before between settlers and soldiers, but Velasco, where the Brazos River emptied its muddy brown waters into the blue brine of the Gulf, below Galveston Island, was the site of the first pitched battle.

The Mexican fortress was built of logs and sand in a circular configuration, its cannon atop an earthen embankment in the center, trained toward the Gulf but capable of swinging in any direction. Around the outside of the wall a deep ditch was intended to slow or stop any attack from land, though it had always been anticipated that any serious confrontation would come from warships in the Gulf. The Texan forces were under the divided command of John Austin — no relation to Stephen F. — and Henry Brown.

Shortly after James and the others arrived to reinforce the considerable number of fighting men already gathered beyond range of the fortress and shouting for a fight, a "committee of invitation" was sent to the commander of the fort, Colonel de Ugartechea, suggesting that he surrender the garrison. His curiosity much aroused, James took it upon himself to go along with this group under a white flag of truce. Though he did not understand Ugartechea's words until a translation was made, the colonel's grim visage told him the suggestion was refused.

The interpreter said, "The colonel conveys his regrets, but he says his orders are specific. Part of his duty is the protection of Anahuac. To give up this post without a fight would be to desert Anahuac and compromise his dignity as an officer."

One of the Texan leaders declared, "If it's his dignity he's worried about, he could put up a show of a fight, then surrender. Down in Mexico City, they would never know."

The interpreter relayed the message. The colonel remained adamant. The interpreter said, "*He* would know. He says the schooner shall not pass."

The head of the committee said, "Tell him we respect him as an officer and a gentleman. Then let us withdraw and be about the business we came for."

James had never seen a cannon so large as the one on the center of the raised mound inside the small fort, nor had he ever seen one fired. He shivered to an involuntary chill, though the June day was warm. For a moment he wondered if Shipman had been right: He had no business here. But he saw no such reservations in the men around him. They appeared a strong-minded, determined set of men spoiling for a scrap. The mood was contagious, and his moment of doubt passed. He was almost glad Ugartechea had not capitulated.

We're fixing to see a hot old time around here, he told himself. He was glad to get back to his rifle and feel the comfort of its wood and cold steel in his hands. It gave him a feeling of power, even invincibility.

"Them Mexicans ain't much for fightin'," he heard one of the men say. "One of us is good for five of them."

James hoped they fought better than that, or the contest wouldn't amount to much.

The plan was announced while the men waited for darkness. The attackers would split into two groups and advance upon the fort under cover of night. They would take up and fortify positions but would not attack until the schooner *Brazoria* appeared in the morning and brought its two new pieces of ordnance to bear upon the post. The Mexican garrison would then be caught between fire from the water and riflemen on the land. A group under the command of Austin were to carry spades and wooden planks to the open side of the garrison and build a set of breastworks during the night. The second group, under Brown, was to circle the garrison and take positions behind a protective pile of logs and other driftwood cast up by past rises of the river.

James was chosen to go with Austin's group. He could see the dark and ominous shape of the fortress in the night as they advanced. He wondered that the soldiers inside did not seem to see the Texans' approach. It would have been far better, he thought, to be able to move in the dark of the moon.

He heard a man named Robinson say that his wife had been bitterly opposed to his joining this expedition. "As I was leaving, the last thing she said to me was, 'I hope them Mexicans shoot you dead!' "

James wished the sentries in the fort might

be asleep, but that quickly proved to be a forlorn hope. He and the other Texans had just begun digging and setting up the protective planks when powder flashed atop the wall, and a bullet whistled past. That shot was followed by others.

"Hold your fire, men!" came Austin's order.

But the man named Robinson, either misunderstanding or out of panic, fired back. A volley responded instantly, aimed at the point where his rifle had flashed. James heard the sickening thud of a bullet and a surprised cry, then a long, agonized moan as Robinson slumped to the ground, mortally wounded. James rushed to his side and knelt, but a gurgling sound in the man's throat told him nothing could be done. He felt sick at his stomach and turned away.

"I reckon he's made his wife happy," somebody remarked.

James felt a surge of anger and would have challenged the man were he not trying so hard to hold down the little bit of supper he had eaten.

Fire from the fort became so intense that some of the men began to run away. Angry threats from those who remained did nothing to slow their speed. Bullets smashed through the planks that had been raised for protection. There had not been time enough to shovel up an earthen embankment adequate to reinforce them. The Texans returned fire for fire.

James involuntarily ducked each time he heard a bullet snarl by, though he realized by that time it would have been too late had it been intended for him. Every once in a while he heard a man cry as he was struck. The stench of gunpowder was so sharp that at times he could hardly breathe. He choked, his nostrils afire, his lungs burning. He could hear screams from inside the fort and knew the Texans' fire was as deadly as that from the Mexicans. The only saving grace was that the big cannon could not be lowered enough to bear down upon the attackers. It thundered and belched fire over their heads.

He found himself more than once looking back over his shoulder, wondering if he could make it to safety were he to jump up and run, as others had already done. Here, at least, the planks and the earth provided at least a modicum of cover. Better to stay in the little hole he had dug for himself than to take his chances out in the open.

He felt a tug at his sleeve and a sharp, fiery pain along his left arm. A Mexican bullet had grazed him. He felt with his right hand. The place burned as if he had run against a hot poker, but it bled only a little.

"They hit you?" a man next to him asked anxiously.

"Just enough to make me good and mad." But nausea came over him, and he lost most of his supper after all.

He had heard many stories about many battles, but somehow they all fell short of the reality he was experiencing here. The stories had always made the fights seem bloodless and without pain except to the enemy. But he felt pain now. He could hear the cries of the wounded and dying, both in the Texan line and within the beleaguered fortress.

He heard a voice from somewhere behind him, trying to shout and whisper at the same time. "James Lewis! James Lewis! Where the hell are you at?"

James had just finished scooping dirt over his own vomit so he did not have to smell it. He replied, "I'm here. Watch your head."

He knew the voice. In a moment Sly Shipman dropped down on his belly beside James. A bullet kicked dirt into his face. Rubbing it from his eyes, he asked anxiously, "You all right?"

"I'm all right. What're you doin' here? I thought you said it was a damnfool idea, comin' to this place."

"I ain't changed my mind about that. It just goes to show that there's two damn-fools in our partnership." He touched James's wounded arm, and James flinched. "Looks to me like they've already proven it to you."

"Lucky shot," James said, not wanting to admit error.

"Been a bunch of lucky shots from what I've seen. This outfit's pretty bad shot up."

"So are those Mexicans. Every time one of them sticks his head up, almost, he gets his brains blown away. Everybody said they wouldn't fight. Why the hell don't they give up?"

"Because they've got guts. And because they've got the same contempt for Americans as a lot of Americans have for them. They're fightin' for their honor."

"Damn little good honor'll do you when you're dead."

"That's a funny thing for *you* to say. You're the one always spoilin' for a fight. Well sir, you've found one. Enjoy it."

"What did you do with our mules?"

"Left them with a farmer. He said he'd take care of them for us."

"What if we both get killed?"

"Then I reckon he's got him a good set of

mules." A bullet whined just past Shipman's head, taking off a little of his hat brim. "Move over, James, and give me room. For people who weren't goin' to put up a fight, they're doin' a right smart of a job."

James knew the cover wasn't enough to guarantee safety, but it was the best he had. He inched to one side, giving Shipman a share of the hole he had gouged into the sand. "I still don't see what you came here for," he said. "You were dead set against me comin'."

"I tried to go on without you, but them mules wouldn't let me. They look on you as kinfolk. You *do* have a lot in common. They kept tellin' me I'd better come see about you, that you'd probably fool around and let the Mexicans kill you if I didn't lend you a hand."

"I don't see you doin' any shootin'."

"I ain't mad at anybody — except maybe you."

James felt a warm glow inside. Shipman would not admit it in a hundred years, but he had come to rescue James if he could, and protect him if he could not. "Thanks, Sly."

"Thanks for nothin'. When we get out of here I'm goin' to whip you within an inch of your life."

James had to smile. "You and how many others?"

Dawn's approach gave a rosy color to the water where the Brazos flowed into the Gulf. The marksmen's aim improved on both sides. Around him, James could now see several dead among the Texans, and many more wounded. He could see a couple of Mexicans lying across the garrison wall, shot dead as they had raised up to fire. Some soldiers, fearing the Texans' deadly aim, raised rifles over the wall and fired blindly, keeping their heads down. Even this did not protect them from harm. A rifle exploded as a Texan bullet struck it, and a Mexican screamed over his shattered hands.

"This," Shipman said grimly, "is what a battle is all about. It's men dead or shot to pieces and spillin' blood and guts all over the ground."

"I didn't ask you to come."

"Neither one of us has got any business here. I hope you know that now."

James heard the sickening thump as a Mexican bullet drove into Shipman's body. He heard breath gust from the man's chest, followed by a moan. Shipman quivered.

"Sly!" James cried. In his anxiety he raised up too far and felt the wind as another bullet sang by his head. He dropped back down and turned Shipman over. Blood spilled from a hole in Shipman's homespun shirt, high in the shoulder. Shipman gasped for breath.

"Damn you, Sly, don't you die on me. I got you into this. For God's sake give me the chance to get you out of it."

He tore a sleeve from his own shirt and shoved it tightly against the wound, trying to stanch the blood. He knew it was useless to call for help. Others needed help as much or worse but had not received it. So long as the fire continued hot from the rim of that fortress, there was little help for anybody.

But as the day broke, the fire from the fortress became desultory, finally sputtering and dying. Each time soldiers had tried to man the artillery pieces, sharpshooters from the Texan ranks had cut them down. The riflemen had done far more damage than the schooner *Brazoria,* its cannons loaded with scrap iron and pieces of chain in lieu of proper cannonballs. Dark smoke curled and did a devil's dance over a scene of despair and ruin. In due course, a white flag was raised over the garrison wall. The Texans, those still able on both sides of the fortress, gave a round of cheers, then went silent in contemplation of the carnage wrought around and among them.

James had managed to stop the bleeding of Shipman's wound. Shipman was semiconscious, fighting to hold back the darkness that threatened to overtake him. "Hold fast, Sly," James told him, gripping his partner's hand tightly as if that would keep him from slipping away. "Maybe we'll have help here directly."

Help did come, after a while. Someone brought a jug of Mexican whiskey for Shipman to drink, to deaden the pain. James watched a portly, black-clad man work with other men, as badly wounded or worse than Shipman. After a time he responded to James's urgent beckoning. "You a doctor?" James demanded.

"I am a minister," the man replied. James noticed for the first time that he wore a leather patch over one eye. "My first concern is for healing lost souls. But from time to time I have been called upon to help heal wounded bodies. Let me see what the trouble is here."

He tore Shipman's shirt open. "If that bullet had gone an inch or so farther to the inside, the best I could do now would be to pray for the young gentleman's soul. But let us see if we may give the Lord some help here."

He bade Shipman drink some more of the

whiskey. "Ordinarily I do not hold with spiritous liquors, and this smells particularly vile, but there are times when it has its uses. Drink all you can, young gentleman. The less you know about what I do here, the better for you. I shall return."

He went on to treat other wounded while Shipman drank himself into a stupor. When he came back he heated the blade of a long, thin knife over an open fire and probed the wound, seeking the bullet. Shipman cried out and fell unconscious. James decided the minister would do better to confine his doctoring to horses; with just one eye he probably could not see what he was doing, anyway. But after a minute that seemed an hour, the minister brought out the lead ball that had done the damage. He poured into the wound the whiskey that Shipman had not already drunk.

"He has a good chance now that the bullet's out of him," the one-eyed man said. "That is, if he does not take blood poisoning. But he's going to be a long time getting back to the man he used to be. He will need the Lord's blessing and a lot of care. I shall seek the blessing, but the care will be up to you and his family."

"He's got no family that I know of."

"Then the responsibility falls upon your

shoulders, young gentleman."

You don't know how much I'm responsible, James thought.

The minister looked at the long crease across James's arm. The blood had long since congealed and dried. "It would appear you could use a little attention yourself."

"I've had yellowjackets sting me worse than this. Go see after them that needs you, preacher. And thanks."

The minister moved away to do his work upon other wounded. From a distance James watched him cut away part of a shattered leg. He tried again to retch, but nothing was left in his stomach.

James did not go into the fortress; he did not want to leave Shipman that long. He took it for granted that the scene inside was as terrible as the one outside, for several who went to see came back white-faced and shaken.

The Mexican commander Ugartechea surrendered his sword to Austin and Brown. A night of fierce hostilities seemed to have burned away most of the enmity on both sides. The surrender was cordial enough. The Mexicans were allowed to retain their sidearms and personal property upon Ugartechea's promise that they would leave Texas. They were to take their wounded with them, but they would bury their dead here.

The schooner *Brazoria* moved past the garrison, its sails set for Anahuac, though some of its rigging had been shot away.

James did not know for certain how many had died on the Texan side. Some said seven, some said more. He found that he did not really care to know. He wanted only to put this place behind him and forget. But he knew he never would. Even if he tried, he would have Sly Shipman to remind him.

Concerned settlers brought wagons after a time, hauling part of the wounded to a farm some distance from the scene of the battle. Others, who did not live far away, were carried to their homes. It was out of the question for James to take Shipman back to Louisiana in this condition. He helped carry his partner and a couple of others into a cabin owned by a generous widower who offered the use of his farm home for however long it took the men to be able to travel farther.

James was not sure the first night that Shipman was going to make it. After being white and cold in the beginning, he began to run a fever that had him ranting out of his head. James wiped sweat from Shipman's face and forehead with a cool, damp cloth and alternated between cursing himself and praying for divine intervention. Shipman's talk was unintelligible at times. Other times he was talking to the mules or berating James for his rashness or talking to his mother in the language of a small boy. Twice James heard him talk to Annie. He wondered if the woman in Shipman's fevered dreams was Annie Lewis or some other Annie from times past.

The fever began to subside the second day, and Shipman came to consciousness off and on. Each time he did, James had to explain to him where he was and what he was doing there. Toward sundown of the second day, the fever was mostly gone, and Shipman was fully awake. He stared at James but said nothing. James looked for blame in his eyes but did not see it.

Tension building to an intolerable point, he finally declared, "I wish you'd say it and get it over with. You told me so!"

"I ain't said nothin'," Shipman replied in a weak voice. "Ain't figured on sayin' nothin'."

"You got a right to. If it hadn't been for me, you wouldn't be layin' here."

"I've been shot before. It ain't like they'd done somethin' brand new. What're you goin' to do about our mules?"

"Who cares about mules at a time like this?"

"I do. I ain't goin' to lay here forever."

"I'll go fetch them when I see you're out of trouble."

"I ain't been out of trouble since I was six years old. I want you to go see about them mules. Tell the farmer who's keepin' them that we ain't dead and we'll be after them bye and bye."

James decided that Shipman wouldn't rest until that chore was taken care of. The next morning, following Shipman's directions, he set out on Walker to find the farm where the mules had been left for safekeeping. Along the way he came upon half a dozen horsemen, riding from the direction of the fortress at Velasco. He recognized them as veterans of the battle and held up until they reached him.

"Any news from Anahuac?" he asked. "Did the schooner make it down there all right?"

"Yes," was the answer from the tall man who had led him to Velasco in the first place. "Turned out it wasn't needed. Colonel de las Piedras had already gone to Liberty and then up to Anahuac and turned Bradburn out of office. He agreed to right the wrongs that Bradburn visited upon us."

"Then Travis is free?"

"Travis and all the others Bradburn had imprisoned."

James felt his stomach start to tie itself into a knot. "When did all this happen?"

"Before the battle of Velasco. We just didn't know. Ugartechea didn't know."

James slumped in the saddle, thinking of Shipman, thinking of all those dead, all those wounded. "So the battle was for nothin'."

The tall man shrugged. "It wasn't a total loss. We got to shoot hell out of some Mexicans."

"And got the hell shot out of us, too."

"Life doesn't give us anything free." The man lifted one hand as a way of saying good-bye and proceeded upon his way, the other men following in silence. James watched them for several minutes, his stomach roiling in frustration and anger and regret.

He began to wonder if Michael *would* have gone.

CHAPTER 15

James was reluctant to leave Shipman, but his partner was adamant, even angry when James seemed to try to stall the mission. Following Shipman's directions, he found the farm where the mules had been left, rewarded the farmer with a jug of good Kentucky squeezings and then proceeded to peddle most of the assorted goods out around the area for a small but welcome profit. Though the Mexican soldiers had prevented him from working his farm, he had not been idle. He had a little money deposited with Baptiste Villaret in Natchitoches, probably more than he could have hoped to make out of one year's crops in Austin's colony. Nevertheless, it scratched in his craw that they had robbed him of that chance. It was the end of June now and much too late to start a crop even if he *were* to return to the farm.

Memories of his aborted attempt to settle

on the Colorado set him to thinking. From here it was not really very far. On horseback, he could make it in maybe three days without pressing Walker too much, four or five if he took it slow for Shipman's sake. It was considerably farther back to Louisiana, and there would be no one to see after Shipman at their cabin except James. For help he would have to carry the wounded man all the way to Natchitoches. A trip of that length could kill him. Among the Lewis family, Shipman would receive the care he needed.

He didn't know what Annie's reaction might be. She had seemed to have mixed feelings about Shipman the last time, but James never had paid much attention to what Annie said.

By the time he returned to the farm where Shipman lay recuperating, James had made up his mind. As soon as his partner appeared fit to ride, they would go to the Colorado. He had to circle around San Felipe, of course. That Mexican officer had a long memory, from what Annie's letters had said. And James might have to sleep in the woods instead of in one of the Lewis cabins, but that was all right. He had been spending more nights under the stars than under a roof anyway. At this time of year it was no hardship.

He found a visitor at the farm, the one-eyed minister. Round of belly and gray of hair, the man came out to the horse pen to greet James as he rode in, leading the string of mules. "Well, young gentleman," he said pleasantly, "your packs appear to be about empty. Commerce must be thriving."

James doubted the minister would approve if he knew that some of those trade goods were whiskey.

"I done all right," James admitted. "How's Sly?"

"Mr. Shipman is doing quite well, praise the Lord, considering how near he came to confronting his Maker and accounting for all his past transgressions."

James frowned. "What do you know about his transgressions?" He wondered if Shipman had been talking too much. A man in their profession could not afford to be overly free with conversation, at least about their business.

"Fear not," said the minister. "I have no truck with the authorities. I am contraband here myself, you might say. As a Protestant servant of the Lord, I am in Texas in violation of Mexican law. It forbids all but Catholics, as you must know."

James was not a church-goer, particularly,

so that restriction had not caused him any personal inconvenience. He was aware of it, though. "I'll make a pact with you, preacher. I won't talk to the law about you, and you don't talk about us."

"A fair trade, sir." The minister stuck out a large, rather puffy hand. "I am the Reverend Fairweather."

Fairweather. The name struck a chord, and James searched his memory. It seemed he had heard Andrew and Michael speak of a minister by that name, a one-eyed preacher. "I'm James Lewis," he said, waiting to see if the name meant anything to Fairweather. It did. The man studied James with one critical eye. "Yes, I can see the resemblance, now that I look for it. You would have two brothers by the names of Michael and Andrew."

"You know them, then."

"Our trails have crossed more than once. The first time, I fear, I was about the devil's work. But the Lord did smite me hip and thigh and show me the error of my ways. We have since had better relations, your brothers and I. But they are farming out on the Colorado River. What are you doing in this part of the country, running contraband past the noses of the authorities?"

"I had a mite of trouble with the convict soldiers. I had to leave."

"Unfortunate. That is good land where your brothers are. You should be there raising crops to feed the hungry, with a family to share the bounty of your labors."

"I'm goin' back."

"And what of the soldiers?"

"To hell with the soldiers!" He thought better of his language. "I beg your pardon, preacher."

Fairweather shrugged. "There has been but one of us who was perfect, and He lived a long way from Texas. Let me feed your animals while you see about your friend. I believe you will find him better than you left him."

Shipman was pale and drawn and had dark circles under his eyes, but those eyes were livelier than before. He assumed the worst before James had a chance to say more than hello. "I suppose you lost money for us on our merchandise?"

"As a matter of fact, I did pretty good. There ain't much cash in this colony, but I got a little of what there is. I thought it was better than tradin' for goods, because we're not apt to go back to Natchitoches for a while."

"Why not? I'm ready to travel."

"The hell you are. I'd be buryin' you before we got halfway to the Sabine. But maybe in a few days you'll be up to makin' a shorter trip. I'm takin' you to my family."

Shipman did not seem to know whether to accept that as good news or bad. "That sister of yours, she may not take kindly to me."

"She probably won't. She's got a temper like a cat that's had its tail stepped on. So we won't ask her. We'll just show up."

Shipman pondered a while. "I can't abide bad temper in an ugly woman. But I can stand it if she's good-lookin' enough. And your sister's good-lookin' enough."

James waited three more days before undertaking the trip, giving Shipman time to gain strength. He disliked imposing on the farmer's patience and hospitality. When Fairweather departed to see after other souls, James gave the farmer two jugs of Kentucky whiskey which he had retained for that purpose from the supply of trade goods. The jovial farmer seemed to feel that this was excessive payment and insisted upon sharing at least one of the jugs with James and Shipman. Shipman was still carrying a glow when James helped him upon his horse and they set out westward.

He took more time than necessary, carefully watching for sign of soldiers but seeing none. He considered spending a night at the farm of Marcus Caldwell, the rusty-haired settler who had befriended him on his flight toward the Sabine. The only thing which gave him pause was that he still remembered his run-in with Caldwell's red-headed daughter Libby. Unlike Shipman, James had little patience with bad temper in any woman, no matter what she looked like.

He had to hunt a little before he found the place, but he recognized the long, rambling log house, the well-tended rail-fenced field where corn waved green in the wind. He found farmer Caldwell and his sons out hoeing their corn, as befitted good farmers. Caldwell laid down his hoe and gave a shout. When his sons tried to follow his example, however, he quickly set them back to work. "You'll have time enough to greet our company," he said, the wind carrying his strong voice to James. "They'll be stayin' all night with us, you can be sure."

James looked back at Shipman. His partner looked tired and pale. They would be spending the night, all right. Maybe two nights.

The farmer remembered James's name without prompting. "I knew no brother of Andrew's and Michael's could be kept out of Texas unless they buried him. Welcome back to God's paradise." He shoved out his big hand and nearly crushed James's bones. His attention went then to Shipman. "What's this? A man hurt?"

James said, "We got ourselves caught up in a scrap over at Velasco. Sly Shipman there, he taken a bullet."

Caldwell frowned darkly. "We heard about that fight. Was it as bitter as the stories make it out?"

"It was bad enough," James said grimly. "I was sure wishin' I was someplace else after the shootin' started. It wasn't what I thought it would be."

"I've been in a couple of bad scrapes myself, in my wilder days. I decided bein' a farmer was better than bein' a fighter. Maybe you're gettin' the same notion?"

"It's come to me several times. Didn't seem like there was much else we could do, though. Bradburn had Travis and some others in jail and was goin' to see to it that they was shot. We couldn't just stand by and let him get away with such as that."

"I suppose not. Never met Travis myself, but I've heard of him. Seems like from what folks say that he hunts up trouble if it doesn't hunt for him. He ought to've left Bradburn alone."

"Maybe so. But he didn't, and we set out

to turn him a-loose. I just didn't figure on it bein' so mean. I figured they'd see we meant business and back away. People kept sayin' the Mexicans wouldn't fight."

"Folks say lots of things. You can't believe them all. Yes, the Mexicans will fight. How else do you think they won their freedom from Spain?"

Oddly, James had never thought about it in that light. "I wish I'd talked to you before I went."

"And while we're talkin', now, your friend is sittin' there sufferin' on that horse. Let's get him up to the house." Caldwell called his oldest boy to come with him. "You others, keep choppin' weeds till you hear your mama ring the supper bell. Come winter, you'll be glad you raised somethin' to eat."

Mrs. Caldwell had seen them coming. She stood waiting on the porch, wadding a cotton apron in her hands. "Land's sake, Libby," she said to her red-haired daughter, "it looks like we've got a hurt man on our hands."

James said, "He's been wounded, ma'am."

He felt Libby's blue eyes examining him coolly. She had gotten no friendlier since his last visit here. She said, "Can't say I'm surprised. Look who he's with."

James hoped one night here would rest

Shipman enough to continue the trip. He tried to ignore Libby and said to her mother, "If you've got a place for him, ma'am —"

"Certainly. We'll *make* a place."

Libby asked, "You still runnin' from the same soldiers? Or maybe a new bunch now?"

"You don't see me runnin', do you?"

"I'll bet we would if some soldiers were to come ridin' over that hill yonder."

James could not deny that, but he tried not to dignify it with an answer. "I sure don't want to be any trouble to you, ma'am. But Sly Shipman here, he got hurt on account of me."

Libby declared, "I sure can't say I'm surprised."

Mrs. Caldwell led the way to a room at the end of the log building. James knew by the look of it that her sons slept there. "Libby," she ordered, "you go fetch some hot water and clean cloth. I'll fix this poor young man's dressin'." She frowned. "Looks like it hasn't been changed in a day or two."

James said apologetically, "We been movin', ma'am."

When Libby brought the water and cloth, her mother ordered her to go busy herself in the kitchen. A girl her age had no busi-

285

ness seeing a young man's body naked from the waist up. It wouldn't be seemly. James was relieved; a little of the girl's barbed comment was enough to serve him from now to Christmas. He and Caldwell removed Shipman's badly-abused cotton shirt and then the bandages that the Reverend Fairweather had put on. James shook involuntarily at sight of the wound. It still looked angry and dark, though it had improved from the last time he had seen it. He said, "The preacher was afraid he might get blood poisonin'."

Mrs. Caldwell answered, "Since he hasn't already, it's not likely he will. But you'll need to keep the wrappin' clean."

She set about cleaning and rebandaging the wound. "Now, young man," she told Shipman, "we'll get a good supper into you after a bit, and you'll look and feel a lot better."

"I feel better already," Shipman told her gratefully. "If ever a time comes that I can do you a favor —" He turned to James. "We got any of our goods left?"

"Nothin' but a jug or two of Kentucky whiskey that I kept in case somethin' comes up."

"It's come up. Fetch it."

They ate supper. James sat across the table

from Libby Caldwell and tried to ignore her gaze, which remained on him during most of the meal. She seemed to be appraising him as if he were a lame mule at a crossroads sale yard.

After supper Caldwell took out an old fiddle he said had been made forty or fifty years ago by his grandfather. The oldest son fetched a homemade stringed instrument not quite like any James had ever seen, but it had a fair to middling twang. Another son had a primitive instrument known as a recorder, whittled from wood. They began to play. Mrs. Caldwell and the rest of the youngsters joined in. Even Libby sang, after a bit. Her singing was much more pleasant than her talk, James thought, for it had a nice lilt and a clarity that reminded him of his sister Heather, back home. Most of the songs were hymns he had heard often in Tennessee. He sang along when he could remember the words and hummed when he could not. Shipman's pale face seemed to brighten to the music, though he did not sing. James figured Shipman did not know the songs. He probably had not been exposed to much church music — or much church, for that matter.

The singing made James feel a little homesick, for it took him back to Tennessee and a far more peaceful time. As he looked at first one and then another member of the Caldwell family he realized what a lucky man Marcus Caldwell was to have that good wife and these several sons and daughters to help him in his work and to comfort him in his leisure.

Maybe someday, he thought. Then he looked at Libby Caldwell and reassessed his situation. It was not all bad, being a bachelor.

James gave San Felipe a wide berth, for the capital of the colony was almost certain to be watched over by at least a few soldiers at any given time. The trip required a day or two more than he expected. He had not taken into full account that the last time he had ridden some of the same route, he had been moving a lot faster. Moreover, Marcus Caldwell had talked them into staying over an extra day at his place to let Shipman rest a bit longer. James suspected the farmer simply enjoyed company and hated to see them leave.

He began to see the familiar landmarks that told him he was nearly home. He crossed over the Colorado to its south side sooner than usual, not wanting to run into any of the Blackwood family. They would call the soldiers down upon him out of pure spite.

At last he saw a small figure sitting on a tall horse, pushing a few cattle westward. He shouted three times against the wind before the rider turned to look, then pulled his horse around and pushed it into a lope. James recognized young Mordecai, Michael's son. As the boy reined up beside him, James squeezed his hand so hard that Mordecai winced. James leaned back in the saddle to take the youngster's measure. "I swear, Mordecai, you've grown half a foot since last I seen you."

Mordecai was trying to cover some disappointment. He said, "I thought at first you might be my daddy comin' home. From a distance, you look sort of like him."

"Michael? Where's he at?"

Mordecai shook his head. "We don't rightly know. A bunch of men came by here a while back lookin' for volunteers to go to Anahuac and set things straight. You know my daddy. He went." Mordecai gave Shipman a moment's curiosity.

James said, "Sly Shipman, this is my nephew Mordecai." He frowned at the boy. "A ways from home, ain't you?"

"I come to gather up my daddy's cattle that strayed down the river. Things can happen to them when they get too far from home. Finis Blackwood can't tell our cows from his own."

James nodded grimly. "A common failin' in that family. We'll help you drive the cattle."

Mordecai observed, "Mr. Shipman don't look like he feels too good. Maybe you-all had best go on."

Shipman did look tired, James thought. He said to Mordecai, "You're right. I'd best get Sly on down to Andrew's house, where Annie and Petra can take care of him."

Mordecai said, "Aunt Annie ain't livin' with Uncle Andrew and Aunt Petra no more."

James blinked. "Did Petra run her off?" That would not have surprised him, given Annie's penchant for running things.

"No, Aunt Annie decided she was a burden, and she wanted to live in a house of her own. So we taken those logs you had piled up, and added some more to them, and we built her a house up there on your place."

"My place? You mean it's still mine?"

"Ain't nobody come and taken it away. I think Aunt Annie would shoot anybody that tried."

"Them Mexican soldiers, they been huntin' me?"

Mordecai nodded solemnly. "Every so often. They poke around a little but leave when they can't find you. They don't hurt anybody. You come to stay, Uncle James?"

"If the soldiers don't catch me."

He rode on, circling far enough around the cows to avoid turning them back. The first cabin was Michael's. He saw the slight figure of Marie Lewis standing in the dog-run, shading her eyes with her hands. She ran a little way out into the open, then stopped, slumping a little. James sensed that she, like Mordecai, had thought at first he was Michael.

He got down from the bay horse and hugged his sister-in-law. "I'm sorry, Marie."

"Sorry for what?"

"Sorry I'm not Michael. I saw Mordecai back yonder a ways. He told me. But I reckon Michael'll be along pretty soon. All the trouble appears to be over."

Her gaze went to Sly Shipman, and James had to explain about the fight at Velasco. He left out most of the details, because they would only intensify her concern for her missing husband.

Trying to change the subject and lift her spirits, he said, "It hadn't been but a little while since we left your daddy over in

Natchitoches. Sly and me, we been part-nerin' with him a right smart."

"I know. It's a wonder you haven't all been put in jail."

By the time James and Shipman had answered her many questions about the parents and the family she had not seen in years, the sparkle had returned to Marie's dark eyes, pushing the worry aside. James enjoyed listening to the French accent he had once thought odd. After the time he had spent in Louisiana, it sounded natural.

Riding away, Shipman said, "She's too pretty to be old Baptiste's daughter. Must take after her mother's side of the family."

James nodded but looked back at the cabin they were leaving behind. "I wish he wouldn't do that."

"Who, do what?"

"Michael, go off and leave her thataway. Andrew says he gets an itchy foot every so often. Can't help himself. Says he's like our daddy used to be, always lookin' for a reason to ride over the hill and see what's out yonder."

Shipman observed, "If it hadn't been for him and his restless nature, there wouldn't none of you Lewises be in Texas."

"I reckon you're right. But that's a fine

little woman back there. I wish Michael wouldn't go off and leave her."

CHAPTER 16

Annie Lewis watched in disbelief as Isaac Blackwood pulled up in back of the cabin, driving two mules hitched to a wagon loaded with firewood. A small boy sat on the seat beside Isaac, his eyes wide and curious as Annie walked out to meet them, her skirt catching in the wind and whipping a little. Isaac doffed his old hat. He was clean-shaven, as the last time. Gone was the dark beard he used to wear.

"Mr. Blackwood — Isaac," she called, stopping a little short because the skirt seemed to be worrying the skittish mules. "What in the world brings you here with that wagon?"

"Howdy, Miss Annie. Well, ma'am, me and the boy here, we been gatherin' up wood for next winter. It come to me that you don't have a man of your own to fetch for you. There's aplenty of dead timber out yonder, and it's easy gatherin'. Didn't take us no time, hardly." He nodded toward the heavy woods which lined the river and stretched beyond it.

The mules' attention had gone to a cow which grazed in a meadow beyond the house, so Annie stepped closer to the wagon. She had not seen the boy before. She judged him to be five or six years old. She thought she could see a resemblance, but she had not heard of Isaac ever being married. "Your son?"

Isaac seemed a little flustered and slow in answering. "He belongs to Finis. But I reckon I've done the biggest part of his raisin'."

Annie suspected that was no exaggeration. She had not seen much of the other two Blackwood brothers, Finis and Luke, but she had heard enough from Michael and Andrew to know their coming to Texas had been an improvement for Tennessee. Finis could not be much of a father for a boy, any more than old Cyrus Blackwood back home had been for his own sizable brood.

She said, "I appreciate the gesture, Mr. Blackwood, but it wasn't necessary. My brothers have promised to lay in a supply for me once they get their fields worked."

"If it comes a hard winter, you'll need all the wood you can get. I'll be unloadin' it for you." He stepped down from the wagon, then took the boy in his arms and set him on the ground, motioning for him to stand back out of harm's way. A small woodpile was already there, thanks to Andrew and to Michael's oldest, Mordecai. The mules stood patiently, switching tails and flipping their ears against the summer flies that harassed them.

Annie vacillated between gratitude and embarrassment as she watched Isaac work. She did appreciate the gesture, but she sensed that Isaac had a reason. She had not been oblivious to the way he looked at her whenever he came around. That he admired her, that he wanted her, she had no doubt. She was both flattered and troubled, troubled because she could not return the feeling. He seemed in all ways a gentleman in her presence, never pushing himself, never saying or doing anything that might give offense. Had he been someone other than a Blackwood, she might have been able to respond. But she remembered too well the reputation that family had back in Tennessee, and knew the reputation Isaac's brothers had here. It had been Isaac's father Cyrus who had betrayed Annie's father to the Spanish soldiers, resulting in his being murdered here in Texas a long time ago.

That, if nothing else, would always stand between them.

She asked the boy, "What's your name?"

He gave her a long, critical study before he answered. "Cyrus."

Give a dog a bad name — But this was not a dog, this was a boy, an innocent boy who had no reason to answer for something done a dozen years before his birth. She said, "I cook up somethin' sweet for my nephews when they come over to see me. I'll bet I can find you somethin' good in the kitchen if you'll come with me."

The boy looked back to Isaac, asking him silently. Isaac nodded, smiling. "Be sure now and tell the lady *thank you.*"

Cyrus was quiet, but his eyes never rested. Annie found him some cookies she had made for Mordecai and Edward, Frank's boy, when they had come over to help weed the cornfield and chop a supply of wood for the cooking. She had used honey, which was relatively plentiful, instead of sugar, which was not. While he munched the cookies, Cyrus walked about the cabin, looking at everything with a lively curiosity, even poking into the wooden trunk in which Annie had brought her few treasures from Tennessee. He took particular interest in a set of drawings she had made of the family back home so she could have them for remembrance. Annie got him a slate she had used in school and asked if he could draw. He lay on his stomach on the floor and went to work. The drawing was crude, but she could tell it was supposed to be a horse, or perhaps a mule.

"That's good," she said. "You could learn to be an artist."

She realized sadly, however, that as Finis's son, following in his father's footsteps, he was unlikely ever to be anything but another Blackwood, lazy, trifling, perhaps even a little dangerous. What a waste that would be.

She realized after a while that the sound of wood falling on wood had stopped. She stepped out onto the dog-run and saw that Isaac had finished. He had stacked the timber as neatly as was practical. "Come on in," she said. "I've made you some coffee."

She did not often make coffee; it was too expensive for every day, so she had gotten into the habit of saving it only for company. It was a small price to pay for a wagon load of firewood. She watched him dust himself off and wash his hands in a small basin, using brown soap she had made from tallow and ashes and such. "You shouldn't have gone to so much trouble, Mr. Blackwood — Isaac."

She found his face not unpleasant when he smiled, and he smiled now. "Wasn't no trouble at all, Miss Annie. And I've told you before, I'm just plain Isaac, not Mr. Blackwood."

She was a bit dubious about so much familiarity, but she said, "If you'll call me Annie. Not *Miss* Annie." She led him into the kitchen, where the boy Cyrus was still on his stomach, sketching a cow that had horns as long as its body. Isaac stopped to look at the slate with some surprise. "I swear, Cyrus, I didn't know you could do that."

Annie said, "You don't know what all a boy can do until you give him the chance. I think Cyrus could be an apt pupil for somebody who wanted to teach him the right way."

Isaac seemed downcast for a moment. "I wish. I just wish —" Then he shrugged. "That coffee sure smells good."

She had been thinking for some time that she needed to get a dog, so it would bark and let her know when somebody or something was coming. The first she knew of company was when she heard a mule bray out in front of the cabin, and an answer from one of Isaac's hitched to the wagon in back. She gave Isaac a questioning glance. "I hope it's not soldiers again." She pushed her chair back from the table and went reluctantly to the door that led out onto the dog-run.

A familiar voice called, "Annie?"

She stopped at the edge of the dog-run, not quite believing what she saw. "James?"

It was her younger brother, all right, leading a string of pack mules. Behind the mules was someone else on horseback, slumped over in the saddle so she could not quite see his face in the dark shadow beneath his hat brim. "James, that's not you!" She realized how foolish that sounded. "It *is* you. Where'd you come from?"

"From Hell, I guess you could say. Mind if I get down?"

"You can do what you want to. It's your place." She rushed to embrace him as he dismounted from the bay horse. He seemed surprised at the warmth of her greeting.

He said, "I was half afraid you'd take a club to me."

"Tomorrow maybe. Right now I'm too glad to see you."

"You don't know where I've been, or what I've been up to."

"You do some fool things at times, but

you're still my brother. Who's that with you?"

The other rider had moved forward. James helped him to the ground. "You remember Sly Shipman. He's been wounded."

She felt a quick sympathy, but she also remembered the last time she had seen Shipman, his casual attitude toward women, and his running away and leaving them to the mercies of Sergeant Díaz. "I suppose he's done some fool thing, too." She allowed a little disdain into her voice.

"It was me that done the fool thing," James admitted. "Sly got shot tryin' to pull me out of it. I was hopin' you'd see your way clear to help take care of him till he's healed up."

That put a different light on the situation. "Bring him, then." She turned and led the way to a bedroom across the dog-run from the kitchen. When they had built the cabin, they had divided that half of it into two rooms so Annie would have her privacy. "This is your room, anyway," she said. "The boys have been sleepin' in it when they come over to help me."

Shipman could walk on his own, but James gave him support, anyway. James said, "His bandage needs changin'. If you'll fix me some hot water, I'll do it."

"No, I can do it." Annie did not like the faded look in Sly Shipman's eyes. She did not know how long he and James had been traveling, but it was plain that he was exhausted. "You said he tried to pull you out of some fool stunt. What were you up to?"

James explained to her about the battle at Velasco. She had heard there had been a battle, but she knew no details. She had feared Michael might have been there. She had not once considered that James might be mixed up in it. She asked anxiously, "Did you see or hear anything of Michael?"

"He wasn't there or I'd've seen him. Me and Sly never did get to Anahuac."

A startled look came over James's stubbled face. Annie turned and saw Isaac standing in the doorway. Isaac asked, "You-all need some help here?"

James frowned. "Isaac Blackwood?" The man looked different with his beard gone, his hair cut shorter than before. James turned to Annie, his eyes asking.

She said, "Isaac brought me a wagon load of firewood."

James was in Isaac's debt for warning him once that the soldiers were coming. Still, an old family enmity was not easily put aside. "Much obliged, Isaac, but I reckon we can

302

handle this all right."

Isaac seemed to accept James's distrust without resentment. "Looks like you folks've got a lot to talk about, so me and the boy'll be movin' on. I need to pick up a load of wood for our own cabin before it gets dark. I enjoyed the coffee, Annie. And I do appreciate your interest in the boy."

Annie walked out onto the dog-run as Isaac brought the boy from the kitchen. She extended her hand, and the boy took it after a moment's hesitation. She said, "You come back sometime, Cyrus. You can draw on the slate all you want to."

Isaac prompted, "Say, 'Thank you, ma'am.' "

The boy responded as told, then turned shyly and trotted toward the wagon. Annie offered, "He seems like a good boy, Isaac."

Sadness came over Isaac's face. "He could be, if —" He let it go at that. "Glad your brother got home. I know you've worried." He was gone in a minute, he and the boy and the wagon.

Annie sensed that James stood behind her on the dog-run. James demanded, "How long's this been goin' on?"

Annie caught a suggestion in his voice and reacted with a flare of impatience. "How long has *what* been goin' on?"

"I don't know what. Maybe you'd like to tell me."

"There's nothin' to tell. Nothin's been goin' on. He's just tryin' to be nice, that's all."

"He's a Blackwood. Blackwoods don't do nothin' without they expect to get somethin' more out of it than they put in."

She felt heat rising in her cheeks. Any more talk would just lead to argument, and James had barely even gotten home. "Your friend in yonder needs care. Let's be gettin' to it."

"I just don't like the idea of a Blackwood sniffin' around here, is all. You can do better than that."

She turned on him, hands on her hips. "Like your friend Shipman, I suppose?"

"Sly's got his faults, but he ain't no Blackwood."

"No, he's just a smuggler."

"A merchant," James put emphasis on the word. "The merchandise is good and legal. It's the law that ain't. And he didn't have to go to Velasco and get all shot up. He did it tryin' to get me to go away from there. I owe him."

"Right. *You* owe him. I don't."

Annie had had no experience doctoring gunshot wounds. This one, despite several days of healing, still looked bad enough to give her stomach a few uneasy moments. She gritted her teeth and went about cleansing the wound, then putting a fresh dressing over it. She could tell that it hurt Shipman considerably, but he did not complain. She stewed over the question a while before she asked it. "Did you really go to Velasco to try to get James away?"

"That was what I figured on when I went. By the time I got there, though, there wasn't any gettin' a-loose. The fight had started real good."

"Seems to me you're pretty good at runnin' from fights."

"The ones I know I can't win? You're damned right. I ain't no fool."

"And James is?"

"He's young and green. He'll grow up if somebody don't kill him first. He's done a right smart of it in the last few days."

"Well, I thank you for tryin', anyway, Mr. Shipman."

"My friends call me Sly."

"Maybe your friends do, but I'll call you Mr. Shipman."

It was the next afternoon that young Mordecai came over the hill and up to the cabin as fast as he could make his horse run. He was shouting before he leaped from the saddle. He took long running strides up to the dog-run. "Uncle James! Uncle James! Soldiers comin'!"

Annie had been in the kitchen, preparing to cook supper on the hearth. She met James on the dog-run as he came out of the room he shared with Sly Shipman. James demanded of the boy, "What's this about soldiers?"

"I saw them myself, Uncle James. There's a big bunch of them, and they'll be comin' over that hill yonder in a minute or two. You've got to take my horse and head for the woods."

"But I haven't even been home a full day yet, hardly. How'd they know?" He frowned angrily. "Isaac Blackwood."

Annie said, "Isaac wouldn't betray you; he's not that kind."

"Finis would. Maybe Isaac said somethin' to Finis."

"We don't have time to argue about it now. Take Mordecai's horse and ride."

James did, but with reluctance. Annie watched anxiously as he crossed the river and disappeared into the heavy timber on the other side. Not many minutes later, a large body of horsemen appeared on the trail that led to Andrew's house and, farther, to Michael's. She said to Mordecai, "If they ask, you're here to help me with my garden. We haven't seen James in way over a year."

"I'm not much good at lyin', Aunt Annie."

"You've lived in Texas long enough. It's time you learned."

Her heart was thumping as she stood at the edge of the dog-run, waiting. This was by far the largest body of soldiers she had yet seen pass this way. She saw the officer who so often had come in search of James, but she saw other officers too, men whose uniforms suggested even higher rank. One of them gave an order, and the procession halted. She thought there were probably seventy-five or eighty men, perhaps as many as a hundred. The officer who had always led the searches seemed to be asking permission of a higher-ranking one. He received a nod and dismounted. He came up to the dog-run with less swagger than he had shown in the past, when he had always been the ranking officer. He had never spoken English, and Annie had learned only limited Spanish from Petra. They had always managed to communicate, however, because she knew what he wanted, and *no* was the same in both languages.

She had to assume he was asking about

James, as he always had before, though the words were unintelligible to her. She was surprised when a man's voice answered from behind her, speaking in Spanish. Sly Shipman leaned against the log wall. The officer asked him several sharp questions, and Shipman replied to them in a matter-of-fact manner that neither challenged nor yielded. The officer was obviously not fully satisfied, but he seemed resigned. He spoke something in a gruff voice that Annie supposed more or less meant good-bye. He walked back to his horse and remounted. The soldiers were soon gone on the trail that led west toward San Antonio de Bexar.

Mordecai had stood silently beside Annie, his gaze moving from the officer to Shipman as each spoke in turn. He asked in awe, "You sure you ain't a Mexican, Mr. Shipman? You sure do talk like one."

"A necessity of the business I'm in." To Annie he said, "The lieutenant says he and the others have been called to Bexar. There's a revolution down in Mexico, and they've got to go fight it. He said he's not forgettin' about James, though, and if he ever gets back up in this country again he'll be huntin' for him."

Annie let go a long pent-up breath. Leaving. It was like a heavy weight had been lifted from her shoulders. "Then James will be free to stay here, out in the open."

"If he wants to. Chances are that officer will never come back."

"He looked at you a little suspiciously. How did you explain what you're doin' here?"

Shipman made a broad smile. "Told him you're my sweetheart. Told him we're fixin' to get married."

Annie felt the blush warm her cheeks. "Why did you tell him such a lie as that?"

"The notion just popped into my head. I figured it'd seem logical to him, a good-lookin' woman like you and a good-lookin' man like me."

Her cheeks warmed even more. She knew she should take offense, but somehow she could not. "You're a shameless liar, Mr. Shipman."

"I only lie when there's a good reason for it. And I'm generally ashamed of myself afterwards."

"I should think you would be."

"But I'm not this time. There ain't nothin' wrong with the notion, except for the mar-ryin' part."

She pointed toward the door. "You'd bet-ter go lie back down, Mr. Shipman, before your notions get you in worse trouble than you've already been."

Shipman went, and Annie was glad, for if he had stayed another few seconds he would have seen her laugh in spite of herself.

Mordecai was not sure how to take it all. "Are you really his sweetheart, Aunt Annie?"

"If I were lookin' to be somebody's sweetheart, don't you think I could do a lot better than him?"

Mordecai shrugged. "I don't know. *I* like him."

CHAPTER 17

James tied Mordecai's horse back out of sight in the timber, then worked his way carefully to the edge where he could hide behind some underbrush and watch the cabin. He was vaguely uneasy, but the soldiers did not put fear into him as they might have done a year or two earlier. He had dodged enough of them by now that he could take them in stride. They did not stay long, which surprised him, and they made no move to search the woods, which surprised him more. He was unable to count them, either coming or going, so he could not safely assume that none had been left behind to watch for him. Prudence would demand that he remain out here until dark.

James had not always been on speaking terms with prudence. He waited a while, then fetched the horse and crossed back over the river. Mordecai came walking out to meet him. "They're gone, Uncle James."

"You sure they didn't leave any spies behind?"

"I watched them awful close. They're gone. They're on their way to Mexico to fight a revolution. Said they got hornets to worry about, and they can't be bothered with gnats."

"So I'm just a gnat, am I?"

Mordecai smiled. "That was him said it, not me."

Annie had returned to fixing supper and asked Mordecai to stay. He shook his head. "I better not. Since my daddy's not home, I've got more chores to do, and Mama to watch over." His eyes were serious. He was still only a boy, but he knew his responsibilities.

James held the tall horse and gave Mordecai a boost up into the saddle. "Thanks, Mordecai, for comin' to warn me. You're a credit to the Lewis family."

Mordecai broke into a broad smile. "I don't think anybody ever told me that."

"I'm tellin' you. Your old granddaddy would be proud to know you're carryin' his name."

James had feared that Annie and Shipman would not get along. Shipman had a tendency to say the wrong thing at the worst possible time, and Annie often said exactly what she thought no matter the cost. To his surprise, however, they appeared to tolerate each other quite well. Annie changed some of her cooking methods to accommodate Shipman's tastes, and Shipman went out of his way to compliment her on everything from the way she combed her hair to the way she fixed corn dodgers. Shipman seemed to heal visibly day by day. He would walk out a little farther each time he ventured from the cabin. He even picked up a hoe to help James weed the field, though James made him put it down.

"You don't want to open that wound up again," he warned. "Them Mexicans could kill you even yet, and not even be here."

With the constant threat of soldiers lifted from him, James began making plans for the farm. His brothers had broken out a small field for him and a garden for Annie. It was too late in the season to plant any more crops this year, other than some vegetables for the cabin, but he stepped off and staked additional acreage which he would break out next winter and have ready for spring's planting season. He went out into the woods and cut posts and rails, dragging them up to start a fence around the field to keep the cattle from straying into it. There was much to do and not enough daylight hours for all he wanted to accomplish. He kept remembering Marcus Caldwell's farm, with its neatly-kept rail fences, its well-tended fields, its long log house.

Give me a few years and I'll have this place looking just as good as that one, he told himself whenever his back began to ache and his eyes burned from the sweat rolling into them.

One afternoon about a week after his arrival, he cut his hand while sharpening his hoe. The cut was deep enough and bled enough that he decided he had better go to the cabin and treat it, lest it become infected and put an end to his work for a while. He walked into the room he shared with Shipman, then stopped in midstride.

Annie sat on the edge of a cot, leaning over Shipman. He had one arm around her waist, the other resting on her leg, her long cotton skirt pulled up above her knee. The front buttons of her dress were undone, and she had both hands on Shipman's cheeks, pressing his head to her bosom. Her eyes were closed, but she opened them wide as she heard James declare, "Damn!" She gave a little shriek and sat up straight, pulling the top of the dress around to cover herself.

Shipman said sharply, "Damnit, James,

314

can't you make a little noise?"

"Maybe it's time I did. Maybe I ought to throw you out of this place right now." He moved toward the cot, his fists clenched. "After we took you in, you go and take advantage of my sister —"

Annie stepped in front of him, buttoning her dress. Her face was flushed. He did not know if it was from arousal or embarrassment. "Before you go tryin' to throw anybody out, you just listen a minute. He wasn't takin' any advantage of me. I had as much to do with it as he did. Maybe more."

"You mean you wanted that — whatever you were doin'?"

"Yes, and we might not've stopped there either, if you hadn't come bustin' in here like a bull in a china closet. We're grown people. What we choose to do is none of your business."

"But you're my sister."

"Yes, and two years older than you are. So don't you be lecturin' me on what I ought or ought not to do."

Angrily he turned. "Then I'll just walk back outside and bleed to death, and you-all can go on about what you were doin'."

For the first time she noticed his cut hand. She was considerably less sympathetic than he thought she might be. "Well, let's see if we can fix it. You don't need any Mexicans to kill you; you'll fool around and do that for yourself."

She had some foul-smelling medicine she had used on Shipman's wound. It burned like it had come up out of Hell or someplace, and she poured it on with a certain amount of grim satisfaction. He clamped his teeth together to keep from swearing aloud. When the burning subsided and she began wrapping the hand, he asked "How long has this been goin' on between you and Sly?"

"There hasn't nothin' been goin' on, any more than what you saw. I guess we both know where the stoppin' place is."

"That's easy said, till you get there."

"What would *you* know about it?"

"I didn't spend all my time in Natchitoches with mules. You figure on marryin' him?"

"I hadn't figured one way or the other about it."

"You might ought to before you let things go much further. You may find out that Sly has notions of his own. They may not be the same as yours."

"We'll see."

She finished wrapping his hand. He flexed it. It had not yet had time to get sore, but it would. "I better go get some more work done while I still can. Is it safe for me to leave you two here with one another?"

"No, it isn't, but you go ahead anyway. If we need you, we'll holler."

James went back to the field. He didn't waste his time listening for anybody to holler.

He decided Annie and Shipman must have talked things over, because Shipman saddled his horse after breakfast the next morning, haltered half the mules and struck out down the river. About the only thing he said to James was, "Half the mules are yours. Since you're goin' to stay here and be a farmer, I figure you can make good use of them."

"I thought you might want to stay here, too. It's good land. I've got enough for you and Annie if you want it."

"For me and Annie? You Lewises are great ones for wantin' people to get married and set down in one place like a fence post." He acted as if he wanted to smile but couldn't. "You were a pretty good partner, James. You took to the business right off. But I can't afford to stay around and keep pullin' you out of the scrapes you get into. Next time you could get me killed. You watch out for yourself now."

Annie stood at the cabin, watching from a distance. Shipman raised his head and glanced in her direction a minute, lifted his hand in a half salute and left. The mules jogged along behind him, one of them breaking wind with every stride.

James walked reluctantly back to the cabin. Annie stood there with a look in her eyes as if she wanted to cry but had made up her mind not to. James said, "There ain't many things Sly is afraid of. But marriage is one."

She said nothing. James tried to think of an easy way to ask the question. "I'm goin' to be worryin' for the next month or two if you don't tell me."

She shook her head. "You've got no cause to worry. It didn't go that far."

He felt relieved. "You stopped him, did you? I'm proud of your good judgment."

"It wasn't me who stopped. It was him. I guess if I had good judgment I'd've stayed in Tennessee." She turned and went into the kitchen, closing the door behind her as a sign that she wanted to be left alone.

He had no quarrel with that. He hitched up two of the mules and went out into the woods to drag poles for the fence.

■ ■ ■ ■

The day Shipman left was the day Michael Lewis came home. With him was his old friend from Bexar, Elizandro Zaragosa and Zaragosa's son Manuel, now about thirteen. After stopping a while at his own cabin to kiss Marie and the children, Michael had gone by Andrew's and Petra's. Finally, late in the afternoon, he and Zaragosa arrived at the cabin James shared with Annie. They were trailed by Manuel and Mordecai, who lagged behind, talking. The boys had become close friends.

Annie had kept her own silent counsel all day. James surmised that she was grieving over Shipman's leaving. But she brightened at the sight of her older brother. Michael had always occupied a special place in her heart. She threw her arms around him and declared, "We were afraid they might have killed you."

"Nobody's ever killed me yet," Michael said, shrugging off everybody's concern over his long absence. He hugged James. "Mighty good to have you home again, little brother. I hope this time you can stay."

"I sure figure on it." James shook hands with Zaragosa. It had always puzzled him a little, Michael's friendship with this dark, leathery skinned Mexican. They seemed, on the surface, to have almost nothing in common. But they had fought side by side in earlier times, and each had saved the other's life. He supposed shared experiences like that might make people forget their racial differences. He wondered aloud how the two had come together this time. The fighting had been to the east. Zaragosa lived to the west.

Michael said, "Elizandro and Manuel were over on the coast sellin' horses when the trouble started. Bradburn figured they were thieves or somethin' and tried to confiscate their horses. I helped them drive the bunch out of his reach."

James grimaced. "That Bradburn. He must be a son of a bitch."

"He's just another little two-bit tyrant who had more power than was good for him. Piedras is a fair man, though. He turned Bradburn's prisoners loose and countermanded a lot of Bradburn's orders. So Bradburn turned in his papers and went back to Mexico. Like as not, we've seen the last of him." He glanced at Zaragosa. "Maybe we've seen the last of our quarrels with Mexico. Looks like we've got them all patched up."

Zaragosa did not appear to share Michael's confidence. "It is to be hoped." But he seemed to doubt.

Michael said, "They've pulled most of the soldiers back down into Mexico. They're fightin' a revolution down there to throw Bustamante out of power. There's a young general by the name of Santa Anna who says he wants to restore the constitution of 1824. I think we'd all be happy with that."

Zaragosa frowned. "I know of this Santa Anna. He is much popular with the people. But he is one who watches always which way the wind blows. If it blows east, he goes east. If it blows west, he goes west. Today it blows for the constitution. Tomorrow?" He shrugged.

James hesitated to bring up the subject with Zaragosa here, but he decided to do it, anyway. "I heard a lot of people talkin' when I was at Velasco. They're sayin' what Texas needs is to be independent from Mexico. Then we wouldn't have to worry about the likes of Bradburn or Bustamante or Santa Anna or any of them. We'd elect our own, and if they didn't do what we wanted we'd vote them out and start over, like back home."

Michael said, "This isn't Tennessee. It isn't the United States. I think most of the old settlers would be glad enough just to have the constitution back. It guaranteed us our rights. Give us that and we've got no quarrel with Mexico."

"But will they give us that?" James shook his head. "I think independence is what we need."

Michael gave him a long, sad look. "Would you be willin' to kill for it?"

James nodded grimly. "I'm afraid I already have."

CHAPTER 18

Sergeant Díaz was disappointed. He had hoped the uprising at Anahuac and Velasco would give the central government gumption enough to bring in an army of invasion and drive the Americans from Texas for once and for all. Certainly it should have opened the eyes of those in Mexico City to the danger of tolerating these *extranjeros* who showed every intention of wresting Texas from Mexico and delivering it into the hands of the United States of the North. He regarded Colonel José de las Piedras as a fool. He should have supported Juan Bradburn and crushed the rebels with an iron will instead of countermanding Bradburn and forcing that worthy patriot to resign.

It was true, of course, that Bradburn had abused his authority, but it was *his* authority, and the central government should have supported him. Rebellion, whatever its motivation, should never be tolerated. Order should always be the first priority. Grievances should be addressed by authority, never by the mob. That had traditionally been the army's view, and Díaz had never questioned it even when his conscience told him that authority was wrong. He was, first and last, a soldier.

In drawing a major part of its soldiers from Texas after Anahuac, the army had chosen for the moment to leave him in the reduced garrison at San Antonio de Bexar. He had mixed feelings about that. In a way he would have preferred to go where the real fighting was, against the tyrant Bustamante who had seized control from the rightful president Guerrero. That fight was being led now by Antonio López de Santa Anna, Mexico's hero of the hour. Santa Anna had promised to restore the liberal constitution of 1824 and end Bustamante's oppression of the people. He was supported by most of the army, so it seemed a foregone conclusion that he would win.

On the other hand, Díaz felt some gratification in being left here in Texas. He could at least watch what the Americans were doing, though he had little hope that anyone in higher authority would listen to his warnings about them. No one paid much attention to a mere sergeant.

He had noted that many Americans, particularly those who had been in Texas for some years and had accumulated property, were vocal in their support for Santa Anna. They were saying that restoration of their rights under the constitution of 1824 would make them happy to remain under the benevolent banner of Mexico. But others, particularly those who had no property and therefore little to lose, loudly advocated that Texas become independent. Díaz suspected that was the true feeling of most American Texans, no matter how often they proclaimed their loyalty. They had been fed generously by the hand of Mexico, and now they were ready to bite that hand like a pampered cat turned surly and mean.

Díaz briefly saw at least a ray of hope. Colonel José Antonio Mexía, who had just captured the city of Matamoros from Bustamante's forces, decided to make an expedition into Texas to determine for himself the true situation. Sailing up the Gulf coast to the mouth of the Brazos, he brought with him some four hundred men. That, Díaz thought, should be enough to whip the Americans into submission if Mexía chose that course. He did not see how the colonel could decide otherwise, once he observed the Texans' perfidy.

What Díaz did not know at the time was that the Texas impresario Stephen F. Austin had hurried to Matamoros to join Mexía, to argue that the uprising against Bradburn had been over personal grievances and was not directed against the central government. Moreover, Austin had sent word to his colonists to make Mexía welcome wherever he went and to demonstrate their loyalty with fervor. By the time the Mexía expedition reached the Brazos River and a grand reception in his honor, the colonel had already been softened by Austin's powers of persuasion. He was feted everywhere he went, treated to the best the Texans could offer in food and drink. With warm feelings toward his hosts, he gathered most of the remaining troops from Texas and ordered them to the interior of Mexico. They were needed there, he decided, to hasten Santa Anna's victory.

Among them now was to be Sergeant Díaz. A native of the Nacogdoches area in northeastern Texas, he had never been to the interior of the country. Texas was his home, and he saw it slipping away a little at a time to people of an alien kind. The day before he was to begin the march, he saddled his horse and rode out to the farm of his old friend and former commander, Elizandro Zaragosa. They greeted one another with the *abrazo,* the embrace of friendship. Zaragosa said, "I heard of your orders. I will be sorry to see you leave."

"And I am sorry to go. I have come to believe that the true fight for Mexico will be here, my lieutenant." Díaz always referred to Zaragosa as lieutenant, though Zaragosa had long since retired from the military and settled down to the life of a farmer on land which had belonged to his father-in-law. "We will be leaving you to the mercy of the Americans."

"And that still troubles you?"

"Very much. You have ridden among the colonies. You have seen them just as I have. What do you see of Mexico in any of them? They have their own government, and it is a government modeled after that of the United States. They have begun to build schools, but they do not teach from Mexican books. They do not even teach our language."

"There are Mexican settlements. Bexar remains almost entirely Mexican. So does La Bahía."

"Islands in an American ocean. When the tide rises, it will wash over them, and nothing Mexican will be left. It is illegal now for

327

more Americans to come into Texas, yet more come every day. The law is like an old watchdog that has no teeth. With the few troops we have, trying to stop them is like trying to stop the geese from going south in the winter."

Díaz observed Zaragosa's son Manuel in a corral, riding a half-broken colt around and around. "If we do not stop them, what will become of your son, and those who come after him? He will be living in an American land, not a Mexican one. If they let him stay here at all."

Zaragosa placed a hand on Díaz's shoulder and nodded toward his front door. "Come on into the house. Let us drink to your safe journey."

Inside, Zaragosa called to his wife Elvira. She brought a bottle of wine made from Zaragosa's own vines. Díaz tried not to stare at her, but he could not help himself, for he had always considered her a rare beauty, with olive skin, raven-black hair and dark eyes that would melt a man into his boots. Would that he had such a woman to come home to at night, to share his supper and his bed. It pained him to think of her someday losing this good home to some grasping American, of becoming a penniless refugee thrown out upon the road. That, he feared, was the fate of all Mexicans in Texas unless the steady invasion could be stopped and the Americans pushed back beyond their own border.

Zaragosa poured three glasses of wine, passing one to Elvira and one to Díaz. He said, "You do not see the Americans as I have seen them. You have never made friends among them."

"I tried, as you will remember. My family tried. All they did was enslave us and kill my sister."

"Are there not Mexicans who would do the same? You judge the many by the few."

"I can only judge by what I have seen, and I have seen that side of their nature. You have been spared that view, my lieutenant, or you would not be so complacent."

"I am afraid this is a subject on which we will always disagree, old friend. Let us talk of more pleasant things. Let us talk of Mexico and better times."

Díaz lifted his glass in salute. "To Mexico, where at last I will see no more Americans."

"To Mexico, and to the constitution. When it is restored there will be no more fighting, no need for rebellion."

Díaz sipped, then raised his glass again. "To Santa Anna, who will restore the constitution."

Zaragosa hesitated, only reluctantly joining the toast. "To Santa Anna. May he be a man of his word, a man devoted to freedom and justice, and not simply another Bustamante."

Zaragosa's attitude caught Díaz by surprise. "Do you doubt him, my lieutenant? They say he is a great patriot."

"But a patriot to what? To Mexico, or to himself?" Zaragosa finished his wine and stared absently through the open window where sunshine lay warm and benevolent over his ripening fields. "If he is only for himself, as so many others have been, I tremble for Mexico. I tremble for Texas."

The peace which followed Mexía's withdrawal of troops was a happy illusion which would not long endure. That fall Andrew Lewis was called to attend a San Felipe convention representing the Texas settlements to appraise existing conditions and suggest improvements. Of the three Lewis brothers, he was considered most likely to sit still for such a session. The restless Michael would probably only stray off somewhere looking for country he had never seen. James was considered still too young and unsettled to ponder with seriousness the affairs of state. Andrew was the statesman, the one most likely to see all sides of a problem and find a path toward settlement agreeable to all parties.

Though conceived with good intentions, the convention planted new seeds of mistrust that would eventually flower into conflict. Such a convention was typically American but contrary to Mexican custom. That the Mexican town of San Antonio de Bexar failed to send delegates might have been recognized as a portent of the reaction in Mexico itself, had the convention been inclined toward that sort of introspection.

Andrew was not surprised to find a considerable division of opinion. A faction largely of the newer Texans talked independence among themselves but did not submit such a radical notion to a vote. The more conservative old settlers, including himself, favored accommodation with Mexico under the original constitution. They named a committee to write a resolution asking Mexico to rescind the anti-immigration law of 1830, which had been largely ignored after the first months but under which later immigrants were considered illegal and not entitled to citizenship. They also asked for lower tariffs on certain necessities and for the creation of a school fund.

The thorniest issue was a request that

Texas be given statehood separate from Coahuila. Though opposed by some of the old settlers, it won majority approval. Andrew cast a vote in favor but wondered how it would fare with Mexican politicians to whom even such a convention itself smacked of rebellion.

His concerns turned out to be well-founded. Don José de la Garza, political chief in Bexar, wrote the governor of Coahuila that the request was but a symptom of mounting insurrection, that "a true Mexican can but bitterly deplore his misfortune and feel sore at the foreign hand that has come boldly to rob him of his rights." In his view, an assemblage to voice public sentiment was tantamount to revolution, for inevitably that was where such meetings had always led in Mexico.

Andrew rode home from the convention feeling that it had done good work, in the main. When all the Lewis families gathered on a Sunday afternoon, which was their custom, he told Michael, James, and cousin Frank, "I think they'll know down in Mexico that we're still loyal to the government, that all we want is for Texas to blossom and grow."

Not until much later would he discern that the effect had been the opposite, that slowly but certainly the stage was being prepared for conflagration.

■ ■ ■ ■

PART III:
TO ARMS! TO ARMS!
1835

■ ■ ■ ■

CHAPTER 19

James worried about Annie. After five years in Texas, she still gave no sign that she was ever going to marry. He could see himself in his old age, supporting an old-maid sister who never had been totally satisfied with anything he did and would probably outlive him just for the cussedness of it. Times, he would almost be satisfied to see her marry Isaac Blackwood. Isaac still came around now and again, doing little favors for Annie, bringing her things like jugs of honey or bear grease for cooking or an occasional backstrap and hindquarter of venison — anything to earn a smile from her. He would go away as happy as a dog granted a few pats on the head.

Nor was Isaac the only suitor. Others came from as far away as San Felipe, for men still outnumbered women in the Texas colonies. Annie gave them even less encouragement than she offered Isaac.

James was pretty sure he knew what the trouble was. She still yearned after Sly Shipman, though she had not seen or heard from him once since he had ridden away that summer day not long after the battle at Velasco. She would occasionally talk about her other suitors. She never mentioned Shipman's name. That was how James knew.

But he had worries more pressing than Annie's lack of romance. He was well aware that the pot was bubbling in Mexico, that sooner or later it would boil over, and that Texas was likely to be scalded. Each traveler passing through the colony, especially if he came from Bexar or the direction of Mexico, was closely questioned for news, for any information that might yield some hint of what was to come. James would not have been overly surprised if he had looked up from his plowing one day and had seen the whole Mexican army marching down the hill toward him.

A second Texan convention, conducted in 1833, had been bolder than the first. Andrew again had gone as a delegate. Into this one strode a new figure, a delegate from San Augustine who towered over most other men. He was Sam Houston, still less than forty years old but already a former governor of Tennessee, recently come into Texas after a long sojourn among the Cherokee Indians in Arkansas. His reputation had preceded him. Even so, Andrew had been surprised and impressed by Houston's eloquence and bearing, his physical size, and by the way he seemed to dominate any room into which he walked.

But there had been something about Houston which bothered Andrew. "There's Stephen F. Austin," he had told James, "the man who brought the first of us into Texas, the man who's held Texas together all these years with sweat and blood and guts, the man we owe everything to. Yet when Sam Houston comes in, it's like Austin isn't even there anymore. It's like he doesn't matter. Everybody's attention goes to Houston."

James had said, "From what I heard, Houston was a great scrapper back in Tennessee. Maybe he's what Texas needs to keep Mexico from overrunnin' us."

"What Texas needs is a calm and steady hand. Austin has been real good for us all these years."

But Texas was to lose Austin's good services during a most critical period in its existence as part of the Mexican nation. The convention not only asked again for separate statehood, apart from Coahuila, but wrote a constitution for that proposed state over

Austin's objections. Against his better judgment, Austin carried it to Mexico City on behalf of the colonies he represented, in company with his friend Lorenzo de Zavala, a member of the Mexican cabinet. As before, it provoked a hostile reaction. It was widely regarded as part of a plot to separate Texas from the rest of Mexico and deliver it over to the United States. Austin was imprisoned, and de Zavala fled Mexico City for Texas. For a year and a half, Austin languished in a dungeon that had been used during the Spanish Inquisition, while Texans quarreled over where to turn and what to do.

The news out of Mexico was discouraging. Santa Anna had revealed the ugly side of his face. After coming to power on a promise of reinstating the constitution of 1824, he repudiated it. The state government of Coahuila had made welcome concessions to Texas: legalization of immigration, lower tariffs, improvement in the mails. But Santa Anna nullified all this. He disbanded Mexico's republican congress and set up a new one subservient to his demands. He abolished the state legislatures and local *ayuntamientos,* declaring that all rules in the future would be written in Mexico City, and that the pen would be his own. When the liberal state of Zacatecas rebelled, he marched in with a force of five thousand men and laid to waste whatever stood in his way, leaving bloody scenes of wholesale rape and murder as an object lesson for any in Mexico who would defy his will. Long a student of France's Bonaparte, he declared himself the Napoleon of the West and turned his attention to the restive north, to Coahuila, which had fallen into chaos and civil war.

He dispatched his brother-in-law, General Martín Perfecto de Cós, with a large body of soldiers to reconquer Coahuila and bring it under the military dictatorship centered in Mexico City. Ahead of Cós, Coahuilan officials and other refugees poured across the Rio Grande, bringing with them their fears and their hatred for Santa Anna. These emotions spread like an epidemic across Texas, finding ready reception among American settlers, who by now were fearful about their own future.

In Texas, after the relative calm which had followed the Anahuac and Velasco affairs, it seemed that history had come full circle, for the central government reestablished its customs offices in those two places. Citizens resisted, blood was spilled, and men were thrown in jail. The time was ripe for William Barret Travis and Sam Houston and others of the war-party persuasion who had long advocated that Texas should break free of the Mexican yoke. Stephen F. Austin could no longer bring his sober influence to bear on Mexico's behalf. He remained in prison, charged with treason for having advocated a constitution. Time was ripe also for those in Mexico who called for taking Texas back from the Americans. The voices of reason and good will were smothered on both sides by the call for war.

James Lewis plowed his field and harvested his garden and cared for his few cattle, but he did so with a needling restlessness, his eyes going often to the horizon. He knew Mexico had remanned its abandoned garrisons. It seemed only a question of time until the soldiers marched across the land to establish for once and all the supremacy of Mexico over these immigrant Texans. Santa Anna had made it clear in Zacatecas and Coahuila: All who opposed him, in even a minor way, would be crushed beneath the boots of his army. He took no prisoners and granted no mercy. No longer was he the liberal savior of his nation. He was its emperor, and he ruled by blood and fire.

James found it hard to accept the relative

calm of his brother Andrew, who spoke little of the troubles but took care of his work, planting and cultivating his fields as if he had no concern for what was happening to the south, out of his sight, as if he knew he would remain on this piece of land forever. "You know how many revolutions there have already been in Mexico," he told a nervous James. "There are a lot of people down there who hate Santa Anna. Chances are that they will rise up against him before the trouble ever gets this far north. Anyway, we're farmers, not soldiers. If they would only let Austin out of jail —"

But James suspected his brother harbored fears he did not want to reveal lest they frighten the women and children. Rumors that summer of 1835 had spread through Texas like a prairie fire, and gloom had laid itself across the land like smoke from that consuming blaze. If wild reports were to be believed, Santa Anna was marching north with ten thousand men, and Mexican agents were out among the horseback Indian tribes, firing them up for war against the Texans.

Michael's reaction was different from Andrew's, as James would expect it to be. Michael continued his work, but he did it with a nervous energy, attacking the ground

343

with the plow as if it were a weapon of war. Like James, he paused often to look to the horizon. James had learned to recognize the symptoms. One morning Marie would rise up to find herself in bed alone, her husband gone to God knew where, to return God knew when. She must sense that herself, for she had been through it before. But Marie gave no sign, nor did Petra and Annie betray any foreboding of the events that were rapidly overtaking them.

James wondered sometimes if the women might not be the strongest of them all.

The crops were almost in when Elizandro Zaragosa arrived one Sunday afternoon with his son Manuel. All the Lewises were gathered at Michael and Marie's cabin. Michael strode out in front of the others to greet his old friend. "Mighty happy to see you, Elizandro. Get down and join us. We'll be havin' supper directly."

Zaragosa dismounted wearily, his face dark with trouble. "I am not happy to be here, Miguel. It is a bad wind that has blown us to this place."

Mordecai rushed shouting to the side of his young friend Manuel, then went quiet as he sensed the gravity in the boy's manner. He shook Manuel's hand and asked,

"What's the matter?" Manuel looked to his father.

Zaragosa stared westward, in the direction from which he had come. "We left in the middle of the night. Ugartechea is in the garrison in Bexar. He has a list — men to be arrested — men who have spoken out — men to be shot as traitors to Santa Anna."

Michael and Andrew exchanged knowing glances. Michael said, "You're on the list?"

Zaragosa nodded.

"And what of the boy? He's not old enough to've gotten mixed up in politics."

"He is sixteen. He is old enough to be shot in my place if they do not find me." To Andrew's and James's doubting looks, he said, "You do not know them. But I have been a soldier. I know them much too well."

Michael asked, "What about the rest of your family?"

"I do not believe they will harm Elvira or the young ones, but I fear for Manuel."

Andrew said, "You're mighty welcome to stay here with us until the storm blows over."

Zaragosa shook his head. "The storm is barely begun. It will come here if we cannot stop it."

"Then where do you plan to go?"

"I am not sure. Resistance is building in

many places. I go to find that resistance and join it."

"But your boy," James argued. "He's not old enough to go a-fightin'."

Manuel stood firm. "I am old enough to fight beside my father."

Zaragosa studied his son with pride. "He thinks he is, but of course he is not. I would leave him here if you would keep him. Even if the soldiers come, they do not know him. He can use another name."

"Papa," Manuel argued, "I want to go with you."

But he could see in his father's eyes that this was not to be. He lowered his chin in sadness. Mordecai put his arm around Manuel's shoulder. He did not speak; he did not have to.

Next morning, when the family awakened, Elizandro Zaragosa had already gone. And Michael Lewis had gone with him.

As the crops were harvested and farmers were freed from the tyranny of the fields, they began to gather in various places, rifles in their hands, unsure what to do but knowing they should do something. Many of them passed James's place, and he itched to go with them, perhaps to find where Michael had gone. But he held back, awaiting direction, awaiting a call.

As if in warning of calamity to come, a mysterious comet lighted the Texas skies that fall, a spectral visitor that chilled brave hearts and set the superstitious to talking about the end of the world. James wondered aloud if it was a bad omen.

Andrew said, "It's just a comet. It doesn't mean anything."

Cousin Frank declared confidently, "Books say comets've been flyin' around ever since Eve pulled the apple stunt on Adam. Even if it meant anything, they're probably seein' it the same in Mexico as we do here. Maybe it means bad luck for the Mexicans instead of for us."

Frank would be the one to know, for he was always the reader in the Lewis family. He knew all manner of things that were of no earthly use to a working man.

James had about made up his mind to take his rifle and go in search of Michael when the wagons came. He and Annie were at Marie's, helping her and Mordecai and Manuel harvest her garden. The wagons came into sight over a rise from the east. James looked up from the work and wondered idly who would be taking wagons westward. That trail led toward San Antonio de Bexar, where Cós and his troops held the presidio, awaiting reinforcements from the interior before venturing out into the colonies to assert Santa Anna's control. Most of the traffic James had seen lately had been coming *from* Bexar, not traveling toward it. But he put his curiosity aside and bent to the work again, for it would take the wagons some time to get here.

He noticed, after a bit, that Marie was becoming excited. "It cannot be," she said, then lapsed into French, something she occasionally did when she forgot herself. She hurried to the rail fence. Though she wore a bonnet, she shaded her eyes with her hand. "Papa?" Her voice was barely a whisper at first, then a shout. "Papa!"

James squinted. Surely enough, he recognized old Baptiste Villaret on the lead wagon, driving a pair of big, strong mules. Marie scaled the fence, skirt flaring, jumped down on the other side and went running. Villaret climbed from the wagon and trotted stiffly to meet her, limping from the arthritis in his deteriorating knees. "Marie!"

They grabbed each other. They were still embracing, tears flowing down their cheeks without shame when James reached them. He had taken his time. For the moment it was as if he did not exist, so far as father and daughter were concerned. They had not

348

set eyes on each other in all the years Marie had lived here.

James heard Annie's voice behind him. "I wish you'd look who's comin' yonder."

The second wagon trailed some distance behind, but James recognized the driver. Sly Shipman. He glanced back at Annie. A broad smile brightened her face to a degree he had not seen in years. But she brought it under control as Shipman neared. By the time he halted the mules and climbed down, the smile was gone. She looked almost severe.

"Back already?" she asked. He had been gone three years.

Marie called her children about her. It was the first time they had met their grandfather. Old Villaret, who seemed grayer and more bent than when James had last seen him, embraced each in turn, speaking French to them and taking delight in their responses. Marie had seen to it that all learned to know French and Spanish as well as English. That was part of their heritage. It had always struck James strange, the times he had heard French coming from young Mordecai's lips. Mordecai was like a young copy of Michael, and James could not picture Michael ever speaking French.

James shook hands with Shipman. Annie

had already spoken all the welcome she was going to give him, at least for now. She moved back to share in the glow that had built around Marie and her father and the youngsters. She had met Villaret briefly five years ago, when she and James and Frank and his family had passed through Natchitoches on their way to Texas.

Shipman's eyes were on Annie. He asked James, "Has she been mad for the whole three years?"

James had to smile. "I've seen her a few times when she wasn't."

"I was hopin' —" Shipman shrugged and said no more.

Marie had gotten over her first excitement. Clinging to her father's arm, she asked, "Papa, why have you come? After all this time, why are you here?"

"To bring the wagons," the old Frenchman replied. "To take all of you to safety in Natchitoches."

"To safety? I do not understand."

"We hear many things in Natchitoches, bad things from Mexico. Your mama and me, we think it is too dangerous for you to stay here. I want you to come with me back to Louisiana. Santa Anna will not cross the Sabine."

"But, Papa, this is our home."

"If you stay it could be your grave."

"There is one grave here already." She pointed up the slope to a little fenced-off spot where a baby lay buried. "We have paid much for this place. We do not leave it."

Villaret stared at her, studying the rigid lines of resolve in her face. "I will talk to Michael."

"Michael is not here. That is another reason I cannot go. I have to wait here for Michael."

"Where is he gone?"

James thought for a moment he saw tears in Marie's eyes, before she blinked them away. "I do not know. Somewhere to fight, I think. I could not go and not know what has become of him."

Villaret put his arm back around her. "Perhaps. We will talk about it some more later. Now, let me love my grandchildren again." They all began walking toward the cabin.

Annie started after them, but Shipman called her. "Annie, just a minute." She stopped but did not turn. He had to walk around to face her. "Annie, he's serious. *I'm* serious. It's dangerous for you-all to stay here with a war fixin' to bust out around you. That's why we came with the wagons, so we can haul you out of here."

"You heard Marie. This is her home. She's raised her family here, buried a child here."

"*You* ain't raised a family here."

"And not likely to, either." Her face creased. "It's twice now you've ridden off and left me. Why didn't you just stay gone?"

"Because I'm scared for you. Because I don't want anything to happen to you."

"And why would you care?"

His face clouded with impatience. "Because, damn it, woman, I love you!"

Her face softened. "Say that again."

"You heard me. What do you want me to do, get down on my knees?"

"No, I heard you. I just wanted to be sure you heard yourself." She smiled and held out her hands. "I don't know one good reason I should love you, Sly Shipman. I can think of a dozen good reasons why I shouldn't."

James saw that he was not needed. He walked away and left them standing there trying to crush the breath from one another.

Time did not change Marie's mind about leaving. All her father's efforts at persuasion went for nothing, though he kept trying for several days. He begged James and Andrew, Frank, Hope, and Annie to talk to her, but it was to no avail. Marie had as much stubborn determination as if she had been born a Lewis rather than married into the name.

They had considerable company during the days that Baptiste Villaret remained, enjoying his grandchildren, hoping their mother might yet change her mind. Horsemen rode by singly and in small groups, all moving toward San Antonio de Bexar.

A familiar face was among them, a portly, one-eyed minister named Fairweather. James remembered him from Velasco. Andrew knew him from much farther back. James asked him, "You fixin' to go fight, preacher?"

Fairweather solemnly replied, "Big events are afoot, young gentlemen. I fear that there will shortly be much need for prayer. I carry the Lord's word where it is needed the most."

A chilling report had come from the town of Gonzales. First blood had been drawn. A force had marched out from the Bexar garrison to retrieve a cannon the government had lent some years earlier to the citizens of Gonzales for defense against Indian attack. The Texans had raised a homemade banner emblazoned with the words *Come and Take It.* Rifles had spoken an even bolder message. The cannon had been loaded with scrap iron and pieces of chain and fired in the direction of the soldiers. The Mexicans had retreated, trailing blood.

Texas had had her Lexington. There could no longer be doubt. The war was on.

James felt a strong urge to saddle Walker and ride with some of the men who passed by. They were on their way to drive Cós out of Bexar, they claimed. But he waited, thinking Marie might yet decide to leave, for if she did, Hope would go, and Annie and all the children, at least. But Marie showed no sign of weakening.

"Michael is probably at Bexar now," she said sternly. "If he were to come looking for us, he would not know where we had gone."

James decided he had stayed as long as he could. He was at the shed, brushing Walker's back to get the bay horse ready for the trip, when Isaac Blackwood rode up. Isaac had his long rifle across his lap, blankets tied behind the cantle of his saddle, a bag of "possibles" hanging down on one side. James sensed at a glance that he, too, was headed for Bexar.

Isaac watched James throw a blanket and saddle upon Walker's back. He asked, "You fixin' to go somewhere?"

"Same as you, I reckon. I'm goin' to Bexar."

"You'd be welcome to ride with me if you

don't mind bein' in the company of a Black-wood."

James nodded. "I reckon we're all in this together."

Isaac looked toward the cabin. "I came by to speak to Annie. She here?"

She was. But so was Sly Shipman. The two had been in the garden together just now, gathering up some vegetables. James did not see them at the moment.

He slid back the rail that served as a gate, led Walker outside and swung up into the saddle. "I expect Annie's in the cabin. We'll go see."

As they rode around the dog-run, he saw Annie and Shipman in each other's arms, oblivious to anything or anyone around them. Annie freed her hand and opened the door to her bedroom, then led Shipman inside and closed the door behind them.

James felt his face turn warm, and he glanced at Isaac. Isaac looked as if a mule had kicked him. He swallowed hard and tore his gaze away from the closed door. "I reckon I'll be goin' on to Bexar," he said weakly. "You comin'?"

James had already said his good-byes. "I'm comin'." He brought his rifle up into his lap and touched his heels to Walker's ribs.

CHAPTER 20

James found Isaac Blackwood to be a quiet traveling companion. Isaac spoke no more than was necessary, riding along with his mind elsewhere, holding counsel only with himself. James suspected he was thinking of Annie much of the time, grieving over lost opportunity. James also suspected there had never actually been any real opportunity. Whatever her faults of temper and impatience might be, his sister was too bright to let herself be trapped into an alliance with a Blackwood, even a benign Blackwood such as Isaac seemed to be. James was relieved when on their first night's camp some other volunteers saw their fire and joined them. Now he had someone to talk to for the duration of the trip.

He found that the old Mexican stone and adobe town of San Antonio de Bexar was surrounded by arms-bearing citizens like himself, most impatiently waiting to do battle. General Cós's Mexican troops were well entrenched. Part of them had taken up positions in an abandoned and partially crumbling mission which had been used as a fortress from time to time ever since Mexico's first efforts to free herself from Spain. Because of the trees which had grown in profusion around it, the place was known by the Spanish name for cotton-wood: *Alamo.*

The sight of so many guns reminded him uncomfortably of Velasco, three years earlier.

He found little here to indicate much of a military organization. These were volunteers. Few had military training or experience at combat beyond in some cases a skirmish or two with Indians. They had come here not so much an army as a ragtag collection of independent individualists who would follow an order only so long as it pleased them to do so. They were free men not suited to any high degree of discipline, one reason they would never be good and willing citizens of a militaristic and authoritarian Mexico.

The bloodletting at Velasco preyed heavily on his mind and did not let him share in the eagerness of so many to open a full-scale battle with the Mexican soldiers. He remembered too well the smell of gunpowder and warm blood, the taste of fear in his mouth. He would fight when the time came, but he would not relish it nor glory in taking other men's lives. Velasco had burned that foolishness out of him forever.

His immediate concern was to find Michael. Isaac Blackwood had come across a couple of acquaintances from an earlier time when he and his brothers had squatted near Nacogdoches, and James left him in their camp to reminisce. He set about visiting every encampment he could find, inquiring about his brother.

He found to his surprise that Stephen F. Austin had returned. James had heard nothing about Austin's release from imprisonment in Mexico City. He had met the impresario a couple of times in San Felipe, but he would hardly have recognized him had he not known beforehand who he was. The Austin he saw in camp was haggard and pale and gray. The shadow of death lay in eyes that James had remembered as lively and quick. Prison had left him a broken man of just forty-two years. To honor him for what he had done on behalf of Texas, he had been chosen to be general of this Army of the People. It was done against his wishes, for he was not a military man and had little knowledge of battle tactics. As he had always done when unpleasant necessity had reared its head, he had accepted the responsibility, only to find a considerable division among the volunteers who ringed the town. Some wanted to try to negotiate Cós and the troops out of Bexar. But others, probably a majority, could smell blood and wanted to see it run. Most of them had not been at Velasco.

Austin was inclined toward negotiation, for that had always been his specialty, but that clearly was not to be. Cós seemed to have the advantage: numerical superiority and a strong, fortified position. But the farmers and frontiersmen whose rifles bristled around this old mission town had something more potent: a fire in the belly and a yearning to be free of Mexico. Even Austin, who had so long advocated conciliation and accommodation, had come to bitter disillusionment during his long incarceration. Independence was the only course for Texas now, he agreed, independence from the internal power struggles and the vacillating policies of an unpredictable government that too often operated for the enrichment and the egos of those who happened to rule at any given moment, as Santa Anna did now.

James found someone else, too. Elizandro Zaragosa was in charge of a company of Mexican volunteers of republican sentiments, men who still remembered the high principles of the Mexican people in their proudest time, in the winning of their independence from Spain. Too often they had seen those principles trampled by one tyrant or another who managed for a while to grab the power of the central government. Santa Anna was but the latest.

James shook hands with the Mexican farmer and ex-soldier, old friend to the Lewis brothers. He felt a warm respect for the courage of this man who had come back to his home in defiance of the proscription list that named him as one of several to be captured and punished for their principles. He looked quickly about the Mexican camp, half expecting to find Michael there.

"Do you know where Michael is at?" he asked anxiously. "We haven't heard from him."

Zaragosa shook his head. "He was at Gonzales when last we were together. He rode away with some other men. I think they were on their way to attack the garrison at La Bahía." Zaragosa tried to keep his grace, not to appear too eager. "What of my son Manuel? Tell me about him."

"He's fine. Him and Mordecai, they're the best friends you ever saw. Where one goes, the other follows. He's growin' up into a fine man. How about the rest of your family?"

"They are well. I should be with them now, but this is more important. If we can force Cós to surrender, to leave Texas, it will be a big defeat for Santa Anna. Cós is his brother-in-law, you know."

James nodded. He had heard that. "You don't suppose Michael is here somewhere, in one of these camps?"

"I cannot say he is not, for there are so many I have not seen them all."

"I'll keep lookin'. You be careful."

"And you also."

James hunted until he was sure he had visited every encampment in the vicinity of Bexar. They ranged from company strength in a few cases to little groups of as few as two to four men. He lost track of the number but knew it ran to seven or eight hundred. People said more than a thousand Mexican soldiers were garrisoned in the town.

He finally had to concede that his search for Michael was futile; his brother was not here. He found Isaac Blackwood and decided the company Isaac had affiliated himself with was as good as any. Isaac asked him no foolish questions; James supposed the answer showed in his face. Isaac said only, "Michael has always known how to take care of himself."

The Reverend Fairweather worked his way from one camp to another, calling men to listen to the Word, offering up prayers for those who felt the need. James had been a disappointment to his mother in the matter of church attendance, but he felt drawn to Fairweather's service. The man's message left him with a measure of peace for a little while.

He felt himself as ready as he would ever be for an assault upon the town. The rest of the men seemed equally primed. But the leadership waited, holding the existing positions, hoping the Mexicans could be starved into submission. Days passed, and dragged into weeks. The men had come to do battle but found themselves conducting a siege instead. That siege stretched into winter's cold. Rations ran short because there was no formal organization to provide for so many men. Volunteers gradually began pulling away to see about their families, left in isolated cabins and tiny settlements all over American Texas. Those who remained grumbled and fretted and shivered against the north winds, for most had left home in warm weather and had no heavy clothing to shelter them from November's cold.

There was talk about a third Texas consultation back in San Felipe setting up a provisional government. James had little interest in politics and paid but scant attention. He did hear, however, that Stephen Austin and two others had been selected as commissioners to travel to the United States and plead for men, munitions, and money to aid the Texan cause. This was work for which Austin was better fitted than the conduct of a military campaign, though his fading health would make traveling dangerous for him. Austin gave up his command of the shrinking Texan army and took the commission without complaint. He had never hesitated to give his all for Texas, and he did not shirk this final duty. The command at Bexar passed to Edward Burleson. Still, the men waited, for their officers thought the Mexican fortifications appeared too formidable. Wait, they said. When the Mexicans had starved long enough, they would lay down their weapons and abandon the town.

James acknowledged that this was probably the wisest course; it was certainly the safest one, but the inactivity, the cold, and his own hunger caused him to begin considering going home as so many others had already done. He was cheered a little when sixty-four men of the New Orleans Grays marched into the main encampment, fresh from a voyage to the mouth of the Brazos on the schooner *Columbus.* They brought with them fresh provisions and military stores contributed by the people of New Orleans. It was the first sign James had seen that people elsewhere, outside of Texas, had an interest in what was happening here.

A few days later a tall, grim-faced adventurer named Jim Bowie took out a patrol. Bowie, an old hand in Texas and Mexico, was already a legend for the huge knife he carried on his hip and for the many desperate fights he was reputed to have won with it. His patrol confronted a Mexican pack train, thought to be bringing fresh provisions to the besieged troops, or possibly even money to pay the men. In a brief, bloody battle, the Mexicans lost some fifty men and all the mules. The victorious Texans tore into the packs, expecting to find food and ammunition, or perhaps gold and silver. They found only grass, cut to sustain the Mexicans' animals inside the city. But the skirmish aroused excitement in the encampment and gave James the resolve to stay a little longer.

The officers were still not sure. To storm the fortifications would result in a terrible slaughter on both sides, some said. The Mexicans were not good fighters and would quickly give up, others argued. They debated at length while the men waited, impatient and angry over the indecision. Burleson and James W. Fannin favored giving up the siege for the winter and retreating to La Bahía, also known as Goliad, to await reinforcements before hitting Cós again in the spring.

Then came a gangly old Texas veteran named Ben Milam, recently escaped from imprisonment in Mexico, embittered as Austin had been embittered, and out of patience with the long delay. He went about preaching a sermon of war and gathering a growing entourage. As Mexican patriots once had raised a *grito* against Spain, he raised a cry of his own. "Who," he thundered, "will go with old Ben Milam into San Antonio?"

A great shout went up. James, caught in the momentum, surprised himself by adding his voice to it. The officers who had counseled caution were helpless to stop the pent-up energy that erupted in the wake of Ben Milam's challenge.

The storming of Bexar began in the dark

of a December early morning, sweeping past Cós's pickets in a rattle of small-arms fire. In little groups the Texans pushed forward, battling at close range for house after house against a stubborn Mexican resistance. Once into it, James felt his blood running hot, and whatever fears he carried into the fight were drowned by his fevered excitement. He heard the exultant yelling of the Texas fighters on either side of him and the defiant shouts of the Mexican defenders, holding their ground until they were killed or swept over.

As daylight came, a pall of dark smoke hung over the edges of the town. Mexican artillery shook the walls with its thunder, and the high, flat rattle of musket fire showed the extent of the battle. James joined other Texans in gathering the spent Mexican cannonballs to be fired back into the fortifications from which they had come. Nearly exhausted, he took rest when he could, rousing himself to go again when the call came to advance.

It was a slow, murderous campaign fought by fits and starts, often hand to hand, knife to knife, Texan rifles and Mexican *escopetas* firing at point-blank range. When artillery and musketry made the streets too dangerous for the men to cross, they used logs for battering rams and drove holes through the stone and adobe walls, fighting from room to room, house to house, inexorably closing in on the Mexicans' main entrenchments. The Texas fighters might have been farmers, but they were also hunters, and their marksmanship was as deadly here as it had been at Velasco. Wherever an enemy soldier showed his head, he was likely to lose it.

The battle continued for four days and was finished without the fiery leadership of the man who had precipitated it. On the afternoon of the third day, old Ben Milam was leading a charge across a street and fell with a bullet in his brain. The battle went on, even as Milam was being buried in the courtyard of the house of the Veramendis, family of Jim Bowie's late wife.

James had known nothing of Ben Milam before Milam had issued his challenge to the men, but he felt the loss as if the old fire-eater had been a lifelong friend. And it brought home to him once again the high cost of war. But the die had been cast. There was no backing away, no retreat now, or all those who died would have died for nothing.

So the fight went on, the Texan vise gradually tightening yard by yard, plaza by plaza, house by house, until on the fifth day a white flag went up in the Alamo. General Cós was surrendering to a force a third the size of his own.

James was caught up for a time in the euphoria of victory. A captured Mexican blanket wrapped around his shoulders, he and Isaac Blackwood and others danced in a dirt street to the music of a soldier's flute. But the glow began to fade when they came upon Elizandro Zaragosa and found the former soldier ashen-faced, his arm bound with white cloth through which a red stain had seeped. Zaragosa sat on the ground, his back propped against the tall wheel of an ox cart. His Mexican compatriots who had fought against the forces of Santa Anna were gathered around him, not mixing with the victorious Anglo Texans. James wondered if this was by their own choice or if they had found that the Texans were not quite ready to accept them even though they had fought side by side. He suspected it was some of both. Though the men of two races who had taken Bexar shared a wish to be free of tyranny, they were of different cultures. They looked differently and spoke different languages. No matter how much they might share, there was a line over which neither would cross.

James knelt at Zaragosa's side. "I didn't know you'd been shot. At least it was just your arm."

Zaragosa tried to smile, but the effort did not succeed. His pain was obvious. "I have been shot once before in this same arm. Always it has been stiff. This will heal."

Isaac had not shaved since they had left the Colorado. He had regained much of the rough backwoodsman look James remembered best. Zaragosa remembered him, too, for he had encountered the Blackwoods before. He gave Isaac a look that said he did not trust him, even though they had fought on the same side. He did not know Isaac well enough to see any difference between him and his two brothers.

Nor did Isaac know Zaragosa well enough to differentiate between him and the soldiers they had fought against. They were all of a dark skin, speaking an alien language. He stood back distrustingly while James visited with the man who had long been a friend to Michael and Andrew.

The smell of smoke still clung heavily over the town. James's eyes burned from it, and he had to rub them. In doing so, he rubbed in dirt from his sleeve and made matters worse. "They say Cós has agreed to take all the soldiers out of Texas and never come back. I guess the fightin' is over."

Zaragosa frowned darkly. "Cós can agree, but will Santa Anna?" He shook his head. "I think not. He does not give up Texas so easily. I think he will be back. I think we must watch and be ready." He rubbed the arm gingerly, flinching a little. "I must go home now. Elvira will know how to treat my arm. Do you go home too, Jaime?"

James nodded. "I don't see no reason to stay."

"Would you please tell my son that he can come back to his family? We are safe, for now."

For now. James felt much of victory's glow go out of him. Zaragosa's pessimism was contagious. "You really think we'll have to fight again?"

"We have beaten only a little of Santa Anna's army. When the grass comes in the spring and his horses can graze, I think Santa Anna will come. I think he will bring more army. We will watch, and we will wait. I hope we will be ready." He reached out with his good hand. "*Buena suerte,* Jaime. I think we will see you and your rifle again in the spring."

Walking away from Zaragosa's camp, Isaac said, "He's liable to be right. We're liable to have to do the whole thing over again when the grass rises."

"Maybe not," James said, trying to show more confidence than he felt. "I've sure had enough of this. Maybe the Mexicans have, too."

The Reverend Fairweather held a prayer service for those who wanted to express thanksgiving. James and Isaac bowed their heads. When the meeting was done, Isaac said, "I expect you'll be goin' home now?"

"I don't see any need to stay. We'd just as well ride together if you want to."

Isaac shook his head. "I got no reason to hurry. Ain't nothin' much waitin' for me there." In the distance, someone was calling a group of militiamen to attention. The response was ragged and slow. Isaac pointed his chin in that direction. "There's some that agree with Zaragosa. They think we ain't seen the last of the Mexican army. I've been studyin' on joinin' a company that's goin' to follow Cós's soldiers all the way down to the Rio Bravo to be damned sure they cross over and don't come back."

"I heard he signed a paper sayin' he would never take up arms against Texas again."

"A paper don't mean nothin'. Anyway, Santy Anna wasn't here to sign it. So I think I'll just stay with the boys. Beats settin' around the cabin all winter watchin' Finis and Luke and Nelly fight." He looked away, toward the east. "Just one thing — you know the boy that's come with me from time to time, over to see your sister?"

James nodded. "Finis's boy?"

"Maybe Finis's boy, maybe mine. If anything was to happen to me — if the Mexican army should come back, I wisht you'd see that the boy gets out all right."

James swallowed. It had never occurred to him that the boy might be Isaac's. But remembering Nelly, he could not be overly surprised. "I'll do what I can."

"And tell your sister —"

James waited for Isaac to finish, but Isaac had said all there was. Isaac turned and walked away from him.

He did not know what to expect when he returned home. He thought Baptiste Villaret might have managed to convince Marie to flee with him to Louisiana. If she had, the others no doubt would have gone as well: Annie, Petra, the children.

But as he rode up to his cabin, he saw smoke curling from the chimney. One of Baptiste's wagons stood out by the pole pens James had put up for his few livestock. "Annie!" he called. "Annie, it's me!"

She came out onto the dog-run into a cold December wind. "James?"

He had not shaved in weeks because of the weather. He knew he probably looked more like a Blackwood than a Lewis. But she came running as he stepped down from the saddle. She threw her arms around him in joy. "We heard there were a great many killed. We were afraid for you."

"There were more killed of them than of us. We won, Annie. It's over."

She pulled away and looked beyond him, as if hoping to see someone else. "How about Michael? Is he with you?"

"I never found Michael. He wasn't there. Hasn't he come home yet?"

She shook her head. "Marie hasn't heard a word. We don't know whether he's dead or alive. It isn't like Michael not to let us know something."

"Yes it is." Andrew had told him of Michael's penchant for riding away and staying gone, of looking always for some new place he had not yet seen. "I'm afraid it's *just* like him."

"But there was fightin' in other places besides Bexar. We heard there was a fight at La Bahía. He might've been killed."

"Does Marie believe he's dead?"

"No. She says she knows he's alive. She

says she can sense it."

"Then listen to Marie and not your fears." He looked around. "I figured I'd find Sly Shipman with you. Where's he at?"

She looked at the ground. "He's gone, wouldn't you know? He went back with Baptiste."

He saw the hurt in her eyes. "I'm sorry, Annie. I had figured you and him would be married by now."

The hurt turned to a flash of resentment. "Me, marry a man who's always up and gone when you need him the most? I wouldn't have him as a gift." She turned away, but not before he saw tears well up in her eyes.

"It's cold out here," she said. "Go take care of your horse, then come on in and get warm. I'll be fixin' you somethin' to eat."

CHAPTER 21

Christmas was not happy for the Lewises on the Colorado River. The weather was damp and unpleasantly cold, and the threat of war still hung over Texas like the leaden clouds of winter. Worst of all, for the Lewises, was that Michael had not been heard from. Though James would not speak of it to anyone else, least of all to Marie, he was haunted by a fear that Michael had fallen somewhere in one of the scattered skirmishes the Texans and the lately-arrived American volunteers had fought with Mexican soldiers from Goliad to the Rio Grande before General Cós's retreat from Bexar.

If that were so, he would join many of the other pioneers to early Texas who had been swallowed up by that vast land and never seen again. James grieved inwardly when he was alone, but he tried not to betray his feelings around the others, except for Andrew. Somehow he felt that with Andrew he could unburden himself, for Andrew had always been the one in the immediate family most able to listen with sympathy, to understand, to offer advice, and help without impatience.

Andrew heard James's fears about their older brother with eyes that could not hide misgivings of his own. He said, "I've had the same thoughts. I've tried to push them aside because it seems disrespectful to think of him as gone, like Papa that time. I remember when we thought once before that Michael was dead, but he finally turned up, when old Eli Pleasant brought him back to Tennessee. You weren't big enough to remember much about it, I guess. Marie still swears she knows he's alive, says she can sense that he's out there somewhere, tryin' to get home. I guess from there we have to take it on faith. Whatever comes, we'll face it as a family."

The Reverend Fairweather came by on Christmas Day and shared with them some venison and wild turkey at Andrew's cabin, where all the families had gathered. "The Lord's bounty is generous indeed," he said, and led them in a prayer for the safety of Texas and for the return of all the missing, especially Michael.

"I ought to be praying for all those men trying to make a new government for Texas over in San Felipe. They argued and fought amongst themselves until I am not sure the Lord will have patience with them much longer. You should be glad you vacated Bexar as soon as you did, James. There arose quite a squabble over putting together an expedition to march on Matamoros and invade Mexico."

"I heard a little about it," James said. "I decided I'd had all the fightin' I needed for a while."

"They're near coming to blows in San Felipe. Governor Smith is against invasion. So's Sam Houston. You know they've made him a general, and he's trying to raise an army. He says he doesn't want any men wasted on a fool's errand. Says they'll all be needed much closer to home. A big part of the Consultation is for an invasion, though. I fear Texas will be so badly divided that the Mexicans can just walk in and swarm over us like hornets."

Andrew asked, "Do you think they'll come back?"

James answered before Fairweather. "I talked to Elizandro before I left Bexar. He believes it's just a matter of waitin' for the grass."

Fairweather frowned darkly. "I fear it may not be that long. I have heard things that shake me to the core. There are reports that Santy Anna even now is marching up toward Laredo with a large army of fresh troops. If that is true, then he will soon meet up with Cós and his thousand soldiers on their retreat. When they put those two forces together, it will be a fearsome thing to behold."

James pointed out, "Cós gave his promise at Bexar that he would never invade Texas again."

"Cós is a general, but Santy Anna is the *presidente.* He can overrule any treaty Cós has made." Fairweather's one eye looked grim. "So you see, young gentleman, the new year may bring great tribulation to this poor beknighted Texas."

Andrew said, "I'll pray that you're wrong."

Fairweather replied, "I have prayed the same thing, many times. But the Lord does not promise to always send us the answer we want to hear."

Fairweather saddled up after resting a while to let his big dinner settle. "Whichaway you headed?" James asked him.

"South. There are Texans scattered along the Rio Grande, watching for Santy Anna and his minions. I expect they'll be needing to hear the Word to gird them for the fight."

Andrew said anxiously, "You'll inquire

about Michael along the way, won't you?"

"That I will. He and I have not always gotten along as Christian brothers, but I respect him as a good and strong man. If I find him I will send word. If possible, I will send *him*."

"We couldn't ask no more," Andrew said.

Cousin Frank came out to stand with James and Andrew as they watched Fairweather ride away, moving in a southerly direction with a cold, damp wind blowing at his back. James shivered, but not altogether from the cold. The good meal had soured on his stomach. "If he's right, what're we goin' to do?"

Andrew said, "I don't see where we have any choice except to fight. That or run." He took a sweeping look at the land around him. "I've put too much into this place now, me and Petra together. I don't figure to run."

The memory of Velasco had faded but little in three years, and Bexar was so fresh that James thought at times he could still feel the sharp bite of gunpowder in his nose. He awakened sometimes in the middle of the night, thinking he felt the ground shaking to the roar of cannons and heard the staccato crackle of rifle fire. Any illusions he might have harbored about the glory of battle had been shattered in Velasco and San Antonio.

"But the women and the young'uns — Petra and Marie, Hope and Annie —"

"We'll have to send them off to safe ground, over into Louisiana. That's why Baptiste left his wagons and teams behind, so they'll have a way if it comes to that. But maybe it won't. Maybe Fairweather's wrong."

The look in Andrew's face told James that he did not really believe it, and even Frank looked deadly serious. It was a bad sign when Frank could not find something to make a joke about.

James said, "I think we'd best oil up our rifles."

Something was wrong with Annie, though James could not determine just what it might be. Since his return from Bexar she had not once berated him for his shortcomings, not once placed any imperious demand upon him. She had been kinder than he had ever known her, and quieter.

It was obvious she was ill.

He came upon her unexpectedly one chilly day when he returned earlier than usual from a trip into the woods in search of fresh meat. He had shot a young whitetail buck that had had the poor judgment to abandon a hiding place in the underbrush and bound away in fright. He hung it for the moment in the dog-run and stepped into the kitchen to warm his hands at the fire before going back out to skin it. He found Annie sitting at the kitchen table, staring at a drawing she had made of Sly Shipman while he had been here the last time. She had not once mentioned Shipman's name since the day James had come home from the Bexar fight and had asked the man's whereabouts. He had thought perhaps she had recovered from her infatuation.

She made a quick move to put the picture away but realized James had already seen it.

James said, "Was I you, I'd stick that in the fire and forget about him. He ain't the kind that'll tie himself down."

Defensively she declared, "I wasn't really thinkin' about him. I was just lookin' at this, thinkin' what a poor artist I am."

"You're a poor liar but a good artist. That picture's a fair likeness. Only trouble is, you ought to've done it from his back side, because that's what you see most, with him ridin' away."

"You worked with him for a long time. Didn't you like him?"

"I got to where I did, after a while. But I

ain't a woman. He's a good friend and partner for a man, but he's got too much travel in him to be good for a woman. Was I you, I'd take another look at some of them boys from over at San Felipe."

Her voice was firm. "I don't need them, and I don't need him. I can get along by myself very well." She started to rise up from the table, then sat down quickly, her hands on her stomach. Her face looked pale.

Worried, James asked, "What's the matter, Annie? You don't look good at all."

"I guess it's this chilly, damp weather. I must've taken a cold."

That made sense. James volunteered, "I'll make you a fire in your bedroom. Maybe you'd ought to drink a little whiskey and then go lie down and wrap yourself up real good and try to sweat the sickness out."

Whatever it was, it seemed to pass in a while. But the next morning she looked sick again. She started fixing his breakfast, then had to sit down and let him finish it.

He said, "I'm goin' over to see Petra. Seems like she's always got some Mexican remedy for just about anything that ails you. Maybe she's got somethin' to get you over this."

Annie argued that it wasn't necessary, that this wouldn't last long, but James went anyway. Andrew seemed concerned and said he would ride over after a while and look in on Annie as soon as he got a few chores done. Petra said little until Andrew had left the cabin.

James asked her. "You got anything that might help Annie?"

Petra studied him with large, dark eyes. James had always thought Petra and Marie had eyes enough alike that they could have been sisters, except that Marie was Spanish and French, while Petra was pure Mexican. Petra said, "Yes, I have something. It tastes bad, but it can help." She knelt before a wooden cabinet and brought out a bottle half full of some dark liquid. It looked terrible. He had no intention of removing the stopper and smelling of it.

"Is it good for a cold?" he asked.

Petra considered a moment before she shook her head. "What is wrong with Annie is not a cold."

"Then what is it?"

"If you were married, you would know."

He stared at her, not comprehending for a minute. When the answer came, he rejected it out of hand. But it would not go away. "You tryin' to tell me Annie's —" He could not say the word, not in front of a woman.

Petra nodded. *"Preñada."*

He felt a flush of heat rush through his body, anger and confusion and helplessness, all wrapped up together. He almost dropped the bottle. He finally managed, "Are you sure? How do you know?"

Petra made a faint smile. "You forget my children? I have only to look at Annie, and I know before she says it."

"Why didn't she tell me?"

"You are a man. You are her brother. She does not believe you will understand."

"I understand, all right. It was that Sly Shipman. I don't know what she could've been thinkin' of."

"She was thinking of love. When there is love enough, you do not think of other things."

"Hell of a fix, a war tryin' to break out around us, and she gets herself in this shape."

"Do not be angry with her. She is your sister. Right now she needs you to love her and be kind to her. It is not a time to blame, to make her more unhappy."

"Does Andrew know?"

She shook her head. "Just Marie and Hope and me. And now you. Andrew will know soon enough. One brother at a time. Now go, take her the medicine. I will come in a while and see what I can do."

James nodded and turned, his feelings still running in all directions. He stopped at the door. "Petra, you're a good woman. I've got to tell you somethin'." He almost wished he had not started, but she was waiting now to hear him out. "When I first met you, I didn't know what to think, you bein' Mexican and all. You weren't like the womenfolk I knew, like my mother and sisters, or my brother Joseph's wife back home. I wondered if Andrew hadn't maybe made a mistake. But I know now that the smartest thing he ever done was to marry you, like the best thing Michael ever done was to marry Marie. I doubt I'll ever be lucky enough to find anybody half as good as either one of you."

She kissed him on the cheek, and he saw a tear run down the side of her face. "Go now, and take care of your sister."

Annie had gone to the hearth and was starting dinner when James walked into the kitchen. He held out the bottle. "It looks pretty bad, but Petra says it'll help."

"Thank you. I feel better now, but it'll be good to have it the next time."

He could not take his eyes from her, and she seemed to flinch under his long study. He asked, "You want to talk about it?"

"No." Regret was in her eyes. "Petra told you, didn't she?"

"I ought to've seen it for myself."

"I'm sorry if you're ashamed of me."

"You're my sister. We've fought a lot over the years, but I've never been ashamed of you for a minute. I'm not ashamed of you now."

"You'd have a right to be, I guess."

"You want me to go and find him? I'll drag him back here by the hair of the head if that's what it takes."

Some of the old determination came back to her eyes, pushing regret aside. "No. I wouldn't want a man who had to be forced."

"Does he know?"

She shook her head. "I didn't know it myself till after he'd left with Baptiste."

"Then I ought to go find him and tell him."

"No. That'd just be another way of forcin' him. I wouldn't want him to marry me just because he had to. He'd resent me, and I'd resent him, and we'd just come to hate one another."

"I'm sorry, Annie. I don't know what else to do."

"There's nothin' you *can* do. I ought to've known better. But I guess you wouldn't know how hard it is when you want some-

386

thin' so bad. Or somebody."

"Maybe I do. I did things in Natchitoches that I wouldn't want our mother to see."

He opened his arms, and she came to him, and they hugged one another while the johnnycake burned on the hearth.

The families gathered on Sundays at one of the homes, usually rotating from Michael and Marie's to Andrew and Petra's, to Frank and Hope's, and finally to James and Annie's. This Sunday was Marie's turn. James and Annie went in one of the wagons Baptiste and Shipman had left behind. James thought it not a good idea for Annie to try to ride horseback, though she tried to argue that in her early stage it posed no risk.

They found Andrew and Frank already arrived and standing in the dog-run, while several of the children ran and played hide and seek out around and behind the wood-pile and the cow pen. James did not like the somber look on Andrew's face. Carefully he helped Annie down from the wagon, holding her arm firmly until she was safely on the ground.

Frank was surprised, for he was used to seeing James let Annie go it alone, either to make it or fall down, however her luck might run. After Annie had gone into the kitchen to join the other women, Frank said, "You're bein' mighty gentle with her this mornin'. Annie have an accident or somethin'?"

James assumed they didn't know. "I guess you could call it that." It wasn't his place to tell them. He gave his attention to Andrew. "Your face looks cloudy enough to rain."

Andrew seemed to shiver, though the winter sun was fairly warm and he was standing out of the chilly north breeze. "Petra and I got here first. We found Marie in a bad state. Petra and Hope've been talkin' to her. I'm afraid it's come to a point that we've got to do somethin'."

James's first thought was that Marie might be in the same condition as Annie. "She sick?"

"In a way. Sick with worry. I guess she's been feelin' it a lot worse than she let on. She's always been a strong woman, Marie has, but it's come down now to a point that she can't handle it by herself anymore." He jerked his head toward the kitchen door. "Come on, let's go talk to her."

James knew at a glance that Marie had been crying. Her face, always thin, was drawn more than usual, and her big brown eyes met his for only a moment, then looked down. She gripped a handkerchief. Petra and Hope and Annie were solemn. James asked, "What is it, Marie?"

She touched the handkerchief to her eyes. "I had a dream last night. I know you all will think it was nothing more, just a dream, but it *was* more. I saw Michael. I heard him. He was bad hurt — wounded — lying on the ground somewhere all by himself. I could hear him calling for me. I could hear him so plain —" A tear ran down her cheek, but she made no move to stop it. She twisted the handkerchief in her hands. "There is something — I don't know how I can tell it so you will understand — always I have been able to sense things with Michael. I have known what he was thinking before he told me. It is like his mind talks to me even when he does not speak.

"Always I have felt that Michael was all right, that he was alive. I still feel that he is alive. But I feel that something is wrong, that he is hurt, that he needs me, and I do not know where to go to find him."

James glanced at Andrew and Frank. "You want us to go hunt for him?"

Marie's eyes reflected her anguish. "I do not know where to tell you to start. And it could be dangerous if Santa Anna comes."

James said, "It'll be dangerous *here* if Santa Anna comes."

Andrew motioned for James and Frank to follow him back out onto the dog-run. His brow was furrowed. He glanced at the door to be sure it was closed, so Marie would not hear what was said. "If it was somebody besides Marie, I'd be inclined to say it was just a woman worried to the point of gettin' a little hysterical. But Marie's never been one for that kind of thing. She's never one to scare at much of anything. You can see she's scared now."

James said, "I wish I knew how we could help her."

Andrew stared out across the prairie, his eyes bleak. "Only one thing we *can* do. We've got to try to find Michael."

Frank nodded agreement. James could not remember his ever disagreeing with Andrew about anything. "But where do we start?"

Andrew declared, "*You* don't start anywhere. Somebody's got to stay here to watch after the womenfolk and the young'uns. If the Mexicans *do* come, and me and James haven't got back, somebody's got to be ready to take the families to safe ground. That's apt to be the toughest job of all."

Frank was a couple of years older than Andrew, and in many families that would automatically have given him the unspoken authority to make the plans, to delegate the responsibilities. But Frank did not argue with Andrew. "If that's what you want me to do —"

"It is," Andrew said. "You're dependable and level-headed, and you've got a wife and kids of your own. You'll do it right." Andrew turned to James. "With all due respect, little brother, you're too young for that job. I'm afraid you might take too many chances. We can't afford that with our families."

James was not offended. Staying with the women and children would not have been his choice, anyway. "So you want me to help you look for Michael."

"There's no use in the both of us goin' together. We've got little enough chance of findin' him even by splittin' up. Texas is a hell of a big country when you set out a-lookin' all over it for somebody lost."

James knew. He had traversed a goodly part of it, first in getting here, then in the period he had spent working the clandestine import-export trade with Sly Shipman, and finally in going to the battles at Velasco and Bexar. "I'll go south," he volunteered. "As I recollect, when Michael rode away from here he was goin' to try to help take Goliad away from the Mexicans. Last I heard. Fannin's troops were there. Maybe Michael's

391

with them."

Andrew nodded. "That suits me. I'll go to San Felipe and see what I can find out. Maybe somebody at the council has got a list of the volunteers. Then I'll find where Sam Houston's army is at. Michael might've decided to join up with it. I don't think he'd've let himself get caught up in a fool's errand like that bunch marchin' off to attack Matamoros."

The look in Marie's eyes had shaken James. He asked, "Do you think we've really got any chance of findin' him?"

"About as much chance as a lamb in a wolf's den. But he's our brother. We've got to try."

CHAPTER 22

James had never been as far as Goliad before. Known by two names, the older being La Bahía, it had long been second to San Antonio de Bexar as one of the three principal Mexican settlements in Texas. The third, far to the north, had been Nacogdoches. Approaching the little settlement, James could see that it had already experienced the war in a painful way. The place was nearly deserted of civilians. Most of its stone houses and its stick-and-mud *jacales* stood empty. Their inhabitants had fled in anticipation of a coming battle between the Texan forces which held the presidio and the Mexican troops even now reported marching up from the south. Most of those inhabitants had been Mexican. They had feared mistreatment at Texan hands as much as the likelihood of their being caught in the crossfire if and when the soldiers from Mexico set out to take back this presidio they had lost in October to the Bay Prairie company of volunteers under Ben Milam and George Collinsworth.

Now Ben Milam was dead, killed in the December battle for San Antonio de Bexar, and Collinsworth had moved on to other duties. The presidio was under the command of James W. Fannin, temporarily serving as head of the provisional Texas government's armed forces while Sam Houston was away among the Indians, negotiating for them to keep the peace and allow the Texans to fight just one enemy at a time. Fannin had marched to Goliad as the first leg of his expedition to Matamoros but had halted here after learning that the Mexicans had greatly strengthened their troop strength at that ancient Mexican town just below the Rio Grande. Goliad was of strategic value to Texas because it lay only some forty miles from the new port of Copano, on the Gulf, and commanded the road between the Gulf and San Antonio.

James crossed the San Antonio River at a shallow ford and rode toward the forbidding high stone walls of the military presidio. They were gray and cold and inhospitable. He found himself hating Goliad on sight. It was the kind of place that made him think uncomfortably of chains and whips and dungeons. He could imagine that terrible things might have happened there in the past. It had been fought over several times in its eighty or so years. It would be easy to envision the ghosts of its past dead hovering over it, casting a dark curse upon all who entered. He did not intend to remain longer than necessary.

He was admitted through the gates without difficulty, for he was clearly American by birth. He suspected that had he been a Mexican, even a lifelong inhabitant of the Goliad settlement, he would have been at considerable inconvenience ever getting that far. He saw men halfheartedly drilling in the open courtyard. There was no Texan uniform. The volunteers wore whatever clothing they had brought with them, homespun cotton or wool in many instances, or buckskins or flannel. They wore boots or shoes or mocassins, and he noted that a few were barefoot. Hell of a thing, he thought, in the middle of winter. But Texas was hardly a rich man's paradise. Most settlers here lived from one crop to the next, one hunt to the next. The wolf of hardship and privation was always prowling, always near.

He had a long wait before he was finally ushered in to see Colonel Fannin. A native of Georgia, Fannin had just enough West

Point training to get him in trouble, some people said. His responsibilities for the army left him little time for helping some farmer find a lost brother, and his impatience indicated that he would rather be doing something else. But he took the trouble to study his rosters, running his finger hurriedly down the pages. "Lewis, you say? A common enough name. I find a Henry Lewis here, and a Matthew Lewis. And there is a Nathaniel Lewis with Shackelford's Red Rovers. But I find no Michael Lewis."

James explained that his brother had come in the early fall and might have been in the short fight that had originally taken this fortification from its thirty or so Mexican defenders. Fannin said, "Scarcely any of the men who originally took this presidio then are still here. They have scattered to other places, other battles."

James felt a letdown, though he had known within reason that he would not find Michael here. In a garrison like this one, with people constantly coming or going, there was no reason for Michael not to have sent word home, to let Marie and the rest of the family know where he was. "Well, sir," he said, "I thank you anyway for your time and trouble. I reckon I'll be movin' on, huntin' for him somewhere else."

"He could be with any number of small companies and scouting parties between here and the Rio Grande. You cannot hope to find them all."

"I'll damn sure make the effort," James said firmly. He started to leave, but Fannin called him back. "Do you know this part of Texas?" he asked.

"No sir. Never been this far south before."

"I'll make you a rough map, and I'll show you where I last knew the various units to be. But I want it understood that you'll memorize this map, then burn it."

"Burn it?"

Fannin frowned. Reluctantly he said, "We must recognize the possibilities, no matter how grim they may appear. By going south there is more than a good chance that you will run afoul of Mexican troops. Should they capture or kill you, it would not do to have such a map found on your person, would it?"

James swallowed. He had acknowledged to himself that his mission carried an element of risk, but nobody had spelled it out in terms quite so raw. "I believe I get your meanin', sir."

It did not take Fannin long to draw the map. On it he included the creeks and rivers and the few settlements at which Texan units might be headquartering, or at least camping temporarily. Handing it to James, he said, "I have to suppose you have taken the probabilities into account."

"The probabilities?"

"That your brother in all likelihood is dead. The fact that you have not heard from him in so long and the fact that a number of men have been killed in skirmishes with Mexican units south of here ever since last fall leads me to recognize that as the strongest probability."

"Us Lewises don't give up till we see the body."

"Do you have any conception of how much land lies between here and the Rio Grande, and between here and the Laredo–San Antonio road?"

James looked at the map. "It doesn't look like so much."

"That is a small piece of paper. Those are not paper miles out yonder." Fannin made a sweeping motion with his hand. "I could use your strong right arm and your rifle here at Goliad. We feel that sometime in the spring Santa Anna and his minions will be coming again. We intend to stop them at these walls and push them back far into Mexico."

"I didn't see that many men out there."

"They will be here. There are only a few hundred now, but I expect to have a thousand more by the time the grass is green and we again face the Mexican soldiers. Even now, we continue to receive recruits from the United States. If you inquire outside you will find that a majority of the men within these walls are not longtime residents of Texas. Those all seem to be home breaking their fields for next spring's planting, or dallying at commerce. These men are mostly lately come from elsewhere, willing to fight to protect the lives of their fellow Americans in Texas. Would that more of the Texans themselves would do so."

James could have told him that many of the old settlers would have been content to live under the flag of Mexico provided the government guaranteed them continued freedom like they had known in the early years here. The loud cry for independence had sprung up mostly from the later immigrants, those who had no memory of a benevolent Mexico that gave them little help but caused them little trouble. He decided, however, that to say such a thing would only start a needless argument. Fannin was known to have begun calling for independence almost immediately upon his arrival in Texas a couple of years ago. Like Travis, but not so vocal about it. Fannin had not spent time in a Mexican jail to pay for his intemperate language.

Fannin said, "Between Travis and Bowie in San Antonio, and Sam Houston wherever he is, and our garrison here, we intend to give Santa Anna such a whipping that he will lick his wounds all the way back to Mexico City — if indeed he survives."

James remembered how many had said the battle for San Antonio de Bexar would be easy, and how they had thought the contest for the little fort at Velasco would be quickly won. They had said the Mexicans would not fight. Fannin, by implication, was still saying it.

Fannin said, "Surely you would like to be part of such a victory. It would be something to tell your grandchildren."

James remembered an old saying: the third time is the charm. He had survived two battles. The third one just might be the last, and he would never have any grandchildren to tell a story to. But he chose to leave Fannin feeling well disposed toward him. After all, the man had given him his time and the map. "If I can find my brother, I just may come back and join you, sir. We both may."

"Then, Mr. Lewis, good luck in your

quest." Fannin extended his hand, and James took it.

Leaving the presidio, he paused for another look at the dark stone walls. They were taller, he thought, than the ones at the old San Antonio mission fortress called the Alamo. General Cós had withdrawn his troops into the Alamo for a final stand, then had surrendered because he considered the place indefensible. Well, maybe Goliad was different. By all accounts it was the best fort the Mexicans had built in Texas. It just might be that a thousand or so well-equipped defenders within its walls could wear down an attacking army, then spill out to crush whatever was left of it: But Fannin was far short of his thousand, and he might be far shorter of time than he expected, too. If Santa Anna did not wait for the grass —

James shuddered at the possibilities.

Matamoros lay almost due south of Goliad. As Fannin had indicated, miles on the ground were much longer than they had looked on the small map James had studied and studied, then burned in a small campfire his first night out. The country was less benevolent than that he had come to know in the regions farther north and along the Colorado. It was dryer, given to some degree to sand and cactus and low-growing chaparral. Just middling to poor farming country, he judged. Probably pretty good for cattle, if anybody had them in considerable numbers. But there was not yet in Texas a big market for cattle because there were already enough to provide beef for the residents and it was too far to drive them overland to the old states for sale. Some were slaughtered at the ports for their hides and tallow to be shipped to New Orleans and elsewhere, but the meat would not keep during such a journey. James wondered if anybody would ever find a use for this part of Texas.

He found one of the outposts Fannin had indicated on the map, and some twenty men stationed there, patroling for sign that any Mexican soldiers were moving back into Texas. Colonel Sesma was south of the Rio Grande, at or near Matamoros, he was told, awaiting orders. Reports from friendly Mexicans indicated that Santa Anna was somewhere south of Laredo, moving northward. Surely, though, he would wait for spring. He could not possibly haul enough corn in his wagons to feed all the horses his cavalry would be bringing. The horses would need grass.

Relying on his memory of the map, James

missed the second outpost he sought and wasted two days backtracking until he found it. Someone there thought he vaguely recalled a Lewis, a tall, gaunt man. Best he remembered, he looked a little like James, except older. It had been two months ago or longer, so he had forgotten if the name was Michael. Could have been, or maybe not. James learned only enough to fire up his hope, yet leave him frustrated and a little angry.

"Can't you remember anything else? Can't you remember where he was goin' the last time you saw him?"

The speaker was not a Texan of long standing. He had come from Alabama back in the fall, just about the time the first blood was being spilled at Gonzales. He had been spoiling for a fight with the Mexicans and, up to now, had seen a lot of Texas but very little of the enemy. "Best I can recollect," he said, "this Lewis went a-ridin' out with a patrol that was headed down to the Bravo to whip up on any Mexican stragglers they could find and be damned sure they went on across the river. Ain't none of that bunch ever come back, as far as I know. Could be they run into too many Mexicans. Me, I'd like to run into a few. I ain't had the barrel of ol' Hickory here good and hot since I got to Texas." He patted the long rifle he cradled across one arm. "I just hope them Mexicans *do* come. Time we get done, what's left of them won't quit runnin' till they get to Mexico City."

If all the reports were even half true, James thought, the Alabaman would get his wish. A man ought to be more careful about what he wished for.

Somewhere north of the river was supposed to be another patrol unit, watching for sign. Fannin had warned that it was not permanently stationed at any one place but remained mobile. It was mobile enough that James almost despaired of finding it. In the end he did not find it; it found him. Three men rose up suddenly out of the chaparral, leveling rifles at him. They startled the bay horse Walker enough that he jumped to one side and almost made James lose his hold on his rifle. One of them shouted a command in Spanish. James had no idea what he said. The men were bearded and dark, but they wore no uniform, so he thought they were probably Americans. He had found that men who spent all their time outdoors, in all kinds of weather, often became dark enough to be mistaken for Mexicans. Probably they mistook him for one.

He raised his hands, his rifle balanced across his lap. "Don't any of you-all shoot."

One of the men lowered his rifle partway. "You're an American?"

"Used to be. I'm a Texan now. Come from over on the Colorado River, west of San Felipe."

The man spoke, and the others let their rifles rest. "We seen you from a good ways off. There's been a report of some Mexican soldiers. Outriders, maybe, scoutin' for a column. For all we could tell, you might've been one. Seen any?"

James shook his head. "Haven't seen a human bein' in three or four days." He explained his mission and described Michael.

One of the men nodded. "I know the man. *Knew* him, anyway. Him and two more, they rode out from camp four or five weeks ago. None of them ever showed up again." He grimaced. "I hate to be the one to carry bad news, friend, but I'm afraid they must've run into somethin' too big for them. Otherwise they'd've been back. I'm afraid your brother is dead."

James felt his throat tightening, and his eyes burned. It was the news he had come to expect, but he had not made up his mind to accept it. "You never actually saw him killed, though. You never saw his body."

"A man falls in this country, you ain't likely ever to find him. All you know for sure is that he's gone."

Us Lewises don't quit till we see the body, he had told Fannin. "You know which direction he rode?"

"No, I was out on patrol myself when they left. Never did hear anybody say. You'd have to talk to Captain Jones."

"I'd like to. Whichaway is he?"

The man pointed west. "Camp's over yonderway about eight, maybe ten miles. Goin' to be a mite hard to find. We keep it hidden so it *will* be." He gave James a little description to help him locate the site. "Good luck to you, friend. Sorry we handed you a scare. I wish I could give you more hope about findin' your brother, but truth is truth."

James thanked him and started west, his hope rising, falling, and rising again as he pondered the man's words. At least he had found where Michael *had* been.

He had just ridden into a wide, brushy draw, splashed through a cold little stream and had come out on the far side, back into the lower-growing chaparral brush, when he saw a dozen or so riders. Instinct told him they were Mexican cavalrymen before he made out the color of their uniforms. He felt a flush of excitement, a quickening of his heartbeat. They saw him at almost the same instant that he saw them, and they came charging from two hundred yards away. He whirled Walker around and drummed his heels into the bay's sides, racing for the heavier brush.

He heard a few shots, which served only to make Walker run faster. The muskets the soldiers carried were notoriously inaccurate at any distance, one reason the sharp-shooting long rifles of the Texans had done so much more damage in Bexar than the defending Mexican troops had been able to accomplish. But James knew the cavalrymen had an answer for that: Get closer. He felt they were gaining on him. He had not given Walker much rest or grazing time since he had left home, and the horse was wearing down.

He hit the heavy brush at a run and was quickly swallowed up in it. He cut to a northerly direction, picking his way through the thorny branches, trying to make as little noise as possible. Were he to continue running, they had only to stop and listen to know where he was. He slowed to a walk, stopping frequently to turn an ear back in the direction where he thought the cavalrymen should be. He could hear the brush crackling as they fought their way through it. He heard shouting and laughter, as if they were hunters in pursuit of a rabbit, trying to catch it before it could drop into a hole.

He wished he were as small as a rabbit. No hole was big enough for him and Walker.

He stopped after a bit, dismounted, and led Walker into a patch of particularly heavy brush that he could not have ridden into. This, he reasoned, was as near to being a hole as he was going to find on short notice. He halted when he came to a tangle of limbs and thorns that he could not lead the horse through. He could still hear the cavalrymen. They seemed to have split up and were beating through the timber in several directions. None seemed close to James. He stood with a hand on Walker's nose, ready to clamp the nostrils shut if the horse gave sign of nickering to the Mexicans' animals. But Walker seemed to sense the danger, for he was nervous, rolling his eyes a little.

The sounds of pursuit gradually died away. They had probably given up and gone after other prey, James thought. But it was also possible that they were setting a trap. He decided to stay put for a while. He took a piece of jerked venison from a pack tied to his saddle and chewed on it. He was not hungry; if anything, the chase had ruined any appetite he might otherwise have had, but he knew he would be needing his strength. These were not likely to be the only Mexicans around. He wished there were some grass in this heavy thicket for Walker, but the density of the foliage during the growing season would have kept it shaded out.

James waited. The brush impeded the cold wind, but he still felt a chill.

Somewhere to the west another Texan patrol should be operating under a Captain Jones. With Mexican horsemen prowling about, however, there was no telling where the patrol might be at any given time, or if it still existed. If the men were not alert, they might have been surprised as James had been, possibly without a thicket to lose themselves in.

He wondered if such a thing might have happened to Michael.

Toward dusk he began picking his way back out of the heavy timber, leading Walker at first, eventually remounting when the brush became thin enough to ride through. He found the creek and let the horse drink his fill while James looked carefully in first one direction, then another. He saw nothing to indicate that the soldiers were still anywhere around.

He had no clear idea just what to do next. He did not want to abandon the search for Michael, but he was beginning to realize that his chances of finding his brother were painfully slim, especially now that Mexicans were patrolling the region. If he remained here much longer, chances were great that he would be caught and probably killed. What Fannin had said about the reason for destroying the map was beginning to take on a new dimension of cold reality. To continue to roam around this part of the country presented a hazard far greater than any chance he had of finding Michael. Regretfully he decided to start back north. Michael probably already had, if he was still alive.

It was almost full dark when he ventured out of the thicket on its east side. He had waited in the edge for some minutes, watching, listening, hearing nothing except the calling of a few birds. His courage girded up, he finally touched his heels to Walker's sides and moved out into the open. His confidence was shaken, however, when Walker swung his head to the left and pricked his ears forward.

James's heart leaped. A horseman charged at him from no more than fifty yards away. They had set a trap, and he had blundered into it. As he wheeled Walker around, he saw the flash of a musket and heard it crackle. Walker missed a step, almost falling. But the horse regained his feet and plunged headlong back into the brush. James could hear the soldier shouting somewhere behind him, calling for help. He could hear responses from farther away.

They had known he had to come out of the brush. They just had not known where.

He felt Walker beginning to falter. The horse was wheezing. Then his legs went out from under him. James kicked his feet free of the stirrups as the horse went down. He hit the ground rolling, scrambling out of the way. Walker's thrashing hoofs could be as dangerous as the cavalrymen's muskets. Jumping to his feet, he turned back toward the horse and saw blood gushing from a wound in the bay's chest.

He wondered how Walker had made it this far. He grabbed his fallen rifle and his shot pouch. He looked for a moment at the dying animal his Uncle Benjamin had given him, a gallant horse that had brought him to Texas and had carried him over a large part of it during the last several years. Now James was losing him. He had no time for grief. He paused to pat the animal on the neck, then took off running afoot through the brush. Branches slapped at him. Thorns clutched, stopped him, dug into his skin and bled him, but he struggled free and kept going. He fought for breath, pausing to lean against a tree and gasp for air when it felt as if his lungs would collapse. He tried to lick his leather-dry lips, but his tongue was just as dry. He could hear himself wheezing as Walker had wheezed. But he could also hear the soldiers hunting for him in the heavy timber. That kept his blood pumping, his feet moving. He heard a loud and exultant shout and knew Walker had been found. He wished he had taken time to retrieve the pack of food tied to the saddle, but he had not thought of it in his haste to get away. He buried himself deep in the brush and lay down flat on the ground behind a tall clump of prickly pear, fighting for breath, fighting against the fear that threatened to paralyze him as he heard the pursuers breaking through the timber, coming closer all the time.

Darkness came as a friend. He heard a horse moving very near, possibly no more than fifty feet away. But James could not see him or his rider, nor could the horseman see James. He held still as death, taking short breaths and holding them. The horseman passed on by and soon was gone.

James sat up, finally, as the moon arose cold and bright over the heavy thicket. He took stock of his situation and found it bleak. Here he was afoot, without food, in a part of the country he had never seen, surrounded by Mexican soldiers on the lookout for him. He had not found Michael and now knew there was no hope whatever that he would. He would do well if he got out alive himself. The only thing in his favor was that he had kept his rifle and his shot pouch and powder horn.

He waited until he had heard no sound of the horsemen for what he thought had been an hour or more. Then he got to his feet and found the creek. If he followed it upstream, it would lead him in a generally northerly direction. That was as good as he could ask for, under the circumstances. Maybe by daylight he could put some miles behind him.

He had a lot of miles to travel.

CHAPTER 23

Isaac Blackwood stood on a narrow riflemen's walkway behind the high stone wall
and stared out over the town of San Antonio
de Bexar, beyond the river that ran almost
beside the mission compound. He could see
Mexican people leaving afoot, in ox carts,
and on horseback, most of them heading
eastward. Rumors had been circulating for
days that Santa Anna had crossed the Rio
Grande at Laredo and was on his way with
a huge army. Most of the officers had taken
the reports with skepticism if not outright
disbelief. It seemed only logical that Santa
Anna would wait for spring, for the grass.
To march northward into Texas now, in the
dead of a wet, cold, and miserable winter,
without fresh grass for the horses along the
way, seemed highly improbable for a man
who had Santa Anna's reputation as a
military strategist. There was a tendency
among some of the officers like Travis to

dismiss any report of Mexican origin simply because it *was* Mexican.

But the Mexican people of Bexar seemed to believe it, for many were putting the town behind them. They remembered too well the storming of Mexican troops by the Texans in December, and the carnage that campaign had wrought. They did not want to stay and witness another like it. Isaac had a cold feeling in his stomach as he watched the exodus. Some would say good riddance; they wished *all* the Mexicans would leave. But Isaac took it as a bad omen.

Down in the open plaza within the fortress walls he watched Elizandro Zaragosa standing with his son, a boy Isaac took to be around sixteen. He had heard him called Manuel. The two were arguing with considerable emotion. Isaac could hear the words but did not understand them, for he had never seen any need to learn Spanish. He surmised by the pointing and other movement of the hands that Zaragosa was telling the boy to leave, and the boy was begging his father to let him stay. At length the argument ended. Isaac watched the two embrace each other. The boy mounted a nice-looking black horse and rode out the open gate, looking back over his shoulder. Isaac thought he was crying. Zaragosa followed his son to the gate and stood watching him as he rode across the wooden bridge toward the heart of the town, the old San Fernando cathedral, and the main plaza. When the Mexican finally turned, his dark eyes were sad.

Isaac moved a little, for his leg had cramped. Zaragosa heard him and looked up, recognizing him. He nodded. Isaac nodded back. He had known Zaragosa by sight almost from the time he and his brothers had come into Texas, back when Zaragosa had been an officer in a more benevolent Mexican army. Until lately, Isaac had been able to develop no particular liking for the man, and Zaragosa had been cool toward Isaac, making no distinction between him and his older brothers. Isaac had never felt comfortable around Mexicans, even though there had been times he wished he could. The Moreno family near Nacogdoches, Andrew Lewis's in-laws, had treated him kindly and generously once when he had badly needed kindness and generosity.

Zaragosa's past experience as a soldier had been called into service here in the preparation of this old abandoned mission for the defense of Bexar. He had helped organize and drill a small company of Mexicans hostile to the tyranny of Santa Anna and to

416

work them into the military apparatus commanded jointly here by the young lawyer Buck Travis and the ailing, hard-drinking Jim Bowie. The fact that Zaragosa's men were Mexicans was conveniently overlooked in the garrison's dire need for manpower. Earlier, Isaac had strongly considered leaving when Travis and Bowie together had a force of only a little more than 140 men. He remembered that General Cós had had more than a thousand, yet he had felt himself unable to hold this post.

Isaac had been put off also by the earlier quarreling between Bowie and Travis over the rightful leadership. They had settled the matter, more or less, by dividing the command. Travis was in charge of his regulars and Bowie of his volunteers. Then thirteen men from the old states had arrived, including one Isaac remembered well from Tennessee, at least by reputation. He had never seen the man before, but he knew the name: David Crockett.

Travis had taken cheer from these recruits and told the men he expected shortly to see the garrison swell to a thousand. Isaac had no idea where another eight hundred would come from, but he had decided to stay and see. Given that many, let Santa Anna come. The Texans would give him a hell of a fight and send him running back to Mexico without his britches on.

But now the signs were bleak. The best Isaac could tell from a rough count was that only about 150 fighting men were within the heavy walls. And despite what the officers were telling the men, the hurried departure of civilians from the streets of San Antonio was an omen too dark to ignore. At times he thought about taking his horse and riding out that open gate, joining the civilians in their flight. After all, he was no soldier. He had joined the fight against Mexico of his own free will, and he could quit it the same way. He wondered what prevented him. He supposed he was just waiting for someone else to start, to be the first. Then he would follow. There should be no shame in running if others were doing it. And when it had come down to the cutting, Blackwoods had almost always run. That was their family pattern. His father Cyrus had run twenty years ago, deserting a young Michael Lewis in the face of danger from Spanish troops. His brother Finis a few years later had ambushed Michael and had run when he missed his shot.

Maybe, at last, it was time a Blackwood stood his ground, to prove that the blood was not all bad. Or perhaps he was just proving another belief widely held about the Blackwoods, that none of them were very bright.

He was surprised to see Zaragosa climb up to join him. If they had not developed a real friendship within these walls, the shared experience had made them tolerant of one another. Watching Zaragosa send his son away had touched a responsive chord in Isaac. It brought home to him the fact that though they might be of different races, different cultures, they were all similar human beings at the core.

Zaragosa looked out across the top of the wall, silent for a moment. He was gazing in the direction Manuel had taken.

Isaac finally asked, "Can you still see him?"

Zaragosa shook his head. "He is gone. I told him he must go."

"He didn't act like he wanted to."

"I told him one Zaragosa in this compound is enough. I told him the danger is great, that he is young, and I want him to live to be a very old man. I told him also that he is the oldest son, and if I am gone his mother will need him."

Isaac grimaced at the tone of that. "You talk like you don't think much of your chances — *our* chances."

Zaragosa shrugged. "I was a long time a soldier. In here" — he tapped his chest — "I am still the soldier. A soldier stands where he is needed, and he fights and does not count the enemy. But you are not a soldier. I wonder why you stay."

"I wonder myself. I guess it's because the others do. And old Crockett down there — I can't even remember the first time ever I heard about him. Don't seem right for one Tennessean to run away and leave another one to do his fightin' for him."

"And your brothers? What of them?"

"Odd thing about them. All these years I've wanted to get away from them and have a life of my own. I always stayed because I thought they needed me. Now I'm here and they're way east yonder, and they ain't sent no message beggin' me to come home. Maybe they don't need me like I thought."

"Perhaps what you do here is for them. If we can stop Santa Anna — if we can even slow him down — perhaps we give the Texas army time to be ready."

"But *is* there a Texas army? From all I've heard it's scattered to hell and gone, what there is of it, and everybody fightin' so hard amongst theirselves that they ain't got time for fightin' Santa Anna."

"I think they will awaken when they see

the enemy coming. They must." Zaragosa's gaze went back to the town, to the flat-topped stone and adobe houses, to the tower of the San Fernando church. He was still looking for his son.

Isaac said, "He's gone. He's a good boy, I reckon. He done what you told him."

Zaragosa made a small smile. "A good son." He turned back to Isaac. "You are a bachelor, I believe. You do not know what it is to have a son."

Isaac looked away, swallowing. "I reckon not." He had tried not to think too much about the boy. He had especially tried not to dwell on what would become of young Cyrus without Isaac there to guide him and only Finis and Luke to model after. If he were now to jump and run from this place, to save himself, it would be to spare the boy that fate.

Zaragosa said, "Perhaps God will smile. Perhaps Santa Anna will turn back from these walls when he sees we are ready." But the tone of his voice did not inspire belief.

Isaac saw a rider spurring hard from the direction of town. He was a Mexican civilian, a man whose face had become familiar to Isaac though he did not know his name. His excited manner brought Isaac to full attention, and automatically his gaze went to the southern horizon, searching.

He heard the distant ringing of the bell in the tower of San Fernando. It was not the time of day for mass, he thought, then wondered why he knew. He had never been to mass. He had seldom been to any kind of church service.

He saw frenzied movement in the distant streets. Men on horseback were hurrying toward the fortress: Texans and volunteers from the United States who had been sleeping in town instead of inside the crowded post. Shortly, a group of Mexican civilian horsemen came pushing a herd of cattle toward the walls, beef to withstand a siege.

Zaragosa said, "It is Juan Seguín and his men. I must go to help them." He turned hurriedly, then paused. "You know what this means. The enemy is upon us."

The cold, damp wind gave Isaac a chill that seemed to go all the way to his boots. "And the grass ain't even up yet."

Lieutenant Díaz had expected to return someday to San Antonio de Bexar, but he had not thought it would be with such a grand army as this one. At least, it had seemed a grand army when it had gathered at the Rio Grande. The steady march into a cold, wet Texas winter had been a grievous ordeal for men afoot and for the horses. There had been little grass from Laredo north, partly because of the dormant winter season and partly because Texan scouts had done the best they could to burn off the old, dead grass that at least would have filled the horses' bellies even if its nutrients had been sparse. Rain had put a stop to the burning, but the grass was brown and empty, and the animals had grown thin.

The *presidente* had gone into a rage over the condition of the horses, almost as terrible as the one in which he had indulged upon learning of General Cós's disgraceful surrender of troops at Bexar in December. The men should have fought to the death, he had shrilled, rather than surrender to such an unholy band of pirates as these accursed *americanos* who would wrest Texas from the bosom of its mother Mexico. But he would show the foreign invaders the power of the Napoleon of the West. They would feel the sting of good Mexican steel. He would put them to the sword, every last misbegotten son of a goat.

The army had straggled badly in the days since February 16, when it had crossed the Rio Grande. There had been a pause at the Nueces for hasty rebuilding of a wooden bridge, evidently burned by Texan scouts in hopes of delaying the invasion. At the Medina, Santa Anna had called a halt for a day of rest, to allow the lagging battalions to catch up. There, friendly arrivals from San Antonio had told the president that the Texans were to have a big dance in town the following night, that it would be easy to steal in under cover of darkness, catch them drunk, and do a quick and easy job of execution. Santa Anna had been intrigued by the possibilities, but a heavy rain and a rise in the river delayed his movement.

It was probably just as well, Díaz thought. The same rain had probably spoiled the Texans' dance. They would be angry enough about that to put up a good fight.

All along, Santa Anna had wondered if the Texans might fortify the old mission Concepción south of town and make their stand there instead of in the Alamo, where Cós had found his position untenable. The walls of Concepción would be more difficult to breach than those of the Alamo. But informants coming from San Antonio said the defenders were still fortifying the Alamo. They had built up new breastworks and filled in gaps in the walls left by the December siege. They had cannon, and they had the long rifles that could reach out and kill a man at two or three hundred yards.

Díaz's thoughts drifted to his old commander, Zaragosa. He wondered what the lieutenant was doing now, if he and his family had evacuated their farm and moved to a safe distance from the battle that was about to take place. Surely the lieutenant had not taken up the Texan cause. The president had declared this a racial war, Mexican against *americano*. It was unthinkable that any true Mexican could hesitate about choosing his side. Yet Díaz knew that many had done so. Men like Lorenzo de Zavala and Juan Seguín had turned against their race, had taken up the call for an independent Texas. That meant an American Texas. There would be no place in it for Mexicans. The turncoats would learn soon enough who their true enemies were, should the unthinkable happen and the Texans win. Once their services were no longer required, the Texans would turn upon them and drive them out, taking for themselves all the properties the disloyal Mexicans left behind.

He could only hope that this was not the case with Zaragosa. There were others in San Antonio who deserved no better, but Zaragosa was a good man, a good soldier, a true Mexican.

As the column approached the town, Santa Anna sent Colonel Mora to take possession of the Concepción mission, to keep it from the hands of the Texans should they decide upon wholesale retreat to a better position than the Alamo. Díaz could hear the sounds of musketry in the distance and knew Mora's troops were caught in a skirmish. It was not of long duration, and a courier soon reported back that the mission was firmly in hand. The Texans who had challenged the column had fled back toward the town, toward the Alamo.

The president was pleased. Now, he said, it was time to show these invaders the shine of Mexican steel, to vindicate the honor of the Mexican army, so besmirched by the unwillingness of his brother-in-law Cós to stand and fight. He ordered his men into full dress uniform.

Díaz carried a small diary in his pocket. In it he had marked the important dates: February 16, crossing the Rio Grande; February 17, the Nueces; February 21, the Medina. Now he took out a short pencil and noted this date: "February 23, 1836. Entering San Antonio de Bexar."

The president himself rode just behind the advance guard, resplendent in his best uniform. As he entered the main plaza, his band struck up a march for the benefit of those inhabitants who had not fled the town. Before and behind him fluttered the banners of the various army units, and the red, green, and white flag that symbolized the glory of Mexico, the eagle with a snake in its teeth, its claws clutching a cactus.

Soon Santa Anna would have a snake in his teeth, and he would administer to these invaders such a terrible defeat that never again would Americans even consider crossing over the Sabine. Never again would military scholars devote all their attention to Napoleon Bonaparte. They would marvel at the greatest warrior of them all, the Napoleon of the West, General Antonio López de Santa Anna.

A red flag of no quarter was raised over the tower of the San Fernando. The eighteen-pound cannon at the Alamo was fired toward the city in reply.

The battle for the Alamo had begun.

CHAPTER 24

Isaac Blackwood was exhausted. For twelve days since the first Mexican troops had marched into San Antonio de Bexar to the sound of Santa Anna's band, there had been a constant bombardment of one kind or another, advances by infantry, sallies by Mexican cavalry, the digging of trenches to let soldiers move into closer range of the Alamo walls under the protection of earthworks. Seldom in that long siege had the defenders been able to sleep for any restful length of time. He guessed this was a part of Santa Anna's strategy, to keep them awake, keep them off balance, wear them down before he attempted whatever his plans called for. The general expectation was that sooner or later he would stage a grand assault. The only question in most of the defenders' minds was why he had already waited so long.

Isaac was hungry, too. Rations had been

reduced to corn and beef, and a short supply even of that, for there were 188 men within these stone walls, and not enough food for half so many. Not since the coming of the Mexican soldiers had he eaten his fill.

For the first few days it had been obvious that new Santanista troops were arriving at regular intervals, adding to the thousands massed outside the walls, throughout the town and encamped on its fringes. They had been strung out along the trail because of the sparcity of grass and decent water as well as because of the miserable weather that had turned roads into bottomless pits of mud. Now and again, one Mexican unit or another would make an attempt at rushing the walls, only to be cut to pieces by Texan rifle fire and a lethal peppering of scrap iron and chain from the fourteen artillery pieces manned within the Alamo. Each time they came, Isaac's heartbeat quickened, and when they retreated it would be a long time slowing back to normal. If it was Santa Anna's aim to wear Isaac down, he was doing a good job of it.

The Mexicans had managed at considerable cost to mount a number of artillery batteries beyond rifle range. These had been fired at the Texan position for days without inflicting serious damage or fatalities. The Alamo defenders had used their own cannon to good effect on occasion. But Travis, now in full command because Bowie lay half out of his head from pneumonia, had been sparing in his use of the big guns. Powder was in short supply and must be conserved for whatever urgent need might yet come.

In the early days of the siege there had been the exhilaration of first combat to keep spirits stirred, and the hope of reinforcements. Goliad was considered the most likely source. Travis had sent out couriers like Juan Seguín in the dark of night to try to bring back help. James Butler Bonham had ridden through the Mexican lines to Goliad, only to bring back word — again through Mexican lines — that Fannin had declined. Fannin said he would need all his four hundred men to hold the presidio at Goliad.

At a low point in the garrison's morale, thirty-two men from the town of Gonzales paraded through the Mexican encampments unscathed and offered their services to the beleaguered defenders. Just thirty-two men, when Santa Anna had thousands massed to storm these walls. But the sight of these new faces brought cheer. If they had made it through, perhaps more would be coming. That, and the fact that the Alamo had lost not a single man despite days of cannonading, lifted spirits for a time.

Now, dog-tired but unable to sleep, Isaac lay with his hat for a pillow upon the bare ground and stared up at a cold, dark sky. He could smell the smoke of the Alamo's campfires, where men huddled for warmth against the night's chill, and from Mexican campfires just beyond rifle range. The odor of gunpowder was mixed in it, too. Midnight had passed. The thirteenth day had begun, though it would be hours yet before the sun came up. He wished for sleep but could not find it. His troubled mind ran riot with a hundred images, memories of the past, dreams he had once entertained and none of which had come to pass. That they could ever come to pass for him now he realized was unlikely. The Mexicans had tightened their ring of steel until he knew there was no possibility of reinforcements getting in, even if any were on their way. It seemed no longer a matter of whether the Mexicans would make a frontal assault but simply when. Sentries with spyglasses had seen troops building ladders yesterday, and there had been considerable activity in the Mexican ranks. A fierce bombardment had left a serious breach in the north wall. Then, suddenly, the firing had stopped. After all these noisy days and nights, the Santanista guns stood quiet.

The eerie silence was as nerve-wracking as the cannonade. Isaac wondered if that might also be part of Santa Anna's strategy, to grind them mentally as well as physically.

Again, he thought of dropping over the wall under the cover of darkness and trying to slip away alone. Earlier, he might have managed. But only one had made any move in that direction, a foreign mercenary named Rose. He was nòt a Texan, not even an American; he had no dedication to this fight. As for the rest, whatever the cause — valor, patriotism, defiance, or just plain inertia — nobody seemed even to consider going over the wall alone, so neither did Isaac, not seriously.

Now the Mexican noose was drawn too tight. He doubted that a dog could get through that line, much less a man. To try it would almost certainly result in sudden death. But to remain here would mean no less; it might just take longer. He had seen the red flag that still flew from the church tower on the main plaza, and he had heard trumpeters play the *degüello,* the call of no quarter. The garrison, if conquered, was to be put to the sword. He shuddered at the thought of cold steel.

He had wondered several times if Travis might decide their situation here was impossible and try a massive breakout. Though the cost would have been high, some probably would have made it through to fight again somewhere else. But Travis had chosen to make his stand here, and the fighting men seemed to have concurred. So long as the Alamo stood, Santa Anna was delayed in making a devastating sweep across the rest of American Texas. If a Texan army was building somewhere, and he hoped to God it was, each day they delayed Santa Anna here was a day longer that army would be able to recruit volunteers and prepare itself.

Isaac thought of Tennessee. His had not been a happy or an easy childhood, for his father had been lazy and cowardly, his mother embittered and mean of spirit. He had often had to fight his brothers for a fair share of anything except the work; they had always been willing to let him have his part of that and theirs as well. Coming to Texas with Finis and Luke, he had been sorely tempted to leave them and find his own destiny. But they had needed him, so he had remained with them to his sorrow. Now, damn them, it looked like they would have to make their own way without him after all.

He thought of Annie Lewis. He knew that from the beginning she had been a forlorn hope. The Lewises might have killed rather than let a Blackwood join the family. Michael especially. Of all the Lewises, Michael had more cause than any to hate the entire Blackwood clan. Isaac had always understood that, and he had never really blamed Michael for his feelings, hard as they might have been on Isaac himself. But he had wanted Annie as he had never wanted a woman before. To see her hand-in-hand with another man had brought a shattering end to a desperate dream.

First and last, he thought of the boy Cyrus. It had taken him a long time to win any affection from the youngster, for real affection was a rare commodity in the Blackwood family. Cyrus certainly had inherited none from Finis, if indeed Finis was his father. It was plausible that the boy was Isaac's. Slow-minded Nelly had not been particular with whom she shared a bed. As the years went on, Finis's meanness had turned the boy more and more toward Isaac, who offered him shelter, who gave him guidance and understanding and love.

What would become of little Cyrus now?

In the gloom, Isaac could see Elizandro Zaragosa dozing with a rifle across his lap, a sword at his side. At least Zaragosa had been able to talk to his son, to hug him tightly, before he turned to face whatever fate awaited him within these walls. Isaac envied him that. He wished he could have Cyrus here now, just for a minute. He wished he could say to him things he had said in his mind a hundred times but had never brought himself to speak aloud.

I thought I had all the time in the world. He measured time now in hours, in minutes.

From atop the wall he heard a quick buzz of conversation, then a shout. "On your feet, boys! They're comin'!" He heard men running, shouting all over the garrison, rushing to defend the walls. In the distance he heard a trumpet, commanding the Mexican troops to charge.

Isaac hurried to his post. Under the dark sky he could make out vague shapes moving across the opening. They looked like tall grass waving in a night wind. But these were men, carrying muskets and bayonets. He saw the bobbing motion of ladders as soldiers came running, carrying them in the hope of scaling the high walls. Texas rifle fire began to crackle up and down the line, all the way around, for Mexicans were converging on every side. A Texan cannon thundered into the dark faces of the soldiers, its fire momentarily lighting the field. Men screamed as their bodies were torn by bullets, by white-hot chunks of scrap iron and chain. Isaac fired into that surging mass, knowing he could not miss, that he had to have brought down a man. But he could not know which, for they were falling like leaves as far as he could see in the faint light of early morning. Ladders meant for scaling the walls never reached that far, falling as those who carried them fell.

The charge broke off. The soldiers turned and ran for their lives. Those who had ladders dropped them. In the bright light that followed a cannon's blast, Isaac saw bodies scattered near the wall and in the field beyond it, some still, some yet struggling against death.

There was death atop the wall too. Texans had been killed by musketry in that first brave assault, but the carnage had been far greater among the Mexicans because they had had to cross that opening into a blazing Hell.

Isaac reloaded his rifle before he took time to try to recover his breath. His heart was hammering, his blood running hot. His hands trembled so that he lost a little of the powder. He had to get control; there was not so much powder that they could afford any waste.

He looked around, remembering that just before the assault he had seen Zaragosa sleeping nearby. He saw him now, his face bloodied by a musket ball that had grazed his cheek, but Zaragosa was on his feet.

Isaac went to him. "You goin' to be all right?"

Zaragosa nodded solemnly. "Always as a soldier I wished for rifles that would shoot straighter. Now I am glad we never got them."

"We sure as hell beat them off. Maybe they won't be comin' again."

"I think we did not kill Santa Anna. They will come again."

They did, just at dawn. The trumpet sounded the charge, then again the *degüello,* and the soldiers came running, carrying fresh ladders, picking up those that had fallen before. The Texan rifles blazed again, and the cannon belched death. Some of the ladders made it as far as the walls, but no soldiers managed to climb one. The second wave recoiled and fell back. So did Isaac, feeling that he had no strength left to meet another charge.

But he found that he did, for shortly the

Mexicans rallied and came again, shouting their anger for those who already had died. Again rifles and cannons blazed from atop the wall. But this time there were more soldiers, and in the dawn's light they could finally see enough to take aim at the defenders. Despite the Texan fire, despite its deadly impact, there were more soldiers than defender rifles or cannons. For each who fell, ten came behind him, and several thousand feet pounded like thunder across the deadly field.

This time the ladders made it to the wall. They slammed against it, and soldiers scrambled up to be met by bullets, by rifle butts, by sharp knives patterned after the one carried by Jim Bowie. In the moment that they reached the top of the ladder and grabbed for something to hold on to, to pull themselves up, they were vulnerable. Isaac did not have time to reload. He brought his rifle around and jabbed the butt of it against a head, felt the skull break, then shoved the ladder with his foot. It went crashing down. Powder smoke choked him, but he hardly noticed, for his blood was at the boil. He reloaded his rifle, fired again into the crowd, then once more used the heavy butt to stun, to kill.

The defenders along the wall were spread

too thin to withstand the hordes rushing over. Isaac felt them coming past him in waves. He no longer had time to reload the rifle. He found himself standing back to back with Elizandro Zaragosa, who fought now with his sword. For a moment he glanced around, and his gaze met Zaragosa's. He saw a wild exhilaration in the man's black eyes. In these last moments, Zaragosa was not a farmer; he was a soldier again, fighting like a soldier to his final breath.

Isaac smashed his rifle across the head of a man who came charging at him with a bayonet. For a second or two he stood there with the useless, broken rifle in his hands, then flung it away and grabbed a knife from his belt. He heard Zaragosa groan as a bayonet jammed through his heart. Zaragosa fell back against Isaac, knocking him off balance. Isaac surged forward at two soldiers who charged him. He plunged the knife to the hilt into one, then saw the blast from a musket in the hands of the other. He felt the ball drive into his chest with the force of a sledgehammer.

He was numb, half blinded by the fire. He fought for breath but could draw none. He saw the flash of bayonets as two more soldiers came at him. He had dreaded the steel, but he did not even feel it now. He felt nothing except the sensation of floating slowly to the floor. The sound of the battle went dim in his ears.

The last thing he heard was his own voice, calling, "Annie — Cyrus."

Lieutenant Díaz knew it was more than the saber slash across his shoulder that made him feel ill. He was appalled at the slaughter before him in the wide plaza between the Alamo's walls. The dead and dying lay, often in heaps, like rag dolls carelessly flung about by thoughtless children. No man could walk across that ground from the wall to the chapel entrance without stepping in pools of blood. Mexican soldiers, and Texan defenders were intermingled in death. He could hear an occasional shot as a wounded Texan was given a coup de grace, and he saw troopers in a blood frenzy bayoneting bodies to make certain. *El presidente* had ordered that not one male defender be left alive. So far as Díaz could tell, everyone of them had fought until he died or was so badly wounded he could no longer raise an arm in defiance.

Hombres muy valientes. Valiant men, all of them, on both sides.

A shiver ran all the way to his feet, and he

tried to brace himself against the cold. After the heat and fury of the battle, the relative calm gave him time to feel the chill of an early March morning. He could see his breath in the air and wished for a coat or a blanket. Santa Anna had commanded that no man wear a cloak or carry a blanket or anything else that would hamper movement. Díaz could feel the blood still trickling from the wound, and he gripped it with his hand, hoping he might stop the bleeding. He had no idea when he might receive medical attention. So many needed it worse than he.

The firing stopped at last, and the bayoneting. Some of the soldiers began searching the clothing of the dead, looking for money or knives or any other treasure that might suit their fancy. Díaz watched with mixed feelings. The men had fought well, and he supposed they deserved anything they found. But the Texans had amazed him with the ferocity of their defense. He had half expected that when they saw the hopelessness of their fight, those who had survived to that point would try to surrender and beg for mercy. It had not happened. He had not seen a man who looked as if he even considered it. Of course they had seen the red flag and had heard the *degüello.* They knew they were doomed to die; Santa Anna had made it plain that he took no prisoners.

To rob these men now seemed a sacrilege, but he made no move to stop it. He had no energy left, and those who rifled pockets probably would not listen to him, anyway.

He heard a stirring and looked around. *El presidente* had entered the plaza, flanked by several of his subordinates. He had watched the battle from a safe distance, beyond the range of the Texan rifles. Now he came to taste the fruits of his victory. Díaz pushed painfully to his feet and tried to salute, but his wound prevented him from raising his arm that high. Santa Anna gave him only the briefest of glances, anyway. This was the nearest Díaz had ever been to the general. He was, after all, merely a lieutenant, a common soldier who had worked his way up from private to corporal to sergeant and finally to a commission. Santa Anna had lieutenants by the hundreds.

He heard one of the officers say, "We have gained the prize, Excellency, but the cost has been terrible. See how many of our soldiers have died."

Santa Anna betrayed no regret. He said casually, "It gave meaning to their lives. It is a soldier's destiny to die in battle. These, at least, were privileged to die for Santa Anna." He added, almost as an afterthought, "And for Mexico." He turned to a nervous civilian Díaz recognized as the mayor of San Antonio. It was obvious that the poor man had no wish to be here and that he had come only at Santa Anna's command. "I want you to find for me the bodies of Travis and Bowie and Crockett. I want to see them for myself."

An officer asked, "What shall we do with so many dead, Excellency?"

"We will bury our own with honor. As for the enemy, we will burn them. Send a detail into the town and pick up as many able-bodied men as you can find. Compel them to bring wood to make the fire."

One officer left immediately to carry out that order. Another gathered soldiers and had them begin picking up the bodies. The Mexican dead were handled with a certain reverence and care. The Texans were brought to a central place and carelessly flung into a heap. Díaz did not want to look at them, but he could not help himself. He had seen a few Mexicans among the defenders, fighting side by side with the *americanos.* He wondered if there were any he had known during his service in the San Antonio garrison.

He was standing there when they brought down the body of Elizandro Zaragosa from the narrow walkway atop the wall. The men were about to fling it on top of the others. Díaz shivered again and stopped them. "I know that man. Put him down here. With respect."

The soldiers looked at him with surprise, as if he had ordered them to spit upon the flag, but they complied. Díaz knelt before his one-time commander and tried to straighten the dirty, blood-stained coat. Bloody slits showed where bayonets had pierced Zaragosa's chest. The eyes were open. He tried to close them with his fingers, but it was already too late. He supposed it did not matter. Zaragosa had already looked upon his Lord, the Lord of them all.

Why? He did not speak aloud, but in his mind. *Why were you here? Did you not know that the fight was hopeless from the start? Why were you not at your farm, with your family around you? Now a widow weeps for you, and your children cry for their father.*

As Santa Anna had commanded, men from the town came under guard, bringing posts and fence rails and other wood for fuel. The president himself saw to the stacking of the bodies, with layers of timber between them for the burning. The men from the town stared ashen-faced at the horror of the Alamo plaza.

Díaz felt his heart quicken as he recognized one of them, not quite a man, a boy really. He called, "Manuel? Manuel Zaragosa?"

The boy turned at his call. His eyes widened at sight of Díaz, then his gaze fell to the man who lay at Díaz's feet. He cried out in dismay and came in halting steps. "Papa?" He fell to his knees at his father's side.

Soldiers came to pick up Zaragosa's body. Díaz bade them leave it where it lay.

"We have our orders, sir."

"And I have given you another. You will not burn this man."

Santa Anna heard the commotion and strode over to see what the dispute was about. It was the first time he had ever had reason to speak to Díaz. "What is the trouble here?"

Díaz tried again to salute but could not bring his arm up far enough. "I respectfully ask an exception for this man, sir. He has been a good soldier for Mexico. He fought against the Spanish. He was for a long time my commander. This boy here is his son. I ask permission for the boy to take him home to his family."

Manuel turned his grief-stricken face up

to Santa Anna in silent supplication.

Santa Anna was unmoved. "He was one of the enemy, was he not? He fought at the side of the *americanos?*"

Díaz said, "I would ask that you take into account all he has done for his country. Please, Excellency."

Santa Anna's face flushed with anger. "He was a traitor. Burn him!"

The boy Manuel started toward the president. "No, please!"

Soldiers grabbed him and roughly pulled him back. Santa Anna glared at Díaz. "Do you not have duties to perform? Be about them, or I shall have you court-martialed. I have no use for an officer who speaks for traitors."

The soldiers picked up Zaragosa's body and put it on the pyre with the others. Manuel stood in mute shock, staring.

Anger smoldering in his heart, Díaz watched *el presidente* walk away with his retinue about him. He had served Santa Anna with all the dedication and zeal a common soldier could muster. He had believed in him as the savior of Mexico. Now, his mouth filled with the bitter taste of disillusionment, he detested him as he had detested few men in his life.

He put his good hand on the boy's shoulder. "Come, Manuel. I will see you home."

Manuel pulled away from him and stepped back. His dark eyes crackled with fury. "No. You helped kill him. I can get home by myself."

"Manuel —"

The boy's fists were clenched. "If ever I see you again, I hope it is over the sights of my rifle." He turned and trudged toward the wooden bridge and the road that led to town.

Díaz watched him with burning eyes. The shoulder ached, and he brought his hand up to it again.

He wondered why he had ever chosen to become a soldier.

CHAPTER 25

The event would become known in Texas history as the Runaway Scrape, the flight of the Texan settlers to escape the wrath of Santa Anna and his advancing armies. It began as word spread across the land that Travis and his men had been annihilated within the blood-drenched walls of the Alamo. Indeed, Santa Anna purposely set the retreat in motion to clear as many people as possible from the path of his troops. When the guns at the Alamo fell silent, Mrs. Almaron Dickenson was found with a handful of Mexican women, huddled in terror in one of the old chapel's rooms. He sent the newly-widowed woman and her baby forth to carry the news to the town of Gonzales, sure the terrible story she told would throw Texas into panic and simplify his sweep across the rebellious colonies.

The civilian evacuation became a stampede after news of the horror at Goliad.

There the indecisive Fannin, who had declined to reinforce Travis at the Alamo, delayed a retreat ordered by Sam Houston until it was too late. He surrendered his entire force to Mexican troops under General José Urrea, who promised with good intentions that they would be granted mercy as prisoners of war and repatriated to the United States. Santa Anna coldly countermanded Urrea and ordered the captives executed. To the disgust and shame of Urrea, an honorable man, most of four hundred men were marched out of the old Goliad fort on Palm Sunday, lined up, and shot by firing squads. Only a handful escaped by fleeing between volleys, hiding from the lancers who galloped out to overtake them and run them through.

Certain now that Santa Anna meant to slaughter every American who fell into his hands, settler families began a desperate run for safety across the Sabine River. Sam Houston himself sent riders out to warn them and hurry them along. A great many of their menfolk rallied to Houston's army, driven by a cold fury over the Alamo and Goliad, and hoping at the least to fight a delaying action that would allow their families time to escape.

Annie Lewis was in her cabin alone when

young Mordecai came galloping over from the direction of Andrew and Petra's, his face aflush with excitement. He hit the ground running, barely taking time to wrap the reins around a post to keep his horse from running away. He rushed up to the dog-run, where Annie stood in the cold wind, wiping her hands on a cotton apron.

"Aunt Annie, we've got to hitch up the wagon and get away from here, quick!" He pointed excitedly toward the west. "Santa Anna's comin'! He could be here any time."

Annie brought her hands up to her breasts, her throat suddenly tight. "How do you know?"

"A rider just came by. Sam Houston sent him. Mama said for me to help you. Aunt Petra'll be ready for us by the time we get there."

In the back of her mind Annie had known all along that this might happen, but she had refused to acknowledge it by word or deed. "I wish James was here," she said. But neither James nor Andrew had been heard from since they had ridden away in different directions to search for Michael. She pointed toward the river. "You'll have to go fetch the mules. Last I saw of them, they were grazin' down thataway."

As Mordecai reined his horse around the

cabin and struck a long trot toward the river, she turned back into the kitchen, trying to decide what to take. They couldn't put a lot on the wagon, not and have room for her and Petra and Petra's children. Food, of course: cornmeal, what little flour there was, some hog lard, a couple of slabs of bacon, a cured ham. And a skillet and a pot to cook in. Blankets, a few extra clothes because the late-March weather remained wet and cold. And corn to feed the mules. She quickly began gathering these things and carrying them out to the wagon. She had most of them secured by the time Mordecai returned, driving a pair of mules Baptiste Villaret had left behind with the wagon. The wise old Frenchman had feared all along that this situation might arise. He had left the Lewis families prepared as well as he could.

When they had hitched the mules she took a long look at the cabin that had become home. Tears stung her eyes as she realized she might not see it again. She started to climb up into the wagon, then stepped back.

Mordecai said urgently, "We better be hurryin'."

"In a minute." She went back into her bedroom. She glanced for a moment at the bed, remembering Sly Shipman. She thought she should curse his memory, but at this moment she could only take warmth and comfort from it. She dug into a box and came up with several of her drawings, tied together with a black ribbon. They were of family members back home in Tennessee, of her mother. There were sketches of Michael and Andrew and James. And there was one of Shipman.

If the Mexicans came they would probably burn the cabin and everything in it. She would not give them the chance to destroy these. She carried them to the wagon and stuck them between the stacked blankets. She found that Mordecai had pulled the wagon sheet up over the hoops and secured it, for the sky was leaden and promised more rain. There had already been more than enough. The wheels pulled heavily in the mud as Annie clucked at the team and flipped the reins to start them moving. Mordecai rode close beside her on his dun horse.

The second wagon was at cousin Frank's place, for Frank was the only grown man here to supervise the families' flight to sanctuary. It had been agreed beforehand that if evacuation became necessary, this wagon would carry Annie and Petra and Petra's family. Frank would take his own family and that of Marie. Annie said, "Thank God Frank stayed to help."

Mordecai shook his head. "I'm afraid Uncle Frank can't help us much. He's flat on his back with pneumonia."

Annie blinked. "What?"

Mordecai said, "He went out to try to get some fresh meat and got caught in the cold rain. He was runnin' an awful fever when I went by there a while ago. But Aunt Hope and her boys said they'd get the wagon loaded and meet us at Mama's."

Annie felt that clutch at her throat again. For a moment she almost gave in to despair. The only man they had, helpless. Four women, their children, two wagons — and all those long, muddy miles to be traveled. Only God knew how close the Mexican soldiers might be.

She found the boy looking at her with eyes that showed concern but also determination, the same determination she had seen many times in the blue eyes of the Lewis men. At this moment Mordecai looked much like Michael had looked at his age. Michael had been able to take care of himself from the time he was old enough to lift a rifle to his shoulder and hold its heavy barrel steady. If Frank Lewis was helpless, Mordecai was not, and neither was Annie

Lewis. Nor would the other women be.

By thunder, we're Lewises, every last one of us. We don't have to have anybody else. We can take care of ourselves. She straightened her back and shoulders. "Let's be about our work, Mordecai."

Mordecai hollered, and the mules put their strength into the harness. As promised, Petra was ready when Annie got to her cabin. If Petra felt any fear, she did not show it. She was grimly businesslike as she put more blankets, a few clothes, and a little more food into the wagon to add to what Annie had brought. The wagon was well loaded now. The weight of its new passengers forced the wheels to bite deeper into the mud. It tugged at the wheels, slowed their turning, forced the team to strain harder. Mordecai stayed abreast of the mules, shouting at them when they seemed to falter. Annie saw that he looked back over his shoulder frequently. She knew he was watching for pursuit. Like Petra, any fear he might have felt was carefully concealed. By years he might still be a boy, but this day he was doing a man's part. Annie glowed with pride for her nephew. She only wished Michael could know.

They did not have to go all the way to Marie's cabin. Annie saw the second wagon already on its way, angling across to meet them. Like Annie's, its hoops were covered by canvas. Marie had the reins and was talking to the mules in French. Annie did not know the words, but the tone of voice was forceful. Frank's wife Hope sat beside Marie. Both women looked calm.

Annie shouted, "Where's Frank?"

Hope pointed back over her shoulder. "We made him a pallet in the bed of the wagon. He's runnin' a terrible fever."

Marie said, "I think he does not even know what is happening. It is up to us women. We must get by without a man's help."

Annie pointed toward Mordecai. "We've got a man."

Mordecai gave her a brief smile, then set about challenging the mules again.

They had to stop to rest the animals after a while, for the heavy mud made the wagons hard to pull. A reluctant thought came to Annie. "What about the Blackwoods?"

Marie said, "They have a wagon. Or did, if Finis has not sold it for whiskey money."

"But do you suppose they got the word? They live back in the timber. The messengers might've missed them."

She thought mainly of the boy Cyrus, who had come with Isaac more than once to visit her. There was no way to know for certain, but she feared Isaac was dead. The last she had heard of him, through James, he had remained in San Antonio de Bexar. The boy, and the rest of the family, had no one to defend them now except Finis and Luke. Those two were hopelessly incompetent.

Marie asked, "What do you want to do?"

Annie looked down toward the river. "We've got to cross it somewhere anyhow. I say we go down to the ford yonder, then over to the Blackwoods'. It isn't much out of our way."

Marie frowned and looked back to the west, from where the Mexicans would likely come. The horizon was clear. "Michael would not like it. But Michael is not here. Let's be about it."

The river's current was strong. Annie and Marie doubled the two teams, taking one wagon across, then the other, while Mordecai rode close by, ready to take hold if an emergency arose. Annie was a little apprehensive about the mules. Water sometimes threw a scare into them. She kept a firm hand on the lines until the crossing had safely been made.

She lifted a corner of the wagon sheet and looked in at cousin Frank, lying on a folded blanket, trying to fight his way out from under another blanket firmly tucked around him. "I've got no business lyin' flat on my back," he argued weakly. "I promised I'd get you womenfolk and young'uns to safe ground."

Annie felt his forehead and found it hot. "If you get up now you're liable to die just when we need you the most. Lie still. Us womenfolk are doin' just fine. Us and Mordecai."

She was not surprised at what they found when they reached the Blackwood place. Finis was stomping around the poor cabin, showing about as much sense as a chicken with its head cut off, hollering in a thin, high-pitched voice just on the edge of blind panic, flapping the stub that was left of one arm. "Hurry up, Nelly, and get that wagon loaded. Them Meskins are liable to be here any minute."

Annie did not climb down from the wagon. "So you've heard?"

Luke came hurrying out of the house, his arms laden with blankets. He stumbled and went sprawling, spilling everything he carried. He tromped half the blankets into the mud while he picked up the rest, letting them fall out of their folds and trail on the ground. He heaved them into the back of the wagon without any attention to the way they landed. Nelly was screaming futilely at Finis and Luke. Annie knew her only by reputation, having seen her but once or twice and very briefly even then. It was said that she was almost as slow-minded as Luke, and now she seemed to have lost even that in her fright.

Annie shouted, "Where's the boy, Cyrus?"

Nobody answered her. They were all too busy hollering at one another. Annie saw the boy coming out of the cabin, dragging a sack of cornmeal too heavy for him to carry. Annie caught Mordecai's eye and pointed. Mordecai stepped down from his dun horse and went to the boy's aid.

Finis cried to no one in particular, "We lost Isaac. God help us, we lost Isaac. Them Meskins massacreed him with all them others at the Alamo."

Annie saw that the boy Cyrus was crying. She climbed down from the wagon and took him into her arms.

The boy sobbed, "Uncle Isaac. They killed Uncle Isaac."

Annie could only hold him. She knew nothing to say that would lessen the loss.

The Blackwoods had not even begun hitching up their team of mules. Without being told, Mordecai took that chore upon himself. He had them harnessed and ready for the wagon when Finis screamed. Annie jerked her head in his direction. He was pointing toward the trail from which the Lewis wagons had come. "It's the Meskins! They're on us!"

Annie blinked, trying to clear her eyes. She saw three horsemen. At the distance it was impossible to tell anything about them.

Finis yelped, "They'll kill us, Luke! They'll kill the both of us!" He jerked the long lines from Mordecai's hands, threw the collar off one of the mules and jumped up onto its back.

Annie demanded angrily, "Finis, what're you fixin' to do?"

"They won't kill women and children, but they'll butcher us men. Git on that mule, Luke. We got to git out of here."

Luke had always done whatever Finis told him. He swung onto the second mule without even taking the collar off. Finis kicked his mule in the belly and set off in a run, showering mud behind him. Luke followed, taking much of the mud.

Annie forgot whatever ladylike upbringing her mother had managed to give her. Shaking her clenched fist, she shouted, "You cowardly sons of bitches, you come back here! God damn you to Hell, Finis Blackwood!"

Mordecai stared at her in amazement.

Nelly stood looking after her fleeing husband and brother-in-law. She blubbered incoherently.

Annie was about to tell Mordecai he had better run too, for he was old enough that the Mexicans might regard him as a man and kill him. But the approaching riders were closer now. To her relief she saw that they wore no uniforms. They were American. One of them had a familiar way of sitting in the saddle. She blinked hard, trying to clear the tears that persisted in burning her eyes.

"Marie," she cried, "tell me I'm right. Tell me if that's —"

Marie's voice tinkled with glad excitement. "It is. It's Sly Shipman."

Annie laughed and cried, both at the same time. She hurried around the wagon, intending to run and meet him. But she stopped, remembering the hurt, remembering the day he had left her to ride back toward Natchitoches with Baptiste. She had wanted to beg him to stay, but pride had not let her. If he did not think enough of her to remain of his own volition, she did not need him, she had thought. Pride stopped her now from running to him. She retreated back around the wagon. She turned away as

460

she heard his voice.

He hollered before he reached the wagons. "Is everybody here? Is everybody all right?"

Marie responded, "We are fine, so far."

"Where's your menfolks?"

Marie said, "Frank is in the wagon, very sick. The rest rode off to the war. We don't know where they are."

Shipman's voice was anxious. "I don't see Annie. What about Annie?"

Marie did not reply except to tilt her head in Annie's direction. Shipman brought his horse around the rear of the wagon where Annie stood. He swung to the ground as if in a hurry to grab her into his arms, but he held back. "Annie?"

She wanted to go to him but would not. She wanted to tell him she had sorely missed him, but she would not. Instead she looked at him in silence.

He said, "Soon's I heard what happened at Goliad, I came a-runnin' to help you. I went to your cabin, saw your tracks and followed them here."

"What for? We've gotten along real good without you." All the past weeks of sadness and resentment and anger were in her voice.

He answered resentment with resentment. "Maybe I shouldn't even have come, then. Maybe I ought to've just stayed back yonder in Louisiana."

"Maybe you should've."

They stared at one another from three full paces apart. She ached to rush to him, to have him enfold her in his arms, but that stubborn Lewis pride held her where she stood. She looked into his eyes and saw there not anger but anxiety and hurt. She sensed that he wanted to apologize, but there was pride in the Shipman blood, too.

He said, "You look to me like you've put on a little weight."

He had several days' growth of whiskers to show for his long ride, getting here. She said, "You don't look all that good yourself."

Marie leaned down from her place on the wagon seat. Impatiently she declared, "We have all the children we can handle. We do not need you two to act as if you are six years old. You both want to hug each other, so do it and let us leave this place before the soldiers come."

Tears blinded Annie as she stepped forward. Sly Shipman grabbed her into his arms and crushed half the breath out of her. "Annie Lewis! I was scared to death I wouldn't find you at all."

It began to rain. Annie loosened her hold on Shipman and looked up, the drops pelting her face. "Just what we needed, with

462

these wagons to move. More water and more mud."

Shipman said, "It'll slow Santa Anna as much as it slows us." Still holding Annie by the hand, he turned toward Nelly Blackwood and her children. "Let's get these folks on the wagons and get movin'. It's a long ways to the Sabine."

They pulled out, leaving the Blackwood wagon standing in a driving rain.

CHAPTER 26

James Lewis had tried to count the days but had lost track, walking in a northeasterly direction through a part of Texas he had never seen before. He tried at first to move only at night, but he found it painfully difficult making his way afoot through the rough chaparral in darkness. Twice he wandered into thick stands of prickly pear cactus and found himself entrapped. No matter which way he turned, he drove the thorns into his legs until he had to give up, sit on the ground and wait for dawn to let him pick his way through. With his fingers and his knife he pulled out those thorns he could get hold of. The rest would remain until they festered and came out of their own accord.

He knew he ran considerable risk moving in daylight, so he stayed constantly alert for sign of riders. Several times he thought he saw them, and he dropped flat upon the ground, heedless of the stickers and thorns. Once they turned out to be deer, warily picking their way along, browsing on the low-growing brush, then bounding away when they saw him. Once they turned out to be wild horses, drifting toward water. More often what he thought was riders turned out to be his imagination. The wild horses, at least, led him to water.

Having the rifle allowed him to kill game. Otherwise he might have starved or been reduced to trying to subsist on roasted prickly-pear pads, which he had heard was possible. The first time, hungry almost to the point of delirium, he managed to shoot a deer. Fearing that his shot might be heard by Mexicans, or perhaps roving hostile Indians, he laid low for an hour, hardly daring to rise his head above the level of the low chaparral until he was satisfied that nobody was coming in response to the shot. He built a small fire but gave the first piece of venison time for no more than a little scorching on the surface. He devoured it with the ferocity of a half-starved wolf.

He carried along all the meat he could, eating from it for days, until it began to spoil.

Some of the pear thorns became infected, and he began running a fever. He had heard of people using a prickly pear poultice to draw away infection. He singed the thorns from several pear pads, split them open lengthwise, and applied them to the festering places. He had to lie up a couple of days until the fever broke and healing began.

In all that time he kept wishing he had a coat to shield him from the raw and chilling wind. He had left his tied to his saddle. He tried tanning the deer hide enough to use but failed for lack of time or proper materials. He had to discard it when it stiffened and the stench became too much to bear.

He had no idea what was happening elsewhere. He had seen enough soldiers earlier to convince him that Santa Anna's invasion had been no flight of fancy, no figment of imagination by those who seemed always ready to surrender to blind fear. He sensed that the patrols he had seen were but the outriders flanking an army. By now that army had had time to reach San Antonio and there challenge the Texans barricaded in the old mission grounds. He could only guess what the outcome had been. Were he Santa Anna, he would probably leave enough men there to encircle the mission and besiege the defenders until they were starved into submission while he took his main force and proceeded across the colonies, sweeping everything before him as he marched.

If that were Santa Anna's strategy, he could well have traversed the whole of American Texas by now. He could have overrun Austin's colony including the Lewis farms and perhaps have his victorious army encamped on the west bank of the Sabine, daring a return by any of the survivors who had fled to sanctuary on the Louisiana side.

James lay awake nights, wondering what had become of Annie, of Marie and Petra and Hope and the children. Surely cousin Frank would not have let the Mexicans overtake them. For all his breezy outlook on life, Frank was serious when he had to be. Looking back, James was ashamed of his own occasional irresponsibility on the long trek west from Tennessee. Had it not been for Frank imposing a gentle but firm hand at times, they might never have made it into Texas. Frank could laugh easily, but that laugh could quickly give way when something else was called for.

He wondered, too, about Andrew. Perhaps he had returned home when he became convinced he would not find Michael. Or perhaps he had become embroiled in some battle with the Mexican forces and was unable to return home. It could even be that

Andrew had joined Michael among the lost, that James was the only surviving Lewis brother in Texas. Even he was still a long way from home.

Gradually the land changed. It became less of a desert and more benign, like the land he knew along the Colorado. At first he found none of it that showed any sign it had ever been inhabited except for traces of old Indian camps along an occasional creek or stream. One day just at dusk he came across a log cabin much like his own. It appeared to have been abandoned hastily. The door was hanging open. Warily, his rifle primed and ready, he worked his way to it, then stepped through the door. A loud snuffing noise made his heart jump. He swung the rifle around and almost shot a big spotted sow, which grunted and bolted through the open door. She was followed by four small shoats, their tiny hoofs rattling on the hard-packed dirt floor. They had startled him as much as he had frightened them.

He leaned against the log wall for a moment to regain his breath and his composure. He found his hand slick from cold sweat and wiped it on his filthy cotton shirt. When he got over his fright he decided to kill one of the shoats for fresh meat. But he found a cured ham hanging from the ceiling. The people who had fled this cabin had not taken everything with them.

If they had left food, perhaps he might find better clothes than the brush-torn rags that hung from him in ribbons. He searched the cabin but found nothing he could use except an old blanket. At least that would give him some protection from the cold. He wrapped it around his shoulders as he had seen Mexicans wrap a serape. He built a small fire in the fireplace and cooked up some of the ham and some johnnycake from a bit of cornmeal he found. He would have given his right arm for coffee — a piece out of the arm, anyway — but there was none. If these people had even had any, they had taken it with them. If they were like the Lewises, coffee was a luxury not lightly come by and not often used except for special occasions, like Sunday gatherings of all the families, and not always then.

He ate the best meal he had enjoyed in weeks, then spread the blanket on a bed made of posts and a strip of rawhide laced back and forth, front to back and side to side. There was a risk that Mexican soldiers could find him, but he had been running that risk for weeks, laboring his way across the country a few miles a day. It appeared unlikely that soldiers had been here, or he would not have found any food in the cabin, or the blanket. More than likely he would have found no cabin, only charred ruins.

The night brought its damp chill, but he wrapped himself in the blanket and slept his best sleep in weeks. In morning's first light he awakened with a start, not remembering for a moment where he was. He heard something rustling around outside the door. Sleep quickly left him. He flipped the blanket aside and moved to the door, opening it slowly and carefully, the rifle in his hand. The sow and her shoats rooted in the dirt beside the cabin, making considerable noise about it. He heard a rooster crow. Where there was a rooster there ought to be hens, and where there were hens there ought to be eggs. He had not eaten an egg since he had left home. He stepped outside, able now to see the place much more clearly than he had at dusk.

To his surprise he saw a sorrel horse standing by a crude set of pole pens, reaching its head across the top rail. He pulled back quickly against the cabin, wondering who the rider was. Then he saw that the horse wore no saddle, no bridle. It had wandered here, or more likely it belonged here. Probably the people who owned this cabin had left in a big hurry. The horse had been off grazing somewhere, and they had been afraid to take the time to go looking for it.

He slipped back into the cabin, looking for a rawhide or horsehair rope that he might use to catch the animal. He found nothing. He unlaced the rawhide strip that had served as a bottom for the bed, formed a loop in one end of it, then walked out slowly and carefully, making no sudden move that might startle the horse and cause it to run. It pricked up its ears and watched his approach. It turned once as if to move away. James talked in a low, even tone. "Gentle now, boy. Be gentle and stand there. I ain't fixin' to do you no harm. Just stand there, feller."

The horse snorted and jerked its head up, a sign of misgivings and a strong hint that it was about to run. James held the makeshift rawhide rope behind his back with his left hand, raising his right hand carefully while he kept talking. The sorrel's hide rippled as James cautiously touched the neck, and the horse backed off half a step. James ran his hand gently up into its mane and took a firm hold, then brought the rope up and laid it across the animal's neck, forming a hand-held loop around the throat. When the horse accepted that, James slipped the main loop over its head. Now, unless it took a sudden fright and jerked away, breaking the rawhide, the horse was caught.

James could tell right away that it was well broken and dependent upon a kind human hand. He rubbed it along the neck, and the horse nuzzled him. It followed him as he laid the gate open and walked into the pen. Beside a rough lean-to shed James found a corncrib. He shelled several ears into a trough and watched the horse take it eagerly.

"Old boy," he said, "the folks that left you here must've figured this wasn't any safe place to stay. I reckon they knew the situation a lot better than I do, so we're fixin' to do what they did. We're goin'."

He formed the rawhide into a makeshift hackamore, as he had seen Mexican horsemen do. He led the horse to the cabin, picking up the blanket, the ham, and his rifle. He forgot about the eggs. Jumping up onto the horse's bare back, he bade the sow and her shoats farewell. "Don't you-all let the Mexicans catch you," he said. "They'll have themselves a pork roast."

He realized that technically he was guilty of horse theft, but under the circumstances nobody was likely to object. The horse's owners had abandoned it to the Mexicans, who would probably have taken it anyway, had they found it. Having the animal would allow him to make much faster progress.

He kept moving in the same northeasterly direction he had followed during the many days of his long walk. Sooner or later he must come to the Colorado River. There should be no mistaking it when he did. He knew it from well west of his farm most of the way down to its mouth at the coast. North of the Colorado lay the Brazos, and eastward along the Brazos, San Felipe.

The sorrel horse's ears warned him in time to keep him from riding headlong into a large group of Mexican infantry, marching in an easterly direction. He pulled the horse up under some huge live oak trees and dismounted to be harder to see. He was glad the soldiers were not cavalry, for he might have found himself in a horse race. He had no idea how well the sorrel could run; he had had no reason to try him. He could at least outrun the infantry. They failed to see him, so he did not have to put the sorrel to the test.

He gave the infantry plenty of time to pass out of sight before he rode across their back trail. Though the country was beginning to look more and more like the area he knew best, he was not familiar with the dim road the soldiers followed. He did not tarry long to study it.

He sensed the Colorado River before he reached it. He realized as soon as he saw the trees and crossed a familiar road that he had come in west of home. The road showed recent hoofprints. There was no way of telling whether the riders had been Texan or Mexican soldiers, so he moved on down to the river and rode where he could quickly pull into the cover of the timber if need be. He had the blanket wrapped around his shoulders against a light, cold rain. He kept the rifle across his lap and primed, the lock dry beneath the blanket. In this kind of weather, flintlocks often failed because the powder became damp.

His pulse quickened as familiar landmarks told him he was nearing his farm. He considered it unlikely that he would find any of the family there. Surely by now Frank had evacuated them to safer ground. James moved up over a rise and saw his cabin below, and Andrew's well beyond it. Over to his right was Frank's. Michael's lay out of sight beyond a hill. He had half expected to find all of them in ashes, for he had come across several that had been burned, either by the settlers to deprive the soldiers their use or by the soldiers to leave the settlers nothing to come home to. He was gratified to see that the Lewis cabins remained intact.

He remained in the edge of the timber, caution overriding his eagerness to get home. He came across the milk cow with her calf. It had grown considerably since James had left. He always kept the calf in a pen so the cow would come in for milking without having to be hunted down and driven. That the calf had been set free brought him some feeling of relief. It meant the family had left; they were not still here at the mercy of Santa Anna's soldiers.

He watched the house a while before he risked riding up to it. He found some corn at the shed and left the horse in the pen, its nose stuck deep into the feed trough. He saw a pair of twin ruts, cut deeply into the mud and not yet completely washed away, showing where the wagon had moved. On harder ground a little farther out he found no more trace. Rains had washed away all sign. He walked up to the cabin, pushing the kitchen door open and stepping quickly inside as he had done at the first one he had come to. This time no hog snorted at him. The place was empty. He felt of the ashes in the fireplace. They were as he expected, dead and cold. By the look of things, Annie had been gone for some time, possibly several days.

He crossed the dog-run to his own room. There he found an old homespun shirt and a pair of trousers. He also found a thread-bare coat he had once intended to throw away but had decided to save for cutting hogs and other rough work of the kind. He looked into a cracked mirror at his bearded face. In a peaceful time he would have shaved, but such a luxury held no interest for him now. Anyway, the whiskers helped protect his face from the cold and the wind.

He did not stay long at his cabin but picked up the trail that led toward San Felipe. In low spots he saw enough deeply-cut ruts to indicate that this was the direction Annie had taken with her wagon. He found where a second wagon had joined from the direction of Michael's place. He was a little surprised to find indications that they had crossed over the river at the nearest ford and moved toward the Blackwood farm. What had possessed them to go by the Blackwoods' he could not even guess, but he followed, putting the sorrel into a stiff trot. He found the Blackwoods' abandoned wagon standing in front of their cabin, the wagon sheet loose and flapping in the wind. The wagon had been loaded with goods for departure, then abandoned. That worried

James more than a little. He wondered what could have spooked them.

He made a quick search of the Blackwoods' shed and found there two saddles which had to belong to Finis and Luke. He could not imagine why they had not taken them.

He was tired of riding bareback. He picked the strongest-looking of the two saddles and put it on the sorrel. He might argue it out with Finis when and if he ever saw the shiftless reprobate again. Given a good scare, Finis could already be halfway back to Tennessee, he thought.

As he moved eastward he lost the tracks of the two wagons because other wagons and carts had pulled into the same trail. Their wheels had sunk deeply into the soft mud, leaving a trace that would probably remain at least into the dry months of summer before they finally filled with dirt and covered with grass.

He had traveled several miles when he heard the distant sound of a shot. The sorrel horse swung its head to the right, its ears pointed forward. James saw a horse moving as fast as its rider could make it run. They were perhaps half a mile away, moving in a direction that would converge with James's course a little farther on, near a patch of woods. A couple of hundred yards behind the rider, three more horsemen were in pursuit. James could make out no details. They were only dark silhouettes, but he guessed that the three were Mexican cavalrymen. He put the sorrel into a run. Perhaps he could help the fugitive. In any case it was only a question of time before the three soldiers saw him and made him a target, for he was in the open.

He reached the little patch of timber ahead of the lone horseman. He waved his hat to get the man's attention. Two of them, given cover of the small wood, ought to be able to discourage three soldiers caught without cover.

The soldiers saw him, too. One of them pulled his mount to a quick stop, dropped to the ground and fired at the fleeing Texan. The horse stumbled and went rolling. James feared for a moment that the man was down to stay, but the Texan scrambled to his feet and came running, rifle in his hand. James braced his own rifle against the trunk of a tree and fired at the nearest of the three pursuing horsemen. The man jerked, then fell out of the saddle and sprawled in the old brown grass. The other two reined up quickly, circling back to see about their comrade. During those brief moments, the fugitive reached James in the edge of the timber.

He wore a month's ragged growth of whiskers, and his clothes were muddy from the fall, but he looked great to James. This was the first person he had seen in weeks other than Mexican soldiers. The man gasped for breath but dropped to his knee and brought up his rifle while James quickly reloaded his own. The downed soldier's riderless horse ran in a frightened circle, then discovered James's sorrel tied at the edge of the wood and came toward it at a fast trot.

The man said, "Friend, you look prettier to me than a whole roomful of blushin' young ladies. My horse was givin' out on me, and I was callin' to the Lord somethin' fierce. I reckon He must've heard me holler."

James nodded toward the soldier's black horse, which had come up to the tied sorrel, nickering. "Looks like He sent you a fresh mount, too. You must stand in with Him pretty good."

"I doubt that, but I made Him a lot of promises that'll be damned hard to keep." He shoved out his hand. "Name's Pete Johnson. I was out scoutin' for Mexicans."

"James Lewis. Looks like you found them

all right."

"Lewis." Johnson stared at him. "That beard covers your face, but your eyes remind me of a Lewis I knew one time over by Nacogdoches. Andrew, his name was."

"My brother."

"Him and me and some others, we had us a scrap with a bunch that called themselves the Fredonians. You look like you was ripped out of the same piece of cloth. I'm mighty glad it was you I ran into." Johnson eased over to catch the Mexican horse and tie him securely. "How come you to be out thisaway?"

James told him, leaving out a lot of unnecessary details. He said, "You're the first man I've talked to since I left that patrol down close to the Rio Grande. I've got no idea what's been happenin'."

Johnson blinked. "You don't know about the Alamo or Goliad?"

James could read disaster in Johnson's eyes. "No."

He was saddened and angered by the melancholy events as Johnson related them in a strained voice. He remembered the battle of Velasco, fought for Travis and others after they had already been released from Mexican custody. Now Travis was dead, and Bowie and all the rest. And Fannin at Goliad, where James had gone first in his search for Michael. So many men, such a terrible loss. Its magnitude was staggering.

The two Mexican soldiers acted for a while as if they contemplated charging the two Texans, but they gave up and rode westward. Johnson said, "They'll be fetchin' help to get us, more than likely. I'd as soon disappoint them."

Johnson rode the black horse out to where his own had fallen. James helped him recover the saddle, which he preferred over the cavalry saddle on the black. They moved eastward then at a good steady trot.

James asked him if there was any kind of Texan army left. Johnson said, "Sam Houston was puttin' one together over at Gonzales. He's been retreatin' to the east lately, stayin' ahead of Santa Anna. Some of the boys are afraid he'll retreat plumb into Louisiana, but I think Ol' Sam is just lookin' for the right place. When he finds it, he'll turn around, and we'll give that Santa Anna the worst case of snakebite he ever had. We could use a fightin' Lewis. You want to join my outfit?"

James studied on it a little. A few years ago he would have been eager. Now he had seen enough fighting to sicken him. "I'd like to find my family first and be sure they're safe."

Johnson pointed northeastward. "They'll be thataway, more than likely. There's been thousands of them, pushin' through the mud, tryin' to get over into Louisiana. In wagons, carts, horseback, afoot — Houston's been keepin' himself between them and the Mexicans to give them time. There's so many of them, you're apt to have trouble findin' your own."

They came to a parting, after a while. Johnson rode toward a rendezvous with his company. James followed the track of the refugees. It was plainer now, for they had been funneling together in a bigger and broader mass. Wheels had left deep scars in the rain-softened ground. James could imagine that much of the time the people had been pushing by hand, having to help the teams move their wagons and carts through the black mud. In places the sorrel sank almost to its knees in the muck.

He finally began overtaking refugees, some in wagons, some in spoke-wheeled carts, some using the solid-wheeled Mexican-style carts that groaned and squealed like something out of a nightmare as wood rubbed against wood. Some vehicles were drawn by horses and mules, some by oxen. He passed a woman pushing a small handcart, her mud-spattered children following behind her, leading a milk cow. Almost without exception, the people he passed asked him how far behind the Mexicans were. Their anxiety became his anxiety, for he feared that some of them would be overtaken if nothing happened to halt the Santanista advance. Enemy patrols like the one he and Johnson had encountered could not be far in the rear.

He came eventually to a broad plain where it appeared that hundreds of families had come together in a miserable, sodden encampment. Inquiry revealed that they were waiting for a ferry, which could take but a few at a time. Some had already been here several days, awaiting their turn. He inquired about the Lewises, but nobody seemed to know. He found a great deal of sickness, not just among children but adults as well, for the flight from the Mexican advance had been arduous and mean, wet and cold, unmercifully wearing on everyone who had made it. He found one family burying a child in a muddy grave, a victim of typhoid. There were more, the grieving parents said.

He came after a while to a familiar face, that of Marcus Caldwell. The farmer did not recognize James until James told him who he was. Caldwell apologized. He had not been able to see through the beard, he said. The rusty-haired farmer was not the same contented, smiling man James had known before. He was haggard and drawn, his eyes dulled with pain.

"We lost our littlest one," he said in a breaking voice. "He was already ailin' when the word came that we'd better pack up and get out. The rain and the cold were too much for him. We buried him back yonder, two days ago." He rubbed a tear from the corner of his eye. "We marked the grave, but I don't know if we can ever find it again. All that rain —"

James put his hand on the man's trembling shoulder. "I'm awful sorry. Whichaway's your wagon? I'll go speak to your missus."

Caldwell went with him. Mrs. Caldwell was dull-eyed, like her husband. James suspected she was sick herself. She spoke to him, but she seemed withdrawn, off in some distant place of her own. James suspected he knew where that was.

Red-haired Libby Caldwell had no insults for James this time. She watched him with sad eyes that reflected the ordeal she had endured. She had seemed but a girl when he had last seen her. She was a woman now, matured before her time.

He felt helpless in the face of all this trouble. He could not think of a thing he could do to lessen this family's tragedy, to ease the misery in which they found themselves. All he could say to Libby was, "I'm sorry."

She nodded an acknowledgement. "You don't look like you've had it easy yourself."

He told her briefly what he had been through, what he had seen. "If I can find my family and be sure they're all right, I'll go join up with Houston's army."

Her eyes were worried. "You don't really think they can whip Santa Anna and all his soldiers, do you?"

He shrugged. "Maybe we can keep them fought back till everybody here is across to safe ground. Then we can follow."

"But we'll lose Texas," she said.

He nodded regretfully. That thought was bitter.

She touched his arm. "You take care of yourself, James Lewis. Maybe we'll meet again sometime, somewhere."

"I'd hope so," he said.

He looked back over his shoulder a couple of times as he left her.

He found his family waiting up toward the

head of the line, nearing their turn for the ferry. Annie was the first to recognize him and come running. She threw her arms around him and squeezed him with all her strength.

"Careful," he said worriedly, "you don't want to be hurtin' yourself. You're not in a shape to be takin' chances."

"I'm not that fragile," she said, smiling and crying at the same time. "We'd been afraid you never would come back."

He looked over her shoulder. He could see Marie and Petra and the children. The wagon sheet had been pulled back because it was not raining, and Frank sat in the wagon bed, a blanket wrapped around him. Hope knelt beside her husband.

Marie and Petra came up. He dreaded what he had to tell Marie. "I never did find Michael. I found where he'd been, but he was gone. I'm mighty sorry."

Marie put her arm around his shoulder. "It's all right, James. I know you tried." He felt a wetness as she laid her cheek against his.

Petra was next. "I never saw anything of Andrew, either," he told her.

She said, "Andrew is with the army, with Houston."

Annie told him, "He was lookin' for us

when we got here. He made sure we were all right, then he went back."

Relief washed over James. At least one brother was not lost. "I'm glad we left Frank to get you-all away from the place in time. I was afraid —"

Annie said, "You were afraid a bunch of women couldn't take care of ourselves. Shows how much you know about Lewis women, James. Frank was too sick to help. We thought for a while that we might lose him. We did just fine, us women and the children. And we *did* have a man." She beckoned to young Mordecai. She put her arm around the boy. "Michael would've been proud of him."

Mordecai gave James a thin smile as James shook his hand. Then he said, "We'd best move the wagons up. The ferry'll be ready to load us soon as it gets back from the other side." He spoke with authority, the way Michael would have spoken.

James felt a glow. He said, "I'll see you onto the ferry, then I'll be goin' to find the army. I owe it to Michael."

Annie lost her smile. "You owe it to Isaac Blackwood, too. Isaac was in the Alamo. We brought Nelly and her young'uns with us." She pointed. James had not noticed them before.

"What about Finis and Luke?"

She frowned. "What do *you* think? They lit out and left Nelly standin' there."

"It runs in the blood."

"Not all the blood. Not Isaac's."

James walked along, leading the sorrel horse as Annie and Marie pulled the wagons up to the ferry landing. He had to explain to Mordecai what had happened to Walker and how he happened to have a different horse than he had left home with.

He noticed a man standing at the landing, watching the ferry's return across the water. The stance was familiar. When the man turned, James knew.

"Sly Shipman."

Mordecai nodded. "He caught up to us at the Blackwoods. He's stayed with us the rest of the way."

James wondered if Shipman knew about Annie's condition. Annie started to climb down from the wagon. James watched the gentle way Shipman helped her. He knew.

"I ought to kill him," James muttered.

Mordecai looked surprised. "Why?"

"You're too young to understand."

"You'd make a widow out of Aunt Annie if you did."

"A widow?"

"They found a preacher in camp right

after we got here."

James's mouth dropped open. "They're married?"

Mordecai smiled. "They stood out in the mud while the preacher married them. Wasn't nothin' fancy, but they sure did draw a crowd."

Shipman saw James for the first time. James walked up and shook his hand. "Mordecai tells me you're a Lewis now."

"I taken a wife. I didn't take a new name."

"As strong-minded as Annie is, she'll have you thinkin' you did. You goin' to take everybody to your place up on the Sabine?"

"No, I'm seein' them onto the ferry, then I'm goin' to find Houston's army."

"I was figurin' on the same. We can ride together if it's all right with you."

"I got no objection." He studied James intently. "You don't look as eager as you did that time at Velasco."

"I'm older now. I hope I'm smarter."

As the ferry pulled in, James shook hands with Frank and the youngsters, then hugged the four women. Annie and Shipman said a long good-bye, holding one another until the ferryman shouted that he was in a hurry.

The two men stood together, watching the ferry pull away. James said, "We've got a long ride ahead of us."

Shipman nodded, taking one last look at the ferry and its precious cargo. "Let's be gettin' about it, then." They mounted their horses and started south.

CHAPTER 27

Sam Houston's troops looked nothing like James's idea of an army, certainly nothing like those of General Cós whom he had faced in the siege of San Antonio de Bexar. There were no uniforms, save for a few imaginative getups worn by officers who had followed their individual fancies. The men wore all manner of clothing, from buckskins to the muddied and torn remnants of what had probably once been suits fit to wear to a wedding. They wore wool hats, skin caps, wide-brimmed Mexican sombreros. They were farmers, hunters, trappers, old Texas settlers, and new volunteers from almost every part of the United States. About the only thing they had outwardly in common was that they were bearded and dirty, muddied from the struggle that had carried them across a large part of American Texas, retreating, halting, retreating again in the face of Santa Anna's relentless march. They were hungry-looking, for rations were short. Only a few of the luckier ones, mostly officers, had tents to shelter them from the chilly April rains. They exhibited little of the discipline James had witnessed in the Mexican soldiers under Cós.

Riding into the camp with Shipman, he watched an officer trying in vain to draw his company into formation. Those who complied did so indifferently, and others ignored the officer completely or told him they would fall in when they felt like it. These were free men, proudly individualistic, unwilling to abandon their personal freedom to anybody for anything. But they would fight. James had seen that at Velasco and San Antonio.

His and Shipman's arrival occasioned little notice, for many latecomers had been riding in to join Houston's force. Others, with and without permission, had been riding out to see after their families, as James had seen them do during the siege of San Antonio. These were soldiers only by individual consent and only for however long they felt like staying. Fortunately for Houston, most were inclined to stay and have it out with Santa Anna. Many were impatient because it had not been done already: They had wanted to fight him at Gonzales, then at San Felipe. Now, near the town of Harrisburg, they were spoiling again to confront the Mexican army. But Houston had stalled, retreating despite the grumbling by officers and men that he was afraid, that he had no intention of facing around and giving Santa Anna a taste of Texas steel.

James had never seen the man, though he had heard the name often in the past year or two. Houston was not one to go about quietly and unnoticed, for his was always a commanding presence. James was sure he recognized him standing in front of a tent. He was a square-faced giant of a man, well over six feet tall, his face framed by muttonchop whiskers. He wore a much-abused black dress coat. The broad brim of his hat was turned up in three-corner style. On his feet were a pair of decorative moccasins that indicated an Indian woman's hand. That fitted with what James had heard about Houston being at one with the Indians, particularly the Cherokees, and able to treat even with the wild Comanches. Houston seemed greatly displeased about something, for he was shouting at a subordinate in language that would peel the skin from a mule.

James had heard that the Mexicans sometimes referred to Houston's men as *soldados God dammes.* It was not difficult to imagine why.

Houston spied James and Shipman and hailed them. "You two! What is your outfit?" His manner was gruff and loud.

James replied, "We don't have one. We just got here."

"Where from?"

"I come from out on the Colorado. Shipman here's my brother-in-law. We just saw our family onto the ferry. We've come to join up."

Houston surveyed them critically. "I don't suppose you fetched along any grain for those horses."

"No sir. I reckon they'll have to get by on grass."

"There's damned little of that. I have eight hundred men in this camp, and sometimes it seems that half of them have horses. Doesn't anybody want to be infantry anymore?"

"I'll be whatever you want me to be," James said, a little put off by the man's brusque manner. He was not used to being spoken to in this way. "I walked most of the way from the Rio Grande to the Colorado River. I reckon I can walk some more. Horse ain't mine, anyway. I just taken the borrow of him."

Shipman said stiffly, "Well, *this* horse is mine, and I ain't about to give him up."

Houston appeared disposed to give Shipman an argument. James put in quickly, "I have a brother here somewhere. I'd like to join up with whatever bunch he's in." That headed Houston off with nothing more than a scowl for Shipman. He called to a junior officer. "See if you can help this man find an outfit. That other insubordinate son of a bitch, too." He turned back into his tent.

Shipman frowned. "If he treats his own men that way, he must be hell on his enemies."

The younger officer made a thin smile. "It's not personal. You'd be quarrelsome, too, if you were a bulldog and had a bunch of yapping little terriers nipping at your heels." He beckoned the two into another tent. James told him he was looking for Andrew Lewis. Searching through a set of rosters, the officer said, "We were on the point of a mutiny from some who wanted to march right out and attack Santa Anna without any thought to the consequences. But the general has wanted to delay until the families had time to get to safety. And he's wanted to pick his own battleground. I believe he knows what he's doing."

James worried. "He said eight hundred men. I heard Santa Anna has got several thousand."

"He does, but not all in one place. Our spies tell us he has moved out ahead of his main force. He wants to cut us off before we can cross the Sabine to safety."

James looked at Shipman, whose face reflected James's own disappointment. "Is that what we're fixin' to do?"

"You'd have to ask the general, and he wouldn't tell you. But I don't think he has any intention of crossing the Sabine. There are some in camp who still call him a coward, but I prefer to believe he is baiting a trap."

The officer found that Andrew had joined an infantry company and had relinquished his horse to an officer of cavalry. "I reckon I can do the same," James volunteered.

Shipman said, "Be damned if I give up a good horse. Anything that can't be done a-horseback ain't worth doin'. Put me with a cavalry outfit."

James found Andrew without much difficulty. The two embraced each other fiercely, for each had feared the other was lost to the enemy. Shipman stood quietly, holding his horse, until the two brothers had finished their greeting. Andrew finally took time to shake hands with him. "How'd you leave Annie?"

"It wasn't easy, but I saw her onto the ferry with the rest of the family."

James said, "You'd be proud of them, Andrew. Petra, Annie, Marie, and Hope — they did real well. And Mordecai." He felt sadness welling up. "I never did find Michael. I'm afraid we may never know what happened to him."

Andrew's sober face told James he was already reconciled. "He wasn't in the Alamo. Manuel Zaragosa told me that."

"Manuel? When did you see him?"

"He's here. He came to Houston's army after the Alamo fell. He's with Juan Seguín's Mexican company."

"But Manuel is just a boy."

"There are a lot of men in this camp who would be boys anywhere else." Andrew grimaced. "We lost a good friend in the Alamo. Manuel saw his father's body there after the battle. Isaac Blackwood was there, too."

James nodded. "I figured he was. I didn't know about Elizandro." He had not gotten to know Zaragosa well, but he knew the Mexican had been a staunch friend to Michael and Andrew. "We've lost a lot of good men. What do you think of our own chances?"

Andrew took his time in framing an answer. "I won't lie to you. We've gone about as far as we can go. If we march much farther we'll be backed up against Galveston Bay. Looks to me like we'll fight or swim. If we fight, we're outnumbered. If we wait for the rest of Santa Anna's troops to come up, they'll have us outmanned by four or five to one. If you were Sam Houston, what would you do?"

James searched Andrew's face but found none of his brother's usual cheerfulness. "I'm glad I'm not him."

"If we fight and win, he'll be a great hero. If we lose, there'll be three widows in the Lewis camp instead of one. And they'll curse Sam Houston's memory."

Houston did not even know the name of the field where he had chosen to fight. He asked and was told that it was San Jacinto, Spanish for saint of the hyacinths. While his cavalry swam their horses over the wide expanse of Buffalo Bayou, he crossed his walking army on Lynch's ferry and camped it in a grove of moss-strewn live oak trees before the broad, open plain of San Jacinto. Even as late as April 20, his command suffered from dissension in the ranks, jealousy among his officers, and doubt about his intention to fight. The men were weary of the long marches, the cold and boggy campgrounds, the pervasive illnesses that swept the army, intensified by hardships of hunger and exposure to the weather.

A chill was still in the air that cloudy day, and few if any other than Houston knew for sure what was in his mind. James, an infantry private far removed from the center of command, knew only that many of the men were complaining. They saw no sense in this endless retreat. What they *could* see was the enemy, moving into position to cut them off. Behind the Texan troops lay boggy Buffalo Bayou. To the east lay the even wider San Jacinto River. In front of them, south and southeast, were the Mexicans. The only opening for further retreat was southwestward, and Santa Anna could close off that avenue in short order if he so chose.

A forty-man Texan cavalry patrol early that morning had encountered Santanista scouts and had killed four of them in a running skirmish, then had watched Santa Anna's column leave a small settlement known as New Washington. The Mexicans moved into an encampment of their own, not a mile from Houston's.

With Houston now were two recently-arrived cannons, which the men were calling the Twin Sisters, bought and paid for by donations from the citizens of Cincinnati. Houston ordered these rolled out in front of the grove. Santa Anna, feeling contemptuous of the undisciplined Texas force and confident that he now had it trapped, sent out a company of skirmishers and wheeled out a twelve-pound cannon by way of challenge. The cannon's shot went over the Texans and splashed harmlessly into the waters of Buffalo Bayou, behind them. The skirmishers fired their muskets without effect, for the range was too great.

The Twin Sisters answered the Mexican cannon shot for shot, finally striking the Mexican gun carriage and killing two mules. As the Mexicans began to retreat, dragging the cannon with too few mules, a Texan cavalry unit sallied forth in an effort to capture it. The resultant heated skirmish failed to take the Mexican cannon but enlivened the fighting spirits in the Texan camp.

James and Andrew huddled over a campfire that night, listening to the telling and retelling of the day's two cavalry skirmishes. Sly Shipman had been among the horsemen involved, but he was not talking much. While around the encampment the Texans were making heroes of the participants, Shipman came to the Lewises' campfire and avoided the celebration. He sat moodily staring into the flames.

James asked him, "What's the matter? People are tryin' to give you a medal, and you look like somebody had taken a whip to you."

Grittily Shipman said, "I don't feel like a hero. Fact is, I was scared half out of my britches there a time or two. All I could think of was Annie, and wonderin' if I was ever goin' to see her again. Or that baby on the way, and wonderin' if I was ever goin' to see it at all. If they could know what I was thinkin' they'd be callin' me a coward."

Andrew said, "You've been dodgin' Mexican soldiers a big part of your life. Haven't you ever been scared before?"

"Not this scared. Maybe I didn't ever have so much to lose before. There's Annie now, and our baby."

Andrew poked up the fire a little, adding more wood. "I'll bet you half the men in camp are thinkin' along the same lines. That's why they're makin' so much fuss over what you-all did. It gives them heart, and helps keep their minds off what's likely comin'."

Shipman asked, "What do you think *is*

comin'?"

James said, "A fight. It'll be tomorrow. It has to be."

"Why?" Andrew asked.

"This camp is ready. It reminds me of when we had the siege on San Antonio last December. We'd sat there and waited and waited while the officers argued over what we ought to do. All we needed was a spark to touch off the powder. Along comes old Ben Milam and furnishes the spark. He raises a holler, and half the camp follows him into San Antonio.

"I think the general is probably ready for a fight now. Even if he isn't, it'll come anyway, because there's aplenty of men in camp ready to do just what Ben Milam did. They'll raise a holler, and off we'll go."

Dawn of April 21 found the skies clearing and the cold wind dying down after having blown hard in the last hours of darkness. Nine more volunteers arrived in a small cutter they had rowed up from the bay. James could see twenty or thirty campfires sending up their smoke along the four hundred yards or so of the Texan encampment. To the southeast, no more distant than perhaps a mile, James knew the Mexicans were camped in another patch of woods. He could not see them because of a gentle rise in the open prairie that separated the two armies. He had never regained track of the days after his long walk across Texas. He asked Andrew, who said it was Sunday.

James expected at any time to hear a command for the troops to fall in, to prepare for battle. The command did not come. He saw Sly Shipman and some of the other cavalrymen leading their horses out into the open to graze. Perhaps he had been wrong. Perhaps there was to be no fight.

The hours wore on, and a new report swept through the camp. Santa Anna's forces had been reinforced early this morning. Texan scouts had counted some five hundred of them marching in from the direction of Vince's bridge across Buffalo Bayou. At the head of the column was the same General Cós who had defended, then abandoned San Antonio in December. This would bring Santa Anna's strength to something like fifteen hundred men, the scouts reported. And the main force was still marching up from the south. When it arrived, the Texans would be hopelessly outnumbered. With their backs to the wide, deep bayou, they would be even more vulnerable than the men of the Alamo.

None of the officers had solicited James's opinions, so he kept them to himself. He

503

was aware that Houston and several of his field officers conducted a long council well into the afternoon. An officer he did not know came to his company and asked the men if they would rather attack the enemy across the open plain or wait in the woods and let the enemy come to them. There was no argument. If a dissenting voice was raised, James did not hear it.

"Let's go and get them!" somebody shouted, and a chorus of voices was raised in support.

Looking at the sun, James guessed it was past three in the afternoon when an order was relayed along the length of the encampment. *Form up!*

James and Andrew and the other men afoot made a double line just beyond the edge of the wood. Cavalry units were interspersed, with one on each end of the long, long line that James guessed must stretch eight or nine hundred yards. Just in front of the line waited the Twin Sisters, the cannons which had seen their first fire in combat the day before.

Though the Mexican camp was out of sight beyond the rising ground, James felt sure that sentries or scouts must be watching. Yet tall Sam Houston, parading back and forth in front of the line on a big white stallion, was preparing to lead these men in a frontal assault against Santa Anna's superior force. James could hear him shouting orders and encouragement, but he could not make out many of the words. Someone repeated a few of them, and the words echoed down the line: *"Remember the Alamo! Remember Goliad!"*

A short distance down the line James could see the dark-skinned men in Juan Seguín's company of Mexican volunteers. Seguín had missed being in the fall of the Alamo because Travis had sent him out as a courier in search of reinforcements. James could see the slight form of young Manuel Zaragosa and wondered what thoughts must be running through his mind now as he prepared to take vengeance for the slaughter of his father and so many others.

The breeze brought him fragments of distant music, fifes and a drum. And it brought him Houston's thundered order: "Trail arms! Forward!"

The line began its awkward movement away from the woods and out upon the open plain, most of eight hundred men marching to free Texas or die.

James's mouth was dry, but his hands were wet and slick against the rifle. At any moment he expected the Mexican guns to open up. He expected Santa Anna's big twelve-pounder to begin blowing holes in this ragged Texan line, followed by a rush of Mexican cavalry. It would be easy, he thought, to outflank this unwieldy formation and cut it down as a farmer might cut a row of wheat with a scythe. But, incredibly, it did not happen. He watched, hardly believing, as the artillerymen towed the Twin Sisters in front of the infantry line. He wondered how many times artillery had ever charged into battle like foot soldiers.

They had topped the rise and were almost upon the Mexican camp before the first alarm went up. James realized with amazement that they had caught Santa Anna and his men at Sunday siesta. So contemptuous had *el presidente* been of the Texans that he had neglected even to post a normal guard. It had been unthinkable that Houston would be foolhardy enough to attack such a superior force across a mile of open ground. Yet this was exactly what the Texans had done.

James would later learn that Santa Anna was in his tent, amusing himself with a pretty young mulatto slave girl he had captured at a nearby plantation. Not even the first sounds of scattered musket fire from his own troops brought him out to investigate. By the time he became alarmed, it was too late.

At a range of some two hundred yards, the Twin Sisters opened up on the Mexican camp. The infantry and the cavalry moved out of a walk and into a run. Mexican *escopetas* were answered by Texan rifles and shotguns. The cavalry ripped into the Mexican flank with a fiery vengeance as foot soldiers burst into and over Santa Anna's outer guard.

Around him as he ran, James heard men shouting the cry that Houston had raised: *"Remember the Alamo! Remember Goliad!"*

Manuel Zaragosa and the others in Seguín's company took it up in Spanish: *"Recuerden el Alamo! Recuerden La Bahía!"*

James tried to stay close beside Andrew as they rushed into the fringes of the Mexican camp. In front of him, he saw rifles stacked for siesta. Some of the suddenly-awakened soldiers rallied and grabbed their weapons. Others, demoralized, began to run headlong toward the south, unarmed, spreading panic like wildfire as they went. James saw Andrew's rifle bring down a soldier. Another soldier who had already fired came rushing with a bayonet. He would impale Andrew if James did not stop him. James shot him in the stomach. The soldier stumbled and fell, writhing in agony.

As at Velasco and San Antonio, black powder smoke quickly clouded the battleground like a dark fog. James paused to reload his rifle, his hands trembling. He choked on the pungent smoke, and his eyes began to burn. He saw Andrew prime the pan on his rifle and start moving again. Though not ready, James quickly followed, trying not to spill powder from his horn.

For a few minutes a portion of the Mexican force rallied and put up a brave resistance. But too many had fled, and those who tried to stand and fight were quickly run over by the rush of the Texans, whipped to a blood frenzy. At a distance James saw a Mexican officer gallantly standing by the twelve-pound cannon, trying to rally the crew into firing it point-blank at the charging enemy. A shot from one of the Twin Sisters struck the Mexican cannon's water bucket and knocked down some of the men. The officer made one more effort, then folded his arms and stood in solemn defiance until Texas bullets cut him down.

After those first few brave minutes of self-sacrifice by a relative few, the resistance crumbled. It was no longer so much a battle as a runaway and a slaughter. Soldiers who had rifles threw them down and dropped to their knees, begging for mercy. But there had been no mercy at the Alamo and none at Goliad. Little was shown at San Jacinto, not for a while. By the dozens, then by the hundreds, the Mexicans were killed wherever sword or bullet or rifle butt could reach them. In blind confusion, many jumped into the bayou and tried to swim. Their bobbing heads made easy targets, and the muddy brown waters turned red.

Andrew halted after a while, dropping to his knees, heaving for breath. James stopped beside him. The Texan line had long since lost any semblance of formation. The companies mixed without any attempt at retaining identity. All that mattered now was to pursue the Mexicans. Let none get away.

"What's the matter, Andrew?" James asked anxiously. "Are you hit?"

"No, I'm just given plumb out. I've run as far as I can. You go on, if you want to. I've had enough." He took a sweeping, horrified look around him. Dead and dying Mexican soldiers were scattered as far as he could see. "God yes, I've had enough." He looked as if he might throw up.

James saw that most of the Texan force had swept on ahead of him. He felt compelled to move forward, to try to catch up.

But shortly he came upon a familiar figure. Young Manuel Zaragosa stood with a smoking rifle at arm's length, looking down upon a Mexican officer who lay on the ground, one hand clutching weakly at the air. Blood ran from the officer's mouth. James recognized the man even before Manuel turned his tear-streaked face upward to tell him, "He was my father's good friend. His name is Díaz, and I shot him. Now I wish I had not."

James remembered. This was the Díaz who as a sergeant had given him and the family so much trouble when they had first entered Texas, who had jailed James and Frank for a time in Nacogdoches, before Andrew and Elizandro Zaragosa had come to free them.

He knelt. The bullet had taken Díaz high in the chest. He was still alive, but barely.

Manuel asked in a breaking voice, "Can we help him?"

James shook his head. "I don't think so, but we can try."

A couple of men in buckskin came trotting up. They gave Díaz a quick glance. One of them said, "That Meskin's not dead yet."

The other one pointed his rifle at Díaz's head and fired. James jumped back at the explosion.

"Now he's dead," the second man said. He gave Manuel a suspicious look. "This boy is Meskin too. Is he one of them?"

James moved quickly in front of Manuel. "He's one of us. He's with me."

"One of them brown-skinned bastards looks just like another one to me," the man said. "We ought to kill every one of them while we got the chance."

James brought his rifle up, pointing at the man's belly. "You'll have to kill me first."

The first man tugged at the other's sleeve. "There's aplenty more ahead yonder. Let's go."

Manuel had paled at the shot that killed Díaz. Now he turned and lost what little he had eaten that day. James waited. He saw no reason to go any farther after the rest of the Texan troops. The outcome was no longer in doubt. Let those who still had a taste for blood continue the chase. The battle had been won.

"You'd better stay with me," he told Manuel. "Somebody else may mistake you for a Santanista and kill you. I think we've both had enough, anyway."

Manuel nodded grimly and turned away from the body of Lieutenant Díaz. James pointed back in the direction from which he had come. "Let's go find Andrew."

■ ■ ■ ■

The shooting went on sporadically until darkness finally forced a halt to the killing and Texan soldiers came straggling back. No semblance of company formations remained. Once the shooting had begun, they had become individual fighting men, each going his own way. Had Santa Anna had a few disciplined cavalry units with him, and these had remained cool-headed, they might have made short work of the disorganized Texas force. On another day, or even earlier in the same day, his foot soldiers might have held the line and turned the Texan advance into a rout. But his men had struggled against the elements all the way across Texas, and they were decimated by illness and fatigue. The reinforcements brought that morning by General Cós were especially weary from a nightlong forced march. Santa Anna's arrogant overconfidence had caused him to let down his guard and had condemned fully half of his force to a violent death. His losses on the field of San Jacinto were comparable in number to the Texan losses in the Alamo and at Goliad.

Ironically, reinforcements not many miles

away would have tripled Santa Anna's forces had the Texan attack waited much longer. But Houston had taken precautions against that. He had sent scout Deaf Smith to burn the bridge over which Cós and his men had marched early that morning. Any further Mexican reinforcements would have had to swim or find a boat.

In burning the bridge, Houston had not only prevented any further reinforcement of Santa Anna's troops but had eliminated any chance of escape for his own, had the battle gone the other way.

Late on the day after the battle, a handful of men brought in some straggling prisoners. One of them was dressed much like the rest of the common soldiers, but at sight of him many of the earlier prisoners began to show excitement. Several said, "It is *el presidente.* It is Santa Anna!"

Houston had had two horses shot from under him in the fight and now lay in pain at the foot of a live oak tree, one ankle shattered by a Mexican musket ball. But with dignity he accepted the president's surrender.

The proud military dictator, who had once declared that it was a soldier's great privilege to die for him, was reduced to pleading that he not be killed. While other

Mexicans cursed him for cowardice, he signed away Mexico's claim on Texas in return for Houston sparing his life.

In camp that night, James and Andrew and Sly Shipman began making plans to return home. It was past time to be planting their corn.

CHAPTER 28

James was concerned about the lateness of planting. If an early frost should come before the crops matured, part or all might be lost. But Andrew had been here more than fifteen years. He said the odds were that they would make a crop despite the late start. Enough, at least, to see them through the next winter. After that there would be another spring, a new beginning, just as Texas had been given a new beginning.

Gamble or not, the Lewis families were more fortunate than many whose homes had been in the path of Santa Anna's advancing armies. What the retreating Texans had not burned to deprive the Santanistas of their use, the Mexicans had usually torched for their own reasons. Evidently the troops had not passed this way, for the Lewises found their cabins, sheds, and pens intact. They managed to find and drive back most of their livestock that had strayed up or down the Colorado River.

James had lost Walker, and he had never seen the borrowed sorrel again once he turned him over to a cavalry officer for the attack on San Jacinto. He did not know whether the horse had survived. If it had, the chances were that it would seek its way back to its original home the first time it was turned loose. Horses had a strong homing instinct. James was fortunate in catching a Mexican cavalry horse after the battle. It had brought him home. Andrew had gotten his own horse back, once the officer who had borrowed him had no more use for him.

Finis and Luke Blackwood finally returned to their place, once they were sure all the danger was past. James had hoped never to see them again, but the Blackwoods were like a bad penny that kept turning up. Finis was indignant over some thieving Mexican soldier having stolen his saddle. James never told him any differently. Finis eventually got himself another. James did not see any point in asking where it had come from. Somewhere, some unfortunate was riding bareback.

James had the whole cabin to himself, for Annie and Sly Shipman had temporarily moved over to Marie's place so Shipman could work her fields for her and do the other tasks that had been Michael's. Young Mordecai did a man's work, but he could not take care of everything by himself, any more than Michael had done.

James got lonesome being by himself. A double cabin like this was a waste for a bachelor. He began thinking perhaps one day he would take a ride over to the Caldwell place, once the crops were in good shape and he could afford to be gone for two or three weeks. He had been thinking some of late about red-haired Libby Caldwell. She had looked a lot different the last time he had seen her. She had matured and taken on the appearance and attitude of a grown woman.

She might not be ready yet for serious thought on marrying, but it wouldn't hurt anything to put in his bid, so to speak. She would be ready, one of these days. And if they were both so inclined when the time came, this cabin would not forever be a poor bachelor's nest.

It was said, though he had nothing in writing to prove it, that the volunteers who had fought for Texas would be rewarded with land by the new republic. Sly and Annie were counting on that, so they would eventually have a place of their own. James and Andrew could add onto their own holdings.

As for Marie —

Baptiste Villaret came down from Natchitoches in June, anxious about his widowed daughter and her children. This time he brought old Mother Villaret for a reunion with her daughter and a chance to meet the grandchildren she had never seen. The Villarets pleaded with Marie to go back to Natchitoches with them. They had property enough there, they said. Marie could live comfortably in surroundings she had known as a girl. Her children, starting with Mordecai, could learn a suitable trade.

This raw country was no place for a young widow, they argued.

"But I am not a widow," Marie had declared. "I know Michael is out there somewhere. I can hear him sometimes, talking to me."

The family members would look at each other and shake their heads. Women had been known to lose their good judgment over lesser ordeals than Marie's. Men, too. The Villarets stayed longer than they intended, trying to win her over.

On Sunday, the day before the Villarets were to leave, James saw Marie walking around over the farm alone, staring a long time at the cabin, the shed, strolling down to the field where the first corn was starting to rise from the plowed ground. Mordecai walked down to join her. She put her arm around her son while the two of them talked for a long time.

When she came back to where all the families waited, she kissed her mother, then her father. Tears glistened in her dark eyes as she said, "Papa, our place is here. All this Michael built, he and I together. Even if something keeps him from ever coming back to me, always he will be here somehow, at this place. I could never leave it, for that would be like leaving him."

She put her arm around Mordecai again. "We are a family. We have paid too much for this land to go away from it now. To you, Mordecai is still a boy. But to us who were with him in the runaway, he is a man. He does not know Natchitoches. He knows Texas. In Texas he should remain."

Villaret accepted her decision without argument, though James saw a deep sadness in the old Frenchman's eyes. Marie's mother turned away, sobbing quietly.

Tomorrow the Villarets would start the long journey back to Natchitoches. It was possible that Marie and her family would never see them again. But they still had today, and all the Lewis families had gathered for Sunday prayers and the sharing of a meal as had long been their custom. It was a quiet, reflective time, nobody talking much. James watched Annie and Shipman sitting together at Marie's long table, touching each other often and trying to make it look as if it had been by chance. Annie was showing somewhat now. The baby would be here long before the first frost.

Frank had recovered from the illness that had almost killed him at the time of the Runaway Scrape, though he was slow in regaining his strength. His boys and Hope had been a big help to him in making up for the weeks lost on their farm.

Petra had spent much time with Marie, for the two had long been like sisters. When one hurt, the other felt the pain and knew how to help. Andrew did not begrudge the time, for he knew the strain and the loneliness Marie had gone through. Without Mordecai, and without Petra's quiet understanding, she would have had a much harder time.

Mordecai's dog began barking while the family was seated around the table. Mordecai got up once and went to the dog-run, scolding the animal. He had not been back in his place long, picking listlessly at a piece of venison, when the dog resumed the disturbance. Mordecai walked back out to the breezeway between the two sections of the cabin. He started to yell at the dog but broke off.

He came back into the kitchen, trembling a little. His voice was shaky. "Mama! Mama, come here!"

James glanced at Andrew, then quickly pushed away from the table. He rushed out onto the dog-run ahead of Andrew. Mordecai pointed. "It can't be. Can it?"

James's breath caught up short. He felt his throat tightening. "It looks like —"

Marie was already running, out past the cabin, running to meet two men riding double on a horse. Mordecai was close behind her, trying vainly to catch up.

James and Andrew followed but did not try to match them. The chubby man in the saddle was wearing a black coat and had a patch over one eye. Behind him, a familiar face showed over the top of the Reverend Fairweather's head.

Fairweather said in a hearty, booming voice, "I wish you-all would look who I found back yonder a ways."

Michael Lewis dragged a long leg across the horse's rump and slid cautiously to the ground. "Marie!" he called, and she was in his arms. Mordecai threw his arms around his father. It struck James that the boy now lacked only a foot or so of being as tall as Michael.

Andrew glanced at James, tears running down his leathery cheeks. "Praise God."

Fairweather dismounted. "Praise God, indeed. I have brought home the prodigal father. I hope you good folks have prepared the fatted calf. I am a hungry man."

It took a while for Michael to get around to hugging his two brothers, then the rest of the family by turns. James stared at him, swaying between gratitude and dismay. He had never seen Michael so gaunt and drawn, his face so pale. He looked to be just two steps shy of death.

James admitted, "We gave you up for dead, Michael, but Marie never did. She always talked like she was sure you'd be comin' back."

Marie said, "I don't know how, but I knew. I had dreams. I heard you calling for me. All the time you were gone, I knew you were out there somewhere."

Michael had made the rounds of all the family. He came back to Marie and held her as if he would never let her go. "And I heard you callin' me. I think that's what pulled me through, hearin' your voice in my head whenever I felt like I was startin' to slip away."

He went into the kitchen, his arm around Marie. She brought him a plate, and one for Fairweather. They devoured the venison as if neither had eaten in a month. Michael finally leaned back in his chair. "I was down there on scout along the Rio Grande when Santa Anna crossed over from Laredo. His outriders took after us, me and two that I was with. They shot the others, and they put a bullet in my back. I managed to hold myself in the saddle till my horse outran them. I must've finally gone unconscious and fallen off. When I came to I was lyin' on the ground. I didn't see the horse any-where.

"I wandered a while, till an old Mexican with a burro came across me and took me home with him. It was like twenty years ago, all over again. Remember, Marie, when the Spaniards shot me, and old Mother Moreno and her boys helped me? This old man and his wife, they took care of me the same way. They said Santa Anna had executed two of their sons down in Coahuila. They hid me when the soldiers came around. I came so close to dyin' that I could smell the angels' breath. But I'd hear you callin' me, and I'd hold on tight."

"Yes," Marie said, burying her face against his neck. "I called for you. Many, many times I called for you."

"The old man finally came and told me that Santa Anna had been whipped, that all the Mexican soldiers were goin' back to Mexico. By then I felt like I was strong enough, so I started walkin'. It was a long ways for a man afoot. I finally made it to the Willet place this mornin'. That's where I found Fairweather."

"The power of prayer," Fairweather said, "and faith. James, young gentleman, would you mind handin' me that platter of venison? I swear, the Lord's bounty never tasted so good."

ABOUT THE AUTHOR

Elmer Kelton is a native Texan, author of more than forty novels, winner of a record seven Spur Awards from Western Writers of America, Inc., four Western Heritage Awards from the National Cowboy Hall of Fame, and countless other honors.